The Alethean Legacy

By Rob King

Copyright 2016 Rob King
Cover by Andrew McDonnell

Author's Note

This is a work of fiction. Characters, businesses, places, events and incidents are either the products of my imagination or used in a fictitious manner. Character names are something else. These were taken from people who I have met in my life (with their consent), because it adds a layer of realism. You won't find a "Max Power" or "Jasper Selkuckle" in these pages. Any resemblance between a character and their namesake is purely coincidental, I only used their names.

This book is dedicated to my wife Rachel, whose patience knows no bounds, and to my children James and Amelia, who inspire me more than I can describe.

1. Ryan Marshall

i.

1993 A.D.

The vines lapped off Ryan Marshall's face as he dashed through the thick cornfield. The sun was beaming, and he could feel the humidity surrounding him like a hot blanket.

"Newton, stand ready," he panted through his radio.

"Roger that," was the calm reply.

Marshall had almost reached the treeline that bordered the field. He concentrated on his breathing, but was also mindful of the numerous trip-hazards that lay before his destination.

Five hundred metres, he thought. *Should make it.*

There was a rattle behind him. The unmistakable sound of gunfire.

Marshall's radio sprang to life. "Tangos on your six," Newton's voice barked.

No shit, Marshall thought.

At 6'2", Marshall had to run with a slight crouch to stay below the corn. He pressed forward, knowing that engaging his pursuers was suicide.

One hundred metres.

"Do it!" He shouted into the small device strapped below his left shoulder.

As the trees loomed ahead of him, Marshall did not look back as a strip of plastic explosives detonated. A line of fire intersected the gap between Marshall and his assailants; he heard a scream when at least one was caught in the blaze, but he ignored it as he reached the forest.

There was movement ahead. Marshall instantly raised his Browning HP handgun, but realised it was Gareth Bird, a member of his squadron.

Marshall reached Bird. "We can't hang about. The corn'll burn for a while but it won't take them long to circumvent it. Where's Newton?" he asked.

Bird pointed upward. "Up there," he said.

Marshall looked up and saw Newton high up the tree next to him, quickly climbing down.

"Jesus, you're like a bloody orangutan," Marshall quipped.

"Fuck you," Newton retorted as he dropped to the ground.

Rob Newton was a demolition expert. He had spent fifteen years in bomb disposal with the British Army, and the last three years as a member of Marshall's team. He was a few years older than Marshall; his hair was receding slightly and had whiskers of grey, but his physical condition was unquestionable.

Marshall grinned. "Let's move out," he said before being distracted by a faint whirring sound that was emanating from outside the woodland.

In the distance, there was a black spot in the otherwise clear yellow-and-blue skyline. Marshall knew immediately that it was a helicopter.

Marshall holstered his pistol and pulled an AK-47 from over his shoulder. "Move out!" he barked, and the trio ran into the forest.

They ran for almost fifteen minutes before taking refuge behind a group of rocks that lay next to a wide river.

"Bird, get on the radio to Smith and have him call for ex-fil," Marshall said to the man crouched to his left. Bird did not have Marshall's height, and Marshall had initially thought that his slender frame was unsuitable for the Special Air Service. Over the years serving alongside him, Marshall had seen the reasons for Bird's selection first-hand, and he could not help but admire his accomplishment of having joined the Regiment from a Secret Service desk job.

Bird released his radio. "Helo inbound. E.T.A. ten minutes."

Marshall nodded. "There's an Evac point two klicks east, across the river," he said. "Tell Smith to meet us there."

The group made for the river. They were wearing camouflage and each had a rucksack on their back. Coupled with the weight of their weapons, they knew that the swim was going to be tough.

They had crossed almost two thirds of the river when Marshall heard a disturbance behind them. He looked over his shoulder and saw movement. "Down!" he whispered forcefully before diving underwater.

The water engulfed him. He could hear nothing but the mild current and the muffled sound of his squad mates. The water was clean and clear, but his vision was nevertheless impaired. He released the rifle, allowing it to fall freely behind him with its strap as a tether. He swam underwater as fast as he was able, toward the far shore. He needed to get to shallower water so that he could stand, and he could not approach the surface until he was ready, for fear of being seen.

After skimming the riverbed for almost three minutes, Marshall could feel the weight of the water above him beginning to subside. He looked up, and guessed that he was now in as good a position as he was likely to get, given his limited remaining oxygen. He stopped his forward motion and turned himself around.

He needed to stay submerged without swimming, so he exhaled to release his remaining air. He then reached back for his rifle and pulled at the strap. He dragged it in front of him, before pulling his legs toward his chest in preparation for standing.

He was running out of time. His blood-oxygen levels were dangerously low, and he needed his faculties sharp when he made his move. It was now or never.

He pushed his feet down onto the rocky floor and slowly stood up. His rifle and head emerged from the water, but only so far as to allow his nose to clear the surface. He breathed deeply, and fought the urge to open his mouth, which was still submerged.

On the far bank were four men, all of whom were looking across the river. Marshall's mind raced, as his SAS-honed instincts took control. He identified the two closest targets and swiftly brought his rifle to bear on the first. Before taking the shot, he saw something in the corner of his eye, and realised that Newton had the same plan and was peering out of the water to Marshall's right. His split-second distraction passed and he pulled the trigger. The first target dropped to the ground, and the second man was dead before he realised what had happened. The other two joined their comrades less than a second later, thanks to Newton's sharp aim.

Marshall brought his mouth out of the water and took a deep breath. The oxygen swam through his bloodstream and he felt a moment's dizziness, though it passed as quickly as it started.

Marshall thought he saw something else moving in the wood opposite, but before he could move his rifle, he saw a man appear and fall forward to the ground. Marshall looked at Newton, who was not aiming down the barrel of his gun, then glanced left to see Bird rise from the water.

"Good job I'm here," Bird whispered loudly enough for both of them to hear.

Marshall pursed his lips and refrained from responding. *Always a cheeky bastard*, he thought.

The men scanned for more enemy units, but were soon satisfied that the area was clear. Marshall stood upright and carefully walked backward to the bank.

"Tell Smith we'll be a few minutes late," Marshall said after fully emerging from the water.

Bird nodded and relayed the information. Smith had waited in the jungle as their point of contact for evacuation. Marshall assumed he would be at the clearing by now.

Marshall and his team arrived at the small open space less than ten minutes later. Smith was nowhere to be seen.

"Get him on the radio," Marshall said.

A voice rang out from behind a small tree on the perimeter. "No worries, I'm here," Smith said as he emerged.

"How the fuck did you stay hidden behind that thing?" Marshall asked with wonder as he pointed at the tree whose width appeared less than Smith.

"Magic," Smith replied with a smile.

Marshall sighed. "Send the flare," he said to Newton.

The flare disappeared above the canopy. There was only a two-minute wait before the helicopter could be heard approaching, and shortly after that it was visible directly above and it began its descent.

"Did you get him?" Smith asked Marshall over the increasing noise of the helicopter's rotors.

Marshall nodded. Their mission was the assassination of a Mexican arms dealer who had been supplying the IRA. Marshall had successfully eliminated him, but a silent alarm triggered by the target had led to Marshall being chased from the compound.

The aircraft landed, and the team climbed aboard. As they rose above the forest, Marshall looked out toward the field where the blaze had spread significantly.

Despite five years in the Regiment, Marshall still got the same adrenaline rush that he did on his first mission. With the operation complete, that adrenaline made way for fatigue.

He had no family, having never found time to settle down, and had very few friends. Marshall filled his life with his work, and rarely stayed in one place for very long. He promised himself after every mission that he would take some leave, but it never happened.

He joined the Regiment after serving tours in Northern Ireland, the Falklands and the Persian Gulf, where he excelled and rose quickly through the ranks. He loved the Royal Marines, but had always wanted to join the SAS so upon his return from the Gulf he applied.

Marshall mopped his brow. The wind blowing through the open-sided helicopter was hot, so did little to relieve the humidity. *Note to self,* he thought. *Mexican heat at this time of year is unbearable, especially when trying to outrun a group of thugs who are trying to kill you.*

2. Discovery

i.

Marshall arrived at headquarters in Hereford for his 8am meeting with fifteen minutes to spare. After passing through security, he made his way to the briefing room that was located on the second floor at the front of the building.

The room was small with a rectangular central table surrounded by eleven seats, five on each side and one at the far end reserved for the section chief. The entrance was in the centre of the wall opposite the chief's chair; to the right was a large window that ran the full length of the wall. The room was empty when Marshall arrived, so he walked over to the window and gazed at the car park outside. After several minutes had passed, he checked his watch, which read 8:01. He was irritated; he did not like waiting. At 8:05, the door opened and a number of people filed in, most of whom Marshall knew but some he did not recognise.

Marshall scrutinised the two men and one woman. Each was dressed in an expensive-looking, impeccably tailored business suit. They walked with rigid backs, and the woman carried a leather briefcase. *Ruperts*, Marshall thought.

"Good morning," said General Howells, a broad man in his late fifties who had been Marshall's supervisor since he joined the service. Howells walked directly to the chair at the head of the table and sat down. Marshall took a seat to the General's left while the three new people faced him. Her male colleagues flanked the woman. She set her briefcase on the desk, opened it, and removed a folder bearing the black and gold emblem of the Secret Intelligence Service. She put the folder on the desk and placed the briefcase on the floor to her right.

General Howells opened the meeting. "Marshall, Ms Taylor and her associates have joined us from MI6," he said as he gestured to the woman. "She is here to brief you on your next assignment."

Taylor nodded to the chief and then fixed her gaze squarely on Marshall. After a slight but noticeable pause, and a smile that appeared false, she started. "We believe that the Iraqi leadership has sanctioned the construction of chemical weapons in a compound south of Basra. We need eyes on the compound, and if their presence confirmed then the compound must be destroyed."

Taylor pushed the folder across the table to Marshall. "The assignment is simple. Go in, confirm the Intel, deal with the weapons and get out."

Marshall perused the document then turned to the General. "The conflict over there is finally subsiding, and now we're sanctioning an assault on of one of their compounds? It's going to royally piss them off."

Taylor interrupted. "This is not open to debate. Everything

you need for the mission is detailed in that document. You can choose your team from anyone in this room, and I will be seconding my colleagues here to oversee the operation."

Taylor waved an arm in the direction of the men flanking her. They nodded in acknowledgement but said nothing. "You leave at 0800 tomorrow."

When will we learn? Fucking numpties, Marshall thought as Taylor went through the document with the group.

Marshall decided to take Bird, Newton and Smith with him, plus the two men in suits. If there were confirmed presence of chemical weapons, Newton would take care of them. Bird would be required if there were any technology that needed identifying and extracting, and Smith would serve as translator.

Of the three men, Marshall knew Andrew Smith the least, having only served with him during the recent mission in Mexico. He had read Smith's record, and was impressed by the unconventional soldier's achievements.

Smith had gone off the grid five years earlier and had been declared Missing in Action. Earlier this year, he returned to England having completed an undercover assignment with the Provisional IRA in south Belfast. The intelligence he had been feeding back to England had been instrumental in the prevention of terrorist attacks against the British military. Smith was a skilled computer programmer, but his specialty was as a linguist with seven languages in his repertoire.

Marshall had read in his profile that he was known to be a little hot-headed. Marshall made a mental note to keep an eye on him.

The two secret service men were Hughes and Gardner. Marshall read their files intently and learned that Gardner had served with MI6 for almost a decade, while Hughes had transferred in from the British Army less than a year ago. The pair had advanced weapons training, and Hughes was especially proficient with a sniper rifle. They were also highly skilled in close quarters combat and had plenty of field experience between them. He had to admit that they would be assets to the operation.

ii.

It had been thirty-nine hours since the group left England; it was now 23:45 local time. The team had managed a couple of hours of sleep on the plane, but the hike from the drop-off point to the target compound had been tiresome and Marshall was still feeling it.

Marshall was prone on the ground, halfway down the bank of a hill that led to the compound. He was peering through a thermal-view headset that allowed him to see the heat signature of anyone inside the perimeter. Smith was to his right and Bird to the left. Newton was further along the ridgeline scouting the area.

Hughes and Gardner had dropped back approximately 100 yards up the hill and crouched behind a large boulder. Their sniper rifles were deployed on tripods and they were awaiting orders.

Marshall scanned the area. The compound consisted of a large rectangular building with a courtyard surrounding it. A chain-link fence with only one opening protected the perimeter, and that opening was facing Marshall and his team. The building had no windows on the faces that Marshall could see, and only one entrance that was in line with the gap in the fence.

Marshall could see a man on either side of the door to the main building. Three patrolled the front courtyard, two more flanked the front gate, and there was one in each of the four watchtowers positioned in the corners of the compound. After several minutes, another man came into view at the back, patrolling the other side. He had a dog on a leash that was dragging him around the open space.

Marshall activated his two-way radio. "There are four in the towers and seven at the front. There's at least one more at the back. Let's assume there's another three to six that we haven't spotted."

Pausing for a moment to finalise the plan in his head, Marshall was sure of their next move. "Hughes, track around to the side of the compound. Get eyes on any other guards and report in."

"Roger that," Hughes responded.

Marshall waited on the hillside, looking through the

binoculars for any other targets. Thirty minutes had passed when Marshall's radio came to life. "Six tangos confirmed at the rear of compound. Four on patrol, two stationed either side of an entrance to the building."

"Stand by," Marshall replied over the radio.

A few minutes passed in silence as Marshall considered their options. *Water treatment plant, my arse,* he thought. *Whether it's Weapons of Mass Destruction or something else, something important is going on in that building. Something that warrants a dozen armed guards.* He had doubted Taylor when she delivered the brief, but he was now convinced that she had been right.

"There's no way we're getting in there without engaging," he said to the men flanking him. "The best way forward is stealth. They outnumber us three to one, so our first job is to thin the ranks."

He squeezed his radio, "Newton, make your way around the ridge and be ready to go in from the other side. On my signal we go loud, but not a moment before. Hughes, on my order take out the two watch towers nearest you. Gardner, take the other two. When the towers are neutralised, I need the pair of you to take out the two guards on the front gate and then cover us. Sort that mongrel out, as well"

He released the button and turned to Bird. "Once they're down, we'll move in and deal with the men around the back. We'll rendezvous at the rear entrance once the area is clear."

iii.

The past six months spent on this research project had often seemed like a waste of time to Sayid, but it finally paid off just under two weeks ago when he and his team finally managed to activate the device.

As he made his way across the impeccably clean and brightly lit lab, he thought about the last project he had worked on. It was in Museh-quala in Afghanistan. An archaeological discovery indicated that there had been intelligent life on Earth over 600 million years ago. The discovery of an artefact deep underground had led to his recruitment; and he quickly confirmed that it was electronic in origin despite being ancient. Electronics was not a skill that many of his compatriots had, but he was fortunate enough to study the field during a stint in Pakistan in his youth.

It had been discovered that the artefact was a recording device. After months of research and experimentation, he had successfully played its contents and uncovered evidence suggesting that a race of intelligent beings had lived on Earth before the evolution of Humanity. He learned that they had suffered some form of disaster that forced them to evacuate the planet, but he never completed his investigation. Upon presenting his findings to his superiors, he was declared a heretic and exiled. He was fortunate not to have been executed, but his disgrace saw him cast out of his home and his work destroyed. He spent the years that followed living on the streets of neighbouring countries, scraping together what food he could muster.

Everything changed when his current employer found him. He was brought to this laboratory and had spent every day since investigating the object that sat in front of him.

The device was mounted on a small plate that was attached to the table in front of him. A light blinked as he activated it, and Sayid stepped back in anticipation.

Sayid felt sweat running down his back. Suddenly, there was a loud noise, an explosion from the entrance to the room, and the world went straight to hell.

iv.

Marshall watched through binoculars as, almost simultaneously, the four watchtower guards dropped vertically, their brains no longer contained by their skulls. *Damn, they really are good,* he thought.

He was quickly on his feet and in a crouched position. He signalled Bird and Smith to do the same. They moved down the hill as fast as they could, raising their MP5 sub machine guns into position for immediate reaction to enemy contact.

They reached the bottom of the hill as silenced sniper fire passed through the two guards' heads and their lifeless corpses dropped to the ground with a sandy thud.

The three men in the courtyard were not alerted as their colleagues fell; however, one of the guards at the door spotted the incident and shouted the alarm.

"Go loud! Go loud!" Marshall shouted.

The rear of the compound lit up with the fire and bang of incendiaries thrown in by Newton. As planned, the guards in the front courtyard were distracted, so Marshall and his team got in and took them down with relative ease. The three Englishmen moved to the southeast corner of the building and spread out, moving around to support Newton and take down the remaining guards at the rear.

As they crouched, Marshall heard the snarl of a dog only a second before he saw the animal in mid-air hurtling toward him.

As Marshall instinctively raised his arms, there was a squelching sound as the midriff of the canine exploded to the right in a crimson burst. The animal immediately fell to the ground.

"Sorry," Hughes said through the radio. "Meant to get him sooner."

Marshall smiled with a combination of relief and gratitude.

He composed himself and brought his focus back to the mission. "Newton, move in. Gardner come around to assist Hughes; take out any tangos you see out the back."

As they reached the rear of the building, the team took up positions behind a set of barrels that were standing at the northeast corner. Gardner contacted Marshall. "In position. I can see five bodies, no sign of the sixth."

"Copy," Hughes replied.

"Keep watching," Marshall said. "Newton, go around the outside and flank. Switch to night-vision; there'll be too many false positives from the fires for thermals."

Marshall raised his weapon and moved around the wall into the rear courtyard, his hand making a gesture to indicate that Bird and Smith should follow him.

As they reached the centre, they could see Newton approaching from the other side. There was no sign of the missing guard.

"He must have retreated inside," Marshall said.

Newton reached the group. "No sign of him, he m-" The familiar sound of gunfire from an AK-47 rang in Marshall's ears. He dived to the ground and scrambled to the nearest cover. He knew the sound had come from behind Newton, so he trained his weapon in that direction. The night vision goggles and the scope on his gun gave him a distinct advantage over their assailant, and they now outnumbered him six-to-one.

Five-to-one. Across the courtyard where he had been when the gunfire started, one of his men lay face down. A distinct pool of liquid was visible even in the green fuzzy view offered by his headset. Only Newton had been facing that direction; it had to be him. Anger swelled in the pit of Marshall's stomach. *How the hell did the bastard get the drop on us?* He thought. He peered out from his cover, scanned the area, and spotted movement. He took aim, opened fire, and the target fell. He stepped out from his cover, swiftly approached the body and confirmed the kill with a double-tap to the head. He gave the all clear and the team regrouped at the door. Gardner and Hughes arrived moments later.

"Newton is dead," Smith confirmed.

"What the fuck happened?" Marshall demanded.

"He must've gone around the north-west corner to the front of the building," Gardner offered. "When Newton came around the back he was out of sight. I was already on my way to assist Hughes. He doubled back and attacked."

"That's an amateur-hour mistake; we can't afford for it to fucking happen again," Marshall snapped, and the team nodded. "For some reason there are no backup guards coming out of the building. Don't think for a second that'll be all of 'em, so we go in expecting resistance. Gardner and Smith go around the front and wait for my signal. On my order, we go in. Hughes, Bird, we'll take this door."

Marshall ran over to Newton's body and removed the bag of plastic explosives from his back. He checked the contents and threw the pack at Hughes. "You're our new demolition expert. I want C4 planted around the entire building. Once it's clear, move Newton's body in there. It'll have to go up with the rest."

With a nod, Gardner and Smith left. The remainder of the team prepared to breach, and two minutes later Smith confirmed that they were in position. Marshall gave the order to move in.

With Bird on the left of the door and Hughes on the right, Marshall stood between them. Marshall kicked the door through and Bird moved in, crossing to the right side followed by Hughes crossing to the left. Marshall followed. They swept the small rectangular room and found nobody. The secondary team confirmed via radio that the other entrance was also clear.

Marshall was surprised by the lack of resistance. "Strange," he muttered to himself. Bird and Hughes looked at him. "Press on," he ordered.

The pair nodded and joined him at a door on the opposite side of the room. There was a window in the middle, through which Bird peered.

"Clear," Bird said after a moment. He stepped away from the door with a frown.

"Don't keep it to yourself," Marshall said impatiently.

Bird's lip curled. "It's just a large open space with a small rectangular building in the middle. Never seen anything like it."

"And there's nobody guarding it?" Hughes asked sceptically.

"Nobody at all," Bird replied with a shake of his head.

Marshall grabbed his radio and activated it. "Gardner, are you ready to move?"

The radio crackled to life. "We are."

"We'll rendezvous at the entrance of the structure in the middle. Move out."

"Roger that."

v.

Marshall's team moved toward the square structure and lined the wall next to a re-enforced locked door. They repeated the breach tactic used to enter the building, but this time with C4 to remove the door. There were five men in the room, three of which they took down in the initial assault. The fourth was hidden behind what looked to Marshall like an airline drinks trolley, and the fifth was dressed in a long white coat with his arms in the air. He appeared to be unarmed in the moment before he dived for cover and went out of sight. Marshall, Bird and Hughes took cover behind a large table near the entrance and signalled to Gardner and Smith that they needed assistance.

The firefight soon turned into a standoff. The guard had no way to escape, but his vantage point meant that if the team attempted to move in he would cut them down in seconds. Marshall considered a grenade, but the room was clearly a laboratory so he decided against it. Gardner and Smith arrived at the doorway and stood behind cover outside.

"Gardner, you got any smoke?" Smith asked from one side of the door.

"Yeah, here," he replied, throwing a smoke grenade across the gap.

Smith pulled the pin and threw the grenade into the room toward the guard, and then ran straight at him only a second after it detonated. As he ran, Smith aimed his rifle toward the area where the guard had been hiding and sprayed it with bullets. The smoke cleared seconds later and the group saw that the target was down.

"Smith! What the fuck was that? Are you insane? He could have mowed you down with blind fire!" Marshall shouted with disbelief.

"Yeah, but he didn't. We don't have time to piss about; something needed to be done."

Marshall held back his retort, conceding in his mind that time was short so they should leave this argument for later. He made a mental note that there *would* be a 'later'.

There was one target left. "What is your name?" Marshall shouted.

"Sayid... Please, don't hurt me."

Marshall nodded to Bird as a signal that he was going to stand up. He turned to face the bench and slowly extended his legs. His rifle and his focus were intently on the room. "I'm coming out. Are you armed?" he asked.

"No."

Marshall was now standing and Bird had joined him. Sayid was also coming out from behind a chair that was effectively useless as cover.

"Where is the weapon you're working..." Marshall stopped in his tracks. He had seen something behind the scientist that he could not initially comprehend. In the corner of the room, approximately seven feet tall and two feet wide, was a doorway like nothing Marshall had ever seen before. It was fuzzy, like static on a television that was not tuned to any channels.

"What the hell is that?" Marshall shouted incredulously at Sayid.

"I don't.... My English..." Sayid replied.

Smith moved over to Sayid and repeated Marshall's question in native tongue. Sayid explained the answer to Smith, who translated it to English for the rest of the team. "It's a doorway. They haven't been able to work out the location of the other side, but it is like nowhere they have ever seen before. At the very least, it is a teleporter. He got it working, but he doesn't understand the science behind what it does or how it works. He says he only knows electronics."

Marshall could not believe what he was hearing, but at the same time he could see the "portal" with his own eyes. "Are there more of your people on the other side of that doorway?"

"Yes."

"How many?"

"Six. They are not scientists like me; they are from the military. An offshoot; this isn't an official operation," Sayid replied through Smith.

Marshall could see a device about the size of an audio cassette tape on the table near the doorway. "Does that control it?" he asked.

"Yes."

Marshall crossed the room and Smith joined him. He almost reached the device when there were two gunshots behind him. He turned in time to see Bird and Hughes drop to the floor with holes in their heads. Gardner had his weapon raised and was turning to aim at Marshall and Smith.

Quickly raising his weapon, Marshall took cover behind a desk. He dragged Smith with him as bullets began flying overhead from Gardner's weapon, which was now in full automatic mode. Sayid was caught in the maelstrom; his body had been destroyed by the onslaught, and he was thrown against the bench before dropping to the ground.

Marshall returned fire, and Gardner continued his barrage whilst taking cover himself. After a minute, the weapons went quiet.

"Drop your weapons," Gardner demanded.

"Gardner, what the fuck are you doing?" Marshall shouted across the room.

"We have what we came for. Time to go."

"*This* is what we came for?"

"Of course it is! Do you think we care about WMDs that are thousands of miles away from our shore? My God, you are either incredibly naive or just plain stupid. I'm taking the device back to England."

"This was your mission all along? What about Hughes?" Marshall said after a moment.

"He was deemed expendable. My orders are that nobody leaves here but me; the C4 that Hughes planted will see to that. Look, I have no quarrel with you Marshall; I'm happy to let you disappear. I'll tell everyone back home that you were killed in the assault. Throw me the device and let me leave. I won't come after you."

"Bullshit! You would shoot us at your first opportunity."

There was a pause. "You have no other way out, Marshall. You have to trust me."

Marshall looked at Smith and raised his chin toward the portal. Smith nodded with understanding.

"You made a mistake, Gardner," Marshall shouted, addressing the turncoat. "You let me assign Hughes to C4 duty. I never trusted either of you, so I kept the detonator."

Marshall took a small device out of his pocket, raised his weapon over the trolley, and fired several shots in Gardner's direction. As he stood and sidestepped toward the device that was sitting only a few metres away on the bench, Smith also stood and opened fire. Marshall grabbed the device as they ran backwards toward the portal, which they reached at the same time. Smith hesitated; Marshall shouted, "Go!" and pushed him through. Marshall hit the detonate button as he followed his comrade.

vi.

As he emerged, Marshall found himself staring at the same image of static that decorated the other side of the portal. The transition had been instantaneous. Instinctively, he dived to his right and covered his head with his arms. A second later a foray of debris came flying through the portal, but he noticed that the heat from the explosion had not transferred through with the objects. There was a crackling sound before the gateway rapidly shrank horizontally until it was nothing more than a line, then shrank vertically and was gone.

Smith stared at the space where the portal had been with his mouth hanging open.

With the portal closed, the room in which they found themselves was very dark. The only light source was two small lights above a doorway at the opposite side. Marshall could not make out any features in the room other than the door, so he took a torch from his pocket and shone it around the area. He could not make out much detail, but he determined that it was approximately twenty square feet in size.

Getting to his feet and crossing the room, Marshall approached the door with Smith following closely behind. "Get ready. Sayid said there are six hostiles here somewhere."

Marshall spotted a control panel on the wall; it was at chest height on the right side. After inspecting the panel, Marshall moved to the right side of the door. He readied his weapon, and confirmed that Smith was in position on the left. He pressed the central button on the panel. A latch moved inside the door, and it slid open with a mechanical hum.

A dimly lit corridor greeted Marshall and Smith. It was about fifty metres long with a high ceiling, and wide enough for two people to stroll side by side comfortably. They crossed the threshold and made their way down the corridor; there was a door in front of them at far the end. Approaching the next door with caution, Marshall and Smith took positions on either side and Marshall pressed the button on the frame. The door slid open to reveal an empty lift.

"Great," Marshall said as they entered. "Where are we supposed to take this?"

Smith moved to a panel with two buttons on it on the wall next to the door, and read the markings. "It's Arabic. There are no floor numbers but this word means, 'Alert', and this one means, 'Signal'," he said, pointing to each of the buttons.

"We can't use either of them until we eliminate the hostiles. We need to find a stairwell or a ladder, and clear one floor at a time. There must be a fire escape somewhere; it makes no sense that a lift be the only way off the floor."

"We could hit the alarm and wait for them to come to us," Smith said.

"No. We are outnumbered; right now our biggest advantage is surprise."

Smith nodded. They stepped off the lift and began their search.

vii.

The walls were matt silver, clearly metallic but unusual. Along the right wall of the corridor, there were several detachable sections that revealed pipes and cabling. Marshall and Smith made their way from one end of the corridor to the other checking each section. It was when they were almost back at the first door that Smith signalled to Marshall that he had found something.

Marshall crossed the corridor. Where a panel had been, there was a gap that contained a ladder leading through both the floor and the ceiling.

"Up or down?" Marshall asked, more to himself than Smith.

"Down is most likely to be the way out. Up is more interesting," Smith offered with a smile.

Marshall's decision was made. He checked his weapon and moved toward the ladder. "Up it is. We aren't leaving until we get some Intel on where we are, and what the hell this place is."

Marshall took the lead as the pair started climbing.

Marshall and Smith climbed for several minutes before they reached the top of the shaft. They stopped and each wrapped an arm around the rung closest to shoulder height; Marshall was above Smith.

"We need to remove this panel quickly. Taking it off by hand will give anyone on the other side too much time to cut us down. Explosives will alert anyone on the floors below," Marshall whispered, pausing to think. "Let's try something. Can you reach this panel?"

"Yeah, just," Smith replied.

"I want you to tap on it every 5 seconds, hard enough to let anyone on the other side hear it. Make sure your timing is right. It wants to sound artificial, like something has come loose and is rattling around. Hopefully anyone on the other side won't know this is a ladder shaft."

"Okay, ready when you are," Smith confirmed.

Marshall readied his weapon and signalled Smith to begin. It was eleven knocks later, shortly after Marshall started to think the other side must be clear, that there was a noise. The panel was being removed from the wall.

viii.

"Activating primary engines," the computer said to Rimoon in Arabic. *Finally,* he thought. "We need to find a way to steer this vessel. Naseeb, go and get reinforcements. We need experts in technology, sciences, and engineering. Get them from anywhere in the world, and use whatever means necessary to secure their cooperation."

Naseeb nodded and made his way toward the lift in the corner of the room; he collected his AK-47 on the way, having left it on a workstation earlier. He reached the door and summoned a car. As he waited, he heard what sounded like knocking coming from his left. He turned to face the strange sound, raised his weapon, and approached it with caution. He walked along the wall slowly, noticing he had gained the attention of several of his comrades who were scattered around the room.

"Naseeb, what are you doing?" Rimoon asked.

Naseeb waved his hand up and down in the direction of Rimoon without looking away from the source of the sound. Rimoon fell silent obligingly. Naseeb continued toward the sound; his knees were bent to almost a crouch as he reached his destination. He moved close to the wall and put his ear against the surface. He was certain that something was knocking on the wall from the other side.

Naseeb and the others had used the ladder shafts to get around the ship until they had learned how to operate the lift. The wall panel before him was the access point to the ladder shaft for getting to and from the bridge. *Why would anyone still be using the ladders?* He thought as he knelt down. He placed his weapon on the deck. Rimoon approached with a weapon he had collected from a nearby bench, and within moments he was standing behind Naseeb in silence.

Naseeb removed the panel from the wall. It hit the deck with a clang and he slid it to the right to get a view of the source of the knocking.

ix.

Marshall opened fire. Smith grabbed his weapon from where he had rested its barrel on a ladder rung and fired through the opening. The panel fell to the ground. Marshall had put a bullet through the neck of the handler of the panel, but was caught off-guard by the other man towering behind him. Fortunately, Smith had a good view of the second man and opened fire on him immediately. He dropped unceremoniously, hit square in the chest by at least five rounds. Marshall now had a restricted view of the room. He could hear the shouting of at least two men. He crawled out of the shaft and, while keeping low, ran toward what appeared to be a large table that stretched the length of the curved left-hand wall. The table was around a metre away from the wall itself. Marshall dropped behind it and waited for Smith to join him.

Smith wasn't far behind. Gunfire had erupted from the far side of the room but it was wild and missed its target. Marshall and Smith remained crouched for several seconds before they split up. Marshall remained at the near end of the bench whilst Smith made his way around the room's periphery, always crouched behind the protective barrier. The pair could still see each other. Marshall nodded to Smith and the two men simultaneously swept their weapons over the bench, took aim, and downed their two assailants. The room was clear.

Two left, Marshall thought

It was a moment before the adrenaline subsided. Marshall stood with his back to the curved wall and looked around the semi-circular room. He realised that the furniture that had served as cover was not simply a table, but was in fact a curved bank of workstations that faced where he was standing. Against the rear wall there was a rigid metal chair facing him in the centre. Marshall counted four high-backed metal chairs equally dispersed around the interior of the arched workstations. Behind him there was a large screen in the centre of what he deemed to be the front wall, and stretching out on either side of the screen was a long strip of glass that appeared to have some form of shutter on the outside blocking the view.

The rear wall had two screens mounted one on either side of the centre chair, though Marshall had never seen a screen as thin as they appeared to be.

The workstations were all powered down except for two on the main console and one on the rear wall to the left of the chair. The chair had a panel of its own on the left arm; Marshall noticed a glow around it, which led him to conclude it was also active.

Marshall was confused by the technology in the room. There were what appeared to be computer screens everywhere but he could see no sign of any keyboards or other input devices.

The pair investigated the room for several minutes. Smith was at the rear, looking at the active station on the wall, while Marshall was attempting to read the text displayed on one of the front console's active screens. He glanced at the uncomfortable looking chairs that lined the bench; they were angular with no upholstery and had severe edges at each join in their structure. Smith called for Marshall to join him, so he made his way to the rear of the room.

"Again it's all in Arabic. We must still be in Iraq."

Marshall nodded, "This room is laid out like the bridge of a ship, but it makes no sense why Iraqis would be so interested in anything like that. Very odd. The furniture too; it all looks very uncomfortable," he said, his brow furrowed.

"It could be the command centre of some sort of military bunker. That would explain the Arabic language and all the workstations in here," Smith said.

"It might also explain the strange metal that the walls are made of," Marshall said. "If it's a military bunker, why are there only six of them? Moreover, where did they get all of this tech? Iraqis are hardly renowned for pioneering technology."

"Hmm," Smith responded.

A voice surrounded them; there was a distinct lack of emotional intonation. It was male and it echoed loudly in the large room. "Language recognised. Reinitialising to English interface."

The workstation next to Marshall and Smith flickered and was now rendered in English. Smith looked at Marshall with his eyes wide, and the two men stood in the strange room completely mesmerised.

x.

Marshall and Smith spent several hours going over each of the workstations. They had determined that they were on the bridge of a ship, as the leftmost station on the main console controlled a weapons array of some sort. The rightmost displayed details of a communications system that was currently offline and the one at the rear had readings from the engines. The panel on the left arm of the centre chair had a status report of key systems throughout the vessel. *Life support?* Marshall thought when he read the list of primary systems. *Surely, it's not a submarine!* He thought. The display indicated that all systems were offline except for life support, atmospheric control, and the engines.

Marshall was amazed to discover that each station had a touchscreen interface. He had never seen technology such as this and it heightened his curiosity even further.

Reluctantly, he decided to suspend their investigation until they had neutralised the remaining enemies. They had been here for longer than he had planned already.

"Smith, it's time to go. We need to secure this place before we investigate any further."

Smith stood up from the communications station on the main console and met Marshall at the ladder shaft on the right side of the room. "It's definitely a ship of some kind. I've found an area in the computer that has technical instructions for many of the systems on board. It's all gibberish; it needs the eyes of an expert. What's useful is the instruction manual for the computer. I found out how to get the lift to work, it's actually laughably simple. We could have saved ourselves a climb," Smith said with a smile.

Marshall was pleased. The news meant they could clear out

of the ship much more quickly. He joined Smith at the entrance to the lift that was only a few metres to the right of the ladder. There was a car waiting.

The pair entered the lift. Smith waited until they were both in position and had their weapons ready before stating, "Ship," there was a chime from the ceiling, "deck two." There was another chime and the lift started moving. It was only two-seconds later that it stopped and the doors opened.

Marshall was surprised by the speed of the lift. He was grateful that there were no hostiles on the other side of the doors, as he was not quite prepared to arrive so soon.

The two men swept the corridors and rooms throughout the deck. They found nobody, and no rooms of particular interest. The deck comprised primarily of crew quarters. From the size of them Marshall concluded they were for the senior staff. There was a door at the end of the main corridor, and to its right there was a panel that read, "Controller". Marshall studied the panel inquisitively for a moment before he tapped the button and the door slid open. He entered the room to find it fairly spacious. To his immediate right against the wall there was a desk with a rigid metal stool. Directly in front of him against the opposite wall was a piece of furniture shaped like a sofa, but made of metal with sharp angles similar to the seating on the bridge and likewise fitted with no upholstery. The sofa and two similar chairs surrounded a low table. An archway to Marshall's left led to another room, which was empty bar the rotten remains of what looked like some form of cocoon. *What the fuck is this place?* Marshall thought as he stared at the cocoon. He was uncomfortable near it, so he hastily returned to the living area.

Marshall noticed that the slanted wall behind the sofa had a window similar to the one on the bridge. It spanned the width of the room, but a shutter blocked the view. To the right of the window there was a panel; he approached it and tapped the single button.

There was a hum from a motor as the external shutter retracted upwards. Marshall was stunned. The large blue and green sphere of the Earth filled the unveiled vista, surrounded by a sea of blackness and the flickering light of distant stars.

This has to be a screen of some kind, he decided. He needed to confirm what he was seeing, so he turned and left the quarters immediately and went into an adjacent room. In this room he spotted a window, which was also closed. He approached and opened it to reveal the same scene.

"My God", he whispered.

Marshall left the quarters and met up with Smith. After describing what he had found, he showed Smith and they both stood for several minutes staring at the view.

"Now what?" Smith eventually asked.

"I have no idea," Marshall replied truthfully.

After a prolonged silence, Marshall exhaled. "Let's clear out the rest of the ship and take it from there," he said.

Smith nodded. "Agreed."

The two men hurried back to the lift and continued to Deck 3 where they found smaller crew quarters, but no signs of life. The next three decks were identical to Deck 3. On Deck 7 they again met with no hostiles, but they did find a medical bay. The room was dark, its workstations inactive and the beds empty. Marshall noted again the lack of coverings on the three beds that lined the wall opposite the entrance. There was a large number of instruments scattered on a bench spanning the left hand wall, and next to the bench was a door that led to a storage room. Marshall approached the bench; he examined the pile of tools to find that they were mostly knives of various shapes and sizes, and a number of other items that he did not recognise.

On Deck 8 there was an array of escape pods lining the hull, along with a cavernous bay area, which contained two vehicles, that Marshall supposed were shuttles or drop ships. There was a door spanning the width of the room; he suspected that it led out to open space but he did not want to verify the theory.

On Deck 9, a corridor led from the lift to a large compartment, which contained a vast number of computer workstations. In the centre was an object that Marshall supposed was the engine core. Before entering the room, Smith heard a voice coming from the far corner. He signalled to Marshall and they dropped to a crouch and entered silently.

It took only a few seconds to reach the area where two men were leaning over a computer monitor. Whatever was on the screen had completely absorbed their attention.

Marshall and Smith crept behind their targets and took out their knives. Simultaneously, they grabbed the men by the chin and jerked their heads upward to expose their necks. In a swift motion, they opened their throats, intersecting the carotid artery on both sides.

Dropping the lifeless bodies to the deck, Marshall turned to face Smith. "We need to check there's no more of them, but that should be the lot," he said, stepping over the corpses to reach the console that the two men had been studying. "We also need to know what they were looking at; it could help us figure out what this thing is."

They swept the remaining decks, which were mostly empty storage bays. There was no further sign of life. Once the sweeps were complete, Smith returned to the Engine Room while Marshall went to the Bridge. The most important thing now was to determine how to get the ship under their control, and to find a way to get a portal open so they had the option of going home.

xi.

Marshall sat at the desk in the Captain's Quarters, which he had claimed at the end of their first day aboard the ship. Both he and Smith had worked through as much of the ship's library as they could, but most of the contents were baffling. *They might as well have been left in their native language*, he thought.

The library detailed the original mission of the ship, and

Marshall had discovered that its name was A-327, which he found particularly sterile. He learned that an alien race called the Aletheans had built the ship, and that they had been studying Earth for many years. Marshall read the mission logs intently. He became so absorbed in the files that he did not notice over four hours pass.

What the fuck is a holo-mesh? He thought as he read the reports.

Realising the time, Marshall got up and began to pace the room. He was hungry. For the past few days, he and Smith had been living on field rations, and not only was he sick of them, but they were running out. He decided that his top priority must be to find food, or at least to work out how to get the portal open again so they could go back to Earth for supplies.

He returned to his seat and scanned the library's index. There was no mention of a food storage area, but he found the instructions for the portal system and started reading.

xii.

Smith was confused and irritable. The engineering manual was too technical, the communications array was offline, and the bridge had so many workstations and systems that he did not know where to start.

Marshall called him on the radio and requested his presence on Deck 10. Smith made his way to the lift, reached deck 10 in a few seconds, and found Marshall at the other end of the corridor walking toward the room where they had first arrived on the ship.

"What's up?" Smith asked as he reached Marshall.

"There's no specific room where the portals are opened; the ship can open them anywhere we want."

Marshall pressed the wall control and the door opened. "One room we didn't find on our search of the ship was the armoury. I looked in the library, turns out it's here."

The pair entered the room. It was as dark as they had left it.

"Ship, lights on." Marshall commanded.

The ship acknowledged with a low-pitched beep, and the room was immediately illuminated. Marshall's earlier guess of twenty square feet had been almost perfect. The flanking walls were lined floor to ceiling with storage lockers. At the far end, a bench stretched across the full length of the rear wall. The only other item in the room was a workstation to the left of the entrance; it was at chest height with no chair and was currently inactive.

Marshall approached a locker. He pressed a red button located in the centre of the door. The light changed to green, and a latch slid aside before the door fell ajar. Marshall fully opened the locker to reveal a number of assault rifles; he reached in and took one from its cradle.

The rifle looked very similar to the new American P90 submachine-gun. With a very short barrel, its trigger on the underside at the front, and a short plastic-like stock, it was relatively short and light for a rifle. Marshall was impressed with the feel of the weapon; the weight made it extremely portable but it felt solid and well balanced. He noticed on the side that there was a switch that he had presumed was the safety catch; however, next to it was a small LED.

Smith had crossed the room to join him. He removed another rifle from the locker and examined it.

Marshall opened a cover on the shoulder rest at the back of the rifle, revealing a slightly recessed button underneath. He pressed the button. The rifle made a sound similar to a defibrillator charging, and the light next to the switch on the side immediately lit up green. With a glance at Smith who had looked over when he heard the rifle activate, Marshall pressed the safety catch and realised it had more than two positions. The first click switched the light to yellow; another changed it to red.

"If only we had a firing range," Marshall said with a smile, before pressing the button on the rifle hilt to deactivate the weapon. Smith grinned and they secured the rifles in the locker.

Marshall turned to face Smith, "We need help. Engineers, physicists, astronomers, and at least one doctor."

"We aren't going home then?" Smith asked.

"No. This ship is too valuable to abandon, and after what happened with Gardner there's no chance in hell that I'm handing it over to the government," Marshall said, inviting no further questions on the subject.

"Do you have anyone in mind?" Smith asked.

"There's an engineer I met a couple of years ago who might

be able to understand the ship's systems. Aside from him, I know a doctor that we can trust, and a pilot who could probably fly this thing given time. I don't know any scientists or astronomers, and the only tech specialist I can think of is Bird," Marshall said with a grimace. "You?"

"I know a couple of physicists, but no astronomers. No professionals anyway."

"Okay, we get the engineer, pilot, doctor and physicists on board. We'll explain the situation, and hopefully between them they can bring in people to fill the gaps."

Marshall took a small piece of paper from his pocket. "Ship, open a portal between this room and coordinates." He looked at the paper. "Latitude 55.0245429 mark -1.5679427. Longitude 55.0245429 mark -1.5679427."

After an acknowledgement chime from the ship, a portal formed creating a vertical line that extended from its centre point at waist height in both directions, until it met the floor and stood just over two metres tall. It then widened to form a full doorway identical to the one that the pair had used to board the ship. Marshall looked at Smith with a smug grin. "I figured out how to get these things open. They use a coordinate system that I found in the ship's computer."

Marshall reached into a pocket in his jacket, and took out two devices identical to the one used on Earth. "These tell the ship to open a portal that will bring us back," he said, handing one to Smith.

"I'll go first. There's one man I need to bring up here before we go any further. We can't risk leaving the ship unattended, so I need you to wait until I get back. I'll be out of contact, but I intend to return within the hour. If I don't, use the same co-ordinates to open a portal from here," Marshall said before handing the paper to Smith.

"Are you expecting trouble?" Smith asked.

"No, but if this device doesn't work that's where I'll be waiting. Open a portal and I'll come through."

Smith acknowledged before Marshall stepped through the vortex and disappeared.

3. The Aletheans

i.

1657 A.D. (Earth Calendar)

Thousands of indigenous life forms inhabited the lush green world of Alethea Prime. The dominant species were the Aletheans who had evolved from reptilian forbears.

The Aletheans had been travelling in space for centuries. With a population of 4.6 billion, Alethea Prime was the most densely populated of all Alethean worlds, and remained a central hub of activity despite the expansion of their domain over the last two hundred years. They had successfully terraformed and colonised several planets and moons in their local star systems, and had more recently moved into neighbouring clusters.

The Aletheans were bipedal and averaged seven feet in height. In their youth, their skin was a rough grey flesh, and as they aged they grew an exoskeleton, which gradually covered their upper body and skull.

The exoskeleton served as protection from the wide variety of wildlife with which they shared Alethea Prime. For centuries, there had been heated debate amongst the Aletheans as to whether they should segregate the more primitive life from their society, but ultimately the agreement had always been to allow them to co-exist without interference.

Despite being a largely peaceful people, conflicts of varying severity littered Alethean history. Most of their disputes had been over land or religion, though there had been the occasional coup d'état.

Three hundred years ago, an asteroid had threatened all life on Alethea Prime. The inhabitants had worked together to prevent the impact, and succeeded. Since that time, they had enjoyed a unity unparalleled in the history of their species.

Their newfound ability to work together inspired Project Pathfinder. The purpose of the project was to catalogue the galaxy, searching for planets with similar attributes to their own.

They had spent 200 Alethean years (an Alethean year is equivalent to 1.6 Earth years) on the project, and several times in the early days it had almost been cancelled when it failed to yield results. Despite this, the scientists and astronomers persisted until they confirmed their first match 184 years ago.

The ultimate goal of Project Pathfinder was to locate habitable planets and establish the status of the dominant species. Any solar system containing a planet worthy of further investigation was designated a "candidate", and survey vessels were dispatched to investigate further. To date they had discovered 12 primitive worlds that were capable of supporting life such as their own, and they now had a ship in orbit of each planet conducting research.

The captain of each vessel was in charge of the mission; however, it was ultimately the responsibility of the Alethean central command to decide the suitability of a "candidate".

ii.

Vessel A-327 was one of the newest in the Alethean fleet. At 189 Alethean years old, her commander was middle-aged. With almost half of his life spent in the military, he had been in command of A-327 for a relatively brief time when the assignment to survey "Candidate 11" was given to him.

The journey from Alethea Prime had taken many years, but the findings on this world had exceeded his expectations. He sat in the command chair on the bridge, studying the latest report from the primary survey team.

The world around which they were now in orbit had been declared suitable by central command, subject to a holo-mesh, which was to remain in place until the dominant species achieved atomic power. Because of recommendations submitted by the team aboard A-327, command had agreed that Controller and his ship should remain for 40 more years, at which point a relief ship would replace them and they would return home.

The holo-mesh was currently under construction around candidate 11 by a team of engineers from A-327. The purpose of the mesh was to project a holographic field, which would display a pre-prepared view of the outer galaxy, thereby preventing the native population from making discoveries for which they were not yet ready. Over the coming years, the mesh would be modified as their development progressed, gradually allowing more of the real universe to become visible.

When complete, the mesh would comprise thousands of small emitters scattered evenly around the world below. At a distance of 400,000 kilometres from the planet, it would encompass the natural satellite and a portion of local space. By the time the inhabitants had developed a manned vessel that could achieve that distance from their home world, they would be ready for first contact and the mesh would be dismantled.

"Controller," Executive said as he approached, "is that the report from the primary team?"

Executive was physically similar to Controller, although the bone structure of his face did not have such strong definition. This was due to his age; at only 103, Executive was not due to start development of an exoskeleton for at least another decade. Controller looked up and smiled at his colleague. "It is," he said. "They are a fascinating species. Every day it seems there is something new to read about in these reports."

"I'm sorry, Controller, but I disagree," Executive said bluntly.

Executive's discomfort was obvious. "You are always welcome to speak freely, my friend," Controller said kindly.

"This planet is an unsuitable candidate. Its inhabitants are barbaric. They fight each other given any excuse, and they have not yet even grasped the power of simple electricity. We should not be here. There must be superior options for us to survey," he said quickly, his passion evident.

"You have never raised such objections before. What has brought you to this sudden conclusion?"

"The reports! Look at their recent history; their disregard for life is beyond reasonable comprehension."

"You are mistaken. They have shown unique inventiveness. Only recently, I read a report of a significant leap in their understanding of logarithms and astronomy. I estimate they are only 30 of their years away from realising the basic principles of physics!"

Executive frowned, "You must also consider the loss of a full third of the population of one of their largest countries. And what of the war that lasted for almost 20 years?"

"30 years. We are in orbit of their world now; we should use their units of time."

Realisation that Controller was fully aware of the content of recent reports made Executive pause for thought. "I meant no disrespect, Controller," he said, "I simply wish to air my reservations about this candidate."

"I appreciate your honesty," Controller replied, "but I think that in a few years you will come to see that this world is not only worthy, but in fact it has the highest potential of any candidate yet."

iii.

1687 A.D. (Earth Calendar)

Controller strode onto the bridge; his rotation was about to begin. With the holo-mesh online, and the science team now forming a strong foundation of a report for command, Controller was pleased with the progress of the mission.

As he approached the command chair, the communications officer informed him they had received a transmission from Alethea Prime.

"Put it on the main screen," Controller ordered.

The screen came to life. It displayed an elderly Alethean whose white exoskeleton fully covered the flesh of his face. "I bid you well from all here at central command. This message is being simultaneously transmitted to all survey vessels, though when you receive it will be dependent upon your distance from home world.

"I bear grave news. A pathogen has swept across the Alethean system, with virility unlike anything previously reported. To date, we have seen 60% infection with a total mortality rate. On average, the infected progress from initial symptom onset to death within five months. The incubation period is abnormally long, estimated at around 11 years; however, it is infectious from the point of contagion.

"We believe that this outbreak originated from a sample collected on one of the candidate worlds. Almost certainly harmless to the native population, it has proved deadly to ourselves and so we must initiate a system wide quarantine to prevent it from spreading further.

"We have no reports of any survey vessel succumbing to this virus, though all colonies have confirmed cases. Central command hereby orders all vessels to remain with their candidate until further notice. You are under no circumstances to return to Alethea Prime or to rendezvous with one another.

"Only five of our expeditions contain a hatchery. They are located at candidates two, three, four, seven and ten. You are our best hope of survival; you must begin fertilisation at the earliest opportunity. If we fail to contain and cure this virus, your hatcheries may be our species' only chance of survival.

"All of you, your mission must continue. We ask that you take all necessary steps to prevent contamination of the candidates. We will contact you again in due course. Good luck."

The screen deactivated, returning to a star field. Controller absorbed the words from home before addressing the crew. "Everyone is dismissed. Secure your stations and clear the bridge," he said.

Except for Executive, the crew obeyed the command leaving the two senior officers alone.

"What shall we do?" Executive asked.

"We have our orders," Controller replied softly. "We will allow the crew to come to terms with this news, and then continue with our mission," he replied.

"We have some of our finest scientific minds aboard this ship. We must return home at once!" Executive exclaimed angrily.

"You heard the orders from command!" Controller shouted, raising to his feet and stepping toward his subordinate. "Know your place, Executive!" he finished.

Executive appeared to shrink in height. "Yes, Controller. Apologies."

"This news is distressing for all of us. Return to your quarters. There is nothing more to be done today. When morning arrives, we shall all discuss our next move."

iv.

The crew of A-327 continued their mission as ordered. A week after receiving the transmission from the home world, Controller convened a meeting with six members of the physical sciences team. He knew each of them well, and respected them more than any other members of his crew.

"Thank you for coming," Controller started when the team had taken their seats in the conference room. There were a series of nods before he continued.

"Would I be correct to assume you are all aware of the Causality Pact?" he asked.

Each member of the meeting nodded. The Causality Pact was standard reading at the science academy. It was drafted over 100 years earlier and ratified by the leaders of the home world and the colonies. The purpose of the pact was to prevent the development of any form of technology that would enable time travel, by making all research into the subject illegal with a punishment of life imprisonment.

"Please, do tell me why the pact was created," Controller said.

After a pause, one of the scientists spoke up. "The risks involved with any form of time displacement are too great and the laws of temporal causality too unpredictable. For that reason, development of such technology was deemed too dangerous to permit," he said.

Controller scoffed. "Just as I thought. What your textbooks have omitted was that time displacement technology has already been invented, and through blind fear central command created the causality pact based upon speculation and conjecture."

The room fell silent; the gathering stared at Controller intently. He stopped for a moment to gather his thoughts. "One hundred and twenty-four years ago, I was an eminent member of the physical science community. I was at the peak of my profession and had dedicated almost thirty years to unlocking the secret of time travel. On a day I will never forget, I discovered the missing part of our equations. We were so excited, my colleagues and I, that without hesitation we began to construct the device.

"Central command demanded regular updates on our work, and we were ecstatic to be reporting that we had made a monumental discovery. When command reviewed the report, their reaction was one we had not predicted.

"Rather than celebrating our discovery, they sent an enforcement team to our laboratory to arrest us and confiscate our equipment. I was held for many days before an officer of the court interrogated me. He insisted that I hand over all research documents to him. I was rather pleased with myself as I had successfully encrypted and hidden the data before they took me in, and I refused to co-operate with the officer throughout my stay in detention.

"After many weeks, considering my lack of co-operation, I was given a choice of either a life in the military away from Alethea Prime and the colonies, or life imprisonment. Some fabricated charges would find themselves pressed against me, as I had in fact done nothing illegal.

"I chose the military, and since that time I have served aboard a number of vessels whilst never being allowed to return home. The causality pact was ratified less than a year after my exile, and I never spoke of my former life again."

Nobody in the room spoke for almost a full minute, and then the same scientist who had responded earlier asked, "Controller, did you ever resume your research in secret?"

"No. Central command had been watching my movements ever since I left home world. They do not realise that I am aware of them, but until approximately forty years ago, I picked up on several of their agents monitoring my activities. I think they may have finally lost interest in me."

"May I ask why you are telling us this now?" the scientist asked.

Controller chuckled, though no smile was visible beneath his exoskeleton. "Ah yes, the point of our meeting," he said. "I have pondered possible solutions to the crisis on the home world, and I believe there is a course of action which will guarantee our success in eradicating the virus.

"I believe that we should rebuild the time displacement device, then go back to before the virus reached Alethea Prime and warn them not to visit the source world. If we are successful, we will stop the plague before it starts and save not only everyone on home world, but also all those who have already died."

The team looked at each other wide-eyed. "You still have the research?" one of them asked incredulously.

"I do," Controller answered, opening his hand to reveal a memory unit. "We can use the data on this to reconstruct the device. The first was not complete but the specifications are all on here."

"Controller," another said, "this is an illegal action. We all face imprisonment if we are discovered, and the research you carry is highly dangerous."

"True, but given the circumstances I believe it is a risk we must take. I cannot do this alone. You represent the finest our scientific community has to offer. I have not practiced science for over a century and have no access to home world's libraries. I need your help," Controller pleaded.

There was hesitation in every member of the team. Controller decided to press his argument further. "Not only are our families in danger, but the survival of our entire species is at risk. We are left with no other option. I cannot order you to carry this out, but I ask you to volunteer. If you refuse, no shame shall befall you."

After several glances were exchanged, everyone in the room nodded their ascent. Controller wished them luck and dismissed the meeting.

v.

Several months passed after Controller began his quest to complete the work he started over a century earlier. The science team worked covertly on the device, shrouding their true intentions with a facade of investigative work aimed at the planet below.

Controller was on the bridge when Executive approached and asked him for a meeting to discuss the mission. He obliged Executive immediately, following his colleague into the conference room. The room contained a long metal table that stretched from one end to the other. Metallic seats surrounded it, and behind the chair at the near end of the table was a recessed counter upon which a bowl of water sat. The entrance was to the left of the recess.

"A moment," Controller said before he stepped toward the recess. He stood in front of the bowl and jerked his head downward, submerging it in the cold water. Executive waited patiently as Controller gulped down almost half of the bowl's contents, before he stood upright and turned to face Executive. His head was dripping wet, but he did not attempt to dry it.

"Please, be seated," Controller said.

The two officers sat opposite each other at the near end of the table. Controller waited silently for Executive to state the purpose of the meeting.

"Controller," he began, "I must ask you to explain to me what the physical sciences team has been working on for the past four months," he stated bluntly.

Surprised by their discovery, Controller carefully formulated a response. "They have been researching the method by which a renowned scientist on Earth derived his conclusions for a recent publication. It is quite fascinating. This Newton describes-"

"That is enough, Controller," Executive interrupted. "I have been observing the team's movements and have found a great deal of irregular activity. Material requisitions, approved by you for purposes undisclosed. Visits to areas of the ship that the nature of their assignment cannot explain. An increased interest in our power output capabilities. Tell me, Controller, why would a team investigating scientific literature require an induction coil?"

Controller felt a wave of discomfort. "Why indeed? Have you asked them? I do not busy myself with the everyday activities of the crew. That is your job. Your line of questioning re-enforces my belief that you are very thorough."

Executive straightened in his chair. "Controller, we have worked together for a long time. Tell me what you have them doing," he said.

Controller considered bringing his friend into his confidence, but decided it safer for both of them that he remained ignorant. "The science team is working on standard research functions. More than that, I cannot say."

Executive's shoulders visibly sagged, his gaze dropped from Controller's eyes to the table in front of him. "I know what you are doing," he said, adding nothing further for several seconds. "After all this time, I thought you had actually given up on this."

Controller could barely contain his anxiety. Executive was still staring at the conference table as he continued. "I have served by your side for almost forty years," he said, looking up. "I have followed your orders, and aided you in many arguments with command despite any personal reservations I may have had. As I came to know you, I believed you had changed from the man you were at the science academy."

Controller looked at his colleague with interest. "And what kind of man is that?" he asked.

"A reckless one, motivated by self-interest with a wilful disregard of anyone and anything that gets in the way of his theories. A man with such blind determination to become the most famous scientist in history that anything in his way would be cast aside, even the risk of universal destruction."

"I was once the man you describe, but no longer," Controller said calmly. "After my exile, I pursued my military career with the same passion I once had for science, but I have become a far more considerate officer than I ever was as a scientist. Tell me, how do you know of my past? And what prompted you to investigate the science team?" he asked, already suspecting the response.

"You already know the answer, Controller," Executive responded.

Controller had been correct. He was a spy for central command, placed alongside him to observe his activities and ensure that he adhered to the agreement he made all those years ago. "Since the beginning?" he asked.

Executive nodded.

"So what happens now?" he asked.

"I take you into custody. Protocol dictates that I return you to Alethea Prime for trial; however, given the current situation that will not be possible for some time. Until the pathogen crisis is resolved, you and the physical science team will be confined to quarters. I sent a security detail to arrest them earlier."

"You fool!" Controller shouted, rising to his feet. "This is the one chance we have to save our people! You read the report last week, we could be all but extinct in months!"

"The law is clear, Controller. You violated your agreement and thereby forfeit the freedom you were granted as a result of it."

"[Untranslatable] the law! We are on the verge of extinction and you are concerned with a ruling that was passed over a century ago!"

Executive stood slowly. "We cannot use our current predicament as an excuse for the flagrant abuse of our laws. Our biological science teams both here and on home world will find a cure for the pathogen. There is no need to carry out your illegal experiments, especially when the cost could be the universe itself!"

"That will not happen. With care, we can use it safely," Controller said.

"The argument is moot; I have had your device destroyed just as your first attempt was."

Rage swelled in Controller. "No!" he screamed as he jumped over the table, colliding with his full weight against Executive.

The two men fell to the ground loudly, Executive's chair spinning across the room and colliding with the bulkhead under the window.

They struggled in a mutual grapple for several seconds before Controller pushed his upper body into the air. Executive was trapped between Controller's legs, which were clamped tightly around his torso. Controller swung a fist into Executive's face; the younger man's exoskeleton was too underdeveloped to absorb the force. Before Executive could react, he threw a second punch with his other arm. Executive went limp; Controller climbed off his subordinate and rose to his feet.

Straightening his uniform, Controller approached the exit. When he reached the door, it opened automatically to reveal two security officers in the opening with their backs to him. Hearing the door, they turned, and seeing Controller alone they instinctively raised their weapons. Controller considered a lunge, but realised quickly that the distance between himself and the pair was too great, and unarmed he would stand no chance of victory. He slowly raised his arms. "There's no need for alarm, I surrender," he said.

vi.

With Controller and his team secured in their quarters, and the time displacement device destroyed, Executive was initially pleased that he and the crew could again focus on curing the pathogen and completing their mission at Candidate 11. His satisfaction was erased five months later, when A-327 received a transmission from Alethea Prime informing them that the pathogen had eradicated the general population and only remnants of life remained on the planet. The colonies had been lifeless for several weeks, and with this final transmission, they confirmed the end of their civilisation.

As he detailed the update to Controller who sat on the end of the cot in his cell, Executive was overcome and collapsed to the deck. Controller stood and approached him. "Believe me when I say I understand your actions, my friend," he said, placing a hand on the shoulder of his former colleague. "But you see now why my way is the only solution? It is not too late for our people. We must rebuild the device and complete my work."

Executive looked up at Controller. "It is too late. Upon receipt of the latest update, a significant number of the crew succumbed to their anguish. They completed the rite of Al'sharai."

"Al'sharai?" Controller repeated. *How?* He thought. Al'sharai was a suicide ritual many Aletheans performed when facing terminal or degenerative illness. It was less common now than in days past, but without an ocean, he could not understand how it could be completed here. A moment of panic struck him. "Gods, you did not allow them to go down to the candidate?!" he demanded.

"No, Controller. Our people believed the ocean of stars to be a suitable alternative," he replied.

Relieved for a moment before the reality of what had happened returned, Controller enquired further. "How many?" he asked.

"Twenty-three. When we conclude our conversation, I intend to join them," Executive said sternly.

Over half the crew, Controller thought. He returned to his bunk and sat down. "Executive, I formally request my reinstatement as Controller of this ship. You need not complete Al'sharai, there is still time. As long as we have this ship and the science team we can complete the work."

Still in a seated position on the deck, Executive's head dropped. "As I said, it is too late," he reiterated. "I released your team some weeks ago. I believed that without your influence they could be trusted to return to duty until we could return to Alethea Prime. When news arrived of home world's demise, they all took part in the ritual."

"All of them?!" Controller asked urgently.

"Yes."

Young fools, Controller thought. *Their choice has cost us everything.*

vii.

Executive completed the rite of Al'sharai two days later, with Controller in attendance. Mourning the man who he had called friend for many years, Controller assumed command of the ship and ordered the remaining crew to continue their mission at Candidate 11.

Controller's mourning did not end with Executive. For the remainder of his life he thought about his people, of their demise, and of how he could have prevented it.

As the years passed, Controller was often astounded at the scientific leaps the people of Candidate 11 were making. With the invention of the electrical capacitor, the steam engine, and the battery, the dominant life forms were truly taking their first major steps toward realising their potential.

In 1804 A.D. the serving Executive (the third to bear the name aboard A-327) completed the rite of passage for Controller after he died in his sleep. Controller's body was wrapped in gauze and launched into space toward the local star. Executive was the last Alethean to serve aboard A-327; he died on January 14th 1846 at the age of 291.

viii.

1945 A.D. (Earth Calendar)

The standing orders of Controller before he died were to reprogram the holo-mesh to reduce its coverage over the years that followed, as the Aletheans knew that without a hatchery they would not live to see their mission to completion.

In 1945 A.D., the mesh detected thermonuclear explosions on the surface of Candidate 11. This signalled the emergence and realisation of atomic physics on the planet below. As instructed by its creators, the mesh launched a pair of devices capable of opening a portal to A-327 toward two separate regions of the candidate.

The Aletheans had no way to predict how much time would pass before the inhabitants discovered the devices, but they were certain that one day they would be found.

4. Odyssey

i.

1993 A.D.

Marshall emerged from the portal on Folly Lane in Hertfordshire. He was here to see John Medforth, who had lived in the quiet suburb since moving out of the Regiment barracks less than a year earlier. In the five years since they met during SAS selection, where Medforth had served as his instructor, the pair had become friends. There was nobody that Marshall respected more than Medforth, so when he realised he needed help aboard the ship there was only one name that came to mind.

Six, eight, ten, Marshall counted along the row of houses. *Typical*, he thought, as he looked at the other side of the road where the odd numbers sat. *Even with a bloody teleporter, I need to walk.*

A vehicle with an excessive sound system drove past at high speed. He watched the car disappear into the distance before crossing the road, whilst cursing the elderly woman who was driving. He arrived at the door of number twenty-seven, and knocked without delay.

A very short woman answered. At the sight of Marshall, her eyes widened and she slammed the door shut before locking it.

Marshall was surprised, but after looking himself over he noticed that his appearance was a little startling. He had an unkempt beard, filthy clothes, and he realised that he still had the residue of camo cream plastered over his face.

"I'm not here to beg!" He shouted. "Is John there?"

There was a pause before he heard the door unlock. The woman re-opened it slightly, and moved between the edge and the wall; her face was only partially visible.

"What do you want?" she asked sharply.

"I'm looking for John Medforth. This is where he lives, isn't it?" he asked.

The woman, who had long brown hair and a thin face, looked him up and down before replying, "What do you want him for?" she asked suspiciously.

"I have a job offer for him. I need to speak to him right away," Marshall replied.

The woman was considering him for a moment, when a voice erupted from behind her. "Caroline?" The woman looked back into the house, and the door closed.

Marshall stood in the street, confused. He knocked again but there was no answer. He stood for half a minute before the door opened and a man emerged.

"Marshall!" Medforth exclaimed, his initially tense demeanour instantly relaxing.

Marshall nodded. "Morning."

Medforth limped out onto the street and the two men shook

hands. In Medforth's left hand was a walking stick, upon which he rested heavily.

"How've you been?" Marshall asked.

Medforth curled his lip. "Not bad. I've been out of the country for the past couple of weeks, overseeing some stuff in the jungle. What the fuck happened to you?" he asked with a gesture at Marshall's face.

"Long story. Actually it's part of the reason I'm here. Can we go inside?"

Medforth glanced at the house before replying, "I'd rather not. Caroline is in a pissy mood. To be honest I'm glad of an excuse to go out, so you can buy me a pint at the Flying Scotsman," he said with a gesture toward the pub at the end of the street.

"Caroline? She's new," Marshall replied with a cheeky grin.

"She's my sister, you arse," Medforth replied bluntly with a slight frown.

Marshall was surprised. "In five years you've never mentioned her."

Medforth's eyes dropped momentarily, but he quickly composed himself. "We hadn't spoken in almost fifteen years before last month. We lost our dad, and she called me when she heard."

"You didn't even speak after the accident?" Marshall asked.

"No," Medforth replied bluntly.

Marshall knew when to end a conversation. A little over a

decade ago, Medforth had lost his family in a car accident that also left his leg partially paralysed. It gave him an arching scar that ran from his temple and around the back of his skull. His hair had been recently cut, so Marshall could see the mark clearly.

"I can come back," Marshall offered.

"No chance. She's annoying as hell; I need a break."

Marshall smirked. "The pub it is, then," he said before a realisation dawned on him. "I've actually got no money with me," he admitted.

"Given the state you're in, that's no surprise. Don't worry about it."

Medforth shouted into the house that he was going out, reached for his wallet on a nearby table, and then closed the door without waiting for a reply.

"You look like you've come straight from the field. What's going on?" He asked as the pair walked along the path.

"I suppose that's exactly what happened. I've been in Iraq, on a mission that went belly-up. I'll tell you all about it once we've got a pint. I'm parched, I haven't had nearly enough fluids these last few days."

They arrived at the entrance. Marshall opened the door and held it open for Medforth who walked past him.

As Marshall followed Medforth into the smoke-filled pub, he noticed that it was busy for a weekday afternoon.

Medforth looked at him. "Lager?" he asked.

"Yeah, Stella. Cheers," Marshall replied.

The two men waited a minute for the round to be served. Medforth paid, and they picked up their drinks before moving to a small table at the end of the bar. "Tell me about it then," Medforth said.

"I came to offer you a job," Marshall replied.

Medforth's eyebrows rose. "I have a job, thanks," he said lightly as he took a drink.

"Not like this one."

Medforth set his glass down on the table, and listened closely as Marshall explained what had happened over the last few days.

Medforth relaxed back into his chair. "Okay. It's a nice story, but you know science-fiction isn't my thing," he said.

"I'm being serious. This isn't a wind-up."

Medforth paused as he thought about what had been said. "Let's see it then. Open one of these portals and show me the ship."

Marshall drained his drink and stood up. "No problem. We need to go somewhere inconspicuous."

The pair left the pub and walked down a quiet side street. Marshall took the portal device from his pocket, and held it in his open palm for Medforth to see.

"Ready?" he asked.

Medforth nodded, and Marshall was sure he was amused by the situation.

After checking the area was clear, Marshall pressed the button on the device. A portal opened several feet in front of the two men.

"Holy shit!" Medforth shouted as he took a step backward.

"This is nothing. Wait until you see what's on the other side," Marshall said with a grin. He raised his arm toward the portal as a gesture to Medforth that he should approach it. Slowly, his friend walked over to the vortex. After a fleeting glance at Marshall, he stepped through.

Marshall followed, and the two men found themselves in a small room. Medforth's eyes were wide as his gaze scanned the area.

"We're in the armoury. There isn't much to see in here. Follow me," Marshall said.

Medforth silently followed Marshall to the lift at the end of the corridor.

Marshall noted his friend's bewilderment. "I'll give you a proper tour later. First, I want you to see the bridge."

Medforth nodded. "It's pretty amazing already."

The lift took them to the bridge almost instantaneously. The door slid open to reveal the semi-circular room occupied only by Smith.

"I didn't even feel it move," Medforth said with wonder.

"It manipulates the gravity system to move us around. No motors, no cables. It's quite something."

Smith approached the lift.

"This is Andrew Smith," Marshall said. The men shook hands as Smith welcomed Medforth aboard.

"Get the shutters," Marshall said to Smith.

Smith returned to the curved console and tapped a button. There was a mechanical whirring in front of the trio, followed seconds later by the shutters that filled the entirety of the forward window retracting upward into the hull. The receding cover unveiled a star field, with Earth filling the leftmost quarter of the vista.

Medforth gasped loudly. "I'm in," he said quickly.

ii.

"I can't say I entirely agree, but I do see your point," Medforth said, after Marshall explained why he was keeping the ship's existence hidden from Earth.

The pair were sitting at the end of the conference room table, facing each other. They had been discussing Marshall's discovery in more detail, while Smith attended to the bridge.

"It may, or may not, be the right decision, but it's made," Marshall asserted.

"Fair enough. So what's next?"

Marshall sighed. "One thing's for sure; I can't run this thing on my own. I need a crew. I've put together a list of people that I think we could do with recruiting, and as my Executive Officer I need your approval before bringing them aboard."

"Executive officer!" Medforth blurted with a loud laugh.

Marshall smiled. "Why not? First-mate doesn't have quite the same ring to it."

Medforth shrugged. "Whatever. Titles don't mean shit anyway."

"Exactly. Anyway, I need help with the selection process, and that's something you're amply qualified for."

Medforth nodded. He had spent almost a decade as Directing Staff in SAS selection, during which time he had garnered a reputation amongst the candidates. Marshall had learned first-hand how tough Medforth could be.

Marshall reached out to the table and opened a thin folder.

Inside was a stack of paper, grouped by paperclips that bound the top left corner. There was a photograph of a man in the upper-left quadrant of the topmost sheet, next to which was a grid of data.

Marshall swivelled the paper to face Medforth and pushed it across the desk. "We'll start with this guy. His name is David Costello, a soldier from the north-east that I met a couple of years ago. His career was exceptional; he actually made Colonel by the time he was thirty."

"Wow," Medforth said with a raised brow. He reviewed the document and studied the photograph. Costello was thirty-five years old, but looked younger. He had blonde hair brushed across the top of his head with a slight quiff at the fringe. As the photo was a headshot, his physique could not be easily determined, but as a military man of almost twenty years he was undoubtedly fit.

"He seems ideal. What job have you got in mind?"

"We need a strategy going forward. Costello specialises in tactical planning, and he's led dozens of military operations with great success," Marshall explained.

"So why isn't this a straightforward decision?"

Marshall's lip curled. "The mission where I met him was in Northern Ireland, where his unit assisted the capture of an IRA cell who had attacked one of our bases. During the operation, Costello captured a teenage kid, who was in the graveyard where we set up the ambush. I don't know what exactly happened, because he was alone, but he let the kid go. It turned out that the lad wasn't involved with the attack at all, and was just in the wrong place at the wrong time, but Costello didn't know that when he released him. The mission was a complete success, in no small part due to Costello's unit. They were well co-ordinated, and well drilled. When I heard about what happened, I put in a good word, but the brass didn't take his actions lightly. They decided to make an example of him, so he was court martialled and found guilty of 'wilfully allowing the escape of a prisoner'. He was sent down for ten years."

Medforth grimaced. "Why would he let the kid go? It sounds like he has impaired judgement."

"He said that the kid reminded him of his troubled younger brother. To be honest, I don't know the exact reason. I'm only going off the official records. It's because this happened on my mission that I took an interest; I don't know him personally. He probably doesn't remember me at all."

Medforth's gaze wandered toward the large window that ran the length of the room. He was literally staring into space.

"What do you think?" Marshall asked.

"I think that being two years into a ten-year stint means he has nothing to lose by joining us."

"My thoughts exactly."

"I also think that he did something exceptionally stupid, and it makes me uneasy."

"Nobody is perfect. Putting the incident aside, he was an exceptional soldier. His skills are exactly what we need."

"I think you've made your mind up, and my reservations aren't strong enough to veto him, so let's put him in the 'yes' pile and move on."

Marshall smiled. "Good," he said. "The next one is easier," he added as he slid Costello's profile aside.

"Next up is Julia Harrison. She's a surgeon at the National Hospital for Neurology and Neurosurgery in London."

Marshall paused while Medforth examined the document. "How do you know her?" he asked.

"I met her in Sierra Leone a couple of years ago. There was a hostage situation in a hospital where she was volunteering, and I was part of the team sent in to resolve it. I'd like to say I was a hero who saved her life, but it was actually the other way around."

Medforth was nodding as Marshall spoke, but was clearly distracted.

"What is it?" Marshall asked.

Medforth shook his head as he continued to look at Harrison's profile. "I've met her too," he said.

"Really? When?"

"She was a student when I was in rehab. When I hit some of my lowest moments, she helped me a lot."

"So I assume you approve?"

"Without a doubt."

"Great. That's the easy two out of the way," Marshall said as he added Harrison's profile to the pile with Costello.

Medforth interrupted Marshall before he could pick up the next item. "Before we go any further, I could murder a cup of tea," he said.

Marshall grinned. "No kettle."

Medforth was visibly disappointed.

Marshall's expression turned sarcastic. "How do you propose we power a kettle on an alien space ship? When we first arrived we couldn't even operate the lift!"

Medforth expression lightened.

"Wait here a minute," Marshall said before standing up. He rounded the table and approached a bench that spanned the wall at the end of the room. After tapping in a number of commands into a control panel, he looked back into the room before pressing a final button. A portal opened behind Medforth.

"Wait here, I'll only be a few minutes," he said as he strode through the portal. It closed a second later, leaving Medforth alone in the silent room.

Medforth waited patiently, wondering what Marshall was doing. Less than five minutes passed before the portal reappeared and Marshall emerged.

"Here you go," Marshall said as he handed Medforth one of the two cups of tea that he was carrying.

"Where did you get this?" Medforth asked.

"Your kitchen. It's a tip by the way."

"You went to my house!?" Medforth asked with alarm.

Marshall's smile widened. "Why not?"

Medforth's initial outrage subsided, and was quickly replaced with embarrassment at having Marshall see his untidy home. "I'll go next time," was all he said calmly.

Marshall nodded and sat down. He placed his cup to the left of the folder, and then grabbed the next profile. "Next up, Ricky Singh. You might recognise him," he said as he handed it over.

Medforth read the file. "Can't say I do," he muttered.

"He was in my group during selection. I didn't fall for your interrogation tactics, but he did, so he failed."

Medforth shook his head. "I've seen hundreds, maybe thousands, of candidates over the years, and most of them failed. I'm sorry to say I don't remember him."

"Fair enough. He is an RAF pilot based at Leeming. I've known him for over fifteen years; he's a good man and a great pilot."

"He looks young for thirty-two," Medforth observed. "But if

he got as far as the interrogation stage, he must be tough."

"His demeanour is soft, and he is overly pleasant, but mentally he's as strong as anyone I've ever met."

Medforth pointed at the document that was now resting on the table. "He has a glittering career, a girlfriend of five years, and if he's as nice as you say, he'll have plenty of friends. Why would he take the job?"

"He is as driven as he is clever, and he can't say no to a challenge. If anyone is going to accept, it's him."

"Fine, he's in," Medforth said quickly.

"As easy as that?" Marshall asked with evident surprise.

"This isn't the Regiment. We need the right people, but what they'll have to cope with is entirely different."

Marshall was pleased that Medforth approved, as he had expected resistance given Singh's failure to pass SAS selection.

"Lastly I want to talk about this guy," Marshall said before handing Medforth the only remaining document in front of him.

"Howells?" Medforth asked when he saw the name in front of him. "Is he a relation of the General?"

Marshall nodded. "His son. Until a few years ago, Chris Howells was a Formula One engineer, working for MacLaren when they won pretty much everything in '89. I think he can help with figuring out how to operate the ship, and how the tech works."

"This file is very brief," Medforth noted.

Marshall hesitated before continuing. "He's an alcoholic, a

drug addict, and has a pretty bad gambling problem."

Medforth's eyebrows raised and he looked up at Marshall, who continued. "A few years ago he was out of his mind on God knows what, when he got himself into a fight, and knocked the other guy to the ground. There was some sort of head injury, and the guy died, so Howells found himself facing the death penalty for Murder – it happened in Vegas. The General contacted me and asked me to go over there and break him out. There was no chance of Chris getting away with what happened because it was all on camera, so his dad saw no alternative. I accepted the job and spent several months getting the guy across the Mexican border."

"You aren't selling him very well," Medforth interjected.

"We got to know each other quite well. I think I got through to him about his problems, and hopefully he sorted himself out after we parted company."

"So you didn't stay in touch?"

"No. He doesn't even know my real name; I was Pete for the duration of the trip."

"Engineering is probably the most important post of all. Are you sure you want someone like him in charge?" Medforth asked.

Marshall's lip curled. "If he can stay clean, he can do it. I suppose we won't know for sure if he can cope unless we give him a shot."

"If he wants it."

"If he wants it," Marshall repeated.

"It's your call, but this guy sounds like a liability. What if he gets drunk and starts telling people on Earth about what he's up to?"

Marshall shook his head. "I think if we can keep him sober, and confined to the ship wherever possible, he should be fine. When I left him he assured me he would stay clean, and it's been over three years so hopefully he's already turned things around."

Medforth's lips pursed. "We'll see," he muttered.

iii.

"Are you sure you don't want me to go with you?" Medforth asked.

"I'm sure," Marshall replied as he entered the armoury. "He's a handful, but I can certainly manage him. I'll be back within the hour."

Marshall opened a portal and disappeared.

He emerged to find himself in a dark room. It was approximately 11pm local time, so there was no sunlight coming in through the metre square window to his right, but there was light from a nearby street lamp giving the room an eerie yellow hue.

Crossing the room, Marshall could make out a sofa along the far wall, and a small coffee table to its left with the silhouette of a lamp on top. He reached out to the lamp and attempted to turn it on, but nothing happened. He cursed under his breath and looked around for the main light switch.

After finding it next to a door to the right of the sofa, he pressed the button. A ceiling strip flickered into life, illuminating the room.

The sight that greeted him surprised Marshall. He was standing in the living room of Howells' flat, with the sofa to his left and another door on the wall opposite. The floor was covered by a stained carpet that was littered with lager cans, spirit bottles, and an astonishing number of pizza boxes. On the table to the left of the sofa was an overflowing ashtray; next to which was a bag of white powder. Lying face down on the sofa, wearing only jeans, was the man Marshall had come to see.

Marshall approached Howells, who had not stirred when the lights came on. He reached over and shook the unshaven and generally grubby looking man, but got no response. He could see that Howells was breathing, but he may as well have been in a coma.

The smell from the bins was starting to make Marshall feel queasy. He did not want to stay in the flat any longer than necessary, so he hoisted Howells over his shoulder. He immediately regretted the decision, as Howell's had put on significant weight since the last time they met.

Marshall activated the portal and returned to the ship.

Howells opened his eyes and was blinded by the overhead lights. He squinted as the glare intensified the pounding thud that was coursing through his head. He turned to his left and looked around the large, well-lit room in which he was lying.

Damn, that was some good shit, he thought.

A woman entered the room. She noticed that he was awake and strode toward him. She said something, but he could not make out what it was. There was a reply from a male voice that he vaguely recognised.

The woman approached the bed. "Chris, how are you feeling?" she asked.

Howells squinted whilst trying to focus on the woman. Gradually her long blonde hair and friendly face came into focus. "Du ah knw yu?" he mumbled, slurring his words while trying to summon some saliva into his dry mouth.

"My name is Julia Harrison. I'm a doctor. You are here courtesy of Ryan Marshall. Do you remember him?"

Howells did not recognize the name. "Nd watr," he said groggily.

Harrison picked up a bottle from a nearby tray and put it to Howells' mouth. He drank greedily, and when he had drained the contents he looked Harrison in the eyes and attempted to focus further. "Cheers. My mouth was as dry as Ghandi's sandal. Where am I?"

"You are in the medical bay of a... ship. You were dead-to-the-world, so Captain Marshall thought you should stay here until you had slept it off. You have severe dehydration, and you'll feel like shit for the rest of the day, but otherwise you're fine."

The fog over Howells' mind was slowly lifting, but confusion was still heavily set in. "What do you mean 'a ship'?"

"Captain Marshall will explain; he's on his way." Harrison replied with a smile. She turned and left, and a minute later Marshall entered the room through a door directly opposite the foot of the bed.

Marshall gave the room a sweeping glance, and then approached Howells. "Chris, you look better than you did fifteen hours ago!" he said sourly.

"Pete? What's going on here? What does the doctor mean by 'you're on a ship'? I feel like I'm on Knightmare," Howells said.

"Everything's fine. You *are* aboard a ship... but not at sea... We are in space, in orbit of Earth at an altitude of 36,000 kilometres." Marshall explained.

Howells' laughed. "I'm not high, Pete, at least not right now. Don't bullshit me, I can't be arsed with it."

"My name isn't Pete, it's Ryan," Marshall said.

Howells looked away. "Doesn't surprise me," he said softly.

"Look, here's how it is," Marshall started.

Marshall explained the situation aboard the ship whose crew was slowly growing.

"So," he continued, after giving Howells a minute to think about what had been said, "I want you to join the crew. We need your engineering expertise. What do you say?"

Howells shook his head slowly. "Are you sure you want to do this? Look at me. I'm hardly at the top of my game."

"I know what you are capable of, and we can help you get clean. If you can do that, I'm happy to have you on the team."

Howells sat quietly for a moment before accepting the offer.

iv.

1994 A.D.

"Fold," Costello said as he threw his cards face down onto the table.

"Me too," Smith said.

"I'll call," Singh said with a smile. "Just you and me again, Doc" he added as he looked at Harrison.

Harrison put her can of McEwan's Export onto the table and reached for her chips. "Raise to 500," she said with a blank expression.

"500!" Singh exclaimed, having called only fifty.

Harrison's face remained emotionless. "Typical Yorkshireman. If you don't have the balls for it, you'd best fold," she said.

Smith laughed loudly. "Ouch."

Singh was holding his cards. He squirmed in his chair, which was of the original Alethean metal variety, and stared at his hand while considering at length whether to stay in the game.

"I'm not going all-in with a straight, so I fold," Singh said with frustration as he dropped his cards face up.

Harrison smiled when she saw the Jack-high Straight. "Good decision," she said as she discarded her hand and collected her chips.

"What did you have?" Singh asked.

"It would've cost you 500 to find that out," she replied with a smile, wanting to keep her bluff to herself.

"I reckon she had a flush," Smith said.

"No way," Costello objected. "High pair at best."

"You'll never know," Harrison said as she gathered the cards and shuffled them for the next hand.

"Did anyone invite Chris?" Costello asked before he drained his own can.

Smith shook his head. "I thought a night of beers, cigars and gambling would be a bit of a challenge for him. Besides, the good Doctor has banned him from the crew lounge."

"Really?" Costello said as he looked at Harrison with a raised eyebrow.

"It's for his own good," Harrison answered sternly.

"Banning him from what is the only social area of the ship is good for him? I don't see how; especially when he lives up here full-time," Costello said with disbelief.

Harrison waved the deck of cards in the direction of the far end of the room. "In that corner is a pile of alcohol that's taller than me. I don't want him anywhere near it."

Costello glanced at the corner despite knowing what was there. Stacked neatly were dozens of crates containing cans and bottles of McEwan's, Guinness, John Smiths and Newcastle Brown Ale. Next to the pile there was also a plethora of liquor and mixers.

"I'm not saying he should be left in here to his own devices, but an outright ban is a bit harsh."

Harrison shook her head. "Trust me, none of us want him around any temptations," she said softly as she gathered her new cards from the table. "Maybe next time we should do this in somebody's quarters and get him to come along. I'm sure we can manage a game without a drink."

Singh scoffed loudly. "Speak for yourself," he said with a chuckle.

Harrison smiled. "Well there you have it."

"Check," Costello said, refocusing the group onto the game.

"Raise to fifty," Smith followed.

"Call," Singh said quickly.

"Call," Harrison added.

"Fold!" Costello said with annoyance. He hadn't had a single good hand all night.

As each remaining player received new cards, Costello thought about how much his life had changed over the last few months. Since accepting Marshall's offer, he had lived aboard *Odyssey* and spent a lot of time with his new crewmates. He had enjoyed the experience immensely, but he was starting to suffer from cabin fever, as he had not left the ship since he arrived from prison.

"How are you finding the balance between working up here and living on Earth?" he asked Harrison.

"It's good," Harrison said without hesitation. "My husband knows what I'm doing and where I'm going so there's no double-life or any of that kind of drama. I leave the house before my shift and return afterward, so aside from the fact that my commute involves a portal to a space ship it's the same as any other. The kids have no idea where I am, nor would they even think to ask at their age, and my friends on Earth have very different careers to me so they are none the wiser."

"Sounds ideal," Costello said with obvious envy.

Harrison did not want to upset the tactical officer, so she tried to lighten the sombre mood Costello appeared to have adopted. "I'm sure Marshall will let you portal back down to your cell if you ask nicely," she quipped.

Costello grinned. "Thanks," he said sarcastically.

"It'll make a big difference having your husband in on what you are doing," Singh interjected. "Stacey has no idea what's going on. I know it sounds bad but I can't trust her to keep her mouth shut," he said with a curled lip.

"That's certainly not ideal in the long term, mate," Costello said.

"I don't think it'll matter in the long term to be honest. Things aren't great between us and I'm tempted to just move here full-time."

"I wouldn't rush into that. Trust me. Ask Chris if you want a second opinion," Costello replied.

"You do know you can go back to Earth whenever you want, right?" Smith asked Costello rhetorically.

"Hardly. I'm an escaped convict!"

"Yeah, in England you are. You're thinking in terms of how the rules of life were before, but now that we have *Odyssey* at our disposal things have changed. I agree you would be daft going to England, but there's an entire planet there for you to pop down to whenever you like. You're hardly Charles Manson, your arrest warrant won't extend beyond the UK. Besides, if anyone spots you, you can just portal back to the ship and that's the end of it. We aren't confined to border crossings or anything like that anymore."

Costello hadn't considered the option and was excited by the possibility. "You're right. I'm going to speak to Marshall about it in the morning."

"Actually, I think I will too," Singh interjected. "I didn't really think about it like that. I could up-sticks and move to Colombia and it would take me ten minutes using portals."

Smith smiled. "Exactly."

"Are you living up here?" Costello asked Smith.

"Marshall and myself are presumed dead so we can't go home any more than you can, but once I get my head around the ship's computer and settled in a bit more I intend to have a home on Earth somewhere. I certainly won't be living up here indefinitely."

The group fell silent. The poker game had paused for the duration of the conversation.

"I'm not ashamed to admit that I don't have a great deal of money, so setting up fresh somewhere isn't going to happen overnight," Singh said. "Marshall said I'd be looked after financially, and so far he's paid me well for my time aboard the ship, but it isn't going to buy me a Hawaiian beach house."

"Money isn't an issue," Smith said confidently. "None of us are on a salary per se, we're just given whatever we need to have a comfortable life on Earth without raising any questions."

"What's that supposed to mean?" Singh asked.

"It means that you are an Air Force pilot, so if Marshall gave you ten million quid people would want to know where it came from. As a dead man nobody is going to notice me flaunting some cash about, but in return I can't go home, visit my friends and family, or have any kind of official identity."

"Are you saying Marshall has given you that sort of money?" Costello asked.

Smith laughed. "I wish. No, what I'm saying is if you want a beach house in Hawaii then we have the means to sort that out for you. We can arrange its purchase on your behalf and you can move in whenever you like."

"How can you say that?" Singh asked.

"Because it's my job to acquire funds for this operation. That beer over there wasn't free, or stolen; it had to be paid for. I'm using the ship to get into the networks of some pretty big banks and rearrange their finances for our benefit. Also, it's amazing what uses you can put a portal system to when you need to get into a vault full of cash."

"You haven't..." Singh started.

Smith had a broad grin. "I have."

"Shit," Costello said softly.

Smith was beaming as he leaned closer to Costello. "It's a lot of fun watching piles of bearer bonds and raw cash fall through a vortex and land next to you," he said quietly, but with enough volume for everyone to hear.

Other than Harrison, the group chuckled.

"Are you alright, Doc?" Singh asked Harrison who was staring vacantly out of the window behind Costello.

Harrison's attention snapped back into the room. "Yes, I was just taking in the view."

"What do you think about all this? The money situation."

Harrison hesitated as she pieced together the parts of the conversation she had heard. "I get an equivalent amount to what I would have earned if I stayed at the hospital, plus a reasonable bonus. I can't complain."

"You don't fancy a beach house?"

"You guys who are supposedly dead or on the run are lucky to have that option, but it's too high a price for me," she said with a shake of her head.

"Fair enough," Costello conceded.

"Beer?" Smith asked as he stood.

There was a round of nods, and Smith proceeded to walk over to the refrigerator that was located to the right of the alcohol stash.

"It's you to act," Costello said to Harrison.

Harrison took an audible intake of breath. "I raise to two hundred."

"Oh for fuck's sake," Singh exclaimed.

"What?" Harrison asked.

"You keep raising by so much you are basically bullying people out of the game."

"Call then!" Harrison retorted.

"I fold," Smith called from across the room.

Singh glared at Harrison. He was one card short of a flush with one change to go. "I call," he said.

After receiving a new card, Singh had completed his flush. Harrison bet three hundred, which infuriated him, so he went all-in instantly.

"I hope you have something. I call," Harrison said with a confident grin.

Singh revealed his Flush. Harrison dropped her cards onto the table to reveal a Full House.

Singh's heart sank. "You're shitting me," he said to himself.

"Sorry," Harrison said with obvious insincerity as she collected her winnings.

"Well I'm out, so on that note I'm off," Singh said as he finished his drink and left the new can Smith had placed in front of him on the table.

The remaining players wished Singh a good night before he left. Harrison gathered the cards and began to shuffle the deck. "I think-," she started before a beep sounded from Costello's walkie-talkie.

"Costello, it's Medforth," a voice said from the Costello's belt.

Costello grabbed the radio and raised it to his mouth. "Costello, go," he said.

"Are you busy?" Medforth asked.

Costello surveyed his colleagues for a moment before answering. "Nothing important," he said with a wry smile.

Smith and Harrison exchanged a glance as the conversation progressed.

"If you are sober, I could do with a hand on the bridge. I know you aren't on duty so don't worry about it if now's a bad time."

Costello hesitated but replied quickly. "Now is fine. I wasn't doing very well anyway. I'll be there shortly," he said before re-attaching the walkie-talkie to his hip.

"See you later, ladies," Costello said before he stood, downed the contents of his almost-full can, and strolled out of the compartment.

"Shots?" Smith asked Harrison.

"Definitely," she replied.

v.

Eight months later

It had been a year since Marshall found the ship that had been christened *Odyssey*.

"What do you mean corrupt?" Marshall asked with obvious irritation.

"Exactly that," Howells replied bluntly. "The data is knackered. I don't know with any certainty whether it's degradation over time, or intentional destruction. Either way, it's gone."

"How much?"

"About a third." Howells replied.

Marshall took a deep breath and looked at the ceiling of the conference room. "Can you get it back?" he asked.

Howells shook his head. "I don't think so. We'll do what we can, but you need to run with a no."

"Fuck."

Howells was distraught. Since his arrival aboard *Odyssey*, his life had turned around. Despite Marshall's insistence that he had accomplished this by himself, he felt that he owed it to the man he called Captain. To let him down in this matter had left him deeply perturbed. "I'll keep working in it," he said.

Marshall nodded slowly. "What about the problem with the engines?"

Howells was pleased to change the subject, but the mention of his latest dilemma left him dismayed. "The news there isn't great either," he said sheepishly.

A look of distinct sarcasm played across Marshall's face. "When is it?" he asked.

Howells rolled his eyes, and before he even felt his change in mood occur, he lost his temper. "Look, this shit is pretty fucking advanced! What are you expecting of me?" he demanded.

Marshall was unaccustomed to being spoken to in this manner, but he quickly remembered that Howells was not a military man.

"Chris, I need this ship deciphered," he started with a softer tone. "Whatever it takes. You know that more than anyone."

Howells' expression tightened as he looked away for a moment before replying. His frustration was swelling. "I'm not sitting on my hands down there. You need to understand that this shit is complicated, and it's going to take time."

Marshall frowned. "Do you think my expectations are unreasonable?" he asked.

"Yes."

Marshall sighed. "Shit," he said deflated. "I'm sorry, Chris. I have a plan for where I want this to go, and sometimes my ambition blinds me."

Silence fell.

"Tell me about the problem with the engines," Marshall said after a minute had passed.

Howell's mood lightened instantly at the prospect of returning to the subject of engineering. "There's a break somewhere in the power system. I can't find it."

"Which systems does it affect?"

"The portal drive. If I can fix it, we should be able to generate portals big enough for the entire ship to pass through."

Marshall's eyes widened. "The ship?"

Howells smiled. "Yes. According to the specs, we can get half way to Mars without any trouble. After the jump we'll have to recharge; I don't know exactly how long that will take until we try it."

"That sounds-," Marshall started, but was interrupted when a chime sounded from the ceiling. Marshall pressed a button on the meeting table. "Go ahead," he said.

"Captain, it's Dr Harrison. Sorry to interrupt, but we have a three o'clock. Is it still on?"

Marshall glanced at his watch, which read 15:08. "Sorry, Doctor. I completely lost track of time. I'm on my way."

"See you soon," Harrison replied with her exasperation imperfectly disguised.

Marshall tapped the button and addressed Howells. "We can leave this for another time. Continue with your work on the engines, and keep me updated."

Howells nodded. "No problem."

vi.

"Sorry again, Doctor," Marshall said honestly as he entered the medical bay.

"Don't worry about it," Harrison said with a shake of her head.

"As I recall, you wanted to see me about some Alethean logs you've been reading?"

"Yes. I've discovered a device that is capable of scanning brainwave patterns. Having found schematics and a thesis on its operational theory, I've slowly come to understand the machine. It is fascinating".

"In English please," Marshall said impatiently.

"Essentially, the device is designed to both read and manipulate brainwave patterns, in such a way as to alter memories."

"Interesting. Could it be modified for humans?"

Harrison looked grim. "There is conclusive evidence that the Aletheans already used the device on human subjects."

"What?" Marshall exclaimed.

"Look," Harrison said as she indicated toward a terminal to her right."

The display read 'Bio-analysis findings C-11'.

Harrison pointed to several areas of the screen. "The Aletheans must have been studying us for years. There's no doubt about it, these are human brain scans."

Marshall frowned. "There are plenty of people who claim to have been abducted by aliens," he offered. "Having said that, the Aletheans have been dead for almost two hundred years."

Harrison took a deep breath. "According to the specs, this thing can manipulate memory patterns as well as read them. If the Aletheans brought people aboard, they could have erased any memory of the experience."

Marshall nodded. Suddenly his eyes widened. "When was the last subject brought up here?" he asked with alarm.

Harrison manipulated the controls on the console as she searched for an answer. "One hundred and eighty-nine years ago," she said after translating the alien time period. "What's the matter?"

"When did they learn about the virus? I'm sure it was before that," Marshall said.

"I don't remember. Hold on," Harrison replied. As she retrieved the ship's logs, a sense of dread washed over her as she realised what was concerning the Captain.

"Three hundred and seven years ago. 1687," she said with dismay.

"They brought humans up here despite the risk of contagion? That can't be right," Marshall stated.

"There's a gap in the research logs spanning more than a century between their being told about the plague and the next experiment. They obviously didn't take the decision lightly, but I suppose it was their only hope of finding a cure."

"Desperate measures," Marshall said softly.

Harrison nodded.

"Keep this evidence to yourself for now, Doctor. I don't want everyone distracted by this information."

Harrison agreed uneasily.

vii.

Marshall sat in the Captain's chair on the bridge considering a plan that he had been formulating for several days. He was wearing the standard uniform that he had decided upon only a week earlier. As he had never cared for the formality of military uniforms, and had enjoyed being spared such attire during his service with the Regiment, he had decided upon khaki cargo trousers and a plain black fitted t-shirt for bridge crew, and casual clothes for those who worked in the engine room and science labs.

On the wall behind him to his left there was an engineering status monitor that was largely left unattended. A similar screen on the other side gave an overall status report of ships systems. Medforth manned that post, and was the place that Marshall had become accustomed to finding him.

In front of the Captain's chair was the large curved bank of workstations that were occupied by the remainder of the bridge crew. The far left station was tactical where Costello was sitting.

To his right was Singh at the helm. Next to Singh was a co-pilot about whom Marshall knew nothing other than her name. Finally, there was Smith at the sensor and communications station.

Marshall originally had a small command interface on the left arm of his chair, but as he was right handed he had Howells move it across. Except for this, and the seating having been upholstered, the bridge was unchanged from how it was found.

The Chief Engineer entered the Bridge with a broad smile.

"What is it Chris?" Marshall asked as Howells strode quickly across the room.

Howells looked excited. "I've fixed the power regulation issue on the ship's portal drive!" he said as he stopped to catch his breath. "I think it's ready for a field test."

Marshall's surprise was obvious. "That's great news!" He said with excitement. "What was the problem?"

"Does it matter?"

Marshall paused. "Not really. Is it safe? I'm not risking everything on some half-baked experiment."

"All the simulations ran without a problem, but no test is going to be one hundred per-cent safe."

Marshall pondered for a moment, but found his curiosity getting the better of him. "Okay, go for it."

Howells nodded and left the bridge, his smile even wider.

"Are you sure this is wise?" Medforth asked as he approached Marshall from his station.

"Nope," Marshall replied with a chuckle.

viii.

The following day, Howells contacted the bridge to confirm that he was ready to begin the test.

The engines powered up, and a distinct hum began pulsating through the ship as it moved out of orbit.

The fuselage of the ship was shaped like a round-headed bullet that had been squashed in a vice. From the front, the blunt nose looked like it had been pulled down from the centre to form a point. Wings protruded from either side of the ship, stretching out in a straight line before bending downward almost ninety degrees in the final quarter.

Between the wings, in the centre of the primary hull, there was a large circular hole in which a sphere was held in place by a single pylon running through the middle. The sphere was spinning at high velocity to generate a gravity field for the crew.

The rear of the ship had thrusters protruding from the otherwise flat surface, and along the front of the wings there were cuttings in the metal where the gun ports were located but were currently closed.

Odyssey pulled out of Earth's gravitational field and headed into open space. After several minutes Singh brought the ship to a halt. His gaze never wavered from his console as he made an announcement. "Activating portal drive in three...two...one...mark."

A moment later a portal, identical to those that the crew were using to travel to Earth, opened ahead of the ship. Singh reactivated the thrusters and the vessel accelerated into the vortex.

Odyssey emerged on the other side instantaneously. "Report," Marshall ordered.

"Scanning the area," Smith replied from the sensor station. "Receiving telemetry. We appear to have travelled nearly thirty-million miles!"

There was a stunned silence across the bridge.

Howells' voice filled the room. "Bridge, Engineering. The portal has closed behind us. Early indications are that the drive will need about an hour to recharge."

"Acknowledged," Marshall said. Medforth noted that he had never seen the Captain smile so brightly.

ix.

Costello slammed the side of his fist against the desk at which he sat in his quarters. He was frustrated at failing to understand the ship's defence systems, despite months of study.

He stood up and marched out of the room, making his way to the crew lounge.

When he arrived, he said hello to those who were already in the relatively small space before heading to a bench, upon which there was a kettle. He made a cup of hot black tea, before collapsing into a chair near the window that spanned the length of the room.

As he gazed into space and admired the beautiful view of Earth, he thought at length about the task that he had been assigned, wondering if he were suitable for the job.

He had been sitting for only two minutes when he decided to speak to Marshall. He stood and left his steaming drink on the table.

x.

"What do you mean you want to leave?" Marshall asked.

"I mean I don't think this is working out," Costello replied.

"Where has this come from? I'm surprised, and that doesn't happen very often."

"Basically, I don't think I'm right for the job. You've got some good people up here working on the ship, trying to figure out how it all works. You brought me aboard to help with tactical and operational tasks, but you have no need for the former and Medforth has a handle on the latter."

"No need for a tactical officer? How do you figure that?"

"We have nobody to fight! On a naval ship the tactical officer is a crucial member of the crew, but we are up here alone with no enemies and no combat in sight. What use do you have for that role?"

Marshall laughed. "Well I can't argue with your logic when

you put it like that, but I see a far wider scope than you do. It isn't just about fighting; we also need to stay hidden from Earth, so keeping the ship close to the planet while avoiding any satellites or gaps in the holo-mesh is a vital job."

Costello sighed. "Yeah and I've been doing that. I'm perfectly capable of that part of it, but a much bigger job is getting a grip of the defensive systems, figuring them out and getting them under our full control. I'm just not qualified for it. I have no idea what I'm doing. I'm no engineer, Howells could probably do it but he has enough on his plate."

Marshall's lip curled. "If you've been struggling so much, you should have come to me sooner," he said.

"Well, you know pride is a tough thing to swallow. I'm not used to failing so badly."

Marshall grinned. "I believe you once told me that learning a bit of humility was the one thing you got out of your time inside."

"Yeah, well it's that same humility that has me sitting in front of you now."

Marshall nodded. "You are right that Howells has taken on too much already, but he can almost certainly spare you a few of his people. I'll arrange for at least two engineers to assist you in the technical aspects of the defensive systems, under your direction. I should have done that from the beginning. I won't stop you if you want to leave, but I'm asking you to reconsider."

Costello's tension had subsided considerably during their

conversation. "Thanks."

xi.

There was a rap at the door to Costello's quarters.

"It's open!" Costello shouted.

There was a short silence before the knock repeated.

Costello sighed when he realised that sound would barely travel through the dense airlock. He rose from his desk, crossed the room, and pressed a button to the right of the entrance.

The door slid aside with a mechanical hum to reveal Howells. "Evening," he said with a smile. "Marshall said you could do with a hand."

Costello pursed his lips. "I explicitly told him that you had enough on your plate. He said he would get me a few support personnel from your team, nothing more."

Howells chuckled. "I'm off-shift, and I have very little else going on. Feel free to pick my brain."

Costello's shoulders dropped slightly. "Thanks. Please, come in."

Howells stepped into the room and made his way toward a sofa lining the opposite wall, underneath a panoramic window.

"Can I get you anything to drink?" Costello offered. Before Howells could answer, he quickly added, "Tea, coffee, Coke."

Howells laughed at Costello's addendum. "Coke would be good, cheers."

Costello hurried toward a small fridge that Howells had rigged into the ship's power systems, and retrieved a can for the engineer. He handed over the drink before sitting in a chair perpendicular to the sofa.

"So what are you struggling with?" Howells asked.

Costello sighed. "It's the technical stuff. The physics. It's baffling."

"Hmm, I can't really help you with that. I don't understand it either! Howells said with a chuckle."

Costello was shocked. "So how can you maintain the systems?" he asked.

"I've come to understand the technical manuals, and the mechanical theory behind the ship's major systems, but I have no idea how the physics works. That's what I recruited physicists for! To fix a car engine you need to know how it works, but you don't need to know the particle theory of combustion."

Costello nodded in agreement.

"I think you've been looking at this from the wrong angle," Howells continued. "You need to plan around what features you have at your disposal. You need to understand what everything is capable of, and from there the rest will fall into place."

Costello took a deep breath. "I think you're right, but I want to at least understand the basics."

"Okay. At the most fundamental level, there's Kyrocite, an ore that exists on several planets in the solar system, especially the asteroid belt. *Odyssey's* outer hull is made of a Kyrocite/Steel alloy, and refined Kyrocite powers the reactor core."

"Yeah I read about that, but I don't understand how the same stuff can provide enough energy to power a reactor, and at the same time serve as hull material."

"When refined, Kyrocite gives off tremendous amounts of energy, and that's what the ship's reactor harnesses. For the hull material, it needs to be rendered inert, and the Aletheans built some incredible methods of doing that. In its raw form, Kyrocite is highly radioactive, so that also needs to be dealt with before it can be used safely."

Howells leaned forward and placed his can on the low table in front of him. "I need to take a step back if I'm going to explain this properly," he said before relaxing on the sofa.

"So, back at the beginning of Alethean space exploration, they discovered Kyrocite below the surface of one of their moons. Fortunately, they realised how radioactive it was before they sent a manned expedition, so they studied the material using remotely controlled robots. They quickly realised how powerful it was, and they spent decades researching ways of shielding themselves from the radiation.

"The next challenge was getting the stuff out from under the moon's surface. You, Marshall, and the everyone else assume that *Odyssey's* Ion Cannon is part of some advanced weapons system, but in actual fact *Odyssey* doesn't have any 'weapons' at all. There's an array of mining tools that just happen to be very effective at destroying things, and the Ion Cannon is a part of that system."

Costello's eyebrows raised, but he remained silent as he listened intently.

"The Ion Cannon is designed to drill deep chasms into planetary bodies. It requires a tremendous amount of power, so it's only fired in short bursts before recharging. The next step is to fire a torpedo into the chasm, which detonates below the surface and blows a chunk of Kyrocite into space. Finally, the rail guns break the chunk into smaller, more manageable pieces."

"Where did you find out about this?" Costello asked with a furrowed brow. "I've read all sorts of documents and manuals about the Ion Cannon and rail guns, and they didn't mention any of it."

"The manuals won't; they just deal with the technical side of the systems. Like I said, you've been concentrating your efforts in the wrong place."

Costello felt chastised, but knew that Howells was correct.

Howells continued without pause. "Have you ever been to the hangar bay?" he asked.

Costello shook his head. "No, not yet," he said.

"You should. It's massive, with an outer door spanning the width of the room. It houses a couple of small shuttles, which are also equipped with rail guns because they were used to chip away at the debris even further. Once the rocks were small enough, the ship would then scoop them up using the hangar as a receptacle. Get yourself down there some time, you'll see scuffs all over the walls."

Costello pondered Howells' words. "The shuttle bay must be lined with radiation shielding then?" he asked.

"Yes, the entire room is. There's a chute that leads to storage pods at the bottom of the ship; that's where the raw material for the reactor is kept. The rest is rendered inert by equipment right there in the hangar."

"Hold on a second," Costello interrupted. "If Kyrocite can be broken apart so easily by the ship's mining tools, then surely it's a shit choice of hull material?"

Howells smiled. "In its raw form, yes, absolutely. It's the process of rendering it inert and creating an alloy with steel that makes it so strong. To my knowledge, there's no substance stronger than a Kyrocite/Steel alloy."

"Wow," Costello said.

"Obviously the outer hull is battered by debris that misses the hangar door during the collection process. The reason there are no marks is because it's protected by an energy shield. I assume you read about that?"

"Yes," Costello answered quickly. "Again, I have no idea how it works."

Howells pursed his lips. "What did I say before?" he asked with a smile intended to take the edge off his mildly patronising tone.

Costello scoffed. "That I don't need to know the physics."

"Exactly. The rule applies to the shields and the cloaking grid, just as it does to the weapons. You need to know what they are capable of, not how they work. Let engineers and scientists figure that out."

"You've made your point," Costello said sternly.

Howells drained his can before sitting back. "So, do you feel any more confident?"

Costello considered the question for a moment. "I feel like I have more direction than I did before."

"Great. Is there anything else I can help you with?"

"Not for now, thanks. I've got a lot to work on, I'll give you a shout if I get stuck."

Howells smiled. "No probs. I'll be off then," he said before standing.

Howells turned to leave before Costello stopped him. "Actually, there is one thing," he said.

"Yeah?"

"The cloaking grid is like the holo-mesh, using a web of emitters to project a holographic field around the ship. Since the ship's grid also generates its shield, does that mean that Earth has a massive energy shield around it?"

Howells grinned. "No," he said. "A holographic projection doesn't need a great deal of power to generate, relatively speaking. That means that the holo-mesh emitters can operate using solar energy and a micro fusion reactor. To generate an energy shield is a different matter entirely, it requires massive amount of energy that only a full size Kyrocite reactor can provide."

"Ah."

"It would be cool if it did though," Howells added with a broad smile.

xii.

Medforth awoke with a start. He had been dreaming about the accident that had ended his career in the field. *Not again*, he thought as his head cleared.

He climbed out of his sweat-soaked bed and made his way to the head. Only a week earlier Howells had filled the water tanks using a pipe strewn through a portal to Earth, and activated the on-board reclamation system. With running water now available throughout the ship, Medforth was pleased that he would no longer have to resort to a cold dowsing from a bottle over the sink.

He checked his watch. It was 0437. He was due at a meeting with Marshall at 0800 but he knew he wouldn't get back to sleep. He showered and dressed, grabbed his notepad, and made his way to the Bridge.

Medforth arrived to find only Singh, Smith and Costello on duty.

Medforth had initially been placed in charge of recruiting personnel trained for infiltration and covert ops. To date, the recruits had been solely used to acquire supplies from Earth, using the portal system to enter secure facilities and extract the required materials. Medforth's intention had been to develop their role further by training them to defend the ship against any potential threats. As his plan began to develop, Marshall had decided to delegate the leadership role of this group to Costello. Medforth's workload was high and he was glad of the relief, but he was also a little disappointed as this was his area of expertise.

He approached Singh at the front of the Bridge. "Good morning. Anything going on?" he asked.

Singh looked up from his console. "Not really. I'm monitoring our orbit, and trying to calculate how many portal jumps we would need to reach Alpha Centauri."

"Isn't that an astrophysicist's job?" Medforth enquired.

"Yeah, but do you know how boring it is just sitting here monitoring our orbit? I need something to do," he said with a smile.

"Fair enough, carry on," Medforth said as he left Singh and moved over to observe Smith at Communications.

"Hi," Smith said as Medforth approached. "Can't sleep?" he asked.

"Something like that. Are you picking anything up?"

"Nothing up here, but I can tap into pretty much any radio transmission on the planet. It can be quite interesting," Smith replied with a mischievous smile.

"Anything of use?" Medforth asked lightly.

"No," Smith replied, his expression now sheepish. "There is something I am looking into, although I don't have much yet."

"Well, don't keep it to yourself," Medforth said with a hint of frustration creeping into his voice.

"I found a sensor log that references something called 'S-327'. The description said that in 1947 it suffered 'a critical power failure in the primary core'. I searched everywhere for details on what this S-327 is, and found only one further log entry. It states that shortly after its reactor core went offline, S-327's orbit around Earth degraded and it crashed on the surface."

"Could it be another ship like *Odyssey*?" Medforth asked.

I have no idea. I think the details of what S-327 is, or was, must be amongst the corrupt data in the library computer. I cannot find it anywhere."

"Is it retrievable?" Medforth asked.

"Howells says not. I'm scanning local space for any sign of debris, in the hope of finding some remnants of the ship. The problem is that Earth's orbit is full of litter from human exploration, so the readings are muddied."

The door to the Bridge opened, and Marshall stepped onto the deck with a large mug in his hand. He strode across the room toward Medforth. "Good morning. You're early," he said.

"So are you," Medforth retorted with a smile. "Do you want to start now?"

"I don't see why not," Marshall replied, he turned and started walking toward the rear of the bridge. Medforth nodded to Smith. "Let me know if you make any progress with this," he said before he joined Marshall.

There was a door on the port side that led to the conference room, inside which there was an elongated metal table with four high-backed leather chairs on either side, and one at each end. Marshall made his way to the near end of the table and sat down. Medforth sat in the first seat to his left.

"So, we need to discuss the long term plan," Medforth started.

"Tell me where we are now, and take it from there," Marshall said.

"We've come to grips with the ship, and on the whole the crew have been remarkable. I've spoken to each of them recently; the consensus is that they want to test some of the systems more thoroughly. Most notably, Howells wants us to go to Mars to give the portal drive a good run out. According to astrometric data, the best window for the trip is February, giving us another five months to prepare. At that point its orbit brings it closest to Earth, they called it the 'opposition', whatever that means. Do you have any objection to us taking the ship out there?"

Marshall had been reluctant to travel too far from Earth, as a system failure could leave them stranded years from home. As a professional risk-taker, he had surprised himself with his reserve. "I have no problem with that; Howells knows what he's doing. I want everything checked a hundred times before we embark," he said. "Schedule it in for next February; if we get there without a hitch we can potentially go a little further, but for now just plan a straight forward round-trip."

"Okay," Medforth replied. He glanced at his pad for the next item on the agenda; his lips thinned, as the item was crew morale. "The morale is generally very good. That was all I had to say on the matter, but when I was on the bridge just now Ricky made a comment about being bored at the helm. I can see why. We're spending a lot of our time in a high orbit, so he just sits there making a few course corrections. On a day-to-day basis, the ship is pretty much flying itself. This mission to Mars will give him something to focus on, and that's great, but I think we need to consider either secondary duties or perhaps coming up with some sort of patrol route. Even if all that accomplishes is keeping him awake it'll be worth it. The ship has practically limitless power so it would cost us nothing."

Marshall nodded. "Agreed. Get Costello to sort out a flight plan. Also, ask Singh if he has any interest in other departments aboard the ship; there's no harm in broadening his horizons."

Medforth made a note and moved back to the main purpose of the meeting. "So going forward, what're your thoughts?" he asked.

Marshall took a deep breath and spread his hands out on the desk. "I've been thinking about something for a while now," he started. "I think we should start thinking about building another ship."

Medforth glared at him, taken by surprise by the suggestion. "You think we are ready for that? It's only been a year."

"I realise that, and I don't think for a second that it'll be accomplished overnight. I just think it's something we should put some serious thought into. Get Howells to put a team together, and set them about working through the logistics of building a replica of this ship. I'm not expecting miracles, but make it clear that I want a small fleet of ships in the long term."

Medforth laughed. "Well, nobody can accuse you of lacking ambition."

Marshall smiled. "True. The fact is, if we're going to explore the solar system and beyond then we certainly need more than one ship. Space is big, so we need to think big. Simple as that."

Medforth agreed, although he maintained that it might be too soon. "I'll sort it out," was all he said.

The pair discussed a number of proposals, including some experiments conceived by Dr Harrison, and the meeting was concluded. They exited the briefing room and Medforth left Marshall on the Bridge, while he made his way to the engine room to inform Howells of Marshall's idea.

5. Stefan Deschamps

i.

"Who, the fuck, do you think you are?" Stefan Deschamps bellowed at Marshall.

Marshall glowered at the Frenchman. He had no idea what had been shouted at him in the man's native language, but the tone and volume gave him a good indication.

The two men sat facing each other in the conference room. Smith sat to Marshall's right, while Medforth was next to Deschamps.

Smith looked at Marshall. "He wants to know what gives us the right to do what we are doing," he translated loosely.

Marshall locked eyes with Deschamps. "You need to calm down," he said measuredly.

Deschamps jolted to his feet, and in English barked, "Calm down? You have taken possession of advanced alien technology, and hidden it from everyone on Earth!"

Marshall ground his teeth. "As I already explained, we have very good reasons for doing so."

Deschamps scoffed. "And I do not accept your reasons."

"Please, sit," Marshall said.

Deschamps complied slowly. "I find it inconceivable that your government are unaware of this ship's existence."

"I assure you that not only are they unaware of the ship, but they also believe me dead."

"And your entire crew just happen to be British?" Deschamps said with a gesture toward Smith and Medforth.

Marshall sighed. "The crew were initially assembled from our personal contacts," he said. "Whilst they are all British at the moment, your very presence here surely proves that we are trying to be more diverse. We need the best people in the world to join us if we're going to unlock this ship's secrets. You were recommended to me as an eminent astrophysicist who would relish the opportunity, by someone who has seen your excellent work first-hand."

Marshall held back a smile as Deschamps momentarily paused. *Go on, follow your ego if nothing else,* he thought.

There was a protracted silence as Deschamps considered Marshall.

"You say these words, but I do not believe them. You will return me to Earth immediately."

Marshall threw a momentary glance at Medforth before asking, "Are you declining our offer?"

"Yes."

ii.

"We knew this would happen eventually. We've been lucky to get this far," Medforth said to Marshall and Smith. They had been joined in the conference room by Costello and Harrison. Deschamps had been secured in crew quarters.

"Do you have any suggestions?" he asked the room.

"Is there definitely no way to persuade him?" Costello asked.

Marshall shook his head. "We did all we could, but he's a stubborn bastard."

Medforth sat forward. "He did raise a good point. We're all British. I think that inviting him onto the crew was a mistake while we are unable to present a multinational front. In all honesty, I can see where he's coming from."

"It's a catch-22," Marshall observed.

"It certainly is," Medforth acknowledged.

Smith added, "I agree that we definitely haven't done ourselves any favours by presenting him with three Brits, but this guy generally came across as a complete arse. I don't think this will happen every time, so I say we press on after we've dealt with him."

"Dealt with him?" Costello asked.

Smith smiled. "No implication intended, I assure you. All I'm saying is that we need to figure out what we are going to do with him, do it, and then move onto the next guy. Our approach is sound, we just picked the wrong person this time."

Costello scoffed. "Well he can't go home knowing of our existence, we can't detain him forever, and we aren't murderers. What's left?"

"We could erase his memory," Harrison said. She had been

silent since the meeting convened.

"And how exactly are we going to do that?" Medforth said bemused.

Costello smiled. "The good doctor wants to beat the shit out of him until he forgets about us," he said lightly.

Harrison glowered at Costello. She had offered the suggestion impulsively, and had immediately regretted it. She looked at Marshall apologetically.

Marshall sighed. He had forgotten about Harrison's discovery, but immediately realised what she was referring to. "There's an Alethean device in the medical bay that can read and manipulate human brain patterns. It's capable of erasing memories."

The room fell silent as the revelation took hold. Harrison shifted uncomfortably in her chair.

Medforth was furious. "Why is this the first I'm hearing of it?" he asked.

"I considered informing you, but I wanted some time to think about it. This device has very dangerous potential."

Medforth was stunned. Marshall continued, "It is not a matter of trust, or anything like that. I just wanted some time to consider what to do with it."

"And what is your conclusion?"

"I haven't reached one."

Medforth shook his head and addressed Harrison. "How confident are you that it's safe?" he asked.

Harrison paused. "I know from the ship's library that it can target a set period of time, and it will manipulate the brain patterns accordingly. The results depend upon the subject's brain, as no two are exactly alike."

"So in other words you aren't confident at all," Medforth said curtly.

Harrison was annoyed because he was embarrassingly correct. "No," was all she said.

"It doesn't matter," Costello interrupted. "It's our best option."

Marshall found himself nodding. "Doctor, what's the worst case scenario?"

Harrison's lips pursed. "He dies."

Marshall's eyes rolled. "Assuming he lives; could he end up with brain damage?"

"If it works as we expect, and the device has remained undamaged in the time it has been left up here, I think the worst case scenario is a greater loss of memory than intended."

Marshall's head tilted back and he looked at the ceiling. He wished there was a fourth option. "OK," he said, his gaze returning to the gathering. "Doctor, prepare the medical bay."

iii.

Harrison needed a week to prepare for the operation. Deschamps was escorted by two security men to the medical bay, where he was greeted by the Doctor and Marshall.

"You can't do this," Deschamps protested. Marshall had previously explained what was going to happen.

"You've left us no choice. I assure you, we will do everything in our power to cause you no harm," Marshall said.

In a heartbeat, Deschamps was on top of Marshall, who fell backward to the deck. Deschamps pushed himself up and grabbed Marshall's throat, as the security men grabbed a shoulder each and hoisted him away. He struggled with futility as the men held him tight.

Marshall's throat was bruised, but he recovered quickly and was soon on his feet. "Put him on the table," he ordered.

Deschamps was dragged to the nearest bed and lifted onto it. He continued to struggle, so Harrison reached for a small device and pressed it against his forearm. Within seconds, he fell limp and his eyes closed.

"What is that?" Marshall asked.

"It's essentially a hypodermic needle, but instead of piercing the skin it uses high pressured air to push through the skin. I gave him a mild sedative."

Marshall nodded. "We'll leave you to it," he said.

"You are welcome to stay. The procedure is non-invasive," Harrison offered.

Marshall looked at Medforth who gave his assent. The two men crossed the room and sat on stools next to a tall bench.

A table hovering several inches from the deck was pulled

toward the bed. On its surface was a silver cube that was glistening under the spotlights of the medical bay. A smooth, rounded arm protruded from one side of the cube, arching over the top and ending with a clamp approximately one metre from the top surface. The clamp was holding a cylindrical rod in vertical orientation.

Medforth winced at the sight of the object. Doubts about what they were about to do flooded his mind, but he suppressed them.

The table was positioned so that the cube was under the bed and the arm reached over the top of Deschamps head.

Harrison was to the right of the bed calling out adjustments, whilst never looking up from her console. Another doctor whom Medforth did not recognise moved the table as per Harrison's instructions.

"Perfect," Harrison said. "We can begin."

The other doctor pressed a contact on the cube's arm. There was a clang as the table magnetised to the deck.

With a brief sideways glance at Marshall for final approval, Harrison entered a number of commands into her workstation before sitting back slightly. The arm on the cube quickly jolted ninety degrees so that the cylinder was pointing at the top of Deschamps' head. There was a beep, and then it partially retracted into the cube leaving the cylinder facing the patient's right ear. Another beep sounded before the arm returned to its starting position. Marshall and Medforth watched intently as the arm repeated the process of jolting to a new position and beeping, until almost ten minutes had passed.

"Doctor, how long will this take?" Marshall asked.

Harrison glanced up. "About forty minutes left," she replied.

The arm continued its frantic motion, punctuated by the high-pitched beep after each step. Marshall and Medforth waited patiently as the procedure progressed without incident.

"I expected laser beams," Medforth quipped quietly to Marshall.

Marshall smiled. "You watch too much science fiction," he said. "You might as well go back to the bridge. I'll stay here and call you when it's over."

"Are you sure? I don't mind staying."

Marshall nodded. "There's no need for us both to be here."

Medforth stepped off the stool and considered Marshall for a moment. "In all the years that I've known you, I have never seen you so distracted," he observed.

A smile played across Marshall's lips, but was quickly gone. "I don't like being unprepared. This is a mess, and what makes it worse is that it was bound to happen."

"Well I can't argue with that."

"We are improvising, when we should and could have had a plan in place. We are all better than this, and it boils my piss knowing that it was preventable."

Medforth rested his hand on Marshall's shoulder. "We fucked up, no doubt. It's how we deal with it that matters."

"Tell that to Deschamps."

iv.

"I can bring him around now, Harrison told Marshall."

"Good," Marshall said before turning to Costello, who was standing to his left. "Get your people ready," he ordered. Costello nodded and left the medical bay.

Ten minutes had passed when Costello returned with Smith and two other men. They were wearing plain black T-shirts, dark jeans, black gloves and balaclavas that were rolled up so that their faces were visible.

Marshall was sitting on a stool next to the left-hand wall when the group entered the room. He placed his teacup on the counter and stood to meet the arrivals.

"Ready when you are," Costello said to Harrison and Marshall.

One of the men lifted an unconscious Deschamps off the bed and hoisted him over his shoulder. With the Frenchman secured, Smith opened a portal from a nearby console.

Harrison handed a medical instrument to Costello. "Press this against any major blood vessel like his wrist or neck, and tap the button. Simple as that."

Marshall stepped toward Harrison. "I'll take that, Doctor," he said with an outstretched hand. Costello gave him a quizzical look.

Marshall turned to Costello. "You are welcome to come along, but I'm leading this one. As Captain, this situation is ultimately my fault and I intend to see its resolution personally."

Costello opened his mouth to protest, but refrained.

Marshall dismissed one of the security men, after collecting his balaclava. He donned it before taking the medical device from Harrison, and leading his people through the portal.

iv.

It was 11:32pm local time when they emerged in a dark alleyway in central Marseille. The only illumination originated from the streetlights on the main road, which was bustling with late night drinkers and a small amount of traffic.

As the man carrying Deschamps lay his charge against the nearest wall, Marshall opened his palm to look at the device Harrison had given him. He looked for the trigger mechanism, and having identified it he pressed the unit against Deschamps' neck and squeezed.

A moment later the man began to stir. Marshall watched him closely as he gained consciousness and a flash of terror crossed his face. "ce qui se passe?" he said with alarm.

Smith stepped forward; his balaclava was covering his face. "What is the last thing you remember?" he shouted angrily in French.

"Manger mon diner." Deschamps said immediately. He was

visibly shaking with fear.

Having his dinner, Smith translated silently. *More direct,* he thought. "What is the date?" he asked.

"Le 2 décembre" Deschamps replied with confusion in his voice.

Three weeks, that'll do, Smith thought. He turned to Marshall and nodded.

Marshall grimaced at the thought of the final part of the assignment. He glanced at Costello and the other security officer, who without need for further comment stepped toward Deschamps and dragged him to his feet.

As the men held Deschamps, who lacked the strength to put up meaningful resistance, Marshall moved toward him slowly. The Frenchman was terrified, and Marshall understood why.

With the exception of Smith, the team was under explicit orders not to speak. Marshall resisted the strong urge to apologise for what he was about to do, before he swung a clenched fist into Deschamps' abdomen. A second punch was thrown, after which he launched a left hook toward the side of his victim's head that knocked him out cold.

Never again, Marshall thought remorsefully

Costello was holding a portal device. He activated it and watched as a vortex appeared before him. He received a nod from Marshall before stepping through, and was followed immediately by both Marshall and the security guard.

Smith was left alone with Deschamps in the alleyway. He

took a final look at the unconscious man before removing his balaclava and sprinting toward the main road.

After reaching the busy street, Smith slowed to walking speed and joined the pedestrian traffic. He was walking with the crowd, but glanced over his shoulder several times to ascertain that nobody was investigating the alley. After walking for two minutes, he spotted a public telephone box and made his way inside.

He dialled 15 and waited several seconds before a female voice asked, "Quelle est l'urgence?"

In French, he replied quickly. "There is a man in an alleyway. I think he might be dead!"

"You are calling from 04 91 02 20 34?" the woman asked.

Smith checked a sticker that was haphazardly placed next to the coin slot. "Yes," he said hurriedly.

"Does the man have a pulse?"

"I don't know… I just… I didn't check," Smith replied with periodic gasps. *I'm a shit actor,* he thought.

"Sir, are you okay? We are sending an ambulance. Please stay where you are and await their arrival."

"Alright," Smith said before slamming down the receiver. His demeanour instantly returned to calm.

Smith waited for the ambulance to arrive. Two paramedics hurried over to him and asked the whereabouts of the victim.

"This way," he said before rushing back down the street toward where Deschamps had been left.

He reached the end of the dark, narrow alleyway, and pointed. "He's down there," he said, with a frantic wave of his arm.

The paramedics immediately ran into the alley. Smith followed, but allowed the distance between them to gradually increase. Deschamps was in sight now, and this gave the pair ahead cause to accelerate.

There was a large commercial bin to Smith's right. He knew that the paramedics could not see past it, and they were too far down the alley for the public to witness what he was about to do, so he activated his portal device.

Smith peered down the alleyway, where the medics were tending to Deschamps. He could barely see them from this distance, but knew he had mere moments before they started asking him questions. Satisfied that the Frenchman was being cared for, Smith ran through the portal and disappeared only seconds before one of the attendees turned around.

v.

Marshall was relieved that the situation had been resolved. Smith had listened to French police radio, and had confirmed that Deschamps' injuries had been attributed to a mugging, and his memory loss to the head wound that Marshall had delivered.

Despite the overall success of the mission, Marshall knew that they would need to be more careful in future, and that their approach to recruitment needed to change.

6. Shipyard

i.

1995 A.D.

In February, *Odyssey* left Earth orbit and successfully completed her first mission to Mars. The expedition proceeded without any problems and Marshall was delighted with the performance of the crew, particularly the engineering team.

In the months that followed, Howells had several meetings with a group of engineering and architectural experts who were drafting a plan for the construction of a shipyard. He had overseen the project so far, and he chaired the panel that would make the final decisions before any implementation began, but he had as yet seen very little of the specifics.

It was almost the end of June before Howells' team was ready to present their final schematics for the facility. They convened in the briefing room aboard *Odyssey*.

"Okay Froede, you have the floor," Howells said after the team had taken their seats.

Patrick Froede, a German architect in his mid-50s who had taken part in the construction of the World Trade Centre in New York City, stood and laid a large blueprint sheet across the desk. He was 6'7" tall and towered over his colleagues.

"The facility will span slightly more than the diameter of this ship. As you can see from the schematic it will have a rectangular footprint, with four support struts for the ship under construction at equidistant points near the corners. The ship will be held above the facility floor by these pillars, and we will use them as a launching platform."

Howells leaned forward to get a clear view of the schematic. It showed a cross-section of the proposed shipyard, including a number of small side-buildings along its left hand border. "Have we decided that Earth is definitely the best place to build it?" he asked.

"Yes. We considered the Moon, Mars and Venus, but without a standard atmosphere it would delay construction by too large a margin. In addition, the gravity would be something that the crew are unaccustomed to, again slowing things down."

"Okay, where exactly will it be built? The Arctic?"

"We considered it, but concluded that a better location would be an area of Mongolia which is unpopulated, never sees human life, and has a less harsh climate for the engineers. To protect the facility against discovery by satellite or aerial craft, we can install a cloaking grid like the one equipped on *Odyssey*. The odds of being found are remote."

"Countermeasures in case of discovery?" Howells asked.

Froede nodded. "Odyssey will monitor the area twenty-four hours a day. If we detect anyone approaching the facility, we'll evacuate the crew and open a portal directly beneath the entire shipyard, the other side of which will be empty space. Gravity on the Earth side of the portal will pull everything through."

And momentum from an object passing through a portal is maintained on the other side. Howells thought. "We sacrifice the entire thing?" he asked, somewhat surprised.

"Yes. This would be a last resort, but it would leave no trace of our ever having been there."

Secrecy is the most important thing, I suppose, Howells thought. "Look into making the whole thing airtight. The damage would then be minimised if we ever had to drop it into space," he said.

Froede made a note.

"Please, continue," Howells said.

Froede nodded. "Using schematics in the *Odyssey* computer, and the knowledge we have gained since our arrival, we believe a ship should take no longer than nine months to construct. We could have a fleet of six ships including *Odyssey* by early 2000."

Pausing for a moment and referring to notes on a pad in front of him, Froede noticed that Howells had raised his eyebrows at the timescale. He repeated, "I believe we can have a ship out of the yard and space borne nine months from now. It will still require some of its secondary systems; these estimates are to make a ship space-worthy and nothing more."

Looking around the room, Froede saw more than one nod of agreement. He decided to continue. "Launching the ships will be a simple matter of opening a portal beneath the support struts of the new ship, and open space just outside of Earth orbit. The ship will fall through the portal and be officially launched when it emerges on the other side."

"What about momentum?" a young woman asked. Froede stopped and looked directly at her. "If we drop a ship through a portal, won't it continue falling on the other side?" she added.

Froede stopped talking and glowered at the woman three seats away.

The woman looked around the table sheepishly. Howells found himself smiling at her inquisitive nature; it had been apparent from the first day she joined the team. He decided to help her, in what he could see was a situation in which she felt more than a little uncomfortable. "A fair point, Kim," he said with a smile, before turning his attention back to Froede.

"Yes," Froede answered quickly. "We will have *Odyssey* waiting with grapple cables so that she can stop the new ship's drift," he said with a dismissive wave of his hand.

Howells chuckled to himself. He knew Froede had not considered this, but he was impressed with the tall man's quick thinking and the confident manner in which he had presented his response.

"The plan appears sound to me," Howells said. "Proceed with the technical detail and give me more information on the necessary resources to make it happen."

Froede spent the next hour outlining the specifics of the plan. Howells admired his attention to detail, although he also realised that the rest of the group were noticeably quiet. He was sure that Froede was presenting many of the ideas laid out in front of them as though they were his own where they had in fact been a team effort. Howells decided after a further thirty minutes that it was enough for one session and dismissed his team. He sat in the chair in the meeting room and went through the schematics once more, before packing up the paper work and returning to his quarters.

ii.

1997 A.D.

Early in the shipyard project, acquiring basic materials for construction was relatively simple for what had become known as the "extraction team", who carried out numerous covert raids of supply depots on Earth.

By early 1996, Smith had taken control of several large hedge funds by hacking into international banks and corporations. Also, several Wall Street stockbrokers and bankers had been recruited; they were tasked with funnelling money out of their employer's books via large employee bonuses, then transferring them to Smith-controlled accounts. Marshall and his crew could afford to buy everything they needed without resorting to any physical incursion on Earth, and so the extraction teams were disbanded.

Construction of the shipyard took the engineering team longer than anticipated, but it was completed in July 1996. The ships were a greater challenge, as they required significant amounts of Kyrocite before they could be constructed.

Singh had discovered early in the expedition that the existence of Kyrocite in the solar system was shielded from humanity by the holo-mesh. There were large deposits on Mars, and the asteroid belt was littered with the ore. Marshall led *Odyssey* on a mining mission that brought home enough Kyrocite to complete the first of his prospective fleet, and gave Costello an excuse to use the Ion Cannon for a practical purpose.

Howells declared the first vessel space-worthy twelve months later, and excitedly made his way to the Bridge to tell the Captain.

"Captain, I have news," Howells said as he crossed the Bridge; his grin was as wide as the ship.

"Well, don't keep me in suspense," Marshall replied with a chuckle.

"We've finished the ship. We're charging the engines, and she'll be ready to launch in eight hours."

Marshall glanced at Medforth, whom was stood next time him. "At the last briefing you said you needed another month." Marshall stated.

"One of the sections of the engine core wasn't as tough to replicate as I thought. We're good to go."

Marshall's smile was now almost as wide as Howells'. "Excellent! I see no reason to put it off any longer, begin launch preparations."

"Yes, sir," Howells said, turning on his heel and striding toward the lift.

"Oh, Chris?" Marshall shouted after him. Howells stopped and turned to face the Captain. "What are you going to name her?"

Howells stood in silent shock, staring at Marshall. "Erm... I... I hadn't thought about it. Don't you want to pick the name?"

"You built her. I'll have plenty more chances, I think this one should be yours," he replied.

Howells thought for a moment before responding. "I think we should name her *Intrepid*."

Marshall nodded. "A fine choice."

"Thanks," Howells said with a broad grin. He nodded toward Medforth and then made his way to the lift.

After the engineer had left the bridge, Medforth stepped to Marshall's side. "He hadn't thought about a name, but he made a choice within two seconds," he observed with a smile that Marshall returned.

iii.

Intrepid sat on her support struts in the centre of the construction facility. The main engines were powered up and her primary internal systems, including life support and the main computer, were fully operational. Howells sat wearing an EVA suit in the Captain's chair on the Bridge, which had been modelled as an exact replica of *Odyssey*.

"Engines on standby," a woman in a matching suit reported from the helm. "They'll be fully operational less than thirty seconds after we emerge."

"All right," Howells replied. "Contact *Odyssey*. Have them prepare to open the portal."

He turned to face an engineer who stood at the rear wall to his right. "Are final checks finished on the defence systems?" he asked.

"Yes," the tall man replied, glancing down at the readouts. "Once we're space borne they'll be online within six minutes."

Howells nodded and turned to the main console where another engineer sat at the sensor terminal. "Life support?" he asked.

"The ship is pressurised and the life support system reads fully operational. We're ready to go."

"Well," he said, his gaze returning to the forward window that presently showed the white of the surrounding ice. "Comms, tell ground crews to get clear of the facility. When they're ready, close the shutters and give *Odyssey* the green light."

"Sending message," the man replied with his hands already entering the commands quickly on his console.

Several minutes passed, and Howells became anxious as the moment he and his team had worked toward for the past year approached.

The man at communications looked up and turned toward

Howells. "Boards read green," he said before his gaze returned to his station. "Portal opening in 3...2...1...Mark."

Howells found himself gripping the arms of his chair tightly; the forward screen had been configured to display a ventral view of the ship that was now showing a large portal growing to engulf the entire view.

There was a jolt, and Howells realised that the portal had just intersected the supporting structure. He felt a lurch in the pit of his stomach as gravity claimed *Intrepid* and pulled it toward the portal.

The next second felt like a roller coaster as the ship accelerated sharply before it crossed the threshold, but once on the other side the acceleration stopped and returned the engineer's stomach to normal.

On the main screen in front of him, Howells could see stars. "Report," he ordered.

"We are 'falling' away from Earth, but we're decelerating because of the planet's gravitational pull. *Odyssey* is approximately 500 kilometres off the port bow, and closing fast," the helmsman reported.

"Brace for grapple," Howells said as he realised he was still gripping his armrests; his knuckles were completely white inside the gloves of the suit.

Odyssey reached *Intrepid* and launched four grapples at her sister; they latched magnetically to the hull and the cables became taut as *Odyssey* spun 180 degrees and moved away. After pulling

Intrepid away from Earth for several minutes, the new vessel's engines were engaged and she was released from *Odyssey*'s charge. With the thrusters online, the ship came to a stop.

There was an eruption of cheers through the speakers in Howells' helmet. He was still sitting in his chair, but he was now smiling and had finally released his grip.

iv.

Four hours earlier...

Making his way through the corridors of the aircraft carrier *U.S.S. Enterprise*, Captain Thomas Batson thought about his current mission. As commanding officer of the United States nuclear vessel, he had been aboard ship for almost a year without a break and he was starting to suffer from cabin fever.

He knew it was his own fault. The brass had offered him leave more than once during his tour and he had declined. He was a workaholic, that much was certain, but eventually sea life had started to take its toll and he requested shore leave. With *Enterprise* on her way to Bosnia, and her return to the homeland not scheduled until December, Batson had resigned himself to the fact that it would have to wait.

As he arrived at the entrance hatch of the bridge, a young officer on his way out snapped sharply to attention and saluted.

"At ease, Lieutenant," he said as he passed the young man,

who nodded and continued his journey.

"Captain on the Bridge," the Executive Officer announced as he entered the command centre.

"Status report," he ordered.

Batson listened as Stowe gave him a summary of the day's events, and he made several notes to follow up some concerning developments in the Middle East. He informed Stowe that his inspection of the engine room had been completed and he was pleased with the outcome, and then handed command of the bridge back to his subordinate.

Deciding that he would take a break in his quarters, Batson left the bridge and walked down the vast corridors of the world's largest aircraft carrier.

The Captain's quarters were located close to the bridge, so he arrived quickly. He entered the room and locked the hatch behind him. As he turned around, he was startled. A man was sat in his desk chair, to the right of the door. Batson recognised him immediately as David Costello, a man he had met several years earlier during the Gulf War.

"Wh- How did you get in here?" he barked, his initial shock replaced by anger at the intrusion.

"Long story," Costello replied. Take a seat and I'll tell you about it," he added with a gesture toward the bunk.

Batson glanced at the bed. He paused momentarily before crossing the room and sitting down.

"Aren't you supposed to be in jail?" he asked.

"Ah, you heard about that?" Costello said.

"'Decorated war hero found guilty of assisting the enemy'? Yeah I heard about it, as did pretty much anyone else with a newspaper or a television."

"It wasn't how it they made it look."

"Did you let him go?"

"The kid? Yeah," Costello said sharply.

Batson was puzzled.

"He was just a kid. It was proved later that he wasn't involved."

"But you didn't know that at the time."

"No, but that isn't the point."

"What is the point? That you are innocent and they were just making an example of you?"

Costello paused. "Well, yes!" he said.

Batson smiled. "You keep telling yourself that. Anyway, that was only a few years ago, how are you out so soon? Any more importantly, how the hell did you get aboard my ship?"

Costello blushed slightly. "I'm free thanks to a man called Ryan Marshall; you won't have heard of him. I actually met him during the mission in Ireland; he read the report about what happened and something about me stuck in his mind. More recently he needed someone with my skillset, and decided he wanted me on the team."

"So he arranged an early release?" Batson asked.

"Something like that," Costello replied.

Batson's eyes narrowed.

"You needn't worry about the circumstances of my release," Costello reassured him. "It isn't a recent occurrence."

"How long has it been?"

"About four years."

Batson's surprise was obvious. "Now that definitely wasn't for good behaviour!"

"No, but as I said, don't worry about it," Costello said with a gesture toward the bunk. "I'm not here to cause trouble for you or your ship."

"Not here to cause trouble? An escaped convict is sitting in my quarters aboard a military vessel, but isn't here to cause trouble?" he said, his anger rising as much as his voice.

"It's important, and it can't wait until your next shore leave. Sit down, and I'll explain."

Batson reluctantly sat on his bunk, and Costello spent the next twenty minutes detailing the events of the past few years. Whilst he left out the names of the crew he did give a full disclosure of Marshall's involvement, as well as his own.

Costello reached the present day in his tale, and fell silent. He waited for a minute while watching Batson, who was sat perfectly still.

"So, the point of my visit," Costello continued, "is that we want you to join us. Come to the ship and I'll introduce you to Captain Marshall."

Batson studied Costello carefully. "I've known you for many

years, but it's been a long time since we last spoke. The young upstart I met back then was very serious, almost too serious. And here you are, having escaped from prison — that much I cannot deny — with a tale so tall I don't know whether to have you arrested or committed."

Costello sighed. "I know how it sounds," he said before standing. "Look."

Batson watched as Costello took a small object from his pocket and pressed his thumb on a contact. He could not believe his eyes when a vortex opened next to the hatch, and Costello's reaction was merely to look at him and smile.

Batson took a deep breath. "Alright, I won't have you committed," he said.

"Are you coming?" Costello asked as he stepped toward the portal.

Batson nodded and followed him through.

v.

Come on, Marshall thought as he sat in the Captain's chair on the bridge of *Odyssey*. He was impatiently waiting for both the arrival of Captain Batson and the launch of *Intrepid*.

"Captain, Costello and Batson are aboard. They arrived in the engine room, Costello wanted to give him a quick tour," Smith said from the communications station.

"At last," Marshall said, standing up. He made his way to the rear of the bridge. "Send them to the conference room when they arrive," he said before he left through the rear exit.

Marshall paced the conference room whilst he waited for Costello and Batson. As they entered, he shook Batson's hand. "Ryan Marshall. Welcome aboard."

"A pleasure. This ship is quite something," Batson said with wonder.

Marshall gestured to the table and took a seat at the head. Costello and Batson sat on opposite sides, and turned to face Marshall.

"Costello's objective was to tell you our story, and to recruit you into our fleet," Marshall started, and smiled. "Your presence here suggests he's been successful?"

"Provisionally," Batson replied.

Marshall paused, taken slightly aback by the response. "And what provisions are there?" he asked.

"I want to know three things. One, what happens if I say no. Two, what exactly is it you want me to do on this ship? And three, who are you really working for?"

Marshall pondered the questions for a moment before answering.

"For a start, we don't *really* work for anyone. This is not a government sanctioned operation, and we have no political allegiance."

"Costello told me you are independent, and that the British government doesn't know you are here," Batson interrupted. "I find that hard to believe. Both of you are English; your allegiance has to be to your country."

"It was, but not anymore. The British government sent me on the mission to find WMDs in Iraq, as Costello will have described," he paused and glanced at Costello who nodded to confirm he had given Batson this information. "But they knew the portal device was there, and they betrayed me and my team in an attempt to acquire it. They can't be trusted, and neither can any other government on Earth. The simple fact is they would all clamour for the technology and power that this ship represents, and ultimately I believe the very knowledge of its existence could start a war. We will keep this ship a secret from Earth until they are ready to share it, equally and properly. That may be a very long time."

Batson shook his head. "It sounds very noble, but I have serious concerns about that stance. What gives you the right to decide when the whole of humanity is ready to have the technology on this ship?"

Marshall was irritated by the American's attitude, but he held his temper. "Look, I'm not here to argue the rights and wrongs of keeping this ship's existence a secret. I'm here to ask you to join us in making the best of it, and its technology. Think big picture. It doesn't matter who controls the ship as long as it's used for the good of all, and not just one nation. The reality is that we cannot trust the politicians on Earth to do the right thing, so for the time being we'll keep the ship's existence to ourselves."

"So you wouldn't hold a preference toward Britain if it came down to it," Batson stated.

"No," Marshall said abruptly.

Batson paused. "Well you certainly *seem* sincere. I'll take you at your word but don't think me a fool; if you start going back on your promise then I'm out."

Marshall gathered his thoughts and continued. "Your first point. What if you say no? The simple answer is you go home. We won't force you to be here, and you are free to say no and go back to your life. We want you here of your own free will. In all honesty we want you here with a passion for what we're doing, you are no use to us if you put in a half-arsed effort."

"I'm here because Costello recommended me, based on our previous working relationship. You have never met me yourself, and yet you trust me not to go home and tell everyone about what I've seen here."

Marshall paused and took a deep breath. "Should you decide not to join us, we do have technology which will allow us to erase any memory you have of the ship and crew. Given the fact that you are the Captain of a United States naval vessel, and were recommended by a senior member of my crew, I believe you will be an asset to the ship so we took the decision to give you the opportunity."

Batson fell silent for a moment; a look of concern was plainly obvious on his face, so Marshall quickly continued in an attempt to put his mind at ease. "Don't concern yourself with that, I think that after I answer your final question you will be saying yes to the offer anyway."

Marshall smiled and stood up. "Please, join me on the bridge."

Batson and Costello followed Marshall as he led them to the Bridge; they entered the room and moved toward the helm.

"Anything?" he asked Smith.

"Not yet, shall I chase them?" Smith asked.

"No, Howells knows his job. Give them another thirty m--"

Smith's workstation beeped to indicate an incoming transmission; Smith listened through his earpiece to the message. "It's *Intrepid*. They're ready."

"Then by all means..." Marshall said.

Several minutes passed whilst the crew carried out their final checks. Marshall stood between the Captain's chair and the helm, flanked by Batson and Costello.

Singh signalled that they were ready and began the operation. "3...2...1... Mark," he said from the helm.

The main screen showed the view in front of *Odyssey*. A portal opened, it was formed for only a second before Intrepid 'fell' through.

"Engaging engines. Intercepting now," Singh said, addressing the entire room but never taking his eyes off his console. "Grapples away."

On the screen Marshall could barely make out the grapple cables that were darting toward the new vessel.

"Grapples locked, reversing course," Singh said moments before there was a jolt as the cables became taut. *Odyssey* moved away until *Intrepid* could power up her engines and bring herself to a stop.

With *Intrepid* successfully launched, the crew on the bridge cheered. Marshall smiled and looked at Batson. "That is *Intrepid*, the first human-built *Odyssey*-class space ship."

"Incredible," Batson said. His eyes were fixated on the screen.

"And I want you to command her," Marshall continued.

Batson eyes widened and his head snapped to face Marshall. "What?" he asked, his mouth remained open.

"The *Intrepid* needs a Captain, and Costello has recommended you. I trust his judgement so she's yours if you want her."

"I don't know what to say," Batson said. "I already have a job, and I can't just disappear from my ship mid-tour without raising any questions."

"We already considered that. Finish the tour, and at Christmas take shore leave before resigning your commission. *Intrepid* isn't finished; she needs another six weeks to be outfitted with her secondary systems. Once you've resigned we'll arrange a cover story for you to go travelling, or something along those lines. We can ensure nobody asks too many questions when you disappear."

"I need time to think."

"No problem, go back to *Enterprise* and think it over. I'll contact you in 48 hours, and you can give me your answer then."

"Thank you." Batson replied with an offered hand.

Marshall grasped Batson's hand firmly. "Would you like a tour of *Intrepid* before you go home?"

Batson's brow lifted at the suggestion.

7. The Laird

i.

1687 A.D. (Earth Calendar)

Alethean survey vessel A-263 had been in orbit of candidate seven for almost sixty Alethean years, having relieved her predecessor who was the first to visit this world. Controller was sitting in his quarters contemplating the latest update regarding the spread of the pathogen on the home world, and found that he was struggling to contain his emotions.

A-263 was one of only five vessels to carry a hatchery, and the infection status of the other four was unknown. It was essential that Controller and his crew find a place to begin the reconstruction of the Alethean species. In the first message about the virus, central command had specifically ordered all survey vessels to avoid contact with both the candidates and each other. Controller considered this at length, but he knew that there would be insufficient space aboard the ship to truly save his people.

Fertilisation of the hatchery and the subsequent birth of the crew's offspring would not pose a problem for the next generation, but unless their population count was to remain stagnant, the confines of this vessel would be prohibitive in the long term.

Controller decided that he was left with no alternative. He must establish communication with the dominant species of candidate seven, and ask for some land on which to establish a colony.

The question now was of the timing of such contact. Recent reports had suggested that the species below were approximately 150 Alethean years away from achieving atomic power. He knew that the introduction of his people to their society could be disastrous if it were too early, yet it was a long wait and time was not on his side.

He decided to consult with Executive, as such important decisions were not to be treated lightly. He made his way to the bridge where his colleague was stood with Communicator.

"We must speak, Executive. Please join me in the conference room," he ordered before immediately turning and leaving the bridge. Executive followed, and the pair were soon sat facing each other.

"I have decided to contact candidate seven and formally request refuge on their world," Controller stated. "I have received absolute confirmation from medical that we are not carriers of the pathogen, so there is no risk to their health. Additionally, they are almost at a suitable level of development for contact. I do not believe we would cause an unacceptable level of disruption to their society. What are your thoughts?"

Executive considered the information. "We are under explicit orders not to make contact. For this reason alone, I believe your intentions are unacceptable."

Silence.

Controller was exasperated. "We have but two choices. We make contact now, or we wait 150 years for them to reach the development level defined in our mission parameters. I am not asking your permission to make contact, I am asking which option you believe is most suitable."

"Controller, neither option adheres to our standing orders."

"The future of our species is more important than our orders. I respect your opinion, and so I have sought it. If you are unwilling to aid me then we shall speak no further on the matter, and I will come to a decision alone."

Executive considered the options once more before responding. "If you insist on this course of action then I recommend waiting, as they are not yet ready. As we speak there is a major conflict developing due to political upheaval in one of their continents."

Controller smiled. "Thank you, Executive. You are dismissed."

ii.

1776 A.D. (Earth Calendar)

For 81 Earth years a cold war had dominated the Laird home world, and then eight years ago the Vrix movement won an election to power, after discontent amongst the population ousted the rival faction. Despite promises during their election campaign that they would end hostilities with the Eastern Coalition, the newly elected government launched an unprovoked attack on their enemy. Since that time the rivals had been bitterly engaged in open warfare that had to date claimed over 250 million lives.

The Eastern Coalition had proven to be a more resilient adversary than expected. When the war had started, the plans in place predicted victory within five years. This estimate was revised after fourteen nations whom the Vrix had counted as likely allies had joined the East.

As General Xon of the coalition reviewed the latest battle reports, he marvelled at how the war was progressing. The Vrix were changing their troop deployment strategy on a weekly basis, which demonstrated to him that they were in disarray.

There was a sound at the door and a man entered. He was 6'6" tall, which was average for a Laird male, with wide shoulders that tapered into a very thin torso to make an almost triangular body shape. Like most of his species, he had muscular arms and legs, a requirement on a world with such a strong gravitational field. Facially the Laird man had two dark eyes, a nose with a single nostril and a wide mouth. His skin was pale to the extreme, and he had thin white hair that was trimmed to a very short length.

The man was out of breath. "General, we've detected a missile launch in from Vrix territory. Intelligence believes it could be nuclear."

Xon jumped out of his chair and ran toward the door. Alongside his subordinate he jogged down the corridor to the war room, where he met the senior command staff.

"General," a woman said as he entered the room. "Telemetry indicates the missile is forty-seven minutes from our shore. We have been unable to determine the precise target."

Another woman at the far end of the room shouted for the General's attention. She informed him there was a call waiting from the leader of the Vrix.

Xon approached the communication device and lifted the receiver to his ear. "This is General Xon," was all he said.

The room fell silent in anticipation as the General listened to the voice on the other end of the line. After approximately twenty-seconds he returned the receiver to its holder on the desk in front of him. He turned to the room, his expression grim.

"Order all assets to do whatever it takes to bring down that missile," he said to the woman before turning to face everyone in the room. "The Vrix claim to have launched a series of warheads. According to their military leader, General Gosha, they are all using stealth technology except for the one we detected. That one was intentionally left visible to prove their existence. We have thirty minutes until the first missile strikes our soil, which is the deadline for our unconditional surrender."

There was an immediate flood of heated chatter in response to the news. Xon walked to the centre of the room and looked at the map of the world, whilst he considered the information he had been given.

"General," the man who collected him from his office said, interrupting his thought process. "We cannot surrender based upon a threat which carries little evidence."

"Is that missile not sufficient?" Xon said, pointing to a marker on the screen to his left.

"We do not know beyond reasonable doubt that it is nuclear, nor do we know that there are any additional missiles," the man replied.

Xon nodded in agreement. "We'll wait for our planes to intercept the warhead and take a decision then."

The following twenty-five minutes felt to Xon like hours. "Sir," a man behind him said. Xon turned to face him. "Air Command report that they have intercepted the missile; it is within firing range. Requesting permission to engage."

Xon nodded. "Fire at will."

The man lifted a receiver to his ear and relayed the order.

Xon and the rest of the people in the room watched the display screens that were scattered around the perimeter, as three icons representing allied aircraft approach the incoming missile. There was a pause, and the missile icon blinked out of existence.

The man with the receiver looked up at Xon. "Air force reports the missile has been destroyed. There is no evidence of a nuclear warhead."

There was a collective sigh and many smiles around the room. Xon looked at the floor for a moment, and released the breath he had not realised he was holding. "Stand down alert status. Get General Gosha on the line," he said.

"Yes, sir. I--"

A klaxon sounded loudly throughout the room. Everyone scrambled to his or her consoles to find the source. A man, who Xon did not recognise, rose slowly from the station over which he had been leaning. "By the Gods," he said. "We have visual confirmation of an incoming missile, impact in three minutes."

"Where?!" Xon demanded.

"Here, sir!" was the response.

Xon maintained his composure as a sickening feeling of panic washed over him. The woman he spoke to earlier answered an incoming call, and she listened to the caller for several seconds before reporting to Xon that further missiles had also been confirmed across allied territory.

Xon's mind was racing. "Get me General Gosha now!" he shouted.

The call was connected within ten seconds. "General, stand down your missiles. We are willing to open a dialogue."

"Do you surrender unconditionally?" Gosha's deep voice replied.

"We are willing to discuss terms," Xon replied.

"Either you surrender unconditionally or this conversation ends now."

Xon knew he was left with no alternatives. If the warheads were to detonate they would eradicate a significant portion of alliance command, plus he did not know how many missiles were heading for civilian targets.

He looked at the screen in front of him that indicated there was less than a minute remaining. "Yes. We surrender unconditionally. Now, deactivate those warheads!" he shouted. The room fell silent, shock and fear were written on the faces of his comrades.

"We accept your surrender. This is a great day for the Vrix Movement. With your meddling in our affairs at an end, we can move on to the next stage of our ascendency. Glory to the leader."

The call ended abruptly. Xon stared at the screen upon which a timer still counted down and passed 20 seconds.

Xon found difficulty in believing the Vrix would wilfully kill so many civilians when they had already won the war. As the counter reached zero, he thought of his family, and silently prayed that the Vrix would treat them well.

iii.

Controller watched in horror as nuclear detonations illuminated the planet below.

His mission parameters stated that when a candidate successfully harnessed control of atomics, they would be deemed ready for first contact. It had never occurred to Controller, or even central command, that such a discovery would lead to the immediate development of weapons. When the Aletheans had first split the atom, there had been wild celebrations across the planet. It was clear that such power could be used as a weapon, but the devastating effect such technology would have on the soil and the seas was deemed too high a price. A pact was signed, and development of such weapons was never again considered.

Witnessing the scattered mushroom clouds first hand as they penetrated the atmosphere, Controller thanked the Gods that his people had the foresight to outlaw such barbarism.

"Registering a total of eighteen detonations, Controller," Communicator reported.

Executive stepped closer to Controller. "This is madness. We cannot make contact with a species willing to do such damage to their world."

"You may be right," Controller said sadly. "But we have little choice. We shall monitor the situation in the aftermath of this event, and when matters settle we will proceed with our plan."

iv.

1781 A.D. (Earth Calendar)

The events at the end of the Laird world war were recorded and edited by the Vrix, who portrayed the Eastern Coalition as a malevolent aggressor. The deployment of nuclear arms was shown to be a last resort, with the coalition surrender following the attack rather than preceding it. The civilian population accepted the propaganda with open arms and celebrated the gallantry of their leadership. There were marches and parties in the streets for several weeks after victory was declared.

Over the years that followed, the political group known as the Vrix Movement evolved into a monarchy, and their leader Artimus Vrix declared himself King. What remained of the eastern countries was absorbed into the Kingdom, and so a single family ruled the Laird people.

The crew of A-263 had watched everything from orbit, having intercepted voice and video transmissions from the surface. Controller had seen the government videos detailing the climax of the war. Although he had doubts as to the extent of the films' accuracy, he had no other sources with which to corroborate the data. This left him with no alternative but to accept the footage as truth.

Controller ordered Communicator to open a radio channel

to the palace of the Laird Kingdom.

"This is Controller of Alethean survey vessel A-263. I bid you greetings from Alethea Prime and her people."

The bridge fell silent as the crew awaited a response. Controller had never before initiated first contact with an alien species. There had only ever been one candidate that had acquired approval from Central Command, and that was before he had even departed from the home world.

After ten minutes had passed, a voice echoed across the bridge. "Alethean vessel, this is Artimus Vrix of the Laird. From where are you speaking?"

"We are in orbit of your planet. We comprise two ships, one is a survey vessel and the other is a support craft. We are explorers. We have been studying your world and have been waiting for your development to reach a predefined level before making contact."

There was another prolonged silence.

"What are your intentions?" the voice said abruptly.

"We are a peaceful people. We wish only to establish a dialogue."

After another pause the voice said in a softer tone. "The Laird welcome you to our world. Would you care to land?"

Controller felt a wave of relief, as the tension in his counterpart's voice had noticeably eased. "Gratitude, but that will not be necessary. We are able to open a portal between our ship and your planet that will allow instantaneous travel. With your permission we will use this to visit your world."

"Please allow us one day to prepare for your arrival. We would appreciate your specifying any dietary requirements so that we may prepare a banquet, as a tribute to your arrival."

"We are honoured," Controller said. "We will transmit the data immediately, and we look forward to hearing from you in one day."

Controller turned to Communicator and nodded, after which the transmission was terminated.

Controller turned to Executive. "Prepare a list of suitable local foods for the meal and have it transmitted to the surface."

"Controller, is it wise for you to attend personally? Allow me to go in your place."

"It is my duty as Controller to initiate first contact, and that is exactly what I intend to do," he responded. He immediately turned and left the bridge, inviting no further debate.

v.

Controller and his three-man security team assembled on the Bridge. Aletheans did not generally wear any form of clothing; however, for this occasion he was draped in a ceremonial robe that was too colourful for his liking. Yellow permeated throughout the brown material, and metallic silver streaks ran down the centre of his back to the hem that brushed the floor.

"The Laird have signalled that they are ready to receive you,"

Communicator said.

A portal opened in the centre of the bridge, and the party filed through.

They emerged to find themselves in what appeared to be a very large, palatial reception area. It was brightly lit by four jewel-encrusted chandeliers, which were hanging from the high ceiling in a square formation. The walls were decorated with various paintings of a man in a military uniform, whom Controller supposed was Artimus Vrix. Opposite the party there was a large staircase that dominated the room. It was dressed with a thick blue carpet, though the floor upon which they were stood was a hard marble-like material.

Standing between the Aletheans and the staircase there were seven men. Five were armed with rifles and stood in a straight line in front of the other two, who Controller could hardly see. Controller's security detail had brought concealed hand weapons as a precaution, something that made him feel somewhat safer.

After a pause, the two men in the centre of the line stepped aside and the hidden pair stepped forward.

An unintelligible noise emanated from the Laird leader. He stood in silence for a moment after his initial address before repeating the sound.

Controller stepped forward and presented the Laird with a translation device, which he took and held in his hand.

The noise was repeated once more, followed moments later by a translation in Alethean tongue from the device.

"Controller, I am Artimus Vrix," he said with a bow. The man was only slightly shorter than Controller, with dark eyes and pale skin. His white shoulder-length hair was swept back in a loose, almost dishevelled, style.

"We are honoured by your gracious hospitality," Controller said. The device reversed the translation for the Laird contingent.

"Please, if you would come with us. Dinner will be ready shortly," Vrix said as he gestured toward a door on their left.

The Laird and the Aletheans made their way through the archway and into a similarly sized room filled with sofas and chairs that surrounded a table. Against the wall facing the entrance, which also had a large window, there was a wooden cabinet containing a host of beverages that could be clearly seen through its glass door.

Vrix pointed to the sofas with an open hand. "Please, sit. Make yourselves comfortable," he said as he simultaneously waved his hand to a small man who had entered the room at the far end. The man quickly shuffled over to the cabinet and poured several glasses of dark green liquid. Vrix sat on the sofa opposite his guests; his silent colleague joined him whilst the armed guards stood near the entrance with their weapons lowered.

Controller cringed at the prospect of sitting on cushioned seats; Alethean elders preferred solid surfaces due to the composition of their exoskeleton. Giving no visible indication as to his discomfort, he sat in the nearest chair with his party next to him.

The frail server placed each glass on a metal tray and carried it to the table. He then set down the tray and handed a glass to each member of the gathering. Controller watched him with interest, taking note of his worn attire and withered demeanour.

When the drinks had been served, Controller thanked him. Without giving a response the man scurried away through the door from which he came.

Controller watched the man leave and considered him for several seconds after he left. He returned his attention to Vrix and noticed the Laird leader was staring at him. Clearing his throat and gathering his thoughts, Controller spent the next twenty minutes detailing the Alethean mission and the data they had gathered over the last century. Vrix listened intently, an occasional sip from his glass the only motion he made.

The small man re-entered the room and approached Vrix silently, never raising his eyes from the floor.

"Ah, dinner must be ready. Excellent," Vrix said with a smile.

The group made their way back to the entrance, crossed the lobby, and entered a room on the other side. Like the lounge, there was a large window covering more than half of the wall opposite the entrance. The key difference in this room was the distinct lack of cabinets or trinkets of any kind. There was nothing but a large fourteen-seat table spanning the length of the room; it was prepared for a banquet and Controller found the attention to detail in the setting impressive.

As the party took their seats, the servant disappeared through a door to the left of the entrance. Controller found himself preoccupied by the man, and he took a moment to compose his thoughts before he sat. Vrix was at the head of the table at the far end, his colleague was to his right and Controller had chosen a seat to Vrix's left. Two of the Aletheans sat to the left of Controller whilst the third made his way around the table next to the Laird.

Food was served as Controller listened to Vrix speak at length of his rise to power and of the war that followed his election. As he bombarded Controller with a list of glorious victories and honours, the Alethean noticed how high an opinion Vrix had of himself and his accomplishments. The level of arrogance he was witnessing was so alien to him that he found it fascinating.

As Vrix continued his relentless boasting, Controller contemplated how he was expected to use the utensils that flanked his meal. After observing the Laird for several minutes, he began to mimic their actions and found the experience uncomfortable.

"You have told me a great deal about your mission to our planet, but little of your ship and her crew," Vrix continued. "I am interested to learn how this portal technology of yours works. We have nothing so magnificent here in my Kingdom."

"The concept is simple, though the implementation is very complex," Controller offered with a smile.

"Please, do indulge my simple mind," Vrix said wryly.

Controller considered the detail he wished to divulge at this early stage. "The portal utilises space folding technology. Consider a piece of cloth," he said as he reached for a perfectly folded napkin that he spread out on the table to the right of his plate. "Folded so that the corners meet," his actions followed his words. "Where once the corners were far apart, now they connect. We fold space in a conceptually similar way, and the portal is an aperture through which we can pass from one corner of the cloth to the other in an instant."

"Impressive," Vrix said, his mouth still full from his last bite of food. "In time I hope you would be willing to share such technology with us. In return for recompense, of course."

"In time, yes. Please understand my intentions when I say that we must evaluate any technology sharing proposal on an item by item basis."

"Of course," Vrix said.

The table fell silent but for the sound of food being enjoyed by all present. Controller was looking around the table when he noticed that Vrix's colleague was chewing with his mouth open, and unlike Vrix he appeared to have no tongue. Controller's brow furrowed with curiosity, but Vrix interrupted his reverie.

"You refer to yourself as Controller, do you have a name as well as a title?" Vrix asked.

"Controller is my name. When we are born, male Aletheans are given the name of their hatch-kin, with a unique number to serve as identifier. When I hatched, there was no number seven, and so it was assigned to me. When we reach the age of enlightenment we are assigned a career. We renounce our birth designations and instead use that of our role. My name was Translator for many years, and it was several others before I became Controller."

Vrix laughed. "How do you tell one Controller from another?" he asked incredulously.

Controller was perplexed. "We are each Controller of only one vessel or facility, so we are identified by our posting. I am Controller of A-263," he said. His tone was unintentionally patronising.

Vrix had noticed Controller's manner but chose to ignore it. "And what of your guards?" he asked.

"They are called Defender. Where more than one role exists in a group, each member is assigned a numeric designation, just as our young are so."

Vrix was intrigued. "I have noticed that you speak of your home world in the past tense," he said. "At first I thought it was simply because you have been away for so long, but I am beginning to suspect that it is something more."

Controller felt a rush of grief at the mention of Alethea Prime. He placed his cutlery on the plate in front of him and looked at Vrix. "Your instincts serve you well," he said.

Returning his gaze to the plate in front of him, Controller continued. "Many years ago, we received word from Alethea

Prime that a pathogen had infected our people and was spreading uncontrollably. When we hea-"

Controller was cut off by the sound of a fork hitting a plate directly opposite him. He quickly realised that the Laird he faced was thinking faster than he could explain. "Do not be alarmed," he said, raising his claw. "We left Alethean territory long before the Pathogen arrived. My crew are not infected, nor do we carry the virus," he said quickly. The man relaxed slightly, but was still sitting at attention. Controller hesitantly continued. "Sadly the same could not be said of our world or our colonies. Within a few years my people became all but extinct."

Vrix appeared stunned. "I am sorry to hear of your loss. Is your ship all that remains of your species?" he asked, his demeanour slowly returning to smarmy and arrogant.

"There are survey vessels at the other candidates. We are unsure which of them, if any, were infected. Our standing orders are to avoid contact with them, so we are effectively alone. Our ship carries a hatchery, which when fertilised will produce offspring that will continue our lineage. Our hope is to do so one day, but now is not the time."

"I see," Vrix said ponderously.

Controller had finished eating, so he placed the cutlery on his plate. His thoughts returned to the servant he had seen earlier. "This was an excellent meal. May I thank those who prepared it?"

"They do not require thanks," Vrix said with a hard tone.

"I insist. We have been aboard our vessel for so long that we have grown accustomed to a very bland and repetitive menu."

Vrix appeared disgruntled. "Very well," he said before pressing a button on a device attached to his wrist.

Moments later the servant entered the room hurriedly.

"Get those who prepared the meal," Vrix barked.

The man nodded and disappeared through the door. Within seconds he had returned with two females and one male following him. The quartet stood in a straight line at the far end of the table, looking at the floor. Controller noticed their attire was similarly ragged, and they were visibly dirty.

Vrix looked at Controller, then flicked his head in the direction of the servants. "There they are," he said with more than a trace of contempt.

Controller looked at the servants with a smile. "I would like to extend my appreciation for the meal that you prepared for us today. It was delicious, you are very talented," he said.

The servants did not look up.

Controller looked at Vrix. "Are they all right?" he asked.

"They are not capable of speech. We removed their tongues when they were brought here."

Controller was horrified at the revelation. "Why?" he said.

Vrix shrugged. "Slaves do not speak because they have nothing of value to say," he said nonchalantly. "By removing their tongues we ensure that they do not waste time talking to each other when they should be working. It is the way of things."

Disgust swelled in Controller, but his ambassadorial training allowed him to subdue it. "I see," was all he said as he glared at the silent man opposite who returned the stare with a neutral expression.

It is merely a difference in culture, Controller thought.

The slaves were dismissed, leaving only the diners in the room.

"This has been an enlightening evening," Vrix said with a polite smile. "Shall we retire and reconvene tomorrow to discuss our future relationship?"

Controller was still anxious about the slaves, but showed no sign of any discomfort. "Indeed. I shall bring Executive with me to our next meeting, where we can discuss the matter at length."

"Would you care to stay at the palace tonight? I'm sure that after so long confined to your vessel you would enjoy the opulence that we have to offer," Vrix said warmly.

Controller had assumed that he would be returning to the A-263, but he found that he was almost excited at the opportunity to spend more time in the beautiful palace.

"I graciously accept your invitation, but I must insist that my detail accompany me."

"Of course," Vrix said with a smile and a slight bow.

vi.

Controller was shown to a room on the second floor of the palace that he was told was reserved for only the most revered guests. He entered the large rectangular space and took in his new surroundings.

The room was tall, with thick cloth drapes over two large windows on the far wall. To the right there was a square object that Controller did not recognise. It was positioned against the wall, and had some sort of fabric draped over it. There were two plush items at the far end, and it rose almost three feet from the ground.

More soft surfaces, he thought with disdain.

Without a cocoon in which to enclose himself, Controller knew he would be unable to rest, but he was trained in psychological discipline techniques so he decided to employ them for the duration of the night.

Before retiring, he opened the door to the room and asked the security team posted outside to contact A-263. They were to inform the ship that dinner had been concluded, and that he would stay on the surface. They complied without hesitation, and he soon found himself alone once again.

vii.

Controller was sitting on the floor to the right of the strange square object. His legs were pulled close into his torso and his head was tucked between them. For almost seven hours he had been fully induced in a meditative state, and he had spent the majority of that time considering the Laird slaves' treatment.

As daylight appeared through the windows that he had not fully covered, Controller broke from his trance and rose to his feet.

Awakening from meditation left Aletheans immediately alert, so without any further preparation Controller approached the entrance to the room and opened the door.

He was surprised to find the corridor deserted. He stepped into the hall and looked both ways before walking in the direction that he knew would take him to the main lobby.

It was only a minute later that Controller reached the staircase and descended to the ground floor. He was yet to see any sign of life, so he entered the lounge and scanned the room before crossing the lobby and entering the dining room.

Artimus Vrix was sitting at the head of the dining table. He looked up when Controller entered and smiled warmly. "Ah, Controller!" he announced. "Please, won't you join me?"

"Where are my crew?" Controller asked.

"Don't concern yourself, Controller. They are merely distracted at present. Please, join me for some much-needed sustenance," he said with a wave toward the chairs that surrounded him.

Controller slowly crossed the room and stood behind the chair to the right of Vrix. "I must ask again. Where is my security detail?" he asked urgently.

Vrix's demeanour remained light, but his tone hardened. "You need not concern yourself, Controller. Your people are in no need of assistance, I assure you. Sit, I insist."

Controller reluctantly complied.

Vrix filled his mouth with food from the bulging plate in front of him. "I congratulate you, Controller," he mumbled with his mouth full. The translator was marginally able to identify his words. "Your people have accomplished much, and I genuinely admire you."

Controller was not fooled by Vrix's platitudes. He was fully aware that he was in immediate danger, and that he had made a grave mistake when he contacted the Laird.

"You see my problem, don't you?" Vrix asked.

Controller remained silent.

Vrix was irritated. "The problem is that you bring with you a risk of contagion from the virus you told me about. I cannot let that go unanswered. You also bring with you a unique opportunity for the Laird Kingdom to stretch its influence across the Galaxy!"

"That is the real prize, isn't it? Our technology. The contagion is merely an excuse," Controller retorted.

Vrix waved his hand back and forth. "It is of no consequence," he said before filling his mouth once more.

Controller felt a pang of panic. "What have you done"?" he asked.

viii.

Two hours earlier

"You look perturbed," Amoria Vrix observed.

"They bother me," Artimus replied.

"In what way?" Amoria asked her husband as she approached her mate slowly from across the room.

Artimus was sitting at the dressing table in his bedchamber. "They have observed us for over one hundred years without our knowledge," he said. "How could I have been so blind?"

"They are an advanced species from another world. You could not have known," she reassured him.

Artimus shook his head. "I know everything that concerns my kingdom. Yet this escaped me."

Amoria knelt at his side. "These aliens cannot be trusted. You must take action immediately," she asserted.

"An attack?" he asked.

Amoria nodded.

Artimus shook his head. "We have no idea of their strength. We must know more before we take such a step."

"No," Amoria stated firmly. "Act immediately. Trust me as you always have."

Artimus smiled. "Your counsel has always been wise," he said, remembering her insistence on the attack that ended the war with the east. "Very well. I will dispose of the aliens and take their ship as our own."

Amoria smiled. "As it is destined," she said.

ix.

Defender 4 stood at attention outside the room that Controller had been assigned. Defender 7 and Defender 8 were standing on the other side of the corridor in silence.

A female Laird approached. She was holding a tray upon which a container of transparent liquid was balanced carefully.

"I have refreshments for Controller," she said.

"We will take them to him," Defender 4 said.

"As you wish," the Laird said as she approached the Alethean slowly and placed the tray in his hands. As he gripped the platter, she quickly grabbed a large knife from under her robe and drove it into his mouth. Without waiting for the tall alien to react, she retracted the blade and spun to assault the nearest of the remaining two guards.

Before Defender 7 realised what had occurred, the Laird slammed the blade into a gap above the shoulder of his exoskeleton. He dropped to the ground as the knife was removed swiftly, and thrust toward the only remaining Alethean in the corridor.

Defender 8 had been caught off-guard, but his reflexes were sharp and he was able to lunge toward his assailant before her weapon was brought to bear.

Having grabbed the woman's arm and using his considerable weight to press down upon her, the Laird was caught off-balance and fell to the ground.

Defender threw himself on top of the woman and the pair struggled. The Alethean had a considerable weight advantage, so he was able to subdue his attacker and pin her to the floor. He told the woman to yield, which without a translator she heard only as clicks and grunts, before he suddenly went limp and dropped on top of her.

The tongue-less personal slave of Artimus Vrix was standing behind the Alethean corpse with a bloody serrated blade held tightly in his hand. The woman pushed the body to the side and climbed to her feet.

"You did well," she said reluctantly.

The slave nodded and looked down the corridor. He gestured to a group of frail Laird who quickly removed the bodies and cleaned the carpet and walls.

x.

"Executive, Controller has signalled he is ready to return," Communicator announced.

Executive was relieved. He had been apprehensive about Controller's visit to the surface, so having him back aboard was a soothing prospect. A portal opened at the front of the bridge. Executive rose from Controller's seat and waited patiently for him to emerge. A group of tall pale aliens appeared from the vortex. There was a shout from one of the bridge crew before the intruders opened fire.

Within seconds, Executive was behind Controller's chair. Pilot had jumped over his console before the Laird had turned around, but the Laird barrage cut down the remainder of the bridge crew.

"Drop your weapons!" Vrix shouted as he emerged from the portal, which closed behind him.

Executive was not armed, and he knew Pilot was not either. "What do you want?"

"Why, your ship of course," Vrix said with a cold smile. "Now come out with your weapons in the air or I will execute your Controller."

"Where is he?" Executive asked.

"He is quite well, sleeping in my palace," Vrix replied.

"I demand proof!" Executive demanded.

Vrix was furious at Executive's insolence. "You demand nothing!" he shouted as he indicated to his men that they should move forward.

Unable to defend himself, Executive was quickly apprehended. One of the assailants hit him over the head with his weapon before dragging him toward Vrix.

Vrix scanned the room to find no survivors, but he heard something from behind a large curved bank of workstations. He looked at his silent slave and flicked his head in the direction of the sound. The man moved quickly with the other Laird around the bench and grabbed the quivering Alethean, dragging him around to face Vrix. Executive was pulled to his knees and placed next to Pilot on the floor in front of the command chair.

"You will show me how to operate this ship, or I will execute every member of the crew and destroy your hatchery. Do you understand?" Vrix said to the pair.

The Aletheans nodded but did not give a verbal answer. Pilot was shaking with fear.

"First you will show me how to open the external hatches, and where the controls for the air supply are located," Vrix said.

A look of terror and realisation covered Pilot's face; Executive seemed to barely register the statement. Pilot shook his head violently, "No!" he said.

Vrix stepped forward and struck the prisoner across the face. It took a great deal of composure to prevent the Alethean from seeing the pain Vrix felt when he made contact, as the alien exoskeleton was surprisingly solid. He flexed his hand as he repeated the command.

Executive's head was beginning to clear, and he processed what Vrix had said. He looked the Laird in the eye. "You will kill everyone. I would rather die than help you."

"You will die," Vrix said menacingly, "but the manner will be determined by the level of your co-operation". He grabbed Executive's wrist and quickly jerked a finger backward, snapping it in an instant.

The Alethean's shrill scream echoed around the room. Vrix stepped back. "You have many digits between the two of you.

Tell me where the controls are located," he said calmly.

Whimpering on the floor, Pilot did not look up. Executive fought to remain strong for his subordinate. Vrix grabbed his wrist again and swiftly broke another finger.

Another scream, and Executive clutched his claw. "I will not help you," he said after a moment of composure.

Vrix was growing tired of punishing the Alethean. He took a rifle from one of his men and pointed it at Pilot. "Your defiance will not be tolerated," he said. He pulled the trigger, and Pilot's head was blown away. Vrix now aimed the rifle at the lower leg of Executive, which was flat against the deck.

"I will ask you one more time, before you lose the ability to walk," he said.

The Alethean shook his head and closed his eyes tightly. After a few seconds, Vrix fired and Executive's leg exploded in a sea of blood and flesh. There was a deafening scream, but it was cut short as the Alethean fell to the deck unconscious.

The bleeding was stemmed by one of the guards using a strip of his sleeve as a tourniquet. After thirty minutes, Executive regained consciousness.

"I will ask you one final time. If you do not answer my question we will work it out for ourselves. If you help us, the pain will stop and we will spare your hatchery. If you continue to resist, then it will be our first target."

That got Executive's attention. He looked at Vrix with hatred. "You will destroy it anyway. My life was forfeit the moment you took the bridge, so you may as well kill me. I will never help you," he said sternly.

Vrix took a deep breath. "Very well. Guards, remove his tongue. Throw him in the corner and ensure that he remains alive and conscious."

Vrix ordered the silent slave to begin work on deciphering the ship's systems. He gave Executive a final look before making his way toward the command chair, in which he sat with a great sense of pride.

xi.

Now

Controller was silent as he struggled to comprehend Vrix's actions.

"We are a peaceful people, in an hour of need. Please, release my crew," he implored.

"Release them? I think not," Vrix said with amusement as he took another bite.

"You cannot access the ship's computer without the access codes. I will exchange them for the lives of my crew."

Vrix stopped eating for the first time since Controller had entered the room. "You are in no position to barter, Controller. You are alive only as long as I permit it."

"What do you want from me?"

Vrix set his cutlery down on the table. "First, you are going to give me the access codes. Second, you will order your crew to surrender, and assist my people in learning how your vessel operates. Third, you will stand with me as I address the nation and announce our new friendship. Finally, you will answer any questions that the people might have, and you will serve as my personal slave until the day you die."

"Why would I agree to such things?" Controller scoffed.

The Laird's smile disappeared. "Because if you don't, I will destroy your hatchery."

Controller was overwhelmed. "You can't!" he shouted.

"Oh, but I can. You see we have already secured several areas of your ship. One such area contains your hatchery."

Controller closed his eyes and dropped his head. For the first time in his long life he did not know what to do.

"Are we agreed?" Vrix pressed.

Without raising his head or opening his eyes, Controller slowly nodded.

xii.

"And so, from this point forward you shall be known publicly as Ambassador," Vrix said to Controller. "In the privacy of the palace, you shall of course be referred to as Slave, as will the rest of your people. You will not be given numeric designations, as you are all the same."

Controller was outraged, but with the hatchery under threat he contained his instinct to throw himself at Vrix.

"The majority of your crew will be confined to the ship, while they teach us about its systems. As a special dispensation, I have forgone tradition and allowed you to keep your tongue. I will extend this privilege to those of your people who prove their value."

"I will address the nation tomorrow. You will meet me in the presentation room at dawn," Vrix concluded.

xiii.

"Loyal subjects of the Laird Kingdom," Vrix started from behind his podium that faced a camera. "Today I bring great news! My family, led by myself, has made contact with an advanced alien species called the Aletheans. These aliens arrived peacefully only two months ago, and already we have successfully brokered a treaty that includes an exchange of technology. This is a great time for the Kingdom and its citizens, for we have met new friends who will help us improve our lives and provide for our future."

Vrix stepped aside slightly as Controller appeared to his left. Vrix smiled at the Alethean before continuing. "The Ambassador has joined us at the palace as the special representative of his people. He will be available for interview by the media when time permits.

"As a gesture of friendship, the Aletheans have kindly donated one of their fine vessels to the Kingdom. We are currently learning how this vessel operates, and we hope to replicate her technology in the future."

Vrix' demeanour turned sombre. "I am saddened to inform you that the Alethean people is dying," he announced, before pausing for effect. "A deadly contagion has swept through their society, killing all in its path. Fear not! The unrivalled strength of the Laird means that we are immune to the disease! I have promised that at all costs we will help our friends in the sky to eradicate this infestation, and as a first step we will build many more vessels with which we will cleanse the galaxy!

"I call on all Laird to aid the Kingdom in this cause. We require materials, hard work, and the goodwill of the people in order to ensure that both the surviving Alethean population, and our noble selves, are no longer threatened by this evil menace.

"This is Vrix, ruler of the Laird Kingdom. Peace be with you all."

The transmission ended.

"You did well, Slave," Vrix said flatly to Controller, before he stepped past him and left the room without another word.

8. Warning

i.

1998 A.D.

With the launch of a third vessel in January 1998, Marshall's vision of a fleet was starting to take shape. Finding a crew for each ship had proved to be as difficult as construction of the craft themselves. Marshall had assigned the task to a team of military recruitment specialists, led by a woman with over fifteen years' experience.

At the end of July, Marshall visited the shipyard on Earth to inspect the next vessel that was a little over five weeks from completion. Visits at this stage of construction were becoming a habit, as he enjoyed seeing new ships without any of the finishing touches.

Howells had given Marshall the usual tour. Very little needed to be said; the ships were identical copies of *Odyssey* so Marshall knew his way around without a guide.

The pair returned to Howells office, where Marshall sat on a sofa whilst Howells took a seat on the opposite side of a coffee table.

"You are doing a great job," Marshall said to Howells. "If you need more people just let me know. Keilthy and her team are having a bit of a nightmare finding people now that our contact lists have been exhausted. If necessary I can have her focus their efforts on engineering staff," Marshall said.

Howells nodded. "Thanks. We have a decent group down here, and I don't want to leave the live fleet understaffed, but it won't do any harm having a few more to hand. You can leave Keilthy's priorities as they are, but don't let her forget about us either," he added with a smile. "Tea?" he asked.

Marshall nodded.

Howells stood and approached a bench on the far side of the room that had a sink and a kettle at one end.

"Chris, I want you back aboard *Odyssey*. You're supposed to be my chief engineer, but you're spending so much time down here we never see you."

Howells turned to face Marshall and leaned against the bench. "I can see your point, but I'm needed here."

"Surely you have someone you can trust to take the reins while you take a more hands-off approach from the ship?"

Howells looked away from Marshall for a moment; the faces of his team ran through his mind. "A couple of names spring to mind, but I'm uncomfortable leaving just yet. We haven't been doing this very long in the grand scheme of things."

Marshall sighed. "Fair enough," he said reluctantly.

"Besides, when I'm done here I have an idea for what should come next, and that will mean me being even less available."

"Oh?" Marshall said with a raised eyebrow.

"Yeah. I've been studying astronomy since all this started, and it's amazing how much you can get through when you're confined to a small spacecraft for four years with no booze or TV," Howells said.

"You do know there's a TV in your quarters, don't you?" Marshall asked.

"Is there?" Howells asked with a look of shock.

Marshall did not know how to respond.

A moment later, Howells burst out laughing. "Of course I know there's a TV, dick head!"

"Tosser," Marshall said with embarrassment as he fought back a smile. "You were saying about astronomy?" he added in an obvious attempt to dismiss his error.

"Right," Howells said as he composed himself. "I have a solid grip of how the portal drive works, so it made sense to me that I be able to calculate journey times, power requirements for getting around, etcetera. I started by reading up on astronomy, and I've managed to get my head around quite a bit of it."

Marshall sipped his tea while he listened.

Howells continued. "The point being that I now know our local neighbourhood, and I know how far away each of our neighbouring systems is. I think we can, and should, visit one of them as soon as possible."

"Another star system?" Marshall asked with surprise.

"Yes, Alpha Centauri. It's the closest to Earth, about 4.3 light-years away."

Marshall stared blankly at Howells.

"About twenty-five trillion miles," Howells elaborated.

Marshall's lip curled. "How long will that take to cross?" he asked.

"Just over two thousand jumps. Each one needs an hour to recharge the portal drive, so that's three months," Howells replied. "I wouldn't want to constantly open portals though, as it would push the reactor too hard. We'd need to factor in some breaks, maintenance periods, etc. I would say it's a twelve month round trip, including time to have a look around once we get there."

"Why are you so eager to go?" Marshall asked.

"Kyrocite. There's a shit-load of it in our local asteroid belt, but it's deep inside the rock and takes quite a bit of time to extract. According to the Alethean logs, at least one of Alpha Centauri's planets is covered with Kyrocite at surface level. We could bring enough home in one trip to see us through the century!"

The prospect was exciting, but Marshall had reservations about the distance. "Whoever goes would be cut-off completely, and on their own if anything went wrong. Do you think you can gather enough idiots with a death wish to man this expedition of yours?"

Howells smiled. "Absolutely," he said.

"And you want to lead it?"

"Don't you?"

"No chance. This sounds like something that was made for you. I'll hold the fort here."

Howells' smile widened. "So we're doing this?"

"I don't see why not, but not until we have more ships. When we have two or three spare, we'll follow it up."

Howells was now beaming.

ii.

Marshall entered his quarters and threw himself onto his bed. He lay there for almost twenty minutes thinking about his conversation with Howells.

His mind was racing. He had never in his life been as excited as he was now. For years he had worked for the Regiment, carrying out endless operations that required him to strategise and plan elaborate ways to accomplish his missions, but he had never been involved in any one task that lasted more than a few months.

He now found himself making plans that would take years to accomplish. Not only that, but he was making decisions with repercussions that could affect everyone on Earth. What if they found life at Alpha Centauri? Howells had told him that it was unlikely, as astronomers on Earth had not even proven the existence of planets in the system, let alone life. But astronomers on Earth also knew nothing of *Odyssey* and the Aletheans. The possibilities were endless, and Marshall was surprised that a subject that had never interested him was now the only thing he could think about.

He had intended to get some sleep, but he was too charged for it so he decided to go to the conference room and wade through some of the reports that he had been pretending didn't exist.

iii.

Two hours and five cups of tea later, Marshall put down the medical report Harrison had given him a fortnight ago and rubbed his eyes. He picked up his empty cup and walked over to the kettle in the corner.

He waited for the water to boil and thought about the next report that he had to review, which was Costello's thick document entitled, "Tactical Analysis of Fleet Deployment". He groaned audibly.

Marshall was startled when there was a loud burst of noise at the other end of the room. It sounded like sparks from a faulty electrical socket, which instantly sent adrenaline surging through Marshall as he subconsciously prepared himself for an explosion. He turned around quickly so that his back was against the tea station.

The crackling had disappeared as quickly as it sounded. Marshall watched the room intently for three or four seconds before it happened again, but louder this time.

He moved away from the wall and approached the meeting table. The sound was repeating consistently now, growing in both volume and duration. He noticed that the hairs on his arm were standing on end, and remembered the effect from school when he had touched a van de graaf generator. That device had created static electricity and caused many giggles amongst his classmates, but in this moment he was anything but joyful.

He rounded the meeting table so that he was standing between it and the large window that stretched the length of the wall. His gaze never left the opposite end of the room.

There was a bright flash at the far end of the table that he judged to be around two square metres in diameter and a metre from the ground. He instinctively raised his arm over his face as he was momentarily blinded, but his vision quickly returned to normal.

The sound was gone, along with the strange electrical sensation in the air. In its place was a man, who was suspended horizontally and appeared to hover for a split-second before falling to the ground with a loud crash. He made no attempt to break his fall, and one of the chairs was knocked across the floor when he collided with it.

"Jesus!" Marshall shouted as he started toward the figure hurriedly. "Are you okay?" he asked as he reached the motionless body lying on the deck.

Marshall knelt down and grabbed the man's shoulder to roll him onto his back. What he saw next shocked him more than any single event of his life.

Lying on the ground and barely conscious, was himself. He appeared to be in his fifties and had put on a little weight, but there was no doubt that the man was Ryan Marshall.

"What the fuck is going on? Who are you?" he asked, still reeling from shock.

The man looked up at him and chuckled. He was regaining his senses and managed to push himself into a seated position. "It's funny being on this side of the conversation," he said with a smile.

"What?" Marshall said.

"Never mind. Help me get into a chair."

Marshall helped the man up. He grabbed the displaced chair with one hand and dropped his counterpart into it.

"I asked who you are," Marshall stated. His eyes bore into the man.

"I'm Captain Ryan Marshall, Earth Defence Force," he replied.

"Earth Defence Force?" Marshall asked.

"That's what we called ourselves, once we had enough ships to genuinely consider it a 'fleet'".

Marshall pulled out a chair and sat down next to the man, who had slouched back against the headrest.

"I knew it would hurt, but not this much," he said.

"What would hurt? Would you just tell me what the fuck is happening here?" Marshall demanded.

The man sat for a moment and stared at the table, contemplating his response. Marshall took in the sight before him. A middle-aged version of himself; complete with open wounds, and an outfit that had seen better days. His jacket was torn, and the collar was stained with blood. The man was also filthy; his face was pitted with what looked like soot, and he had a gash on his forehead that was clearly recent. He looked up at Marshall.

"I have come here from 2016, using a device that we built using Alethean schematics."

Marshall stared at his older self. "How is that even possible?" he asked.

"I don't have long, so just shut up and listen. By 2016, we'd built a fleet of twenty ships. Over the years we've learned a lot more about the inner workings of *Odyssey*, and even managed to improve some of her systems beyond what we found back in ninety-three. We were proud of our accomplishments, and ultimately this led to complacency.

"We had a few extra-terrestrial encounters over the years. Fortunately, only one turned hostile; the rest were either friendly or disinterested in Earth.

"We should have known, especially after our first encounter, that one day we would face a hostile alien force that would require more powerful defences than we had at our disposal. But we were overconfident, and when that day finally came we were totally unprepared.

"The Aletheans, the same race who built *Odyssey*, dispatched a fleet to Earth to eradicate us. We have no idea why, or even how it was that they survived the plague. They simply stated their intention to 'purge our system' and opened fire."

Marshall remained silent.

"It was a short battle. We were totally overwhelmed, and they destroyed the fleet without hesitation. *Odyssey* and *Illustrious* escaped the opening volley, and I used the time displacement system to bring myself back here to warn you of the invasion."

"Everyone is dead?" Marshall asked softly.

"I don't know what happened after I left, but the fleet was gone and there was nothing to stop the Aletheans from destroying Earth's population. They were very clear about their intentions."

"Wow," Marshall said. He stood up and walked toward the window. "What can we do?"

"Build the fleet faster than we did; a lot faster. We built ships and made some incredible scientific discoveries, but we weren't prepared for an invasion. The Aletheans brought one hundred and fifty-seven ships to face our twenty. We had no chance."

"One hundred and fifty-seven ships in eighteen years? That's impossible. We don't have the resources or the manpower," Marshall said.

The older man winced and dropped his head. He remained still for several seconds before looking up at Marshall. "Yeah, with your current setup that's true. You need to increase the ship building capabilities of the current facility, and you will almost certainly need another one, or more. Look, I can't give you a strategy, this only just happened to me. I haven't had time to prepare anything for you, I used the displacement thing as a last resort."

"Are you all right?" Marshall asked when the man winced again.

"No. Our scientists told me this trip would almost certainly be one-way, and they couldn't say how long I would have. The pain is getting worse; I don't have long."

"Shit. I'll get Doctor Harrison."

"No," he replied before he doubled over and coughed. A full minute passed before he regained his composure. "Don't waste time, just listen. Prepare the fleet, build as many ships as you can. The Aletheans' armour and weapons capabilities are the same as ours so you need to get as close to 157 as you can. They'll be here on the 4th of April 2016, so you have eighteen years. The schematics for the time displacement machine are in a kind of memory stick secured behind a wall panel in the science lab. Build the machine, and if you don't stop them then you must do as I have and try again. Maybe you'll be of more help next time. We didn't find the memory stick until 2011, so hopefully with a thirteen-year head start you might figure out a way of not killing yourself doing it too," he said with a smile that soon turned into a grimace as the pain returned.

"I need to get you to the Doctor. She can at least ease the

pain," Marshall said.

With a grunt, the older Marshall lurched forward and collapsed to the deck. His younger self reached out to catch him but did not react quickly enough. He stood up and reached for a panel on the table. "Medical bay, Marshall. I need an emergency team in the conference room."

"On our way," Harrison replied.

Marshall tended to the fallen man, and his heart skipped a beat when he realised that he was not breathing. He reached for his neck, looking for a pulse, but there was none.

For the next two minutes he carried out CPR, and attempted mouth-to-mouth resuscitation, but it was futile. Harrison arrived with his team. Marshall yielded the fight to her, but he knew it was too late.

Harrison pronounced "Future Marshall", as he was to become known, as having died at 14:53 on July 27th 1998.

Harrison rose and approached Marshall who was standing a few metres away from the body next to the window.

"There was nothing you could do. He had massive cellular damage," Harrison said quietly. "This was in his hand," she added before passing Marshall a small cylinder.

Marshall examined the grey object closely. It was smooth with no features other than a small red light at one end.

"Do you know what it is?" Harrison asked.

"No idea," Marshall replied.

"We'll take the body to the infirmary and do a post mortem.

With your permission."

Marshall nodded. He had his right hand tucked under his shoulder and his left hand holding the device in the air as he gazed at it. He jumped as he heard the crackling sound that had accompanied his counterpart's arrival.

"Get back!" he shouted at the medical team who were tending to the body. They immediately obeyed his command, grabbing their equipment as they stood up.

There was an electrical build-up in the air exactly as before. Seconds later there was a flash over the body, and 'Future Marshall' was gone.

iv.

Marshall sat at the desk in his quarters, rolling the small object around between his thumb and forefinger. The light had winked out shortly after Future Marshall disappeared, but it was no less interesting.

Marshall was reliving the conversation with his future self. Medforth had pestered him for an explanation, but he had dismissed the enquiry for later. Other than Marshall, Harrison and her team were the only people on the ship who knew what had transpired in the conference room.

He would follow the advice that he had been given, that much was certain, but he had no idea where to begin.

After staring at the device for thirty minutes, he decided to hold a meeting with his senior crew and the other Captains. He contacted the bridge and had Medforth make the arrangements for 1900 that evening.

v.

The crew of *Odyssey* assembled in the conference room where Captain Batson joined them from *Intrepid* along with his first officer.

Marshall took a seat at the head of the table. Medforth sat to his right and Howells was with Costello to his left. The senior staff occupied the seats, and the remainder of the attendees were spread unevenly around the room.

"Thank you for coming," Marshall said as he pulled his chair toward the desk.

After taking a deep breath, he began. "At approximately 1430 this afternoon I had a visitor," he said, before chuckling to himself as he realised how ridiculous his next words would sound. "It was a time travelling version of myself, from the year 2016."

Marshall's eyes swept the room as he spoke; looking for signs that anyone thought he had gone mad. He wouldn't blame them, but he wanted to intercept any doubts before they could form in their minds.

Apart from a small number of sideways glances, the crew remained still. He was pleased; he pressed on with his story and over the next few minutes he detailed as much of the incident as he could remember.

When he finished, he relaxed slightly and invited questions. Medforth was the first to speak.

"Under the assumption that you weren't high," he said with a wry smile, "we have to take this seriously. This wasn't some random stranger. It was you! It seems to me that our only option is to consider ourselves on the clock."

Marshall was both relieved and a little surprised and by how quickly Medforth had accepted his tale. "I agree," he replied.

Howells leaned forward. "We also need to consider the practicality of building a friggin' fleet of that size in only eighteen years," he said.

"Without a doubt," Marshall replied.

"It took us a year to build *Intrepid*. Now that we've done it a couple of times we can expect an improvement in efficiency, but in the end we still have to go through a procedure, and that takes time. The likelihood of us increasing output by any significant margin is next to nothing. Realistically we are looking at a fleet of thirty ships by 2016."

Marshall was deflated. "He said that we would have made it to twenty ships without the warning, and it wasn't enough."

"What about building another shipyard to speed things up?" Medforth asked.

Howells shook his head. "It's an option, and much more easily completed because it's a traditional building to an extent.

The problem is that whomever we assign to that job isn't working on the ships. Plus, we would need another location."

"We could build it right next to the one we've got. It is relatively small and there's no shortage of space." Medforth replied.

Howells shook his head. "If it were discovered, we'd lose both facilities," he said.

The room fell silent for a moment as the group considered the dilemma.

"We could build a space station!" Smith said loudly.

Everyone's attention turned to Smith, expecting him to continue. He realised that he did not have anything further to add and fell silent.

Struggling to contain a smirk, Marshall looked at Howells. "Feasible?" he asked.

Howells frowned as he considered the question. "We directly copied this ship to make the others; we don't have that luxury with a space station. We would be starting from scratch. In eighteen years? No chance."

Costello looked up. "The Aletheans almost certainly had stations; I bet there are some schematics in the computer."

Howells nodded slowly. "It's possible. I'm just being cautious because the only experience any human has had building a space station is that Russian one, Mir. There'll be ISS in a few years, but that's it. Their design presents the same problems we faced for the facility on Earth; the lack of gravity and the requirement for EVA suits would slow down production so much that the investment in the station itself wouldn't be worthwhile."

Marshall decided to give his crew a break. "Let's leave it for today; we aren't going to come up with a solution in five minutes. Let's reconvene at the same time on Friday and see what we've come up with. Dismissed."

vi.

"Good morning," Marshall said to the same gathering four days later. "So what have we got?"

"I have a suggestion," Howells answered.

Marshall nodded for him to continue.

"Smith's space station idea got me thinking. I definitely think we should build a new facility; I don't see any other way of increasing production. Rather than a space station in the traditional sense, I'm thinking more of a space hangar. When I think of space stations I think of Mir, and that sort of facility wouldn't serve our purpose. Instead, think of a ship, but hollow and much larger than the ones we have now. The inside would be pressurised and have artificial gravity just like *Odyssey*, and from there we'd be working in an Earth-like environment. The hangar would be used to build new ships, and when they're ready we just fly them out of a door."

Marshall was excited by the prospect, but simultaneously

sceptical. "That sounds perfect, and I applaud your creativity, but it also sounds impossible to build!"

Howells chuckled. "Hey, I only thought of it at 4am! I don't know if we can do it, but I do think it's worth looking into. If we loosely base the design on *Odyssey* and replicate the primary systems just as we did with *Intrepid*, we'll have a decent head start. We need to weigh up the resource commitment, because if it takes twenty years to build then it's a non-starter. Unlike the facility on Earth this is a whole new venture. Even with the core technology available, there are still no schematics to follow and no original to copy."

"How would you actually build the thing in the first place?" Costello asked. "It sounds ideal for the ships, but the actual hangar itself?"

"I need to give it some proper thought, but I figured why not build it on Earth just like we do with the ships now, and then drop it through a portal when it's ready?"

Marshall smiled. "Get on it. Let me know as soon as possible if it can be done and what the implications are."

Howells nodded. "No problem."

Marshall turned to Keilthy. "In addition to ships, recruiting personnel will be vital. Our current complement isn't nearly enough. We'll need a crew for every new ship, and they will need to be trained. We don't have eighteen years for this; we can't have recruits going in to a battle with no idea what they're doing. Consider your time limit more like twelve years to get enough people in. You'll need help, so expand your team as you see fit."

"I'll start immediately," Keilthy replied, clearly anxious at the prospect.

"Costello," Marshall said turning to the strategist sitting next to Medforth. "It isn't all about brute strength, it's also about strategy. We're going to work out a solid defence plan. It doesn't have to be done urgently but it needs to be watertight."

"I'll draft initial thoughts, but we should probably leave it until we know how many ships we can expect as it'll have a significant impact on anything we come up with," Costello replied.

"Agreed," Marshall said. "Any questions?"

There were none, so Marshall dismissed the gathering and the room cleared. Marshall joined Medforth on his way to the Bridge. "We're screwed, aren't we?" he said.

Medforth smiled. "Almost certainly."

vii.

Marshall sat in his quarters looking through a proposal that Howells had put together for the new hangar. The vessel would be a large square hollow box, which could house one ship at a time. It was sealed on five sides, with a large airlock door covering the majority of the sixth. Future expansion was possible by adjoining further sections to any of the sides, allowing for more ships to be constructed simultaneously.

Pleased with the schematics, and with the timescale of eighteen months to completion, Marshall noticed the estimated production improvement. After the facility was ready, vessel construction would be increased immediately by one hundred per cent. Expansion of the hangar would take approximately twelve months per module. Each module provided a further production increase, and by the time there were five modules - estimated to be late 2004 - it would be possible to repurpose the sections to specialise in the construction of specific sections of a vessel. Ships could then be launched regularly, rather than in annual batches.

By the end of 1999, only one more ship would be launched but the hangar would be complete and operational. 2000 would see full production underway on the next module and further ships. Two further ships could be expected by the end of the year. From this point construction would increase exponentially through to 2016, with hangar expansion halted at ten modules in 2009.

If the plan succeeded and progressed on schedule, the fleet was expected to comprise approximately 129 ships by the time the Aletheans arrived. The outline was detailed in the report.

End 1999, 0 hangar modules active (plus Earth), 1 new ship, total 4 active

End 2000, 1 hangar modules active (plus Earth), 2 new ships, total 6 active

End 2001, 2 hangar modules active (plus Earth), 3 new ships, total 9 active

End 2002, 3 hangar modules active (plus Earth), 4 new ships, total 13 active

End 2003, 4 hangar modules active (plus Earth), 5 new ships, total 18 active

End 2004, 5 hangar modules active (plus Earth), 6 new ships, total 24 active

During 2005, three modules are to be repurposed for the construction of specific components, whilst two modules are maintained for combining the parts into completed ships. Future modules will add specialist construction services. An estimate of one ship per module per year is a positive yet conservative projection, as efficiency if expected to increase. A review should be carried out annually, with a full audit due after the hangar is complete, and again in 2005 after the repurposing of each module.

End 2005, 6 modules active (plus Earth), 7 new ships, total 31 active
End 2006, 7 modules active (plus Earth), 8 new ships, total 39 active
End 2007, 8 modules active (plus Earth), 9 new ships, total 48 active
End 2008, 9 modules active (plus Earth), 10 new ships, total 58 active
End 2009, 10 modules active (plus Earth), 11 new ships, total 69 active
2010 - 2015, 10 ships per year, total 129 active

For the first time since the time traveller had visited him, Marshall relaxed. With a sound battle strategy, one hundred and twenty-nine ships would hopefully be enough. He was also happy with the margin for error that the report included. It was time to give the idea his endorsement and get started; having seen the work and the timescale involved, Marshall knew that the real work was yet to come.

9. The Purge

i.

"Unforeseen complications? And you only know of this now?" Artimus Vrix shouted aggressively at his Defence Minister.

"Well, I--,"

"How much longer must I tolerate your incompetence?" He was waving in the air a report that he had been given earlier that morning.

"My Lord, it is all we can do to keep the factories running as it is. To achi--"

"Enough of your pitiful excuses!" Vrix screamed. He waved at the guards who flanked the entrance and they approached quickly. "Remove him from my presence," he commanded. "I do not wish to lay eyes on this creature again," he added.

"Sire, please!" the man pleaded as he was grabbed by both arms and dragged out of the room. Vrix generally disposed of those who disappointed him, but he had been hesitant with the Minister, as he had served him well during the war with the East.

Vrix pressed a contact on his desk, and a minute later Slave arrived.

"Where were you?" Vrix demanded when the Alethean entered the room.

"Apologies, Master. I was tending to the kitchens."

"Hmm," Vrix pondered. "I will forgive your tardiness this time."

"Gratitude, Master."

"The Defence Minister has been removed from office. I require a new one. See to it that a suitable member of the council is briefed and appointed immediately."

"At once," Slave said flatly with a bow.

"Go," Vrix concluded with a wave of his arm.

Slave turned on his feet and left the room swiftly, leaving Vrix alone.

I am hungry, he thought. "Why must I do everything myself?" he asked aloud.

He crossed the room and dropped into a heavily cushioned chair. After sitting for a moment, he reached for another contact on his computer console.

There was a beep before a voice erupted from a small speaker in the side of the unit. "Yes, my Lord?" the nervous voice asked.

"Have a slave bring me food. Now," Vrix ordered.

"At once, my Lord," the voice said before being cut off by Vrix when he released the contact.

"I am surrounded by fools," he muttered to himself.

Ten minutes passed before there was a knock at the door. After being summoned, a shabbily dressed female slave entered the room and scurried toward Vrix's desk. She carefully placed the tray of elaborately presented food on the table, before retreating out of the office.

Vrix was motionless until the slave left the room. Once alone, he leaned forward and inhaled the tantalising aroma that the hot plate was producing.

After collecting the cutlery that was wrapped in a towel on the tray, Vrix reached for a piece of bread that was meticulously placed amongst the accompaniments. Before he could pick up the bun, there was another knock at the door.

Vrix felt irritation swell within him. "Who is it?" he shouted.

The door opened slowly and his eldest son, Antillius, entered the room.

Vrix shook his knife and fork in the air. "Can't you see I am eating? Perhaps your vision requires checking," he said insolently.

"I apologise for the disturbance, father. You asked that I attend your office at fifteen o'clock. The hour is almost upon us."

Vrix had forgotten about the appointment. He glanced at the large clock standing to the left of his desk, and sighed as he placed his cutlery on the plate. "Very well. Enter."

Antillius crossed the room and stood at attention, facing his father.

"I wished to speak with you regarding The Purge," Vrix started. "My intention was to inform you that the fleet was finally ready to depart. I have, however, been informed that the project has been delayed by the incompetence of my subjects."

Antillius smiled. "So you will be here for a while longer?" he asked.

Vrix nodded. "Six months, at least. I am appointing a new Defence Minister to oversee the project. He will perform better than his predecessor, or he will also be replaced."

"Your patience knows no bounds, father."

"Quite."

"How many ships are complete?" Antillius asked.

"Two hundred. I was informed that the remaining fifty were awaiting the same component and that they would be finished next week. That appears to have been an exaggeration.

There was a knock at the door.

"Damn these infernal interruptions!" Vrix exclaimed. "Enter!"

Slave entered the room. "Master, you have a public announcement scheduled in twenty minutes. I have your speech ready for review," he said before offering several sheets of paper to Vrix.

"I am busy. It will have to wait," Vrix snapped.

"Yes, Master. Shall I inform the broadcast network that you will be cancelling the event?"

Vrix had never cancelled a broadcast, but he did not want to announce the completion of the fleet prematurely. Under his guidance, the Laird had worked tirelessly for two years to construct a flotilla of replica Alethean vessels, and he wanted to maintain his people's dedication to the cause.

Vrix sighed. "No. I will be there presently," he said.

"As you wish, Master," Slave said with a nod. He left the room without delay.

"He bothers me," Antillius said.

"Slave?" Vrix asked with surprise. "He has proven to be a remarkable servant."

"He is always so calm; like he is biding his time. You should be wary of him, father. He cannot be trusted."

Vrix stood and rounded his desk. He stepped closer to his son and clasped his hands on the younger man's shoulders. "I appreciate your concern, son. But fear not, Slave is quite subservient. It isn't in his people's nature to act as you describe."

"We don't know that for certain, father. When you lead The Purge, you must leave him here."

Vrix smiled. "I do not intend to have him anywhere near me during The Purge, son. You can be assured of that."

ii.

A podium was erected at the front of an overly dressed rectangular room. The occupants were Artimus Vrix, Antillius Vrix, Slave, and a camera operator.

Vrix had been considering his options intently since the meeting with the minister only half an hour earlier. He was standing behind the podium, facing the camera. His son was beside him but was not in view of the lens, whilst Slave was next to the operator.

The operator gestured a countdown from five to one, then dropped his arm.

"My loyal subjects, I bring great news!" Vrix started. "As of today, the Royal Fleet is complete and ready for departure."

Antillius' eyebrows rose at the announcement.

"After two long years of hard work, The Purge may finally begin. The Laird Kingdom will welcome a new era of peace and security, and we can live free in the knowledge that the Alethean virus will never threaten our people.

"The galaxy is large, and the journey will be long. Those of us who leave the home world to carry out our divine obligation shall never return, and for this I am truly saddened. For generations, the brave souls who complete The Purge will live a life of luxury aboard their fine vessels, but they will never again see their home or family."

Vrix glanced down at the podium and paused. The silence became protracted, and then he glanced at his son before looking back at the camera.

"It has always been my intention to lead The Purge personally. Despite knowing that I would be leaving our glorious world forever, I felt it necessary that I oversee the mission first hand.

"I have decided, however, that the need of the people outweighs my personal ambition. To that end, I shall remain here with you, whilst I entrust the safety and success of the Royal Fleet to my son, Antillius, who will lead the crusade as Prince Regent!" Vrix finished with a flourish of his hand as he beckoned Antillius toward him.

Slave was shocked by the announcement. Since the brief pause, Vrix had not followed the script.

Antillius was visibly stunned. It was apparent to Slave that he also had no foreknowledge of the decision.

Antillius stepped closer to his father, who wrapped his arm around the young man's shoulder and pulled him in tightly so that he was in view of the camera.

"This is Vrix, ruler of the Laird Kingdom. Peace be with you all."

The camera operator nodded to indicate that the transmission had ended.

"Father," Antillius said as he shrugged off his father's grasp. "You gave me no warning."

"It was a recent decision," Vrix said with a shrug of his shoulders.

"And the fleet? You said it was delayed."

"I have decided that two hundred ships will suffice. We will then construct a further fleet starting with the fifty that are nearing completion, and dispatch them in a different direction. This will expedite things considerably."

"Why do you not wish to lead the fleet personally?"

"As I said, I am needed here. Do you not wish to go?"

Antillius was offended by the accusation that he may be cowering from his responsibility. "Of course I do, father. And I shall excel! I was merely surprised by the announcement."

Vrix nodded. "Very well, it is settled. You will leave immediately," he said before turning to Slave. "And you will go with him," he added.

Slave glared at Vrix. "Master, my place is at your side," he said.

"Father, I must protest!" Antillius added.

Vrix shot them both a glance. He addressed Slave first. "Your place is where I decide it is to be!"

"Yes, Master," Slave said as his head dropped.

Vrix turned to his son. "And you dare challenge my wisdom?"

Antillius also backed down. "No, father. As I stated earlier, I have strong reservations regarding the Aletheans and their loyalty. I do not trust this slave and I do not want him with me during The Purge.

"It is not your decision to make. Slave knows more about the fleet than you do, and you will need someone to control the Alethean population."

"Other Aletheans will accompany us?" Antillius asked incredulously.

"Indeed. They all shall. I want them off our planet, and I believe they will serve the cause well. After all, the virus eradicated their people. They are invested."

Antillius agreed with the rationale, but was no less unhappy with the situation. "At least I can rest assured that there will no longer be an Alethean presence in the Kingdom. For this, I am grateful," he said resignedly.

Slave listened to the exchange intently. Vrix was afraid, that much was certain. He had insisted from the beginning that he lead The Purge, but when it came to committing to the cause he had cowered behind his son.

Antillius was a strong man with an impressive military career behind him. He was eager to impress his often-disapproving father, but he did not have the passion for the cause that his father had often demonstrated.

Slave had not been allowed aboard A-263 since his capture, and he was overjoyed to learn that he would be returning to his ship. The Purge was designed to see the total annihilation of all known life in the galaxy. This he could not allow. Antillius was right not to trust him, as he had every intention of destroying the Laird fleet at the earliest opportunity. He just didn't know how he was going to do it.

10. Turncoat

2001 A.D.

General Paterson was in his office at Nellis Air Force Base in Nevada. He was sat facing a man who until ten minutes ago he had never met.

The General was a noticeably tall man who stood at almost six and a half feet. The man he faced was also tall but not nearly so much. Paterson had at least five stone and fifteen years' experience on the other, so he was not going to be intimidated by what he had to say.

The general had spent a particularly dull morning wading through a mountain of neglected paperwork. He was glad of the distraction, but what he had been told disturbed him greatly. Either the soldier before him was insane, or he was delivering news that could change the future of humanity.

"Space ships. Alien space ships. In the hands of the British." He stated.

"That's right, Sir," the man replied.

"Rewind a little. Tell me how you came to be involved in this."

The man paused. "I had known Tom Batson for almost a decade when he approached me four years ago. He had an offer of a position aboard his ship. At first I thought it was a practical joke, of course, but then he opened a portal not ten feet away from me. I went through it, after him, and found myself exactly where he described."

"And you accepted his offer."

"Yes. At first I was in a daze over all I was seeing. It is an incredible ship."

"Have you served him ever since?"

"At first I was stationed at comms and sensors aboard Batson's ship. Earlier this year I was reassigned to tactical and intervention aboard another."

"To what?" Paterson asked.

"I am part of a team who organise and execute incursions on Earth when there is a crisis that needs to be resolved."

"You mean this Marshall character is sending troops down here?"

"Yes, sir. Whenever he deems that a situation is escalating out of control, my team are assigned the job of bringing it to a close quickly and quietly."

"Give me an example," Paterson demanded with growing alarm.

The man thought for a moment. "A simple example was a hostage situation last year in West Africa that went on for almost three weeks. Marshall decided that terrestrial forces had failed to resolve it and were unlikely to bring out the hostages alive. My team were tasked with getting them out."

"And did you?"

"Yes. All of them."

"How?"

"My team were sent in using the portal system to drop us in a secluded area. We then scouted the building and pinpointed each of the targets. After transmitting their exact coordinates to the ship, portals were opened beneath them. The other side led to locked crew quarters aboard one of our ships, and gravity pulled them through. The hostages were bound and gagged, with bags over their heads. They didn't see what happened. As far as the African authorities and media were concerned, the hostage takers had fled the scene and escaped."

"What did you do with them?"

"There is a device that Marshall found aboard the original ship that can manipulate human memory. He had all knowledge of the attack wiped from their minds and returned them to Earth. They won't even know they were involved."

Paterson was speechless. He reached out and grabbed his mug of coffee that had now gone cold. He drank it anyway.

The younger man watched the General as he drained his cup. His eyes wandered to the pair of large flags that flanked his superior's high-backed leather chair. An oak bookcase full of hard-backed literature filled the rear wall. The man admired the stately manner of the arrangement.

"You were a willing participant in all of this?" The General asked after placing his empty cup on the table.

The man's lip curled. "I have never been happy with the way decisions are made, but I have followed my orders."

"What exactly do you disagree with?"

"The leadership structure, and decision making process. Marshall is the Captain of the original ship, and overall commander of the fleet. He makes the final call on almost everything."

"It sounds like a normal military structure," Paterson observed.

"Not quite. There is no formal ranking structure, and no military style hierarchy. Each ship has a captain and first officer, and each department has a head, but other than that it's flat. The Captains have formed a council chaired by Marshall, but the reality is that he is calling the shots."

"You have been there for four years. What made you turn your back on Marshall and come here today?"

"9/11."

Paterson swallowed hard at the mention of the attack that had occurred only two weeks earlier. "What of it?"

"For all their advanced technology, nobody in the fleet saw that coming. There was nothing they could have done to prevent it, but in the aftermath there was an outcry that we assist in the rescue effort. Marshall refused, citing the security and secrecy of the fleet being of paramount importance. All of the Captains backed his decision, and I believe they did so out of self-interest rather than genuine belief that it was right."

Paterson paused. "There is more to it than that, isn't there?" he asked carefully.

The man's face turned pale. "My brother was a FDNY fire fighter. He was in the North Tower when it went down."

Paterson steeled himself. "I'm sorry for your loss."

The man nodded.

"You blame Marshall for his death, don't you?"

Anger burned in the man's eyes. "Yes."

Paterson shook his head. "This cannot be about revenge."

The man's anger was evident, but controlled. "Marshall needs to be taken down," he said. "It is as simple as that. He is misusing his power and needs to be stopped."

"What do you propose?"

"I have a plan that will allow us to take his fleet from him. It will take some time, but with your support I know it can succeed."

"And what of this invasion you mentioned?" Paterson asked, referring to the impending attack the man had described at the beginning of the conversation.

"Once we secure the fleet, we will have the resources of the entire U.S. military available to plan our defence. We will have more chance of success than Marshall and his band."

Paterson exhaled through pursed lips. "If this is a practical joke, I will see you discharged."

For the first time since he entered the room, the man smiled. "It is not, Sir."

"Very well, I will take it to the Secretary. But I need proof. Do you have any?"

The man shook his head. "No, but I can get some. It cannot be anything that will be missed. What do you have in mind?"

"Schematics."

"I don't have clearance for anything like that, and have no reason to ask for it.

"Alright. Get me as many photos of the ship's interior as possible. Can you disable any surveillance equipment for long enough to do that?"

"I can."

11. Slaves

i.

1808 A.D.

"I cannot say," Communicator reported.

Controller rose from his seat in the centre of the bridge. "Make another attempt," he commanded.

There was a pause as Communicator's claws raced across the console in front of him. "There are at least one hundred objects, but at this distance it is impossible to say exactly how many."

"Pilot," Controller said with unrest. "Plot a course for the disturbance, have S-112 join us."

"At once, Controller," Pilot replied.

"Controller, portals are opening all around us!" Communicator announced with alarm.

In the cold blackness of space, two hundred portals formed. Almost instantaneously, an Alethean vessel darted from each one.

Controller stared in silence at the large screen hanging on the wall at the front of the room. He was filled with both elation and disbelief. "Impossible," he murmured.

"They are transmitting, Controller," Communicator said.

Controller nodded, and listened as a voice filled the bridge.

"I am Antillius Vrix, Regent of the Laird Kingdom. By royal decree, Candidate 6 has been declared a subject of The Purge. Stand down."

The room fell silent.

Executive stepped forward and was now next to Controller, facing the screen. "Controller, were you aware of these survivors?"

Controller shook his head. "They are not our people, Executive," he said solemnly.

"Those are Alethean vessels, Controller. They may announce themselves as something else, but our eyes do not deceive us."

Controller addressed Communicator. "Can you verify their origin?" he asked.

After checking his console, Communicator looked over his shoulder. "They are of Alethean design. If they are not authentic, they are near-perfect replicas."

Controller turned to Executive. "I agree with your assertion that we are dealing with our own people. This means however that we cannot raise arms against them. There are too few of us left to risk it."

"They said we are subject to 'The Purge'. It is logical to conclude that they are here to eliminate any threat from the virus. That we have been deemed a target would indicate that we are infected, would it not?"

"Indeed it would," Controller replied.

"In which case we should submit ourselves to them?"

Controller's gaze wandered back to the screen. "No. We are not infected, or else we would already be dead. They must know this."

Controller stepped forward and was now standing directly behind Communicator's station. "Open a channel," he commanded.

With a gesture from Communicator, Controller began. "This is Controller of A-112. We left Alethea Prime long ago, and so we escaped infection from the virus. We have remained with Candidate 6 for many years, and have had no contact with any other survey vessel. As it is impossible that we be infected, I submit that we should be exempt from 'The Purge', and that we instead join your fleet on your noble quest."

The room once again fell silent.

"Controller!" Communicator exclaimed, moments before A-112 was vapourised."

ii.

Slave watched in horror, as a barrage of ion beams and torpedoes assaulted both A-112 and S-112. Far more firepower was brought to bear than was necessary to destroy two ships, but the Regent was making a point, and making it well.

Slave was standing behind a beaming Antillius Vrix, who was sitting in the command chair of *The King's Will*. Slave stared unwaveringly at the screen at the front of the room, but in his peripheral vision he could see the unmistakable upward curl on his master's lip.

Slave had spent twenty-seven years at Antillius' side. Over time he had come to realise that Antillius was in absolute awe of his father, and that nothing was more important to him than proving himself worthy of his role in The Purge. Antillius was not as ruthless as his father, and even showed a softer side to his personality on occasion, but Slave could never forget what the Vrix family had done to A-263 and her crew.

Although they were now too far from the Laird home world for two-way communication, Antillius transmitted regular reports to the palace informing them that the mission was proceeding as planned. Slave knew that today's report would be particularly lengthy.

Antillius turned around in his chair. "Father's will, be done," he said with pride to Slave, who did not reply. Antillius peered inquisitively at him. "This does not phase you in the least?" Antillius asked.

"It is not my place to offer opinion, Master," Slave replied carefully in Laird tongue.

"Damn you, Slave. Out with it! Surely the deaths of your people stir up some sort of emotion!"

"Indeed, master," Slave said reservedly.

With a flick of his hand that was characteristic of his father, Antillius returned his attention to the forward screen. "I have no time for your nonchalance," he said dismissively. "Helm, begin bombardment phase."

Slave watched as those manning the curved bank of workstations at the front of the bridge quickly began issuing orders to the fleet. Moments later, the star field on the main screen, along with the visible stars outside the wide forward window, blurred slightly as the ship sharply altered course.

Fifty of the two hundred Laird ships opened a portal and disappeared. Each ship would emerge at predefined points scattered around the planet, and simultaneously launch nuclear missiles toward the surface. The warheads were of Laird origin, but their delivery was facilitated by Alethean torpedo technology. The result would be cataclysmic for the primitive inhabitants, and would render the planet dead and uninhabitable for fifty thousand years.

Slave waited, knowing that it would not be long before the eruptions began on the surface. Sure enough, the detonations lit up the world below as the nuclear fire engulfed the atmosphere.

Antillius stood and approached the primary console. "Dismantle the holo-mesh. Salvage what you can, then regroup and set a course for Candidate 3," he said to the helmsman.

"Yes, your excellency," was the immediate reply.

Antillius turned to Slave. "Would you care to join me for dinner? I wish to celebrate our victory."

"It would not be appropriate," Slave said solemnly.

"I decide what is appropriate! Come," Antillius said before ushering Slave toward the lift.

iii.

Pilot had served his Laird masters as an engineer since the capture of A-263, having revealed his past experience during interrogation.

Uniquely, the Alethean engineers had not been confined to a single vessel. In the last year, Pilot had served aboard seven different ships, carrying out maintenance and upgrades. To signify their status, engineers wore a patch on the chest of their otherwise plain and tattered garments. The patch displayed the crest of the Vrix family, crossed by a pair of multi-function tools that were common on the Laird home world.

Pilot entered the cavernous hangar aboard Vessel 62, and sheepishly approached the Laird male who was manning a workstation.

"What do you want, Slave?" the man asked abruptly when he noticed Pilot's approach.

"Master has commanded me to run diagnostics on both shuttles," Pilot replied.

The man sighed with impatience. "What is wrong with them?" he asked.

"Master did not indicate a fault. I believe it is only a systems check."

The man shook his head and rolled his eyes. He looked up at the towering Alethean. "It is unnecessary. Report that the shuttles passed your tests."

The prospect of being unable to complete his task filled Pilot with dread. "Master would be most displeased if the shuttle's systems were to develop a fault after we reported them satisfactory. I believe it best for us both that I complete my duty," he objected, carefully manoeuvring the Laird into joint responsibility.

The man was instantly enraged. His eyes bulged and his nostrils flared, but just as quickly he disarmed. "There is a reason we remove the tongues of slaves, Alethean. Be mindful of that."

Pilot lowered his head. "Yes, master."

The man growled. "Get to your work! And be done quickly!"

Pilot was elated. "Yes, master," he said with maintained composure, before scurrying across the room toward the nearest of the two shuttles. Without hesitation, he opened the door situated at the rear and entered the small craft.

The shuttle had a passenger section at the rear that could hold eight, seated in two banks of four on each side facing each other. Separating them was a catwalk that ran to the cockpit at the front. Pilot walked along the catwalk that clanked as he stepped on the cold metal, and was soon in one of the two pilot seats. He shifted his weight on the upholstered chair that he found particularly uncomfortable.

After throwing his toolkit onto the accompanying seat, Pilot powered up the shuttle and checked the time on the readout in front of him.

Not long, he thought.

Fifteen minutes passed. Pilot could see the Laird officer on the screen in front of him, which he had set to display the aft exterior of the shuttle. The man had not moved from his station, but he occasionally looked over as though wondering what Pilot was doing.

A light in the corner of the hangar started to blink. It was time.

Pilot entered a number of commands into the navigation console, and the shuttle's engines came to life. On the screen, he could see the Laird officer take note and make his way toward the craft. Only a second after he left his station, he started to grab at his throat. Pilot could see his panicked expression clearly on the screen, but made no move to assist him.

Whilst in the engine room over the past few days, Pilot had entered a sequence of commands into the ship's computer that would be executed in a specific order at the ordained time. That time had come, and step one was to evacuate the atmosphere from the shuttle bay.

The Laird man was now stumbling hurriedly toward the shuttle. He reached it and made his way to the front, his eyes bulging from the strain of breathing. He was attempting to shout something to Pilot, who he could now see through the panoramic window, but the lack of air left him silent.

With the hangar depressurised, the Laird fell lifelessly to the ground. Moments later, the large door spanning the width of the room began to retract upward.

The crew of Vessel 62 would be unaware of what had transpired, as all alarm systems had been disabled in the hangar as part of the program. By the time they realised, it would be too late.

Pilot waited for the door to be fully open before lifting the shuttle off the floor. He engaged the ship's cloaking grid, rendering it invisible to Vessel 62's scanners. Finally, he guided the small craft through the aperture into open space.

His stomach began to churn; partly from the sudden lack of gravity, and partly from apprehension over what was to come next.

iv.

Slave sat opposite Antillius in the Regent's dining room. When the ship had been A-263 this room had been Engineer One's quarters, but Artimus Vrix saw no need for anyone other than the Regent and his family to have special accommodation. After deeming Controller's quarters insufficient for his son's needs, the entirety of deck two was converted into a lavish living area for the Regent.

"You are here as my guest, Slave. Please, let us speak as two leaders of equal standing," Antillius said softly.

Slave shot a glance at the armed guards who flanked the door at the end of the room. "Thank you, Master," Slave replied. "May I ask what I have done to earn this honour?"

Antillius was visibly uncomfortable. After a moment spent shifting in his chair, he smiled and raised his left arm in the air. "It is a great day for the Kingdom. I wish to celebrate!"

Slave remained silent and still. It was customary for the Laird to raise their left arm and touch wrists as a toast, but Slave dared not make contact with his Master.

Antillius lowered his arm sheepishly. Slave was certain that he saw a moment of embarrassment and awkwardness in his Master's demeanour, but dismissed the idea as impossible.

"It will take the fleet fifty-nine years to reach Candidate 3. I will be dead before we arrive, so it is my duty to appoint a successor," Antillius said slowly and solemnly.

Slave said nothing.

"I have selected my eldest daughter, Aurellius. She will inherit the Regency upon my death, but rest assured I intent to retain my command for many years to come."

Slave decided now was an appropriate time to give his master reassurance. "An excellent choice, Master."

A smile played across Antillius' lips, but it quickly disappeared and his expression once again grew grim. "You have been a loyal and obedient servant, Slave," he said solemnly. "My role as Regent requires much of me. There are duties I must complete following the destruction of Candidate 6. Duties bestowed upon me by my father."

Slave had never heard his master speak in this manner, and it was making him feel uneasy.

Antillius continued. "My father stated that after the purge of Candidate 6, or my death (whichever occurred first), I am to eliminate the Alethean contingent of the fleet. He felt that by this stage of our journey we would no longer need you, and that the risk imposed by your presence would by now outweigh your usefulness."

Before Antillius could continue, a male Laird entered the room with a pair of plates heaped with food. He calmly approached the table and set the meals in front of both Antillius and Slave.

"Ah," Antillius exclaimed with distracted glee. "I hope you enjoy this; I am told you found it appetising when you dined with my father."

Slave glared at the meal with contempt.

Antillius began to cut into his food as he continued. His demeanour had lightened since the food's arrival. "You see, Slave, I am left in a difficult position. Personally, I do not wish to carry out my father's orders. I did not trust you when we first left home world, but you have proven yourself over the last thirty years and I have come to think of you as more than a slave. I respect you, and your people. Unfortunately, it is my father's will that binds the fleet. They follow him, and the throne, without question. If I were to defy his will, I could face an uprising. You understand I cannot allow this."

Antillius shoved a large pile of food into his mouth and chewed enthusiastically.

Slave sat perfectly still, his plate untouched.

With his mouth full, Antillius said, "Are you not hungry?"

Slave picked up a utensil and stabbed a small cluster of food onto it. He raised it into the air and gestured toward Antillius before eating the mouthful.

Antillius carefully placed his cutlery on his plate. "I am sorry, Slave. Truly," he said, and surprisingly Slave believed him.

Slave set down his cutlery. "When is this to occur?" he asked.

"Tomorrow, before we depart the system."

"And what of the hatchery?"

"We have no further use of it. It will be destroyed."

Slave remained composed and calm. "I have a request," he said.

Antillius' brow furrowed. He considered the Alethean for a moment before responding. "Go on," he said with a hand gesture.

"I wish to address my people. To thank them for all they have done to preserve the hatchery, regardless of the outcome. And to prepare them for tomorrow."

Antillius took a deep breath. "Your people are scattered across the fleet, with no two Aletheans serving aboard the same ship. You will not be able to incite any form of resistance to what is to come."

"Still you do not trust me?" Slave said coldly.

Antillius grinned. "You may have your announcement, but I shall be listening carefully."

"As you wish."

Antillius stood and wandered casually past Slave to a large mirror that was hanging behind the Alethean.

"I can transmit messages to the entire fleet from almost any room on the ship. It means that when I make my daily announcements I do not have to be in a specific place," Antillius announced boastfully, as though Slave were not already privy to this information. "Join me," he added.

Slave stood and turned to face Antillius and the mirror.

"Just press that button to begin, and again to end," Antillius said, pointing to the activator switch. Slave found his patronising tone aggravating; he had been present at almost every one of Antillius' announcements, so he was fully aware of how the device operated. "Thank you, master," was all he said.

Antillius stepped aside and Slave took his place. He stared at himself in the mirror. *Their vanity knows no bounds*, he thought. He pressed the button and a light above the mirror blinked on to indicate he was transmitting to every screen in the fleet.

Slave took a moment's pause, and then began. "This is Controller calling upon all of my Alethean brethren, hear me now. After many years of hardship and pain, it is time."

Slave pressed the button for a second time.

Antillius' face twisted with confusion, and he asked, "What have you done?"

v.

Moments earlier

"After many years of hardship and pain, it is time."

Pilot watched the image of Controller wink out on the screen in front of him. He was nervous, but also proud of what he was about to do for his people.

He reached out to the control board and redirected all power to the engines, including that of the cloaking grid. The shuttle shimmered into view only seconds before her thrusters burned with every joule of energy at their disposal.

The small vessel darted toward its target, *The King's Will*. Pilot stared out of the window as the large flagship loomed ahead of him. Ten seconds later, the two ships collided.

vi.

"I said what have you done!" Antillius screamed as he grabbed Controller's tunic.

Controller looked down at him and stared him in the eye. "What any slave would do. I have earned my freedom."

Antillius' eyes squinted. He was about to say something when there was a sudden loud noise and the deck lurched violently. All four occupants of the room were thrown with extreme force against the wall opposite the window.

The lights cut out, and the deck shook again. Controller had taken a substantial blow when he hit the wall, but his exoskeleton had protected him.

The shaking subsided. Controller stood slowly and scanned the room, seeing both guards and Antillius lying next to the wall near him. One of the guards was dead, that was certain. He could not have survived having his head twisted in that fashion. Controller approached the other guard and took the Alethean rifle that was strapped over his shoulder. He checked that it was charged, and shot the Laird in the back of the head. He also shot the contorted guard just to be certain.

He turned his attention to Antillius. He stood over his former master's unconscious body and checked for a pulse. There was one, and it was strong. He threw the rifle's strap over his head before hoisting Antillius onto his shoulder. He carried him over to the dining table that was now near the wall. It was upright, but everything that had been atop it was now smashed on the deck.

He threw Antillius onto the table, and then pulled the rifle around from his back. He slapped Antillius across the face several times until the Laird began to stir.

"Wake up," Controller commanded.

"Wh---," Antillius murmured. "What happened?"

"I will tell you. I have waited almost thirty years to tell you. There is one trait common to all Aletheans, and that is patience. Our long lifespan gifted us this, and I have been very patient."

Antillius' head moved from side to side as he looked around the destroyed dining room. He saw the dead guards, one of whom he noticed had almost nothing left of his head, and the other's body was mangled beyond recognition. He began to panic.

"Please! What have you done?"

"I have saved my people. By now, the hatchery is far from here, beyond your reach. You have no hold over us, we are free."

Antillius pushed himself up onto his elbows, but Controller rammed the butt of the rifle into his chest and he immediately fell back.

"You do not have permission to speak," Controller said. "You will listen."

Antillius was shaking with terror. He nodded furiously and remained silent.

"Since the loss of Alethea Prime, the hatchery has been my people's only hope for survival. We do not know the fate of the other survey vessels, so we must treat the hatchery aboard this ship as unique. It means *everything* to us.

"When you enslaved us and threatened the hatchery, we did not resist in fear of it coming to harm. This did not mean that we would not take every possible measure to secure our freedom. For almost thirty of your years, our engineers have served as messengers amongst the Aletheans. It has been a slow process, but over time we prepared everything we needed for this day.

"My transmission executed our plan. One of our engineers has crippled your flagship. Others have eliminated several more in the same manner. Scientists have spent decades lacing the hull plating of your ships with small amounts of explosive compound, all of which have now detonated."

Controller grabbed Antillius and dragged him to his feet. He pushed him toward the window. "That is what is left of your fleet. You can't see the flames, of course. The vacuum has already extinguished them. But you can look out there, at the planet dead at your hands, and the wreckage of your fleet. And know that this is the price of what you did to us."

Controller lowered his head so that he was speaking into Antillius' ear. "Your ship is lost. It has suffered a high velocity collision from which it will not recover. The reactor will overload momentarily."

Antillius was spun 180 degrees to face Controller.

"We have captured two of your vessels, plus a support ship. Well-placed portals programmed by our engineers saw your crews deposited safely into space. Our scattered people were then transported via portal onto the derelict craft. Portals are useful tools, when harnessed properly. We also use a portal to drop the hatchery into the captured ship, and they have now fled to safety. You will never find them. It matters not what happens to me now, it is too late for us both. Soon this ship will explode and we will die with it. A fitting end."

Antillius struggled to form words. "It is not too late. We can escape."

"Escape! I am free. My people are safe, and your fleet is badly damaged. My only regret is that we could not destroy you all."

The deck began to vibrate with increasing intensity.

"That is the reactor going critical," Controller said. "I am not going to allow it to take from me the satisfaction of watching you die."

With that, he stepped back and pointed the rifle at Antillius Vrix's head. "Goodbye, master," he said before pulling the trigger.

Controller lowered the weapon slowly, and then dropped it to the ground. With Antillius dead, his work was complete.

The vibration was now rattling him to the core. Moments later, the reactor breached and A-112 exploded in a nuclear fireball, leaving only a scattering of debris in its place.

12. Intervention

i.

2002 A.D.

For four years the focus of the fleet was vessel construction. The original timescale was reassessed in June 1999, as the hangar proved more difficult to build than had been anticipated. In September 2000 it was completed, and Howells was given command with the condition that he must be available aboard *Odyssey* when needed.

By late 2002, the fleet had grown to number eleven vessels. The Earth-based facility and the hangar were now producing three ships per year.

Marshall had formed a council of which he was chair. The council comprised the Captain of each ship, and a number of senior staff. The council decided on the name *Earth Defence Force* for what they were building, something Marshall had suggested as he remembered his future-self referencing it.

"Calm down, David," Marshall said.

"I'll be calm when people start paying God damned attention!" Captain David Stewart barked. The seething Captain of *Endeavour* sat back in his chair.

Marshall was at the head of the meeting table in *Odyssey's* conference room. The council had assembled to discuss a situation developing on Earth. In the past six months, U.S. bombings over Iraq had increased dramatically, and since May the payload deployment had increased by seven tonnes per month. It was now September, and the total had reached fifty tonnes. The meeting had been called after several crewmembers expressed concern that it could be a prelude to invasion.

"It isn't as clear-cut as you are making out," Marshall said calmly, choosing to ignore Stewart's tone.

"We have the power to intervene. We're talking about hundreds of thousands of lives!"

"I agree that it's an alarming increase," Marshall said. Smith had reported that the change on Earth was not simply an increase in 'Operation Southern Watch', as claimed by the United States government. In the last hour he had confirmed that there was an invasion plan in place, and it was due to begin in early 2003.

Marshall had explained the discovery to the council. There was a murmur of voices around the room at the revelation, before Stewart protested that he had been warning the group of this eventuality for several months.

"Despite this, we cannot get involved." Marshall continued. "The existence of this fleet is something that the people at home simply aren't ready for. If we reveal ourselves and interfere, the US and UK governments will accuse us of treason. It's more than likely that we'd find ourselves on the wrong end of a missile attack."

Stewart scoffed. "We're in no danger from Earth. We could shoot down or outrun any missiles on thrusters alone, never mind the portal drive."

Marshall had to concede the point, but he was convinced that action against the coalition would be a mistake. "Okay so we aren't in physical danger, but I've explained often enough that secrecy is paramount."

"We've gotten involved plenty of times before," Stewart said.

"Not on this scale. It's too risky," replied Marshall.

"Marshall is right," Medforth interrupted. "This is serious, but not enough to give ourselves away. The Alethean threat takes precedence, and dealing with Earth at the same time would screw things up."

Marshall looked at Batson, who was sitting next to Medforth. "Did you distribute the report on your findings to everyone?" he asked.

"I did," the American replied.

Marshall addressed the room. "Did everyone read it?" he asked.

The majority of those present were nodding, but others' eyes wandered with embarrassment.

Marshall sighed. "Arms in the air all those who didn't bother to read the report."

Reluctantly, four hands were raised.

Marshall's irritation was apparent. "In a nutshell, Intrepid and Exodus have been scanning the surface of Iraq for any signs of WMDs. There were clear indications of enriched uranium, and a number of illegal chemical substances in neighbouring nations, but nothing was found in Iraq itself."

"And that is why we must stop the invasion!" Stewart exclaimed.

Marshall sighed. "I just can't see how we could make a difference, shy of revealing ourselves and making some sort of threat."

"Let's do that then!" Stewart retorted.

"Don't be ridiculous!" Marshall snapped.

"I have a more sensible suggestion," Costello interrupted.

Marshall smiled. "Please," he beckoned.

"Instead of anything direct and noisy, how about a standard intervention team going in to remove key players. With the loudest proponents of invasion gone, the idea may just dissipate. At the very least, it'll delay any action long enough for us to think of something else."

"By 'remove', you mean 'assassinate'?" Howells asked.

Costello shook his head. "Not necessarily. We'd simply be removing them from the situation. The best way to do that would be to bring them up here and detain them."

"We're kidnappers now?" Rob Shakespeare, the Captain of *Exodus*, interrupted.

"Call it what you like," Costello replied calmly with a shrug. "But removing these people without harming them is the best and most discreet way forward."

Shakespeare shook his head and looked down at the table.

Stewart spoke next. "Somebody else will take over unless we take out someone like Bush or Blair."

Marshall shook his head. "We're not going to remove conspicuous members of the government, never mind the fucking Prime Minister! That's just asking for trouble," he stated.

"We are looking for trouble regardless," Medforth quipped.

Marshall glowered at him. "Look, the only reason we are considering anything at all is because it's what the council wants. I have no objection to ordering the fleet to do nothing if that's what you prefer," he said sternly.

The room fell silent.

Captain Stewart looked at Marshall. "We need to act. That much is certain. I'm just not convinced that this is enough."

Marshall interlinked his fingers and rested his chin on the top of his hands. "It's as far as I'm willing to go. Like I said before, we're here to defend Earth from a prevailing extra-terrestrial threat, not to be 'world police'. We'll proceed with Costello's idea."

There were several nods around the table, but Stewart was clearly unhappy with the decision. "Draw up a plan," Marshall said to Costello before dismissing the group.

ii.

Costello was appointed mission leader for the extraction operation on Earth. He arrived at the armoury to meet the other nine people who had been assigned to the mission.

"Everyone, over here," he commanded as he entered the small room. "Wilson, you'll lead to Charlie team to Paris. Szeto, you and Fracaro will be Bravo team, going to London. I'll take Alpha to Washington."

Costello approached a weapon locker and equipped an assault rifle, a set of flash bangs and three frag grenades. Once prepared, he turned to face the group who were standing ready. "Charlie team, you go in first. You have your brief; it's a simple extraction. Weapons on Amber," he said as he set his rifle to the non-lethal setting.

"I have a suggestion," Szeto said as he crossed the room to meet Costello. "We shouldn't take these weapons; if we are compromised they would fall into the hands of the enemy."

Costello's reaction was instinctive. "Enemy? We're going to England, France and America. The people down there are not our enemy!"

"Apologies. I meant no offence, but during the mission anyone who isn't part of the team must be considered the enemy, and we cannot let this technology fall into their hands. We should be taking P90s or MP5s."

Costello realised that Szeto was correct, and was annoyed with himself for not having thought of it himself. "You're right. We-"

"I disagree," a voice interjected from amongst the teams. Costello recognised its source as Nick Fracaro, an American security officer from *Exodus*. "These weapons will allow us to neutralise the enemy without any fatalities, while offering more extreme options if needed. We gotta take them with us. Our odds of capture are lower with them than without."

"You make a valid point, Nick, but Szeto is right. We can't afford to lose them," Costello replied. He looked out to the team. "Everyone, stow your weapons and equip P90s from the locker over there," he said as he pointed to the far wall.

The men replaced their ordnance swiftly. Fracaro was last to give up the alien equipment but he reluctantly obeyed his orders. Costello activated the portal and watched as the four-man Charlie team disappeared through the vortex, after which it collapsed. Having opened the portal again for Bravo team, he repeated the procedure once more for his own. He then quickly approached the aperture. "Costello to bridge. Bravo and Charlie have departed. Proceeding with mission now," he said.

After receiving acknowledgement from the bridge he stepped through.

iii.

Marshall sat in the captain's chair, thinking about the extraction mission that he wished he were leading. Standing by while his comrades risked their lives was not something he was accustomed to, and he did not like the feeling.

"Costello to bridge," the tactician started over the intercom. "Bravo and Charlie have departed. Proceeding with mission now."

"Acknowledged. Good luck," Marshall replied.

"I rarely see you stressed," his first officer said as he approached from the communications station where Smith was seated.

"If they're captured..."

"They won't be," Medforth reassured him. "Costello knows what he's doing."

"I know, I just hope the same goes for the rest of them," Marshall thought out loud. He knew much of the crew but there were many new faces on the ship, and even more serving in the fleet. He knew Costello was an exceptional soldier, and he trusted Kielthy's recruitment expertise, but there were ten people out there whom he knew little or nothing about.

"Incoming transmission," Smith announced from the far side of the room.

"On speaker," Marshall replied.

There was a short pause before the loud sound of gunfire erupted from the ceiling and filled the bridge. Marshall could hear several bursts of sustained automatic weapon fire and shouting. He could not make out the words but knew they were spoken in English.

"Costello to Odyssey, we are under heavy fire. Require immediate exfil. Opening portal," Costello's voice was barely understandable over the background noise. Marshall and Medforth exchanged a glance before Marshall ran for the lift. Medforth limped after him, his stick banging quickly on the deck. He entered the car and it descended to the armoury deck almost instantly.

"What the fuck is going on?" Marshall muttered to himself as they exited the lift.

As they reached the small room, Marshall pressed the door activation control and the pair rushed inside. In the middle of the deck, Costello was laid on his back with another man draped across him. The pair was almost a metre clear of the still-open portal. It was apparent that Costello had dragged his colleague through, and was now pinned beneath him. Marshall and Medforth set to approach the struggling soldiers but were stopped by the sound of bullets ricocheting off the metal walls around them.

"Get down!" Marshall shouted at Medforth, and the two of them dropped to the floor. Marshall looked up as several more bullets flew through the portal and bounced around the confined space. He needed to close the portal but noticed that two team members were not present.

"Costello, where's the rest of your team?" Marshall demanded.

"Dead," he replied abruptly.

"Fuck. Ship, close all active portals now!"

The portal shrank horizontally then vertically, and was gone. The room fell silent but for the panting of Costello and the groaning of his fallen comrade. Marshall climbed to his feet and moved over to kneel beside the men.

"Proctor took the worst of it," Costello said.

Upon reaching him, Marshall could see the security officer had at least one bullet wound to the abdomen and a large gash across his calf.

Medforth struggled to his feet and joined Marshall. The pair lifted Proctor from Costello and set him down on the cold deck. Although he did not scream, Proctor winced and groaned with every inch that he was moved. Once he was lying flat, Marshall noticed a further wound to his shoulder.

Marshall stood and ran to a console to the left of the entrance. "Medical, Armoury. Medical emergency!" he said quickly with a raised voice.

"On my way," Harrison replied. Several minutes later, she arrived with another doctor and two nurses who Marshall had never seen before. "What happened?" she asked as she tended to Proctor. The nurses navigated a gurney into the room.

"Fuck knows," Marshall replied honestly.

Harrison was scanning Proctor with a device that Marshall recognised from the medical bay, although he knew nothing of its purpose.

"He has a bullet wound to the shoulder. It's a through-and-through, but it's destroyed much of the collarbone and he's lost a lot of blood. The second wound to the abdomen is more serious. There's internal damage to the stomach and there are two bullets still in there. We need to get him into surgery now or he'll die," Harrison reported whilst simultaneously nodding to the other doctor, who with the assistance of the nurses lifted Proctor onto the gurney.

Harrison turned to Costello and scanned him. "Another through-and-through on the left forearm, but it missed the bone. You'll be fine," she said to her patient.

Costello nodded. "My jacket took the brunt of it."

"What happened down there?" Marshall asked Costello as he took a knee beside him.

"Almost immediately after we arrived they opened fire on us. At least a dozen men were in the room waiting. We dropped to cover but they got Rowley in the first few seconds before she had a chance to move. We held our own for several minutes but a flash bang stunned Milsom. He took a shot to the neck before he could recover. I contacted you for assistance and opened the portal. As we fell back we were both hit. Obviously Proctor took the brunt of it."

The story rolled around in Marshall's head for a minute before he responded. "They knew you were coming. We need to find out what happened to Bravo and Charlie teams and take it from there," he said as he stood and crossed the room to the control panel.

Medforth joined Marshall silently. "Nothing from either team," he reported.

Marshall looked up. "I'm not going to jump to conclusions because they're not overdue yet, but given this mess we have to be prepared for the worst."

"They haven't broken radio silence. That should be taken as a positive until we know otherwise," Medforth warned.

"Agreed," Marshall said as he returned to Costello whose arm was being treated by Dr Harrison.

Harrison turned to Marshall. "I've cauterised the wound and strapped him up. He can report to the medical bay when he's ready. I need to get down there now and assist with Proctor's surgery," she said before nodding to Medforth and leaving the room.

Marshall looked at Costello. "Take as long as you need. When you're up to it I want a full report on the mission," he ordered. Costello was now standing. He acknowledged the Captain then left for his quarters.

Marshall decided to return to the bridge. He had reached the door to the Armoury when he heard the unmistakable sound of a portal opening behind him. He turned and quickly made his way to a weapon locker where he removed an Alethean rifle and threw it to Medforth. He took another for himself and analysed his surroundings. There was nowhere to take cover in the small rectangular room, so he indicated for Medforth to head for the exit where they took up a crouched position outside, using the doorframe as cover.

There was no activity before they were safely out of the room. Looking into the Armoury, Marshall watched as four men stepped through the portal single file, one of whom was carrying a body over his shoulder. They casually moved over to the lockers to stow their weapons and equipment packs.

The tension instantly drained from Marshall. The relief was almost tangible. He stood and entered the room. "Wilson!" Medforth shouted as he approached the leader of Charlie team. Marshall could see Wilson was startled by their sudden appearance.

"Captain, I'm pleased to report a successful mission. We...." Wilson stopped abruptly as he noticed a pool of blood on the floor between himself and his approaching Captain. "What happened?" he finished.

"Alpha team was ambushed," Marshall reported. "Rowley and Milsom are dead. Proctor was seriously injured, and Costello was hit but he's fine."

"Ambushed?" Wilson repeated with wide eyes. "How the hell could that happen?"

"There's only one reason that comes to mind. You had no trouble?" Marshall asked, glancing at the body that had been placed on the floor against a locker to his left.

"Everything went according to plan. He's unconscious but suffered no injuries, and there were no fatalities. He hasn't seen our faces so he won't need any treatment from Dr Harrison before he's returned."

"Congratulations on your success. It's unfortunate that it's been mired by what happened to Alpha team. We haven't heard from Bravo, they're due back soon. Seeing you here safe gives me hope that they will also be successful," Marshall said.

"Thanks Captain. If you have no objections, we'll have a wash and report to the bridge in an hour?"

"Of course. Dismissed," Marshall replied.

Wilson nodded to his team and the four men headed for their quarters.

Marshall turned to Medforth. "We need Bravo team back here now. How long until they are due to report in?" he asked.

"Just over ten minutes," Medforth replied.

The two men waited quietly. Medforth was pacing while Marshall leaned against the wall to the right of the door. The two nurses who had attended Proctor arrived to collect the unconscious body five minutes after Wilson had left. One of them told Marshall that Proctor would live, but he had lost his spleen and would be in recovery for several weeks.

After they left, Medforth and Marshall did not speak until Bravo team were twenty minutes overdue.

"They'll be all right," Medforth said, breaking the silence.

Marshall let out a held breath. "I just hope they haven't been captured."

"Well, if they have, Szeto for one won't give them anything. No matter the cost."

"How can you be so sure?" Marshall asked.

"He was once held hostage in Baghdad. He was tortured and threatened with beheading for almost a year. He gave them nothing, and when he got home it was as if he'd never left. I've never met anyone quite like him. Trust me, even if he has been captured we have nothing to worry about."

"Yeah but it was a two-man team," Marshall said as he crossed the room and activated the intercom. "Bridge, Marshall. Has there been any word from Bravo?" he asked, already knowing the answer but posing the question anyway.

Smith replied over the intercom. "Sorry, no. I'm monitoring radio and satellite signals as best I can. There's nothing so far."

"Have a security detail report to the armoury. Medforth and I will be on the bridge shortly. Marshall Out," he said before tapping the intercom button to deactivate it.

Marshall and Medforth waited for the security team to arrive before they left the armoury and walked to the nearby lift.

"We've been betrayed. For fuck's sake, who would want to sabotage a mission to prevent a war?" Marshall barked.

The pair arrived at the lift door where Medforth pressed the call button.

He turned to Marshall. "The America mission was sabotaged, France went perfectly. England we don't know. For me, we need to focus on the American one, because that's where it started and that's where we know they were waiting for us."

The pair entered the lift and Medforth ordered the car to the Bridge.

iv.

Ray Szeto exited the portal and scanned his surroundings. He found himself in a large dark bedroom. A king-size bed was in front of him, to the right of which was an ajar door leading to an en-suite bathroom. He could see the outline of the toilet basin, but it was too dark to make out any detail of the seemingly small room.

A window on his left allowed in a little light, as the venetian blinds were open, but it was otherwise dark and somehow eerie.

Szeto glanced at Fracaro, who had stepped next to him. He gestured with his right hand toward another door behind them to the left, and Fracaro immediately headed for it.

While Szeto approached the en-suite, Fracaro positioned himself next to the main door with his back against the wall. He watched Szeto cross the room, whilst keeping an eye on the only other entrance to the room.

The room was silent as Szeto crept toward the bathroom. He checked his watch, which read 05:03. *Strange*, he thought. *He should be in bed, asleep.*

They had expected to find the room dark, but the Ambassador was not where they planned.

Szeto used the barrel of his MP5 to fully open the bathroom door. He reached around the opening with his free hand and found a hanging cord, which he pulled.

The bathroom was instantly illuminated. It was empty.

Szeto turned to Fracaro and nodded before joining him at the door. Fracaro reached for the handle, and after counting to three with his free hand he quickly opened the door. Szeto stepped forward and found himself in a perpendicular hallway. He swept left whilst Fracaro crossed behind him and covered the right.

The hall was also dark, but Szeto could see a staircase at the far end, from which a downstairs light was giving a dim hue. Whilst holding his rifle so that he could see down the scope, he released his stabilisation hand and put it in the air. He flicked his fingers forward as an indication that Fracaro should pass him.

His teammate did so, scuttling down the hallway past two doors, one on each side. He crouched at the start of a bannister that led from the corridor and curved round to run alongside the stairs.

Szeto caught up to Fracaro and crossed the staircase to a position on the opposite side of the top step. A wall ran the full length of the left side of the stairs, before opening to another room at the bottom.

His gun was trained on the twelve-step descent, which was clear. After gesturing his intent to Fracaro, Szeto rounded the corner and slowly made his way to the ground floor.

As he reached half way, he could now see a large room on the right, which had a fireplace that was blazing and providing the only light in the house. In front of the hearth was a large rug, upon which matching chairs flanked a three-seat brown leather sofa.

"Good evening," said the man who was sitting in the right-hand chair. He put the book he was holding down on a pedestal next to him, and stared at Szeto.

Szeto paused four steps from the bottom. He trained his weapon on the man, who appeared to be unarmed and not remotely surprised to see him.

"You are not Ambassador Barclay," he said, stating the obvious.

"No," the man replied. "I'm General Paterson. And you must be Szeto?"

Szeto turned pale. "You know who I am?" he asked with incredulity.

There was a cold sensation on the back of Szeto's neck. Fracaro's voice was suddenly in his ear. "Put your weapon down," Fracaro said.

Szeto knew that Fracaro's rifle barrel was pressed against his skin. His mind raced through his limited options, and he quickly concluded that he could make no move before Fracaro pulled the trigger. He relaxed his grip and slowly lowered his own rifle to the ground.

"What's going on, Nick?" he asked Fracaro.

"That is none of your concern," the American replied, before knocking Szeto unconscious with the butt of his weapon.

13. Betrayal

i.

Marshall was asleep at the desk in his quarters when a call came in from the bridge. His neck and upper back ached, as he had fallen asleep while reviewing fleet construction reports. He looked at the clock which read 06:11. He was late for his 0600 shift.

Sitting up and straightening his jacket, Marshall answered the call and assured Medforth that he would be on the bridge shortly.

Marshall washed and changed his clothes. He cursed himself for his tardiness and was forced to admit that he had been working too many hours since bravo team's disappearance three weeks earlier.

He arrived on the bridge and relieved Medforth, who left for his quarters.

"Singh, what's our current position?" he asked the helmsman.

"In high orbit of Earth. We passed over Moscow a minute ago."

"Let me know when we're in portal range of the shipyard," he ordered.

Singh checked the ship's trajectory. "No problem, it'll be any minute now."

Smith looked over his shoulder at Marshal. "Captain, I need you to look over something," he said.

Marshall approached the communications officer and stood behind him.

"I've found discrepancies in the Intel we gathered for the mission to Earth," Smith started as Marshall observed the photograph that was displayed on his terminal. The picture was a profile shot of a middle-aged, slim man with grey hair swept over an obvious bald patch. "The report describes the U.S. Ambassador as one Neil Barclay, who has served in the post for almost five years. His address is a house in central London, where we sent Bravo team, and he lives there on and off for around seven months of the year. He is married, with two grown-up children, but only his wife has ever visited England. She is currently in America."

"So what's the discrepancy?" Marshall interrupted impatiently.

Smith felt chastised. "I was getting to that," he said with a touch of annoyance in his voice. He tapped several keys and the photograph changed to a map of London. "According to the Intel, this is the location of his residence," he said as a marker appeared near the centre. Marshall knew that the area indicated was Knightsbridge.

"But that isn't correct," Smith continued. "The Ambassador lives here," he said as a second pin appeared in Regent's Park."

Marshall was staggered. "What the fuck?"

Smith fell silent.

"Who provided this Intel?" Marshall asked urgently.

"Captain Shakespeare. I imagine it came from his security chief."

"Get him on the line. Now," Marshall said.

Moments later, Shakespeare was on the main screen.

"I need to speak to you immediately. Portal over, and bring your security chief," Marshall ordered.

Shakespeare was visibly unsettled by Marshall's tone. "Okay. I'll be two minutes."

"Just open it directly on our bridge," Marshall added.

"No problem," Shakespeare replied before the image winked to a view of Earth.

A portal formed in front of the screen, and Shakespeare emerged almost instantly. A man whom Marshall did not recognise followed him.

"What's the matter?" Shakespeare asked.

"Look at this," Marshall said with a gesture toward Smith's console. Shakespeare rounded the curved bench and Smith repeated the report he had given Marshall.

Shakespeare looked at his security chief, whose face had turned pale. "Who prepped the report?" he asked.

"Fracaro," the man replied.

"And you didn't check it?" Shakespeare snapped.

"I gave it a once-over, but Fracaro knows what he's doing so I was just looking for gaps. The co-ordinates were critical as they were used for the portal, so I checked that they married up to the address, and they did. I just didn't check that the address itself was accurate."

"Shit," Marshall muttered.

"What do we do now?" Shakespeare asked.

"I don't know, but at least we have an idea what happened to Bravo team."

ii.

Marshall was chatting to Medforth at his station on the Bridge when a klaxon filled the room.

"Intruder alert!" Costello barked from his station. "Unscheduled portal activation in the Armoury. Four unidentified life forms have boarded the ship."

Marshall ran to Costello's station. "Lock it down. Secure the weapon lockers and get a security detail down there immediately."

Costello entered a number of commands into his console and turned to Marshall. "I'll lead the security team myself."

"Go," Marshall said with a nod. He walked back to his chair hurriedly as Costello headed for the lift.

He arrived at the armoury within minutes, to find a team of six equipped in full armour and helmets waiting for him. "Report," he said to the group as a whole.

The reply was from a new security officer who Costello had recruited earlier in the week. She had been working in Germany for a private security firm, and her experience in the British military made her an ideal candidate. "The room is sealed, they have nowhere to go," she said.

"Thanks," he said as she handed him a rifle. "Stand ready."

The team lowered the visors on their helmets and moved into position. Costello pressed the control to open the door, and two smoke grenades were thrown through the aperture. The team moved into the room with Costello taking point.

The room was empty.

iii.

Two days earlier

It was a hot night in Lancaster California. Maxwell Simpson was suffering from insomnia, and had spent the last three hours staring at the ceiling. His mind was refusing to settle, despite him not having anything in particular to think about.

Simpson pondered that the heat may be the cause of his restlessness, although it was not particularly unusual for this time of year. The air conditioning unit in the window buzzed with activity, and he supposed it must be faulty given the current temperature in the room.

There was a noise coming from downstairs. The phone was ringing in the kitchen. He climbed out of bed, being careful not to wake his wife, and made his way through the bedroom and down the hallway. He reached the top of the stairs when the answering machine clicked on and he heard his pre-recorded message playing. As he walked down the stairs that led to the hallway and the front door, he heard a beep before an unfamiliar voice left a message.

"Lieutenant Simpson, this is the office of General Paterson. A car will pick you up at 0800 and take you to Edwards Air Force Base for assignment. You will be briefed upon your arrival."

The machine clicked as the call ended. Simpson was standing at the door to the kitchen, feeling a combination of curiosity and apprehension.

Noting the current time was 04:35 he decided to try for at least an hour of sleep before preparing for his departure.

iv.

Simpson lived a little over thirty miles from Edwards Air Force Base. A black Chevrolet, driven by a man wearing an air force uniform, picked him up promptly at 0800.

The driver did not speak, and Simpson felt more than a little uncomfortable with the whole situation. Upon arrival, he was cleared through security and escorted down a brightly lit narrow corridor to a briefing room.

Although well lit, the room was particularly drab as there were no windows and the cinderblock walls were painted a light grey that was only marginally different to their natural colour.

The room was square, with a projector pointing to the left wall and four rows of chairs facing it. Aside from Simpson and his escort, there were four others in the room. They were either standing around the perimeter, or sitting in the rows of seats, although not together. Nobody spoke or offered a greeting, and overall they appeared to be as uncomfortable and confused as he was.

Simpson's escort told him to take a seat and then left him in the room with the other attendees. After several minutes sitting in silence, the door opened and a group of men and women filed in. The seats quickly filled up, with those who arrived last having no option but to line up along the rear wall. A man who was strikingly tall and broad followed the group and moved to the front of the room facing his audience.

"Good morning," the man started. "I am General Paterson, welcome to Edwards Air Force base."

There was a hum of "Good Morning" from the room, to which the General nodded.

"I apologise to those of you who have been brought in at such short notice, and with little explanation as to the purpose of your being here. This is a matter of national security, so we decided to dispense with the pleasantries," he said as he switched on the projector and began the briefing.

Simpson shifted his weight in his chair. He was still dubious about his current circumstances and was eager to learn more about the assignment.

"Some time ago we learned of a conspiracy involving the British government and a covert mission to Iraq. In 1993, British Intelligence discovered the existence of advanced technology that had fallen into the hands of the Iraqis. They sent Special Forces into the country to retrieve the tech and return it to England."

The General tapped a button on a controller in his hand and the projector promptly flickered to a profile picture of a young man. "The mission leader, one Ryan Marshall, decided that he wasn't going to hand over the tech to his government. Instead, he kept it for himself."

Paterson pressed the button again and the projector screen blinked before displaying three diagrams of a craft of some kind on the screen. The left half displayed a ventral view, while the right was split again vertically, so that the top section showed a frontal view and the bottom was a side profile.

"This space-faring vessel has been under Marshall's control for almost a decade. Over the years he has recruited a large number of personnel to his cause, and more recently he has been building replicas of this ship to form a fleet."

Simpson had no idea what Paterson had said after the words *space-faring vessel*, as his mind became a blur while he comprehended what he was being shown.

Paterson unknowingly continued. "One of Marshall's recruits was an officer of our military, who remained loyal to the United States and reported Marshall's activities to us. Since that time he has been undercover aboard on of the replica ships, and feeding us intelligence regarding Marshall and his people.

"I am now going to hand over to our expert on Marshall and his fleet. Major Fracaro, if you will please continue the briefing."

Paterson stepped aside as a man who had been sitting at the far left of the front row stood and moved to the centre of the room, facing the crowd.

"Good morning. Several weeks ago, Marshall and his advisers decided to use the power of the fleet to interfere with U.S. and U.K. involvement in the Middle-East. The intent was to eliminate key personnel in the military, thereby stalling our plans. I informed the General about the incursion and we acted to contain the intruders.

"There were three teams. One was sent to Washington, where we were waiting and able to swiftly eliminate the squad. The second was sent to Paris. Unfortunately, we could not prevent that mission's completion. The third team was sent to London. I was on that team," Fracaro said with a pause. "Suffice to say, my former team mate has now been transported to Guantanamo Bay where he will be interrogated."

Simpson's brow furrowed. *Guantanamo Bay?* He thought. *Why the hell would he be sent to Cuba?*

He raised his hand. Fracaro looked at him and nodded. "Sir, may I ask why he went to Guantanamo Bay?" he asked.

Fracaro looked at Paterson who had expected the question. "Guantanamo is host to an offshore detention centre designed to hold terrorists and other extremely dangerous individuals. The facility is only a few months old, and its existence is classified. I cannot elaborate further. Suffice to say it is a highly secure facility where he will pose no further threat to the United States or her allies."

Simpson was uncertain about the reliability of the response, but he nodded anyway and Fracaro turned to address the room. "Our task now is to eliminate the threat that Marshall poses by taking out his fleet. We cannot attack them from the ground, as their firepower and defensive capabilities are too advanced for our weapons to breach. Instead, we will send a team to board the flagship and sabotage the fleet from within. Details of the mission are contained in these files."

Fracaro picked up a pile of documents and handed them to the closest officer. "We begin at 0500 tomorrow. Before that, we will be flying to Area 51 to complete preparations. Any questions?"

Simpson had many questions but did not want to become a nuisance. He decided instead to read through the briefing files and speak to Fracaro later if necessary, away from the audience currently surrounding him.

The group was dismissed. Simpson left the room with his colleagues and followed them to a communal area where they discussed the mission ahead.

The flight to Area 51 was relatively short, so it gave Simpson time to read the mission brief again. He had gone over it three times, and felt he was as prepared as he could be.

The team assembled in a staging area comprised of forty-eight people including Fracaro and Simpson. Thirty-eight men and ten women had been split into units of twelve. Everyone was wearing armour and helmets with black visors, so Simpson couldn't distinguish his teammates.

Fracaro lifted his visor and raised his right arm to show the team a small item in his hand. "This is the portal device," he said.

Simpson recognised the device immediately from the brief. It was the device that they were to use to board the flagship. The device had been recovered from the leader of the team that was captured in England, and was set to open at the same location from which it had departed. The brief also indicated that Fracaro and his men shouldn't expect any initial resistance when they boarded the ship, as the armoury was generally unattended and sealed.

Fracaro pointed at three members of Simpson's squad, including Simpson himself. "You three will join me in the initial phase. The remainder of team one will wait for the second portal," he said before he lowered his visor and activated the portal device.

Simpson had over ten years' experience in the military and had seen a lot in his tours of duty, but the sight before him took him by surprise. From nowhere, a dot flashed in the middle of the wall, it expanded vertically to form a line and then horizontally to create a doorway filled with static.

Without hesitation, Fracaro ran through the anomaly. Simpson felt an overwhelming dread coursing through him as he subconsciously held his breath and followed.

He emerged to find himself in a small room with what appeared to be lockers along the flanking walls. His team arrived moments later, after which the portal closed and the room fell silent. Already a klaxon had sounded, and it was loud and sudden enough to make Simpson jump.

"I'll get the portal open. Prepare for immediate Evac," Fracaro ordered.

Simpson recited the mission parameters to himself. The team were to open a portal to the nearest ship immediately after arrival. There would be a computer terminal in the room that would enable them to do this quickly, and they had to be gone by the time ship's security arrived.

He could see Fracaro pressing several buttons on a console at the other side of the room.

A portal opened in the same location as the one through which they had arrived. Fracaro started for the vortex immediately after giving orders to move out. Simpson followed him and ran through.

Emerging from the portal, Simpson noticed he was in an almost identical room to the one they had left. Except for a slightly different tint in the colour of the walls, Simpson could find no difference at all.

Simpson knew this ship was *Exodus*, the ship aboard which Fracaro had served for the last three years.

Unlike *Odyssey*, Fracaro had previously been able to access the computer of *Exodus*. He had installed a program that would disable the sensors in the armoury. The bridge would not be alerted about the portal, and he had also put the internal cameras into a loop so they wouldn't notice the incursion visually.

"Sir, in the mission spec there was no mention of how we masked our destination from *Odyssey* sensors," Simpson said.

"There is no need. Nobody has figured out how to track a portal, or even prove if it's possible," Fracaro replied. "I'm opening a portal to Earth. Clear the area."

Simpson crossed the room with the other two members of his team. He turned and looked back at the wall where they had boarded the ship. Seconds later, a new portal opened and the remainder of team one entered the room. Fracaro welcomed the arrivals and ordered them to stand aside as team two followed. Fracaro ordered the second team to stand ready to disembark immediately.

Simpson processed the remainder of the plan. They were to bring the teams of twelve up to *Exodus* one at a time and distribute them throughout the fleet. If the mission went smoothly, U.S. forces would soon overwhelm the bridge of four vessels and the ships would be secured. After that, they would announce their presence to *Odyssey* and demand her surrender. Simpson was on the team that would remain on *Exodus*, and the last portal would to be set to take him directly from the Armoury to the Bridge.

The first team disappeared into a portal that would deposit them on the bridge of *Endeavour*. After several minutes, the other teams had passed through the room and Fracaro turned to Simpson's squad and ordered them to stand ready. Simpson checked his weapon and moved to the portal location. It opened, and they ran through.

v.

Marshall was standing behind Costello at the tactical station. He was looking at the security footage from the armoury that had been recorded when the intruder alert had sounded.

"There's no way to know who they are because they never remove their helmets, but look at this guy's hand."

"I don't see it. Can you zoom in further?" Marshall asked.

"Yeah but it'll be too distorted. I can tell you what it is; it's a portal retriever. To be precise, it's the one Bravo team were carrying."

"How can you be sure?"

"The ship registered it in the log. There's no doubt."

Marshall scowled. The mystery surrounding Bravo team's disappearance was still under investigation, but since the discovery of Fracaro's involvement there had been no further developments.

"What the hell is going on?" he muttered.

"I have no idea. They were aboard for around a minute and then left through a new portal. They didn't reprogram the retriever, so wherever they went it was a one-way trip."

"Can you get a fix on the destination?" Marshall asked.

"No, we haven't figured out how to do that yet," Costello replied.

"Captain!" Smith said from the communications console, "*Exodus* is not responding to comms. She missed her check-in so I sent out a reminder. I'm getting nothing."

"*Exodus*?" Marshall asked as he crossed the room and approached his chair. Shakespeare was never late for anything, causing Marshall's concern to mount rapidly. "Try again. Singh, lay in a course for *Exodus* and prepare to break orbit."

"Aye, Captain." Singh said as he retrieved the co-ordinates and entered a course to rendezvous with the sister ship.

"Still nothing, Captain," Smith reported

Marshall sat in his chair. "Feed sensor data to my station. Singh, take us to her at best speed," he ordered. He browsed the fleet deployment, looking for the nearest ship to the silent vessel. "Smith, open a channel to Captain Batson, and tell him to rendezvous at *Exodus*."

"Opening portal," Singh reported. "Once through we'll be within weapons range."

The combination of *Exodus'* lack of response and the unidentified intruders aboard *Odyssey* had Marshall on full alert. "Tactical, close the shutters. Activate shield grid and open gun ports," he ordered.

As the ship moved toward a forming portal, shutters covered every window. Simultaneously, an array of rail guns and torpedo launchers were revealed along the front of the wings as large metal coverings slid aside into the hull of the ship. The shield emitters dotted around the hull lit up as they were activated, and the entire craft shimmered as the shields engaged to give it a faint glow.

vi.

The boarding party of each ship was under orders to maintain radio silence at all times. The only way each squad would know the status of another was to open a portal and send through a messenger.

"Sir, all four ships have been secured," a man's voice said from behind his mask.

Fracaro lifted his visor. "Excellent," he said before lifting the helmet off his head and discarding it.

"Simpson," he said, addressing the younger man who was stationed at the weapons console. "Go to *Ulysses* and have her crew evacuated to the shuttle hangar here on *Exodus*. When they are all aboard, do the same for the other two ships. There are no shuttles in there, so there'll be plenty of space for everyone."

Simpson was puzzled by the order, as it had not been part of the mission brief to move the prisoners en masse, but he followed his superior's command without question.

He stepped through the portal and found himself on the bridge of *Ulysses*. "Major Fracaro has ordered that all prisoners be transferred to *Exodus*," he said to the squad leader. "I'm going to the shuttle bay to escort them personally."

The man in the Captain's chair nodded and activated the intercom as Simpson proceeded to the lift.

After travelling in the car for only a few seconds, he stepped into an airlock that was between him and the hangar. As the bay was currently pressurised, the outer door opened without delay. Simpson found himself in the large room that was occupied only by the ship's former crew.

As he entered the room, Simpson nodded to the guards who flanked the door. "Have you received orders from the bridge?" he asked the man to his left.

"Yes," was the reply. "We'll help you get them through."

"Thanks," Simpson said. He raised his rifle and turned to address the room as the man on his right opened a portal. "Okay everybody, listen up!" he shouted, indicating toward the right-hand wall with the barrel of the gun. "I need everyone over here. Now."

The *Ulysses* crew were standing in a group at the centre of the cavernous room. They looked at each other, but did not move.

"Now!" Simpson barked.

Slowly, the group drifted toward Simpson. A portal opened next to him moments later.

"Everybody through," he said calmly.

The tension in the room was tangible.

"Step through the portal. Rest assured, you will be well treated," Simpson said reassuringly.

One of the crowd said, "We aren't going anywhere. For all we know, that thing leads to empty space. There's no chance you'll get us through it willingly."

Simpson sighed. "Look," he said as he walked toward the portal. When he reached the aperture he stopped and looked back at the group before stepping through. A second later he re-emerged. "Satisfied?" he asked.

Everyone appeared surprised by the Simpson's demonstration, but still they did not move.

Simpson threw a glance at the ceiling before exhaling loudly. "One way or another, you will be going through that portal. I would prefer that it was without force."

"Come on," said the man who had previously protested, before shaking his head and storming through the aperture.

The remainder of the group followed quietly.

When everyone had disembarked, Simpson nodded to the guards and joined the captives.

Once through the portal and finding himself in an identical room aboard *Exodus*, Simpson checked that the prisoners had been moved to join their comrades before he lowered his weapon. There were two men awaiting his arrival who moved toward him immediately.

He addressed the guards. "Ulysses is clear. Open a p---"

"Hey!" A voice echoed across the hangar. Simpson looked at the prisoners to see a man walking toward him hurriedly. The guards quickly stepped into the man's path, blocking his approach.

"It's okay," Simpson said. The pair looked back at him before stepping aside.

"I demand to speak to your mission commander," the man said when he reached Simpson.

"Who are you?" Simpson asked.

"Captain Robert Shakespeare, E.D.F. Exodus," the man said formally.

Simpson felt uneasy when he realised that it was this man's ship that had been taken. "I'll ask if he is willing to speak to you, but I make no promises," he said before turning away from Shakespeare.

"You are putting our entire species at risk, you fool!" Shakespeare shouted. "Why, the fuck, are you doing this?"

Simpson was surprised by the Captain's outburst.

Shakespeare took note of his captor's reaction. "You do know about the Aletheans, don't you?" he asked with a softer tone.

"What are you talking about?" Simpson asked before striding toward Shakespeare.

"They haven't told you about the Aletheans, have they?" Shakespeare said sardonically when he recognised his counterpart's discomfort.

Simpson stared wide-eyed at Shakespeare. "I am fully informed about you and your crew. That is all I need to know," he said before spinning on his heel and heading for a nearby control panel.

"The Aletheans are the reason we are here. They intend to destroy all life on Earth, and our sole purpose is to prevent that from happening. Right now, you people are threatening our mission to save the human race," Shakespeare blurted at Simpson's back.

Simpson stopped. He stood still for a moment as he processed what had been said, then turned to face Shakespeare. "I do know of the Aletheans. They built Marshall's ship. There is nothing to indicate that they are hostile."

"Maybe nothing in your brief, no. But it is the truth. They'll be here in fourteen years, and this fleet is all that stands between them and Earth."

"If that were true, we would know about it," Simpson asserted.

Shakespeare chuckled. "Your intelligence might, but that doesn't mean they fed it down to you. Trust me, as one soldier to another; this needs to stop right now before the damage is irreparable."

The man to Simpson's left stepped in Shakespeare's direction. "He's talking shit," he said as he grabbed the Captain's arm.

"Maybe," Simpson said, "but I want to hear him out. I think the Major will too." He raised his rifle and pointed it directly at Shakespeare's chest. "Come with me. If you so much as flinch in that lift I won't hesitate," he warned.

The two men entered the airlock, waited for it to seal, and then proceeded silently to the bridge.

vii.

Fracaro's mind raced. He was sitting at the head of the table in the conference room, to which he had retired to gather his thoughts. He was leaning forward, clutching his forehead with his left hand and squeezing his eyes closed.

"You are doing well," a familiar voice said.

Fracaro opened his eyes and looked up. Standing behind the seat to his right was his brother, Alex.

"Not well enough," Fracaro replied.

"Don't be so hard on yourself. You are here. This ship, and many more like it, is now yours. It's a great achievement," Alex reassured him.

"It's all too soon; I needed at least another six months. If Marshall and the rest of his fucking band had stayed out of our business a while longer, I would have been better prepared," Fracaro replied angrily.

Rage swelled in him as he continued. "But no. The self-righteous prick decided that now was the time to get involved. Thousands of people's lives in clear and present danger isn't enough, but our business in the middle-east is. Who, the fuck, does he think he is?"

"It isn't just him. His people back him at every turn," Alex observed.

Fracaro turned pale. "You are right," he said calmly after a moment. "They are all as bad as each other."

"What you're doing will show them that they aren't all-powerful," Alex said.

"It's still too soon. There are too many of them. We only have five of their ships."

"Then you need to use tactics that they wouldn't consider. Show them that you are without mercy. The fear of losing his friends will make Marshall surrender."

Fracaro stared at Alex, who was wearing a full New York Fire Department uniform, bar a helmet. He chuckled softly. "You were always the smart one," he quipped.

The door to the conference room slid open and a young man entered. "Sir, you are needed on the bridge at once," he said quickly.

Fracaro glanced back into the empty conference room, his brother nowhere to be seen. He blinked hard and shook his head before standing and hurrying out of the door.

"What the hell is going on?" Fracaro demanded.

Simpson was standing in the lift, with Shakespeare slightly in front of him. The bridge crew had their weapons raised and pointing at the pair, whom Fracaro ushered into the room.

Simpson lightly pushed the barrel of his rifle into Shakespeare's back, and the two men stepped onto the bridge. "Sir, this is Captain Shakespeare. This was his ship. He has asked to speak with you," he said.

"I know who he is, and he can ask for whatever he damn well pleases! That doesn't mean you have to oblige!" Fracaro said loudly with contempt.

Simpson shifted his weight uncomfortably. "He has information that I believe you should hear, sir," Simpson said defensively.

Fracaro glanced at Shakespeare with evident frustration. "Go on then, Captain. What information do you have for us?" he asked with a touch of sarcasm.

Shakespeare steeled himself and glanced at the armed men surrounding him before responding. "As you know, the Earth Defence Force is preparing for an invasion by an alien race known as the Aletheans. They built the original ship of our fleet, *Odyssey*, and for reasons unknown they will return to destroy not only the fleet but everyone on Earth as well. What you are doing jeopardises everything we have been preparing for. You must stop now, before it's too late."

"HA!" Fracaro exclaimed, stepping toward Shakespeare. "You actually believe Marshall's bullshit, don't you?" he said as he leaned over the stocky Captain.

Shakespeare was confused by Fracaro's reaction. "Why wouldn't I?" he asked with incredulity. "It's irrefutable."

Simpson was becoming increasingly uncomfortable with the exchange, as he had not been briefed about the Aletheans and it was apparent that Fracaro had known of their supposed threat from the outset.

Without provocation, Fracaro swung an arm at Shakespeare and struck him across the face. Shakespeare dropped to the deck. His face was red and his nose bloody.

"Marshall is a liar and a traitor!" Fracaro screamed at Shakespeare. He grabbed the Captain by the collar and dragged him to his feet, "Do you know the punishment for treason?" he asked menacingly with his face only centimetres from Shakespeare's.

"It depends where you are," Shakespeare said defiantly.

"Where I come from, it's death!" Fracaro shouted. His grip on Shakespeare's collar was tightening.

"Well then I am glad I am from somewhere else," Shakespeare retorted calmly with a slight smile.

Fracaro suddenly released Shakespeare. He was still standing close to his enemy, but his posture and demeanour visibly relaxed.

"You are right," Fracaro said calmly. "The laws back home don't apply here," he said.

Shakespeare felt a sense of relief. For the first time since the incursion began, he felt that he had a measure of control. His reverie was short-lived, as a suppressed popping sound led to the realisation that he was bleeding. Looking down at his chest, Shakespeare immediately saw a large patch of red spreading across his shirt. He felt the strength drain from his legs and he dropped to his knees within seconds. His head began to swim, and he saw Fracaro standing over him before his thoughts drifted into a cloud, and he lost consciousness.

"Major!" Simpson shouted as he saw a weapon being drawn and fired by his commander. Shakespeare quickly dropped to the deck as Simpson knelt beside the injured man, and pressed the palm of his hand against the wound.

"At ease, Lieutenant," Fracaro said. "He is merely a casualty of war, just like the rest of his crew."

Shakespeare looked up at Fracaro in shock. "He's dying!"

"I don't care, he is the enemy," Fracaro said coldly as he turned his back on Simpson and walked away.

Simpson continued to press hard on the wound, but the man was bleeding out heavily and a minute later Simpson could no longer find a pulse. Frantically, he began chest compressions and mouth-to-mouth resuscitation, but after a minute passed he knew it was too late.

He relaxed his arms and stood to see that Fracaro had returned to the Captain's chair. He was in shock from the events of the last few minutes, and did not know what to do or say.

"Clean yourself up and return to your station, Lieutenant." Fracaro said without looking away from his arm-mounted console.

Simpson felt numb. He made his way to the washroom and wiped both his uniform and hands. Thoughts of Fracaro's actions and the lack of reaction from his squad mates were racing through his mind. He filled his hands with water and threw it over his face.

When he returned to the bridge, Simpson noticed that everyone was silently staring at the main screen. Frowning slightly, he looked at the display and felt awash with horror as he saw a flotilla of human bodies floating lifelessly in space.

The crew, he thought as he looked at Fracaro, who was wearing a satisfied grin.

viii.

Odyssey emerged from a portal on the dark side of Earth's moon. The vessel moved toward *Exodus* at full speed. Within seconds, a second portal opened and *Intrepid* appeared with her gun ports open and her thrusters burning at full power.

"Report," Marshall ordered.

"She's intact and energy output is reading normal. *Intrepid* has arrived and is holding position alongside us," Costello reported, his brow furrowed as he read the sensor data. "*Exodus* should be in orbit of the moon, but instead she's outside the gravity field. Something is wrong."

"Full stop," Marshall ordered. "Smith, contact the rest of the fleet and have them rendezvous with us immediately."

The Earth Defence Force numbered eleven vessels including *Odyssey*, *Intrepid* and *Exodus*. Several minutes after Marshall gave the order, seven ships arrived by portal and surrounded *Odyssey*.

"Captain," Smith said from the communications station. "Five ships including *Intrepid* have reported in. *Prometheus* was near Mars, so she'll need at least another hour to recharge for the second jump. The remaining three are not responding."

"Which ships?" Marshall asked.

Smith checked his console before responding. "*Endeavour, Ulysses,* and *Apollo.*"

Marshall navigated his console to retrieve details of each.

"Captain, *Exodus'* ion cannon is charging!" Costello shouted. "I'm reading the same from the others."

In the seconds between Costello's report and the first jolt of enemy fire, Marshall pieced together what happened. *Fuck!* He thought before barking, "Evasive manoeuvres!"

Odyssey spun ninety degrees and accelerated at full speed. Around her, the occupied fleet opened fire on the loyal ships that used their thrusters to avoid the incoming salvo.

On the bridge of *Odyssey*, the crew worked frantically as the vessel weaved through the surrounding ships, narrowly avoiding enemy fire.

"Tactical, I want those ships disabled, not destroyed. They're too valuable to lose," Marshall ordered.

"I'm trying Captain, but they certainly don't have the same disposition," Costello reported.

Odyssey made a sharp turn and opened fire on *Apollo*. Her ion cannon blasted silently through space in a flash of light and impacted the shields of the target. As the flagship veered off and prepared for another run, *Exodus* approached swiftly and fired a volley of rail-gun fire that was deflected harmlessly off the shields.

"*Exodus* has moved away," Costello reported. "Our shields have fully repelled her fire."

Costello was confused by *Exodus'* tactics, as her tactical officer should have known that rail guns would not damage *Odyssey* until her shields were down.

Endeavour approached *Explorer* from above. Her ion canon blazed through the blackness of space and connected with the shield of *Explorer* with a bright glow. As *Explorer's* shield failed, the energy blast connected with the hull and instantly blew a hole in the ship that decompressed several sections. *Explorer* reeled from the blast, whilst *Endeavour* fired her rail guns that decimated her outer hull. *Explorer* soon lost main power and was adrift.

Marshall watched in horror as *Explorer* went dark on the main screen. "Costello, get us within portal range and open as many as you need to get the crew off that ship."

Costello checked his console before replying. He looked up at Marshall. "To open a portal we need to lower our shields. Not a good idea."

Marshall stared at the screen, grudgingly agreeing with Costello. "Alright, we'll just have to hope that Keers and her people can maintain life support for now. We-"

"Captain, incoming transmission from *Exodus*," Smith interrupted.

"Put it on," Marshall ordered.

The large screen at the front of the room blinked from the battle a man who stood in the centre of a bridge identical to that of *Odyssey*. Marshall estimated he was over six feet tall. He was slim and clean-shaven, with a surprisingly shaggy hairstyle for a man dressed in a military outfit.

"Captain, that's Nick Fracaro!" Costello exclaimed from his station. "He was on Bravo team."

Marshall stared at the screen in disbelief.

Fracaro smiled with an obvious smug satisfaction. "By order of the United States government, you are hereby directed to stand down. Surrender your ships immediately, and your crew will be spared," he said as he sat in the Captain's chair.

"Fuck you," Marshall replied. He nodded at Smith then immediately turned his back on Fracaro. He walked toward his own chair as the transmission was terminated.

"'Fuck you'?" Medforth asked with a raised eyebrow.

Marshall smiled. "If there's one thing that confuses Americans, it's English people not behaving like Dick van Dyke. He'll be caught off-balance, and it could work in our favour".

He turned to the helm. "Singh, have the loyal fleet regroup with us. We need to work together to concentrate our fire on one ship at a time."

Singh acknowledged as Medforth approached Marshall. "Aside from *Ulysses* and the other captured ships, we're one down already and while you were talking to that bastard they disabled *Intrepid*. We need to take our gloves off. I understand you don't want to damage the fleet, but if we don't stop them soon there won't be anything left to save."

Marshall sat in silence for several seconds as he processed his options. He stood and ordered Smith to re-establish communication with *Exodus*. On the screen, a grimacing Fracaro appeared. "Have you reconsidered?" he asked smugly.

"Not at all," Marshall replied. "In fact, I am calling to give you the chance to surrender yourselves, before we destroy every ship you have taken.

"We are evenly matched in numbers, *Captain*. And while you appear to want these ships and their crews to survive this engagement, I do not care about yours."

"Perhaps, but we know more about the fleet and its capabilities than you ever will. That'll be your undoing."

"We'll see," Fracaro said. He pressed a button on his console and the screen flickered back to open space.

Anger swelled in Marshall as he stood and turned to face Costello. "Order the fleet to do whatever it takes to disable or destroy those ships, but keep *Exodus* intact. Take out her weapons and shields by all means, but I want Fracaro alive."

He joined Medforth at the rear station and studied his console intently.

"It might be time to break out the torpedoes," he said.

"He indicated that our people are alive," Medforth warned.

"We need to do something. We're too evenly matched. How many do we have?"

"Thirty."

"And he has none?"

"That's right."

Howells had yet to successfully replicate the Alethean torpedoes, so only *Odyssey* had them at her disposal.

Marshall turned to the tactical station. "Costello, target the nearest ship with torpedoes," he ordered.

Costello acknowledged.

Marshall looked at Medforth. "We'll get in close, and when their shields go down we need to open as many portals as possible to wherever our people are being held. Your job now is to locate them. Work with Smith to figure it out."

Medforth nodded and quickly moved to the sensor station.

"I've got a lock on *Apollo* and she's in firing range, Captain," Costello confirmed.

"Aim for an area close to their life support systems. Singh, get us in as close as you can, but keep us out of the blast radius," Marshall specified.

Singh flew *Odyssey* toward *Apollo*, which in turn moved swiftly to avoid the incoming ion cannon blast that passed behind her and disappeared into empty space. As *Apollo* flipped 180 degrees and fired her own ion cannon, three torpedoes were launched by *Odyssey* and hurtled toward their target faster than her helmsman was able to compensate.

The first torpedo impacted the shield of *Apollo* only a second before the arrival of the second and third. Each torpedo had an explosive force capable of destroying an unshielded vessel, but as

Apollo still had hers intact she was able to absorb a portion of the energy. Despite this, the combined power of the trio was too much for the vessel's shield generators, which overloaded causing an explosion that blew a twenty-metre hole in the hull.

Apollo was severely damaged but still operational when *Odyssey* reached rail gun range. *Odyssey* opened fire and the bullets pierced the enemy hull, shredding the outer shell. As *Apollo* lost power, *Odyssey* ran alongside and dropped her shields. A portal opened between *Odyssey's* medical bay and *Apollo's* hangar, and within seconds there was a flood of crewmembers pouring through the gateway. When the crew were safely evacuated, *Odyssey* accelerated away from *Apollo* and headed toward *Ulysses*.

On the bridge, Marshall was looking at a display of ship locations. Fracaro hadn't realised that each ship in the fleet had a live status uplink to the *Odyssey* computer, so Marshall could see precisely how the battle was going. So far, *Apollo* was disabled and *Endeavour* had been destroyed by a combined assault from *Venture* and *Destiny*. Marshall hoped that the crew had been evacuated, but now was not the time to check. Adding to the loss of *Explorer* earlier, the enemy had also destroyed *Trident*.

"Singh, have *Venture* and *Destiny* join us in a co-ordinated assault on *Ulysses*," Marshall said.

Singh acknowledged, and moments later the flagship was joined by its sister ships. They were en route to *Ulysses*, which was regrouping with *Exodus*. The trio of ships reached weapons range and engaged their ion cannons. *Ulysses* evaded, but was caught by the volley of torpedoes that were unleashed from *Odyssey*. The shields rippled and overloaded swiftly. A second volley reached the vessel moments later and impacted with an explosion that obliterated their target.

"Smith, get me a line to Fracaro," Marshall ordered.

Several long seconds passed before Fracaro appeared on the main screen. He was dishevelled, and his demeanour frantic. "Marshall! You traitorous bastard!" he shouted.

"*I'm* a traitor?" Marshall exclaimed. "Lower your shields and surrender the ship. You are defeated," he stated firmly.

"No. We would rather die than surrender to you. You will-" Fracaro stopped abruptly at the sound of a gun being cocked behind him. He turned to his left as the screen flickered and returned to space.

Marshall was confused. He shot a glance at Medforth who shrugged. Costello checked his readings. "Captain, *Exodus* is approximately 1500 kilometres to starboard. Her shields are still up and gun ports are open, but she isn't moving," he said.

"Have all ships hold fire," Marshall ordered.

ix.

Simpson had found maintaining his concentration difficult since Fracaro executed crews of *Exodus* and *Ulysses*. With the battle serving as a distraction he had been able to carry out his orders, but a lull in combat had returned his mind to the events of earlier.

The moments that followed were a blur for Simpson. He had been standing at the engineering station behind Fracaro when Marshall had re-established contact.

Fracaro had declared that he and his people would die for his cause. Simpson reacted instinctively.

He had pulled his rifle around from his back over which it had been slung. He aimed it at the Major whilst simultaneously cocking it, and with his right hand he reached out to the panel on the wall and disabled the communications system.

The sound of his weapon cocking had alerted Fracaro and the bridge crew, and he suddenly found himself with three of his colleagues' rifles raised and pointed in his direction.

"What do you think you are doing?" Fracaro demanded.

"I'm putting a stop to this madness. You've lost control, and we have failed our mission."

"You don't know anything, you idiotic fool." Fracaro scoffed with contempt. "As long as we have this ship, we have not failed."

Simpson looked around the bridge at each of the Americans who were staring at him intently. He knew that if he took any action they would cut him down in a heartbeat. His only option was to make them see reason.

"This man has lost his mind," he said loudly. "Killing Shakespeare like that was a step too far, but ejecting the entire crew into space was madness! He must be stopped before he gets us all killed."

There was hesitation on the faces of his comrades, but nobody lowered their weapon.

"If we surrender now, we live. If we continue to fight, Marshall will bring his entire arsenal to bear and we all die. This man has committed mass murder, a war crime that I for one will not sacrifice my life for."

"You sacrificed your life the moment you committed mutiny," Fracaro said. His lip curled as contempt was replaced with pure hatred.

Simpson was facing Fracaro squarely, when from the corner of his eye he saw the officer with his back to the tactical station lower his weapon.

Fracaro noticed the man's action, and he waved at the other two officers who were behind him. "Arrest both of them on charges of mutiny," he said.

Nobody moved.

"Now!" he shouted, his rage swelling.

The two men behind Fracaro looked at each other before nodding and lowering their weapons.

"Those people are a direct threat to us!" Fracaro shouted with a wave of his arm toward the forward screen. "You are about to hand back the only tool we have against them!"

Simpson's relief was tangible. He was now the only man on the bridge with a raised weapon. "The biggest threat is you. You are relieved, Major. You are under arrest, and you will face a war crimes tribunal," he stated firmly.

"Like hell," Fracaro said. In a heartbeat, he reached for his sidearm and lifted it out of its holster. Without hesitation, Simpson shot the man in the centre of his forehead, ending his life instantaneously. His body dropped to the ground as Simpson rolled his rifle under his arm so it was pointing toward the deck. He walked across the bridge to the Captain's chair.

"Miller, get Marshall back," he said to the man at the helm who hesitantly followed his orders.

The main screen switched to show Marshall standing in the centre of the bridge of *Odyssey*, clearly confused.

"Captain Marshall, this is Lieutenant Maxwell Simpson of the United States Marine Corps. Major Fracaro has been…relieved. I formally offer our surrender. I ask that we meet to discuss terms."

Marshall looked off screen for a moment before he replied. "Mr Simpson, I appreciate your assistance in ending the conflict. Prepare to come aboard *Odyssey* where we will discuss your terms."

"Captain, may I request that you join us aboard *Exodus*?"

"And why exactly would I agree to do that?" Marshall asked. "You and your people hijacked and attacked my fleet, causing severe damage and widespread loss of life. To say that I don't trust you would be something of an understatement."

"I understand. I ask because I want to show you what has happened here, and explain the purpose of our assault on your fleet."

There was a pause before Marshall responded. "Very well," he said, after which the transmission ended.

x.

"You cannot be seriously considering going over there!" Medforth exclaimed.

"I am. They've surrendered. Simpson seems to be level headed and I won't be going alone," Marshall replied as he turned toward the tactical station. "Costello, put together a security detail. Have them meet me in the armoury in ten minutes. I want you there too."

"Ryan," Medforth said quietly as he stepped toward Marshall, whose had his back to him. "This is rash, even for you. Going over there is madness. Send somebody else."

Marshall turned around. "No, we've lost enough people today already. I'm putting an end to this myself," he said. With that, he headed for the lift.

xi.

A portal opened on the bridge of *Exodus* and six men stepped through. They were all wearing full body armour and carried Alethean rifles from *Odyssey's* arsenal.

Marshall led the team and emerged first. He scanned the room to find a skeleton crew scattered around the key workstations of the bridge. On the floor in the centre of the room was the corpse of Major Fracaro. His eyes were open but lifeless. Several metres to the right of the body there was a large bloodstain. A smear led to the conference room door at the rear of the bridge.

"Captain Marshall," Simpson said as he rose from the captain's chair. "Welcome aboard."

Marshall felt uneasy as Simpson approached him with his arm outstretched to shake the Captain's hand. Marshall took it hesitantly.

"Lieutenant. Explain what is going on here. I have limited patience, so out with it. And don't beat around the bush."

Simpson composed himself and began an explanation of his mission.

"Several years ago, Tom Batson recruited Nick Fracaro to serve in your fleet. Fracaro accepted the post, and was later assigned to *Exodus*. Although he accepted the job, Fracaro wasn't happy with the fact that the fleet was being concealed from the people on Earth.

"Fracaro lost his brother on 9/11. I only know what he told me, and what was in our mission brief, which was that he had a serious issue with your refusal to use the fleet to assist with the aftermath. He thought that you had ulterior motives for maintaining the secrecy, and it led to him reporting everything he knew to the U.S. government.

"Under the supervision of General Paterson, Fracaro spent the last year gathering intelligence and planning for today.

"When you sent the ground teams to Earth, Fracaro manoeuvred himself into the one bound for the U.S. Paterson had one of your teams ambushed, but was unable to reach the other. Fracaro's delivery of the portal device, and a prisoner, led to Paterson's sanctioning of this operation."

Marshall raised a hand and motioned for Simpson to stop. "So where is Szeto now?" he asked.

"He's being held in a detention centre called Guantanamo Bay. It's a new facility that is officially designed to hold terrorists. Unofficially, it is purposed to house anyone the government consider a threat to national security, something for which you have been qualified ever since Fracaro's initial report."

Marshall nodded. He would need to formulate a rescue plan but wanted to hear the remainder of Simpson's story. "Please, continue," he said.

"Well, I was called in to take part in the mission to capture your fleet. Neither my team nor me were given any specifics about you or your crew. We were simply told about your existence, and were ordered to infiltrate several ships and use them to force your surrender. Our orders were to capture the ships and detain the crew, so Fracaro had your people taken to the shuttle bay. As far as we were aware, they were to remain there until the mission was accomplished.

"When the Captain of Exodus told me about the Alethean threat, and demanded to speak with Fracaro, I brought him to the bridge. Fracaro had not disclosed the Alethean situation in the mission brief, I'm not even sure if the General knows. Fracaro killed Captain Shakespeare, and soon after that he opened the shuttle bay door with the crew locked inside. I'm sorry Captain, but they are all dead."

Marshall stared wide-eyed at Simpson. His anger swelled and his breathing became shallow. "He executed the entire crew?" he asked softly.

Simpson swallowed hard. "Yes. As far as I am aware, it was never part of the plan. Fracaro took this upon himself, and we couldn't stop him."

Marshall rubbed his forehead with his thumb and forefinger in an attempt to calm himself.

Simpson uncomfortably continued. "My orders were to bring the crew of every captured ship over to Exodus, and secure them in the hangar. Captain Shakespeare's interruption saved their lives."

"How many had you transported before this interruption?" Marshall asked.

The blood drained from Simpson's face. "*Ulysses* was evacuated to *Exodus* before I met Captain Shakespeare."

Marshall spun ninety degrees on his heel and paced away from Simpson. He took five steps, turned, and walked back toward the Lieutenant. When he reached the man he punched him square in the face, sending the American stumbling backward into the Captain's chair.

"Costello, round them all up along with any survivors from the other ships. Hold them aboard *Odyssey* until I decide what to do with them," he said. "Open a portal, I'm going back to the ship. I need time to think."

xii.

Marshall lay on his bed thinking about the day's events. He had lost people before, but never on this scale. Medforth was busy calculating total losses, but Marshall didn't need to see the answer on paper to know that it was high.

There was a knock at the door. Marshall got up and unlocked it, allowing Medforth to enter the room.

"Am I disturbing you?" Medforth asked.

"Yes," Marshall replied sharply. "But it's okay."

Medforth limped further into the room and pulled out the chair under his desk. He sat down as Marshall dropped onto the sofa.

Medforth took a deep breath. "*Explorer* and *Apollo* are knackered beyond repair. Howells is going to scrap them for parts. We lost *Ulysses*, *Endeavour* and *Trident* altogether. The rest of the fleet made it and needs work. The most seriously damaged of them was *Intrepid,* but Howells assures me she is salvageable."

"What about the crew?" Marshall asked, bracing himself for a high number.

"We lost everyone aboard *Trident* when she was destroyed, and you obviously know about *Ulysses* and *Exodus*. Other than that, we got the crew of *Apollo* and *Endeavour* out, and Keers kept everyone on Explorer alive. Excluding the crews of lost ships, and those murdered by Fracaro, there were seven deaths. The injury list varies from cuts and bruises to maiming. Alex Neill, the chief engineer of *Explorer*, lost an eye when a shield manifold blew. His was amongst the most serious."

Marshall sat silently as he processed the information. "We should hold a memorial service for the dead. Can you take care of that?" he asked

Medforth nodded.

"I don't know what to do about our prisoners," Marshall said.

"We should convene the council, what's left of it. Together we can make a decision. It's not on you to take all of the responsibility alone."

"Bullshit. I am the commander of the fleet. I found this damn ship, and I'm responsible for everyone up here."

Medforth decided that the time for tact had passed. "Alright, it's all your fault. You made the Americans attack us, and you killed the crew. I think we should throw a big pity party where only you are invited," he said with an unmistakably sarcastic expression and tone.

Marshall glared at Medforth, his eyes wide with a mixture of surprise and anger. After a moment, the anger subsided and was replaced with embarrassment. "Sorry, tough day," he said with a weak smile. "I'm going to speak to Simpson tomorrow, and try to work out what to do next. When I have any idea what that will be I'll convene the council."

"Fair enough. I'll see you on the bridge when you are ready," Medforth said as he stood and walked toward the door. He looked back at Marshall, "And don't be too long moping around down here, we've got shit to do," he added.

xiii.

Simpson sat on the end of a bunk in crew quarters that were acting as a makeshift cell. He hated to admit it, but he was terrified. Marshall had broken his nose and blackened his eye, both of which had been treated by Doctor Harrison. The doctor had given him pain medication, along with some offhand remarks about being more careful with what he said to the Captain.

The door to the quarters opened and two armed guards entered, followed by Marshall. The guards stood on either side of the door while Marshall looked around, searching for someone. He stopped when he found Simpson.

"Simpson. Come with me," Marshall said as he turned and left the room.

Simpson followed the Captain down the corridor to the next room. He entered the quarters, which were then sealed by one of the guards who remained outside.

"Take a seat," Marshall said with a gesture to a chair next to a desk. "How's your nose?" he asked with a snide grin, as he pulled another seat out from a desk on the other side of the room and sat down.

"The doctor said it'll be fine. Thank you for asking," Simpson replied with a hint of sarcasm.

"I want you to tell me more about the mutiny," Marshall said, changing the subject seamlessly.

Simpson contemplated his response for a minute before speaking. "When Fracaro killed Captain Shakespeare, he had crossed a line that I couldn't follow. Our orders were to capture the fleet by infiltration, with minimal loss of life and minimal damage to the ships. He killed that man out of pure malice, and it was then that he lost me as a soldier and I knew I would have to do something. When he refused to surrender to you, it became apparent that he was again about to do something rash, something which would undoubtedly have led to more deaths including those of my team. So I stopped him.

"I must add, Captain, that not one of my colleagues stood against me. They all allowed me to relieve the Major of his command. Even when he forced me to shoot him, nobody objected or believed my actions to be wrong in any way."

Marshall stared at the American, saying nothing. He swivelled back and forth gently on the chair, thinking deeply. "You understand I could see that your people suffer the same fate as mine. An eye for an eye, and all that."

Simpson took a deep breath and squirmed in his chair. "I do, but I implore you to spare us. We were following orders, and when the mission went beyond those orders we did not allow it to proceed."

"Ah but you did," Marshall retorted. "Fracaro killed Shakespeare before the battle even began. Correct?"

Simpson nodded.

"And I find it unlikely that he killed people from four ships single-handedly. That seems a bit unrealistic, doesn't it? That he needed no help? Why, he could have carried out the whole mission by himself if that were the case, could he not?"

Simpson struggled to respond, something apparent to Marshall who continued. "I find it more likely that your orders were to capture the ships by whatever means necessary, and ultimately that meant killing anyone that resisted your invasion. Isn't that more accurate?"

Simpson hesitated, and then lowered his head. "Yes, Captain. I suppose it is."

"Good. Now that we've established the level of your complicity, I will ask you this: Did you personally have any involvement in the execution of my people?"

"No!" Simpson shouted. "Absolutely not. I wasn't even present. I was... I was in the head when it happened," he finished with embarrassment.

"Do you know how many people he murdered in that one act?" Marshall asked quietly.

"I have no idea." Simpson replied honestly.

"Forty-six," Marshall answered. "Almost the entire crew of two vessels. Forty-six people, gone. Just like that. That is what your military is responsible for, sanctioned or not, and that is precisely the sort of end-result that I am trying to prevent by keeping this fleet and its technology out of the hands of Earth governments. Do you understand?"

"I do," Simpson said truthfully.

"I'm going to speak to the council. A council whose numbers have been halved because of you and your people. Ultimately, they will decide what is to be done, however I will be recommending that you all be spaced."

Simpson felt dread wash over him as the words left Marshall's lip. He felt panic as he blurted out anything he could think of to persuade the Captain to spare his life. "Please, Captain, I ask for asylum aboard your ship, to serve alongside you. I agree with your stance regarding your technology and the governments back home. You are right; my mission is a perfect example. I was following orders; I didn't murder your crew."

Marshall stood and marched over to Simpson. He leaned over so their eyes were level. "I know exactly what your involvement was, Mr Simpson, and I know the result all too well. After I have spoken to the council I will deliver their verdict personally. You had better hope they are more forgiving than I am."

Marshall stormed out of the room without another word.

The council was decimated. The remaining members assembled in the meeting room aboard *Odyssey* and awaited the arrival of Captain Marshall.

Marshall and Medforth arrived several minutes after the rest of the assembly and took their seats at the head of the table without delay. Marshall thanked everyone for coming and the meeting started.

"How's everyone doing?" Marshall asked the room.

The silence was deafening. Marshall took a deep breath. "All right, let's just get this over and done with. I'm going to start with the list of losses," he said with a grimace. He picked up a sheet of paper laid on the desk in front of him and began reading. "The council has lost Captain David Stewart of *Endeavour*, Captain Sylwia Gorzela of *Trident*, Captain Bert Petty of *Ulysses*, and Captain Robert Shakespeare of *Exodus*. Medforth is going to arrange a memorial. You can expect a date from him in due course.

"Having reviewed personnel records of senior officers throughout the fleet, I hereby nominate Captain Batson's first officer Adele Baillie for promotion to Captain, with reassignment to *Exodus* to oversee her re-staffing. All those in favour raise your hand."

Looking around the table, Marshall was pleased to see everyone raise their arms in the air. "Excellent," he said. Hesitantly, he continued. "There is one critical matter on the agenda: What to do with the prisoners. We-"

"The only thing to discuss is when and where their execution will be held," the Captain of *Venture* muttered, his eyes never moving from the table in front of him. Every pair of eyes in the room was immediately upon him, followed quickly by a glance to Marshall who silently stared at him.

"You have something to say, Simon?" Marshall asked.

"Yes," Captain Orton replied. He looked up and glared down the table at the chairman. "We were attacked by that group of men, unprovoked. They are responsible for the deaths of our people, and they must pay for it."

"I've spent some time with Lieutenant Simpson," Marshall said. "He and his team were following the orders of the U.S. military. While they are not blameless, Simpson has told me how his commander, Major Fracaro, was personally responsible for the death of *Ulysses* and *Exodus'* crews. Since Fracaro is dead, thanks to Simpson, he cannot answer for his crimes. With that in mind, I don't think punishing the rest of his men would be just. Especially not the death penalty."

"Bollocks," Orton said.

"Not bollocks. Fact. Simon, you served in the Army for over fifteen years. In that time, you will have followed orders that you didn't agree with, yes?"

Orton did not respond.

Medforth shifted in his chair. "I believe the term 'we were only following orders' has been used before," he said with a raised eyebrow.

"That was different," Marshall said sharply. "Be honest, if you were ordered to attack a foreign target that was perceived a threat, you would carry out those orders without question. And if that meant killing people, well that's just part of the job. Stop me when I start being wrong here…"

Captain Reed, who had survived the capture of *Apollo*, interrupted. "Those people assaulted my bridge, killed many of my senior staff, and incarcerated the crew whilst they commandeered the ship. I have plenty of reasons to want them punished, but Marshall is right. We all lost friends, but they were following military orders. In their position, I would probably have done the same as they did." He turned to Marshall, "Having said that, anyone who assisted Fracaro in murdering our people in cold blood must be dealt with severely. That was a war crime, and they need to pay for it."

Marshall nodded. "Agreed, but according to Simpson it was Fracaro alone who carried out the massacre. What this boils down to is we don't have anywhere to imprison them up here, so we are talking about either releasing or executing them. It has to be one or the other."

"We could throw them out of an airlock, so they can experience what they inflicted on our people," Orton said calmly.

"Sounds good to me," Batson said.

Marshall looked at the American. He had not considered the effect recent events would have had on his colleague who had personally recruited Fracaro.

There were murmurs of agreement around the table. Marshall raised his hand. "Okay, okay. That'll do," he said, and the room fell silent.

Medforth spoke after the silence fell. "There's a third option. Dr Harrison can erase their memories of everything that has happened since they arrived. If we go down that route, we can return them to Earth as a message to their superiors that'll deter them from trying again."

"Not good enough," Batson said.

"We'll take a vote," Marshall said, interrupting the conversations that had once again erupted between those present. "Either they're sent home, or we throw them out of an airlock. I don't want a rash decision, so the vote will be taken two days from now. Dismissed."

xiv.

"Lieutenant Simpson," Marshall said. "Please come with me."

Simpson had been lying on his bunk reading a newspaper that had been delivered to him that morning by one of the security officers. It was a British paper, and he found it full of the same sensationalist nonsense as the papers at home. He had tired of it quickly, but had little else with which to occupy his time in the room he shared with three of his colleagues, as the small talk had dried up several days earlier.

Following Marshall down the corridor to the same room to which he had been taken earlier in the week, he sat in the same chair and waited nervously for Marshall to speak.

"The council have made their decision. They have decided to follow my recommendation," Marshall said curtly.

Simpson swallowed hard and looked at the floor, unable to formulate a response.

Marshall watched the relatively young man. His distress was obvious and Marshall could not let the charade continue any longer. "We are returning your team to Earth," he said.

Simpson's eyes widened. He looked up directly at Marshall who was glaring at him expressionlessly. "All of us?" he asked.

"No," Marshall said abruptly. "You will stay here, where you will work directly for me aboard this ship. You will of course be supervised at all times, and your security clearance will be practically non-existent. Your job will to be to monitor activity on Earth for any sign that there may be another incursion in the future. We haven't paid home much attention over the last few years, and that's going to change."

"Thank you. Really," Simpson said with evident relief.

Marshall nodded. "Your colleagues will have their memories wiped before they are sent back. They will lose all recollection of this ship and the events that have transpired since they left Earth."

Simpson was stunned. "I am grateful that you aren't going to execute them."

"It was considered, but in the end this was unanimously agreed upon. I'll have someone bring you some fresh clothes and assign you proper quarters so you can shower and get changed. When you're done, you will be escorted to the bridge. We have a ruse to plan."

With that, Marshall turned and left quickly.

xv.

Dr Harrison spent several days erasing the insurgents' memories. When the last operation was complete, she summoned Captain Marshall to the medical bay and waited with his unconscious patients.

Lieutenant Simpson, who Harrison noticed was no longer wearing his military uniform and was instead outfitted with plain black jeans and a black T-shirt, followed Marshall into the room.

"Are they ready?" Marshall said.

"I think so. I haven't woken any of them, but everything went as planned."

"Wake them." Marshall ordered. He turned to Simpson. "Are you clear on everything that needs to be said?" he asked his newest recruit.

"I am," Simpson replied.

xvi.

General Paterson had spent almost three weeks waiting to hear from Fracaro, who was supposed to radio in when he had secured the fleet. During his time undercover, Fracaro had impressed Paterson with the punctuality of his reports. Something must have gone awry for Fracaro to be late, but Paterson was helpless to find out any details.

Paterson's office was traditional, with a large wooden desk positioned centrally opposite the door. He was sat in a large high-backed leather chair, and there were two smaller chairs on the other side. Behind his seat there were two large flags that flanked a bookcase full of literature that he had never read. To his left was a sideboard on top which were photographs of his family and an assortment of medals enclosed in wood and glass cases. What could not be seen were the whiskey and cigars that filled its interior.

Earlier in the morning he was given a report on suspected terrorist activity in Madrid that the Spanish secret service had sent him. He hadn't read it, as he was too intently focused on the seemingly failed mission into space.

There was a knock at the door, and a young officer entered and approached the large desk. "General, there's been a breakout at Gitmo. Reports are sketchy; there is word of a vortex of some kind opening in the facility and an armed group of men emerging from it. They freed only one inmate, and left by the same means."

Paterson was on his feet in an instant. "What? That's impossible! Get me a line to General Burton immediately!" he shouted.

The young private left hurriedly. Paterson's mind raced, he had started considering the possibilities when there was a sound in the far corner of the room to the left of the door, followed by the opening of a portal identical to that which he saw his men disappear through weeks ago.

After a delay of several seconds, a line of people emerged single file. He recognised most of them, though they were wearing different attire to when they left, and they were no longer equipped with body armour or weaponry. Paterson quickly moved from behind his desk and approached the team.

"What has happened? Where is Major Fracaro?" he demanded of Sergeant Beattie, who Paterson had known for many years. "I have no idea, Sir. We went through the portal, and I remember emerging in a small room full of lockers, then I woke up in some sort of hospital. When I came around, the others were already conscious and suffering from severe migraines."

Beattie struggled to explain further. "When we had fully recovered, we were introduced to Captain Marshall. Marshall gave me a note to give to you, before he escorted us through the portal that led us here," he said as he passed Paterson a piece of folded paper.

"Have you read this?" Paterson asked.

"No, Sir. He handed it to me just a few moments ago," Beattie replied. He turned and pointed back toward the rear of the group, where the portal had closed while he was speaking to the General. "He also told us to carry that with us," he finished.

Paterson extended his neck to see past Beattie. The group parted slightly so he could see clearly the body bag that two men at the rear were carrying between them.

"It's Major Fracaro, Sir," Beattie confirmed.

Paterson's shoulders slumped. Turning his back on the group, he moved back to his desk and sat down. He unfolded the paper and read the contents.

Dear General Paterson

Your attempt to capture the Earth Defence Force has failed. With the assistance of our operative, Lieutenant Simpson, your men were quickly overwhelmed, detained, interrogated, and returned.

We have known of your plans from conception. Fracaro was allowed to feed you with disinformation and to formulate a plan that was in fact carefully prepared by us. We would like to thank you for the weapons and armour that we have now added to our arsenal.

We have returned your men and women unharmed as a gesture of good will. Unfortunately, not all of them survived the initial fire fight, as they were too stubborn to surrender. I am sorry that this was unavoidable. Those who are with you now have been "cleansed", so they hold no memory of their time with us and they will be unable to help you gather any intelligence. I assure you that they were well treated during their short stay aboard my ship.

We urge you not to attempt any such attack in the future. We are fully aware of all military activity on Earth thanks to the technology at our disposal, and I would hate for there to be any further loss of life.

General, we are here to protect Earth, not harm it. We will not interfere with your state affairs, and in return we expect to be left alone. When the nations of Earth are ready we will discuss the matter further, but for now our presence shall remain a secret and we hope never to hear from you again.

As a sign of my commitment to maintaining the secrecy and security of the Earth Defence Force, I have returned your operative to you in a condition that will be matched by any other agents you send here.

You only had Fracaro up here; we did not only have Simpson down there.

All the best

Ryan Marshall
Captain, Odyssey, Earth Defence Force.

Paterson dropped the letter on the desk in front of him. After a pause, he looked at Beattie. "Did you see Simpson?"

"Yes, Sir. He was with Marshall when I awoke. He told us he had been Marshall's agent all along."

Paterson cursed Marshall. The taste of defeat was almost too much to bear. He ordered the group to report for a medical examination before dismissing them, and began the process of planning what was left of his career.

14. Aftermath

i.

1808 A.D.

Aurellius Vrix was lying on a bed in the medical bay when the Captain of Vessel 143 entered. The room had been cleared of patients upon her arrival, so aside from the doctor and two nurses they were alone.

"Permission to approach, your Highness," the Captain asked.

"Approach," Aurellius replied urgently as she sat up.

"I am sorry to report that *The King's Will* has been lost."

Aurellius closed her eyes. "And my father?"

"There is no sign of him. He was not aboard any of the escape pods, and all ships have reported their survivors. He was last seen on the Habitation Deck of the flagship."

Aurellius felt awash with sadness. Xax stood in awkward silence as she wept.

As Aurellius composed herself, Xax stood to attention.

"So we know what happened?" she asked.

Xax shook his head. "Not exactly. I am expecting a report imminently."

"Return when you have news. I wish to be left alone until then."

"Of course," Xax said before bowing and leaving Aurellius alone.

Xax returned an hour later. His expression was grim.

"Out with it, Captain," Aurellius commanded.

"I have confirmation that the Alethean slaves have revolted. During their attack, they destroyed forty of our ships and commandeered three more."

Aurellius' eyes burned. "How is this possible?" she shouted.

"I will have more details in the coming hours, but initial reports show a number of collisions between shuttle craft and our ships. It appears they were flown by slaves."

Aurellius winced as she swung her feet over the edge of the bed. "Get my clothes," she commanded.

Xax looked for her clothing and found the smoke-damaged garments strewn over a nearby chair. Aurellius had been aboard *The King's Will* when the attack occurred. She had been studying in the ship's library when the evacuation alarm sounded, and had been one of the few to make it off the ship before it exploded.

Xax turned his back on Aurellius while she donned her ruined outfit. "We do not have forty shuttles," she said as she tied her tunic.

"That is correct, your Highness. Some ships simply exploded. We do not know why, but we suspect sabotage."

Aurellius could barely contain her fury. "Have every Alethean rounded up. I want them interrogated."

Like all Laird, Xax was a pale man. Still, his skin found an even lighter shade. "There are no Aletheans left in the fleet, your Highness," he said with disdain.

Aurellius was dumbfounded. "They *all* escaped?" she asked incredulously.

"Or died in the attack," Xax confirmed.

Aurellius paced the room.

"One hundred and fifty-seven ships are more than sufficient. Have the helm resume course immediately."

"Yes, your Highness," Xax said before bowing and leaving the room.

ii.

1892 A.D.

In orbit of the primitive world in a cretaceous period was an Alethean survey vessel and her support ship. For the first time since they had left their home world, the Laird encountered resistance. The Aletheans had fertilised their hatchery and survived, and encampments were detected on the surface in an isolated tropical region.

The current state of the Aletheans was of no concern to an elderly Aurellius Vrix. All she cared about was the completion of the mission, and so she ordered the armada to engage the Alethean vessels.

It was a short battle. Despite employing sound tactics and successfully disabling two Laird ships, the Aletheans were outnumbered one hundred and fifty-seven to two and were vanquished swiftly. Shortly afterward, Aurellius ordered the purification of the planet. Candidate 10 was left a lifeless rock when the Laird fleet began preparations for the next leg of their journey.

Aurellius' father had known that he would not live to see the next candidate. Aurellius found herself in the same situation, but was deeply saddened to know that her only son would also die long before their arrival. Archaelius Vrix was already in mid-life. He had fathered several offspring, but with such a large distance to cover between candidates even they would be too old upon arrival to command the fleet. The duty of overseeing the next purification would fall upon Aurellius' descendants two generations down the line.

Aurellius had spent her life studying her home planet's history. After the fleet had left radio communication range, the records ended, and Aurellius had always regretted that she would never know how her people were faring. With the purification of Candidate 10 complete, her life's purpose was fulfilled. Contemplated her future, she vowed to devote herself to the teachings of Artimus Vrix and reinforce his word throughout the fleet.

As small compensation to her son for the glory he would miss, Aurellius stepped down immediately after the purification of Candidate 10 was complete. As the new Regent, he had the honour of ordering the fleet to proceed to Candidate 11.

15. Exploration

i.

2009 A.D.

In March 2009, Marshall decided to resurrect his long-forgotten mission to survey the Alpha Centauri star system. With the ascent of the council, he personally informed Howells that he could not be spared for the expedition, and after a long conversation the engineer reluctantly agreed that he was needed in the hangar.

After selecting *Intrepid* and *Impetuous*, Marshall assigned Batson command of the mission and needed only to select a Captain for his support ship which had been launched just days earlier. After careful consideration, Marshall decided that Paul Dodd, who was currently serving as first officer aboard *Exodus*, should be promoted to Captain and re-assigned.

Dodd was relatively young at thirty-seven, but he had almost twelve years' service in the fleet during which time he had garnered a reputation for being intelligent, resourceful and more than a little headstrong. After receiving the promotion and offer of command, he accepted without hesitation and transferred to *Impetuous* within a matter of days.

Marshall made a fleet-wide announcement that the mission was going ahead, after which he was inundated with requests to join the expedition. In addition, Captain Batson had personally requested that Simpson, who now served in ship's security aboard *Odyssey*, join the American. Marshall agreed that the experience would be of benefit to the man, who had become fully integrated into life aboard *Odyssey* over the past seven years.

After personally replying to each unsuccessful application, Marshall made a note of those remaining and decided to deliver the news face-to-face.

ii.

After a long day touring the fleet and meeting the volunteers, Marshall had only two names left on the shortlist that he had not yet seen. They were the people from his own crew.

He decided to speak to Dr Harrison first and made his way to the medical bay. Upon arrival, he found her sitting at the table on the left side of the room. Marshall approached and waited for the doctor to finish what she was doing.

"Hello Captain," Harrison said with a smile. "We don't see you down here very often. What have I done?"

Marshall returned the smile. "Nothing, yet. I've come to ask what made you request a transfer to *Impetuous*."

Harrison put down the pen she was holding in her left hand, and turned to face Marshall squarely. "An opportunity to visit another solar system isn't something I would care to miss. Simple as that."

"And you've discussed it with James?"

"I'll tell him when you approve the request."

"When?" Marshall replied with a raised eyebrow.

Harrison's face twisted. "I assume you need a doctor, and I'm the most qualified," she said.

Marshall took a deep breath. "To be perfectly honest, you being highly qualified is a one reason why I need you here, and therefore why I might deny your request. It's for exactly that reason that Howells isn't going."

Harrison paused for a moment, clearly surprised by the analysis. "I see your point," she said. "I would appreciate your approving me for the mission. I very much wish to participate."

Marshall nodded. "I know, but I'm also considerate of your personal position."

"Alex and I have been together a long time, he'll understand."

"This is different."

Harrison's lips thinned. "True, but after Sierra Leone he can't argue that my being in danger is new."

"You'll need to resign from the hospital, and you won't have any contact with your family once you reach the outer perimeter of the system. Are you certain you want to do this?"

"I am."

Marshall wanted Harrison aboard *Odyssey*, but he could not find a good enough reason to deny the transfer. "Alright," he said. "Report to Captain Dodd once you have everything in order here. Seriously though, as your friend I'm urging you to speak with James straight away. This mission isn't worth risking your marriage over."

Harrison's smile returned. "Don't worry, I will. I just wasn't going to broach the subject before I got the go-ahead from you.

Marshall nodded. "Good luck." he said as he offered his hand, which Harrison shook firmly.

iii.

Marshall arrived on the bridge following his visit to the medical bay. He wanted to speak to Singh who was the last name on the list. Singh wasn't at the helm, and Marshall soon learned that he was conducting a test-flight of one of the *Odyssey* shuttles that had recently been upgraded.

He went to the conference room to make a cup of tea, and waited there for the pilot to return. As he waited in the chair at the head of the table, he perused the list of personnel departing on the Centauri mission. Singh entered the room after almost an hour had passed.

"You wanted to see me, Captain?" he asked from the doorway, with the nervousness at his summoning evident in his voice.

"Yes. Please, come in and take a seat," Marshall replied.

"Relax, Ricky," he added with a smile after Singh had taken a seat to his right.

Singh returned the smile and his shoulders dropped slightly.

"I hear you've been testing out one of the shuttles."

"Yes, Captain. They've been retrofitted with new scanning equipment and an improved control interface in the cockpit."

"I know. It was me that asked for the work to be done," Marshall said. "Both of our shuttles have been modified to serve the mission to Alpha Centauri. *Impetuous* and *Intrepid* will receive one each."

Singh nodded.

"You have the more experience with those ships than anyone in the fleet, so it makes sense that I approve your transfer for the mission."

Singh's face lit up as Marshall continued. "Further, I've had a discussion with Captain Dodd and we both agree that you would make an excellent first officer aboard *Impetuous*."

Singh was speechless. He had been second officer aboard *Odyssey* for several years so it was the next logical step in his career, but he had not expected it so soon. "Thank you," he said sincerely.

Marshal smiled. "You deserve it, and you'll be missed here," he said before his expression became neutral. "I need you to do something for me while you are away."

Singh composed himself and listened as Marshall gave him instructions for the mission ahead.

iv.

Twelve weeks later, *Intrepid* and *Impetuous* departed Earth and began their yearlong mission. Staffed primarily with physicists, biologists and astronomers, the seventy-strong crew settled into life in deep space and arrived at Alpha Centauri Proxima five months later.

The mission allowed for two months of exploration and scientific study of the system's largest planet, before they were to begin the journey home.

The most significant discovery was the yield of Kyrocite that existed on the first planet. Such purity and quantity did not exist anywhere in the Sol system, and it was relatively close to the surface so extraction was simple.

After the crew recovered from their New Year celebrations, and the shuttle bays were full of Kyrocite. Captain Batson ordered both ships to set a course for home and they left the remote star system behind them.

v.

The first three months of the return trip were uneventful. It was only when an anomalous signal appeared on the sensor systems that the mission deviated from its original prerogative.

"Captain, I'm picking up an audio transmission coming from deep space," the communications officer reported. "It's Alethean. The ship is translating."

Batson was startled by the announcement. "Play it on loud speaker," he said.

The ceiling-mounted speaker came to life. "Seek any survivors of the Alethean people. We were heading toward Candidate 11 but our reactor is malfunctioning. Please respond… This is Alethean survey vessel A-411; we seek any survivors of the Alethean people. We were heading toward Candidate 11 but our—"

"That'll do," Batson interrupted.

The bridge fell silent.

Batson pondered the situation for a moment before speaking. "Comms, do you know the distance to the source of that transmission?" he asked.

"Roughly 1.5 light-years."

"In the direction of home?"

"Negative. Off-course forty-five, mark twenty."

Batson decided to seek council from his counterpart aboard *Impetuous*. "Open a channel to Captain Dodd," he said.

Moments later the *Impetuous* commander's face filled the central screen. "Paul, have you heard the transmission?" Batson asked.

"I have," Dodd replied with a nod. "I say we investigate. This is our first ever encounter with alien life and it would be a tragedy to miss it."

"It's over two months out of our way. I'm not sure it's wise to go that far off course. Also, that's an Alethean ship, so it's fair to assume they'll be hostile toward us."

"We can't blindly condemn an entire society based on what limited info we have. Besides, they haven't actually done anything yet."

Batson considered the argument for a moment. "Come over, we'll discuss it properly. See you in the conference room," he said. The transmission ended and Batson made his way to the conference room where his first and Doctor Harrison joined him. Moments later, Dodd and Singh emerged from a portal.

"Who wants to start?" Batson asked after taking a seat at the head of the table.

Dodd was to Batson's left. "As I see it, we have an alien ship calling out for help and we should aid them without hesitation. I understand your reservations, but the opportunity to make first contact with the Aletheans is potentially one of the biggest events in human history."

Batson nodded. "I agree, but we must consider the Aletheans as a possible threat to our safety. These are the same people we're preparing to defend ourselves against."

"Not necessarily," Dodd countered. "If the British attacked the French, the French would obviously declare them enemies, but they wouldn't do the same to the rest of the world. Some Aletheans are going to attack us, but that doesn't mean the fellas out there have anything to do with them just because they're the same species.

"Besides, if they are the same group then for all we know, rendering aid could be the act of kindness that makes them realise we are a good people, and don't become our enemies at all. We could avoid the entire invasion by doing this."

Batson shook his head. "Or we could help them, and then they go back to wherever their fleet is and tell them of our existence. This could just as easily be the trigger of the invasion!"

Dr Harrison interjected. "We know from *Odyssey* records that the Aletheans were primarily scientific explorers, so one question we've had from the beginning is 'what would turn them into aggressors?' An answer could be that they had a ship in distress and we did nothing to help."

"We could go around in circles like this all day," Batson warned. "If we change course we'll be late home. We can send the fleet a message, but by the time they get it we would already be overdue."

"We could split up. One goes home the other helps the Aletheans?" Victoria Bellion, Batson's first officer, suggested.

Batson had considered separating, but discounted the option as they had no support this far from the fleet and were too dependent upon each other. "No. We stick together, no matter what we decide," he said.

Dodd nodded his head slightly. He turned to Singh. "Ricky, what do you think?"

"Personally, I would rather take the risk and help them. Helping is the right thing to do, it just isn't necessarily the most sensible," he replied apprehensively.

Batson knew Singh was right, and Dodd's arguments were sound. He momentarily felt a pang of guilt as he realised he had barely considered the moral aspect of the discussion.

Batson sat for a moment as he pondered the options. "Alright," he said with a slow nod, his tone was firm despite his uncertainty. "We'll change course to intercept the Aletheans," he said.

The group each nodded, before everyone stood and left the conference room. Dodd returned to *Impetuous* and within minutes both ships had disappeared through a portal.

vi.

The source of the transmission remained stationary for the duration of *Intrepid* an *Impetuous*' five-week journey. They arrived to find the Alethean vessel adrift, and there was a debris field on its port side that appeared to have once been another ship.

"Sensor report," Batson ordered.

"It doesn't appear to have sustained any battle damage, and the debris field scatter pattern is consistent with an internal explosion. Her power levels are fluctuating all over the place, and there's definite damage to the main reactor but it's still online. Their gun ports are closed and the engines are offline, but their gravity drive and life support are functioning normally," the officer reported.

"Are they still transmitting the recording?" Batson asked.

"No, sir. They stopped when we emerged from the last portal," the communications officer replied.

"Open a channel."

A moment later Batson was told that a video channel was open and would automatically translate his message.

"A-411 this is Captain Thomas Batson, Earth Defence Force Vessel *Intrepid*. We are here to render assistance, please respond."

The bridge fell silent.

A minute passed before the communications officer signalled that the Aletheans were responding. Batson nodded and the forward screen flickered to display the face of the Alethean representative.

The mouth of a rigid face moved, but no sound was forthcoming. Seconds later, the familiar voice of the ship's computer filled the bridge. "We do not understand your name,

Defence Fleet. From where did you acquire an Alethean vessel? Where are our people? From what system do you originate?"

Batson felt momentarily overwhelmed as he realised he was the first human to speak to an alien life form. He cleared his throat nervously before speaking. "We originate from a system we call Sol. I believe you call our planet Candidate 11. This is not an Alethean ship, but a replica of one that we found orbiting our world several years ago. I am sorry to report that your people had already died of natural causes before we discovered their ship," he said a little too quickly.

There was another pause before a response came. "They did not succumb to the virus?" the voice asked.

"No, but without a hatchery they were unable to live beyond their generation."

Another pause. "Although we have a hatchery, our vessel has suffered damage from prolonged use. The reactor is malfunctioning and we require assistance to repair it."

Batson's mind was flooded with questions. "Where have you come from? We were led to believe that your species had perished, and your survey vessels were ordered to avoid each other."

Another pause. "We were surveying Candidate 3 when the virus arrived at our home world. After a time, we decided to disobey our orders, and set a course for Candidate 11. We knew that the ship at Candidate 11 had no hatchery, but we hoped some of the younger crew might have survived to this day. In addition, the early records of your world indicated that your people have more to offer than the primitive natives of Candidate 3. They will not achieve your level of maturity for millennia."

"I see," Batson said with a smile, deciding to take that as a compliment. "We are here to help, and are eager to learn more about your people. We only have historical records for reference."

"We would be happy to exchange information. Would you care to come aboard so we may discuss the matter further?"

Batson was surprised by how quickly the Alethean had opened his ship to unknown visitors, but he was also aware that given the circumstances he must cast aside any preconceived ideas about how this conversation would progress.

"I will consult with my crew, and prepare an engineering team. We will contact you soon."

The Alethean slowly bowed his head and the screen flickered back to a star field.

Batson exhaled forcefully. "Comms, ask Captain Dodd and Doctor Harrison to join me for a meeting at once," he said before nodding to Bellion and heading to the conference room.

Dodd and Singh arrived through a portal within a minute of Batson's arrival, and Harrison was only minutes behind them. They sat down; Batson and Bellion were already seated.

"That was surreal," Batson said. "What are your thoughts?"

Dodd shifted in his chair. "It was difficult to get a read on him. Not only because he's an alien, but also by the time the translator masked his voice it was like looking at a stone."

Batson noticed Harrison and Bellion nodding solemnly.

Bellion looked at Batson. "He offered to have us over to his ship very quickly, don't you think?" she asked.

"Yes, I did notice. For all we know they're a naturally welcoming species. You think he's hiding something?"

"It just seemed odd. As you said, he's an alien so who knows?"

Dodd sat back in his chair. "I think we should take our chances that he's genuine. I stand by my belief that the potential benefits of first contact far outweigh the risks."

Batson had a similar inclination. "Doctor, your analysis?" he asked Harrison.

"Whether he's genuine or not, we can't forget about the virus."

"You think they might have it?"

"Not really. I don't see how they could've survived this long if it ever got aboard their ship. The incubation period is eleven years, so they would have been dead centuries ago. Still, I recommend EVA suits for any boarding party. Also, they should go by shuttle so that there's no risk to the ship."

"Very well. Bellion, put together a six-man team of engineers. I'll lead the mission. Singh, I'd like you to pilot the shuttle. Doctor, I think it wise that you accompany us too. Any objections?"

Silence.

"Excellent. Keep me apprised. Dismissed."

Batson watched as the attendees stood, with the exception of Dodd. "I'll see you aboard *Impetuous*," Dodd said to Singh, who nodded and followed the others out of the room.

Batson was still sat at the head of the table. "Is something bothering you?" he said after the door had closed.

"I wouldn't say in front of the others, but you shouldn't be going over there. You're the mission commander, you need to stay here and let the crew take care of this."

Batson smiled. "I appreciate your concern, but I'm sure I can manage," he said sarcastically.

"Of that I have no doubt, but I would feel very uncomfortable allowing you to go over there when there are other options available."

"Yourself, for example?" Batson asked.

Dodd knew he was being transparent in his intentions. His shoulders slumped. "I've pushed for this encounter from the beginning. This sort of opportunity is what I joined the fleet for," he said calmly, with a hint of resignation. "I formally request permission to lead the mission," he finished, his demeanour resolute but soft.

Batson considered the request for a moment. His gaze drifted toward the desk in front of him. "Why not," he said finally. "I just want to go home, so if you can go over there and get this rescue mission over with quickly and enjoy it at the same time, who am I to stop you?" he said with a smile.

Dodd was both elated and surprised. The two men stood and shook hands before Dodd left for *Impetuous*.

vii.

"Captain, may I have a moment?" Simpson asked Batson several minutes after he returned from his meeting with Dodd.

Batson nodded.

"I request permission to take a security team along with the boarding party. As far as I'm concerned they are entering hostile territory and therefore need our protection."

"Your objection is noted, but I don't want us turning up with an armed contingent. It could send things south," Batson replied.

"Sir, it is my duty to safeguard the security of this ship and its crew. I cannot do that from behind a desk."

Batson agreed with Simpson's assessment, but he had already considered the option and decided against it. "I understand. Please don't think we are ignoring your concerns, in fact you can rest assured that the boarding party will be on full alert throughout the mission. Request denied."

Simpson was visibly stunned.

Batson felt it necessary to explain further. "Dodd knows what he is doing, and ultimately this is a rescue mission. How would you feel if we called for help and a dozen armed aliens came aboard?"

Batson knew Simpson was dissatisfied with his response. "Besides, the shuttle is full," he added with a smile.

Simpson glanced at the deck. "Very well, Captain. I will record a formal protest in the ship's log."

"Quite right. Dismissed," Batson said before turning his attention toward the front of the bridge.

viii.

The shuttle bay was cleared of personnel once the engineering team were aboard and the hatch was sealed. The small craft had a similar appearance to *Intrepid*, but without a spinning gravity drive in the centre, which meant the crew would need to be harnessed during their flight.

With Dodd, Harrison and the six engineers seated along the port and starboard bulkheads, and Singh in the cockpit, the shuttle was cleared for departure.

The engines came to life, resulting in a low-pitched hum filling the cabin. The occupants were all wearing EVA suits so they could barely hear it, but they could feel the vibrations through the deck plating. Dodd was facing Harrison at the end of the row closest to Singh.

Singh checked his controls for what felt like the hundredth time. "Deck is clear. De-pressurising the hangar," he said. Seconds later, a light on his control surface indicated that the shuttle was in a vacuum, and the hangar door began to retract upwards into the hull.

As the door disappeared from sight, the shuttle lifted off the deck and cruised through the opening.

The journey lasted only a few minutes before they passed the Alethean ship and came about to approach the aft hangar door. The door was already open, so Singh wasted no time in taking the shuttle inside.

The shuttle landed and the door closed behind them. As the hangar was pressurised, Singh turned to face his passengers. "We're down. Captain, if you don't mind I'll stay here and use the shuttle's scanning equipment to get a better look at the inside of their ship."

Dodd nodded, but then realised Singh probably couldn't see his head movement through the suit. "No problem. Give us a call when you are finished here," he said.

"Yes, Captain," Singh said. A light blinked on the console. "The hangar is pressurised, and your stomachs have probably already told you that their gravity has taken effect. You're clear to move about and disembark."

The team unclasped their belts, and after gathering their equipment from lockers lining the hull they formed two lines facing the rear hatch. Dodd moved down the centre of the shuttle and stopped at the door. He looked back toward the cockpit and waved for Singh to release the latch.

Dodd was first to step onto the deck. He straightened his back and looked around the cavernous room. Within a minute, the entire crew, with the exception of Singh, had disembarked.

Dodd was stunned as he saw the airlock door open to reveal four Aletheans. They began to walk toward the rescue team and arrived in seconds.

Dodd looked up at the Alethean who had led group. He towered over the Captain by almost two feet. His companions were not quite as tall, but they dwarfed the human.

The leader's mouth moved, and a sound unlike anything Dodd had ever heard came through his in-helmet speakers. It was a piercing high-pitched sound, with intermittent clicks that would sound rapidly then slowly in no discernible pattern. Dodd instinctively flinched, and was immediately pleased that it would be at least somewhat muffled by the suit. The leader raised an arm and offered him a small rounded device about the size of a seaside pebble.

Dodd took the device and examined it, unsure what he should do next. Interrupting his thoughts, he heard the familiar voice of the *Intrepid* computer emanate from the unit. "I am Controller of A-411. Welcome aboard, friend," it said.

Dodd was momentarily mesmerised. "Thank you for your gracious invite. My name is Paul Dodd. I am the Captain of *Impetuous*," he replied.

After a very brief delay, the device played a noise similar to what Dodd had heard from Controller.

Controller replied, "Our atmosphere has only three percent less Oxygen than your own, and marginally more Carbon Dioxide. The Medic has ascertained that you can breathe here for a short time, so your suits are unnecessary."

Dodd hesitated after the translation was complete, as he was unsure how to phrase his response without causing offence. "We are being cautious, perhaps overly so. This is our first encounter with alien life, so we did not want to take any chances. If you have no objection, we will remain in these suits for a while longer."

"As you wish," Controller replied.

Dodd felt uncomfortable, as he was certain that he had offended the alien. "We are here to help in any way we can," he said, in an obvious attempt to change the subject. "Please, show us your damaged systems and we will get to work," he finished with a smile.

Controller nodded and led the group toward the airlock.

ix.

Singh had been studying the sensor readings intently for over two hours. He was so lost in his work that he had not noticed that the lack of contact from the Captain. *Probably enjoying the Alethean's welcome drinks too much,* he thought when he noticed the time.

His focus returned to the sensor display when a spike flared in the readings.

What the hell was that? He thought as he quickly changed the layout to focus on the affected frequency.

The spike reappeared, then again a second later, then several more times in quick succession. The line fell flat. Singh's hands flew across the control surface as he focused the sensor array on the area of the ship where the spikes originated.

The engine room? He thought. But that looks like… *oh bollocks.*

x.

It had been almost two hours since Dodd and the engineering team had arrived in the reactor core. The Alethean who called himself Executive had distributed translation units to each team member when they had first arrived, so they were now busily working with their alien counterparts to identify the source of the problem.

"Captain, may I have a minute? In private," Alex Neill, the engineering team leader, said as he approached from a console in the middle of the room. Neill had a scar that ran down the left side of his face and intersected his eye, which was missing and covered with a patch strapped to his head. The wound had been inflicted aboard *Explorer* during the battle with Major Fracaro.

"Of course," Dodd replied before switching his in-helmet radio to secure mode.

The engineer stood directly in front of Dodd, who had instinctively taken a side step away from the crowd. "Captain, the damage to the reactor is extensive," he said in a lowered voice. "It was clear at first glance that there's nothing we can do for them with the limited resources at our disposal."

The engineer glanced around the room before looking back to Dodd and continuing. "Assuming the Alethean engineers aren't completely incompetent, there's no way they didn't know this before we came aboard. Furthermore, the damage was not caused by age and prolonged use, it was almost certainly sabotage."

Dodd was surprised by the revelation. "If the ship was sabotaged and Controller is hiding it from us, then it stands to reason that he was complicit rather than it being a usurper amongst their crew."

The engineer nodded. "I would say so, yeah."

"Shit. Do they know that you found this information?"

"I don't think so. I was discrete."

Dodd found himself scanning the room. "Continue your investigation. Try to find out what exactly happened."

"Yes, Captain," Neill said before returning to his team.

Dodd noticed Controller stepping toward him, so he switched his radio back to the standard setting.

"Is there a problem?" Controller asked.

"The engineer was simply updating me with the progress of the work. I am no technician, so it must be explained in simple terms," he said with a polite smile.

"I understand," Controller replied.

An Alethean engineer approached Controller and spoke into his ear quietly. Controller bowed his head and the engineer moved back to the central table.

Dodd waited silently.

"Your team are struggling to repair the damage," Controller stated.

Dodd couldn't ascertain the tone of the statement through the monotonous translator, but he could sense a shift in the Alethean's demeanour.

"We have limited resources. I'm sure that with time we can work something out," Dodd said calmly.

Controller's back straightened and his shoulders widened. "Not good enough," he said.

A sense of dread washed over Dodd as he realised what was about to happen.

A weapon appeared from beneath the alien's cloak, and before Dodd could react it had been raised and aimed at the Captain. Controller fired. Dodd was hit in the chest and was thrown backwards. He lost consciousness before he hit the deck.

Within seconds, the remainder of the boarding party joined him.

xi.

"Captain, the Aletheans have engaged their shields," Simpson reported.

"Boarding party status?" Batson replied.

Simpson checked the metrics being transmitted from the team's suits. "They are normal. They--," he paused and his brow knitted. "Their bio-readings just dropped sharply. They're alive but I think they've been rendered unconscious."

Batson stood and crossed the bridge to hover behind the curved bank of workstations in front of him.

"What the fuck is going on over there?" he demanded.

"I cannot tell, Captain," the woman at the sensor station replied.

"Get me Dodd, now!" Batson ordered.

"No response from Captain Dodd," the officer replied.

Batson cursed himself for allowing the mission to proceed when he had such strong reservations.

"Is anyone— "

"Captain, there's an incoming transmission from the Alethean Controller," the officer interrupted.

"Put him on," Batson replied.

The central screen displayed Controller in the engine room. Behind him, Batson could identify several humans lying on the deck who had been extracted from their environmental suits, but he couldn't make out who they were.

Controller's mouth began to move, and seconds later the ship's familiar voice began.

"Captain, we will exchange your crew for one of your vessels. When my people are safely aboard, we will leave you in peace. We will contact you when your team have regained consciousness."

The screen flickered to black.

xii.

Singh sat in the cockpit of the shuttle where he had monitored the exchange between Batson and the Alethean. His mind was racing, but he immediately decided that what he had previously determined to be a rash move was now his only course of action.

After double-checking his sensor readings, Singh implemented his plan.

xiii.

Almost two hours had passed since Controller issued his demands. Batson was sitting in the command chair when there was a signal from the Alethean ship.

"Captain, your decision?" Controller asked. Batson could now see the entire engineering team, including Dodd and Harrison, lined up on their knees behind the alien commander.

"We do not give in to the demands of kidnappers. However, we are open to negotiation of a truce in which all parties are satisfied."

"Unacceptable," Controller said. Without hesitation he raised a weapon that had previously been outside the view of the camera and pointed it behind him without looking. He fired and hit engineer Neill who slumped to the ground.

Controller's gaze did not waver. "When I next communicate, I hope you are more amenable," he said before the transmission was terminated.

xiv.

Singh watched with horror as the events in engineering unfolded. After taking a moment to compose his thoughts, he activated the shuttle's engines and gently lifted the craft off the Alethean bay floor.

xv.

Rage swelled from Batson's core. *Bastard!* He thought.

"Close shutters and activate shields. Have *Impetuous* do the same," he ordered.

As the shutters closed over the windows around the bridge, Batson stood and walked toward the tactical station. "Next time they contact us; I want our weapons on standby with everything we have targeted at their engine room. We will not be held to ransom, even if it means losing our people."

"Aye, Captain," Simpson replied.

xvi.

As the ship hovered in mid-air, with the shuttle facing the Alethean ship's interior, Singh deployed the rail guns that slid out of ventral ports on each wing. They then began to spin.

Here goes, he thought.

Within seconds, the arsenal was unleashed and decimated the wall of the shuttle bay. As the rounds peppered the bulkhead they swiftly broke through and darted throughout the ship.

Singh had targeted the gravity drive, followed by the bridge. It was only seconds after the attack began that his first target was hit, and soon after that the drive failed and plunged the ship into weightlessness.

As the shuttle pivoted in mid-air to acquire a lock on the bridge, Singh entered the co-ordinates for the final assault. The rail gun resumed, cutting through A-411 and reducing the bridge to a mass of shredded metal and empty space.

The shuttle spun to face the bay door and again opened fire. Before a hole was completely formed, Singh engaged the primary thrusters and hurtled the ship toward the target. He braced for impact and moments later the shuttle impacted the surface of what remained of the hangar door before it burst into space.

xvii.

"Captain, something is happening aboard the Alethean ship. It appears to be disintegrating from the inside!" *Intrepid's* communications officer reported.

Batson instinctively looked up from his personal console toward the front of the bridge, but could only see closed windows and the main screen that displayed the stationary alien craft.

"Is it the reactor?" Batson ordered.

"No sir, energy output levels remain unchanged. Wait. Our shuttle has emerged from their ship and is on a direct course toward us."

Batson shifted in his chair. "Put us between the Aletheans and the shuttle."

xviii.

Dodd sat on his knees and watched in silence as Controller made his demands of Captain Batson. He was not a man who would readily accept defeat, though he had to admit that

Controller had fooled him admirably and now had the boarding party exactly where he wanted them.

"Controller, this is unnecessary. We are here on a rescue mission. We will help you in any way we can," he said despite his suspicion that the words would fall on deaf ears.

Controller stepped toward him and spoke into a translator. "We are forced into this course of action. We must get the vaccine to what remains of our people, so that we may reclaim our home world together. We cannot do this without a functioning vessel."

"So why use force? We came to you offering assistance."

"It is clear you are unable to help us. We cannot waste any more time."

"Surely having— "

The deck heaved and threw Dodd aside against Neil's body. He rolled onto his chest and looked up to assess the room.

The deck shook violently for several seconds, throwing both the captured engineering team and the Aletheans around. As the shaking subsided, gravity left them and a jolt from the deck sent Dodd floating toward the ceiling.

As he looked around the compartment, he identified Controller. When he reached the ceiling, he kicked off and hurtled himself toward the alien. When they collided, Dodd reached with his right hand for the sidearm holstered at Controller's waist.

As the weapon came free from the leather-like pouch, Controller grabbed Dodd's hand and squeezed tightly. Dodd yelped as several bones were broken, and then Controller punched him in the face, which caused him to float backwards.

Dodd was dazed but conscious. His mind began to clear just as Controller reached out to grab his arm and pull him back. When in range, Controller gripped Dodd by the shoulders. Dodd knew that he would never beat the Alethean in a one-to-one grapple, so he quickly raised his knee and caught his adversary mid-torso.

Controller shrieked and his grip loosened. Using the moment to his advantage, Dodd threw an uppercut with his left hand that connected with Controller's chin beneath his developing exoskeleton.

As Controller's head snapped back, Dodd pushed the Alethean away from him with every ounce of strength that remained in his left arm. His hand was throbbing, his shoulders ached, and Dodd knew that he had bought himself only a few seconds. Controller was staring intently at him as he floated backward toward a wall against which he could propel himself.

Dodd was floating in mid-air. He looked around the compartment but could find no surfaces that he could reach. To his right he could see a similar confrontation between an engineer and one of the Alethean crew, and to his left there was Dr Harrison struggling to control her movements in the weightless environment. The rest of the team and the remaining Aletheans were scattered around the compartment, either unconscious or dead.

Dodd's focus returned to Controller as he was approaching fast.

"Dodd!" Harrison shouted.

Dodd turned to look at the Doctor and immediately spotted an object hurtling toward him.

The object was a sidearm from one of the fallen Aletheans. Dodd grabbed the weapon with his functioning hand and swivelled in the air to aim it at Controller who was almost on top of him. He squeezed the trigger and watched as the alien's chest burst open and blood floated out into the room. The force of the shot had halted Controller's approach, and he now drifted slowly away from Dodd.

Dodd felt a wave of relief and a sharp drop in adrenaline. He surveyed the room to find the engineer had also been victorious.

xix.

"How long do we have?" Batson asked.

"About an hour. We should start evacuating immediately," Dodd replied. He had just informed Batson that the reactor damage had been amplified by Singh's attack, and the core was now on the verge of a meltdown.

"Will you return by shuttle? Singh is still out there, he can dock and pick you up once you are all back in your suits."

"I doubt that we can get to the bay from here now. Internal scans show massive amounts of the ship exposed to space, and some of the corridors are gone. Without gravity, I don't think we have time. Portals will be the best way."

"Very well. Let me know when you are ready. *Intrepid* out."

As the screen went blank, Dodd looked up to see Harrison conversing with an engineer who she had just awoken. One of the engineers had been killed when he collided with the edge of a workstation as the deck lurched. Another's neck had been broken during a struggle with an Alethean. The remaining three had been rendered unconscious, but would survive with little more than a concussion.

"It's time to go," Dodd said.

"Captain, may I have a moment?" Harrison asked. Dodd nodded and pushed off the desk he was hovering beside to join the Doctor.

xx.

The screen at the front of *Intrepid's* bridge displayed Captain Dodd and Doctor Harrison. Batson had been seated when they first contacted him but he now found himself standing in the centre of the room.

Before Singh's assault on the Alethean ship, Controller had mentioned a vaccine that he and his crew were attempting to take to other candidates. This had sparked curiosity in Harrison, who since the fight had been reading as much as she could in the Alethean medical logs.

The virus had infected the Aletheans surveying Candidate 3 before they left Alethea Prime. Their hatchery had already been fertilised, and they discovered that their unborn offspring had developed immunity to the pathogen. They obeyed their orders to stay away from Alethea Prime and the other candidates, but when the first generation died of the virus their descendants worked tirelessly to develop a vaccine using their own genome as a guide.

They succeeded, and one hundred and seventy-five years ago they decided to depart Candidate 3 and head into space in search of survivors.

The decision to leave had not been unanimous, and resentment of the disregarding of command's orders had festered for almost two centuries, before Executive led a mutiny against Controller.

The sabotage inflicted by Executive's insurrection had resulted in the destruction of their support ship, and critical damage to the survey vessel's main reactor. Controller had emerged from the incident victorious, with Executive and many of the crew dead.

Harrison had just given Batson a brief overview of the Alethean mission.

"Events would indicate that Controller wasn't the villain of the piece."

"That's right," Harrison said. "In fact from what I can see, he'd done nothing out of order until he attacked us. I suppose he felt backed into a corner. He saw no other way of completing his mission."

Batson's lips pursed. "Hmm. So is there a danger to us from this pathogen?"

Harrison and Dodd glanced at each other nervously.

Harrison looked directly at Batson. "The Aletheans we met over here were mostly the generation that followed those with natural immunity. They were immune, but they were still carriers. I've confirmed that the entire boarding party have been infected."

Batson's face went pale as the blood drained from it. "My God. Any their vaccine won't work on humans?" He asked.

"As a vaccine? Possibly. As a cure? No."

"What is the prognosis?" Batson asked.

"The incubation period for Aletheans is eleven years. Since we are the first human cases, it's virtually impossible to guess how long it'll be."

"And once symptoms start, how long will you have?"

"Again, we're the first so I can't be sure. For them it was fatal in every case, and relatively quickly. One thing we do know for sure is that we cannot return to Earth, or even back to our ships."

"That ship's core is about to go critical, you can't stay there!" Batson exclaimed.

Dodd chuckled. "I for one would rather go out in a ball of flames than wasting away in a bed."

"Not an option," Batson said firmly as he began to pace the bridge.

Batson's mind was made up. "Gentlemen, prepare to evacuate your team to *Impetuous*. I'll have her crew transfer to *Intrepid* so there's no risk of exposure. Did any of the Aletheans survive?"

"No, sir. Most were killed on the bridge, and the rest were in here with us," Dodd replied.

"Alright. And Singh, will he be clear of infection?"

Harrison nodded. "Yes, he never left his suit. He'll need to decompress the shuttle to clear anything that might be in the air in the cabin. As a precaution, I recommend he does an EVA over to *Intrepid's* shuttle bay. You can scan him for contamination before you let him through the airlock."

Dodd spoke before Batson could reply. "Tom, we can't come back with you. Don't get it into your head that we're going to follow you to Earth."

"Well I'm sure as hell not leaving you alone out here. You can follow us to the solar system, so you are at least in comm range. We can keep you supplied and in contact until we find a cure."

"A cure!" Harrison said loudly. "Ha! Typical American optimism."

Batson smiled. "Maybe. But with enough support, and the log files from that ship you're on, there's a reasonable chance."

"Perhaps," Harrison conceded.

xxi.

After clearing A-411 and watching from a safe distance as the core exploded, *Intrepid* and *Impetuous* headed toward Earth without further diversion or incident. When they reached Jupiter, *Impetuous* shut down her portal drive and entered a high orbit around the moon Ganymede.

Batson led *Intrepid* home, where the fleet that were in a vertical diamond formation welcomed the lone ship.

Marshall in the conference room debriefed Batson. Singh arrived aboard *Odyssey* soon after to meet with Marshall and Medforth.

"Welcome back," Marshall said as he shook Singh's hand. Medforth followed suit.

"Good to be home. I never thought it would be like that," Singh said as he took a seat opposite Marshall who sat next to Medforth.

Medforth's expression was one of curiosity. "What was the biggest surprise?" he asked.

"The mixed emotions. On the way there it was boring to the extreme. There were literally weeks of doing nothing. At Centauri there was excitement from the science departments that permeated to everyone else. While we were travelling to the Alethean ship the apprehension on both ships was tangible, then there was tension for the entire duration of the encounter. Finally, there was sadness on the way home. To tell you the truth it was pretty awful."

Marshall chuckled. "That's probably the most succinct and honest mission summary I've ever been given. I'm sorry it wasn't as much fun as you'd hoped."

Singh shrugged his shoulders. "I did get to take part in humanity's first contact with alien life," he added with a smile.

"There is that," Marshall replied. "So, to my request that you monitor Simpson. How did it go?"

"I kept an eye on him like you asked, and I actually got to know him pretty well over the course of the voyage. He's a good man. I trust him and I think you can too. He believes in what the fleet stands for, and I'm told he questioned Batson's decision not to send a security detail to A-411 with the boarding party. He was proven right in the end, and Captain Batson should probably have listened to him."

Marshall listened intently, and nodded. "His judgement is something we've questioned given his early actions in the Fracaro incident. As far as I'm concerned he has redeemed himself admirably over the last seven years, so I am considering this his final test before we truly release the reigns. In your opinion, do you think he would make a good chief of security?"

"Absolutely," Singh replied without hesitation.

Marshall beamed. "Excellent. Thank you for your work on this. Captain Batson also reported favourably on Simpson so I think we've found our new chief. Assuming he wants the job."

"Glad to be of help," Singh said with genuine satisfaction.

"Finally, we need to discuss your future. With *Impetuous* effectively lost, you are without an assignment. I have a list of ships that need an executive officer," Marshall said as Medforth handed Singh a sheet of paper. "I also have one that needs a Captain," he added. He let the words hang in the air before Singh realised what he was being offered.

He stared wide-eyed at both Marshall and Medforth. "Captain, I don't think I'm ready for that just yet," he said with a chuckle.

"Of course you are. Your quick thinking saved the boarding party from the Aletheans, and you have a thorough understanding of the fleet. According to Captain Dodd you made an exemplary first officer. I cannot think of anyone more suitable for the post."

Singh smiled. "Permission to speak freely."

"Always."

"I don't want to be in command. I'm a pilot, that's what I'm good at and that's what I enjoy. For prolonged periods I sit at the helm and monitor our orbit, and that can get a little tedious, but when something does happen, like it did aboard *Impetuous*, I feel useful and that I have something to contribute to the situation. Yes, I might be technically able to command a ship, but when the

Aletheans arrive six years from now I know I can serve the fleet better from the helm."

Marshall and Medforth sat in silence. Singh felt uncomfortable, unsure if his rejection of the offer had offended them.

Marshall looked at Medforth who nodded, before returning his attention to Singh. "In that case, I want you back aboard *Odyssey* as helmsman and second officer. Does that sound more appealing?"

Singh beamed. "Yes, definitely!" he said with elation.

16. Progress

i.

Over the fourteen years following what was referred to as "The Fracaro Incident", the Earth Defence Force had been rebuilt and expanded following the original plans. By January 2016, Howells and his team had completed one hundred and nineteen vessels, almost achieving his original estimate of one hundred and twenty-nine.

2016 A.D.

"Cheers!" a chorus rang out, as large glasses clinked and were swiftly drawn to their holder's mouths.

Marshall, Medforth, and Singh lined one side of the table, with Costello and Smith facing them. They were in one of Munich's most popular beer halls. Surrounding them were hundreds of revellers, grouped separately but sharing the long benches. There was a bustle in the cavernous hall whose ceiling was almost thirty feet high, and the smell of pretzels and meat was hanging in the air.

The group had spent the day in the same seat, playing drinking games and catching up on their lives outside the fleet.

Talk of work was prohibited, so Marshall found he had little to say.

"Three. Shit," Costello said with a smile after throwing two dice.

There was a roar of laughter as it was the fifth time Costello had rolled a three, which meant he had to take a drink every time any other player rolled the same.

Smith grabbed the dice and threw them. One rolled off the table, but Marshall quickly caught it before it dropped to the floor. He placed it down to reveal a six. "Eleven he said after seeing the five on the other."

Smith grinned. "Nominate Costello," he said.

Laughs erupted as Costello grabbed his stein. "Bastards," he muttered before taking a sip. He was sure that his selection as the victim of almost every roll had been planned in advance.

Singh stood up. "I'll get another round in. After the toilet." He said before staggering away.

The four remaining men continued the game until Singh returned, carrying five brimming steins of beer.

"I've got something to tell you all," Costello said once Singh had sat down.

Everyone looked at Costello.

"You know I've been seeing Stacey?" he asked rhetorically.

There were nods around the group.

"Well, I've asked her to marry me."

Everyone exchanged glances, each surprised at the announcement.

"Congratulations!" Marshall said after a moment. The others added their approval. "I assume she said yes?"

"Yes," Costello replied with thin lips.

"That came from nowhere," Smith observed.

"Nah, I've been thinking about it for a while," Costello replied. "I just didn't mention it because I wasn't sure she would say yes. You lot wouldn't have let me hear the end of it."

"True," Medforth said sternly. "Are you marrying quickly?" he asked.

Costello nodded. "We have three months left before the Aletheans arrive. No time to waste."

"Ohhh, shop talk! You used the A-word," Singh said. "No excuses. See it off," he added with a smile.

Costello's lips pursed as he glared at the pilot. Without protest, he picked up his quarter-full glass and drained its contents.

"So where are you getting married? Vegas?" Marshall asked.

Medforth clasped his hand on Marshall's shoulder. "You could do it!" he said.

Marshall glared at Medforth. "What?"

"You're the Captain of a ship, you could officiate a wedding for them."

"Don't be daft," Marshall scoffed.

After stepping off the lift, Marshall surveyed the bridge to find Medforth in the Captain's chair. He was noticeably pale, and had a grim expression. "Good Morning," he said to his first officer.

"Morning," replied Medforth.

"How're you feeling?" Marshall asked.

"Like I've been hit by a brick," was the sullen response.

"We know better than to do that on a school night," Marshall said with a wry smile.

"Too right," Medforth replied.

"Any sign of Singh?" Marshall asked with a nod toward the helm.

Medforth shook his head. "He stayed over with that lass he met in Tangerine."

Marshall grinned. "I should have known. Give me a shout when he gets back."

Medforth nodded. "Are you still going to the hangar?"

"Yeah. I'm already late, I just wanted to check in before heading over."

"Do you mind if I join you? In all these years I've never been."

"Be my guest."

iii.

Howells had left a message for Marshall to meet him in module three of the large construction facility, as he was finishing a job he had been working on for the majority of the morning. Marshall and Medforth arrived in module two at one of the predetermined portal formation points, and began the short walk. Although portals could be opened anywhere, it had become customary to designate areas of a ship as entry points, to ensure that they were never accidentally opened in somebody's path. This was particularly important aboard the hangar, where human traffic was continuous and large machinery was in use.

From the outside, the shipyard was a lattice of cube shaped boxes, arranged in a three by three formation. When the tenth module had been added to the top left corner, the facility had started to look like a letter 'b'. Each cube had a door covering almost the entire front face, making the craft look like a grid of grey metal garages.

Module two was built to the same specification as the other ten. It was cavernous, and filled with a wide variety of equipment and engineering personnel that were scattered busily around the room. There was scaffolding wrapped around the shell of the larger components in the middle, and a persistent hum accompanied the sharp sound of metal grinding against metal.

Several years earlier, Howells had completed the task of repurposing each module to specialise in one particular aspect of a vessel's construction. Modules nine and ten focused purely on final assembly.

Module two, which Medforth was now crossing, was responsible for weapons construction. It had been only eighteen months since Howells' team successfully replicated the torpedoes from *Odyssey*, so this module was particularly busy building enough units to equip the entire fleet.

Medforth looked around in awe of the facility and chastised himself for not visiting sooner. He had intended to do so, but it had been only a few months since he had undergone a procedure to correct his limp. Until recently he had been in recovery.

The pair arrived in module three to find Howells lying with a welding torch in-hand beneath a large metal object that Marshall did not recognise. Marshall waited with Medforth until the engineer had completed his work. He climbed out from the curious machinery and joined Marshall in a walk to his office, which was situated against the far wall and looked like a porta-cabin.

"How are you feeling?" Howells asked as they walked toward the office.

Medforth smirked. "Been better," he replied.

Howells laughed to himself. "Being on the wagon has its perks sometimes. When I left my quarters this morning, Kim said you weren't back yet."

"So, will we have any more ships by April?" Marshall asked as they arrived at Howells' office, making no attempt to hide the blatant change of subject.

Howells took the hint and answered the question immediately. "There's one waiting for a weapons array, and another that needs its bridge kitting out. You'll have those two. Around fifteen ships need torpedoes, we are hoping to get them done but it's going to be tight. Can't give you more than that I'm afraid. We've simply run out of time."

"You've done a great job. After our losses near the beginning I thought we'd struggle a lot more than we have. What about the time displacement device?"

Howells reached for his workstation and pressed a few keys before replying. "Dr Millward is on duty; he'll be better able to update you than I will."

Marshall looked puzzled. Howells noticed and continued. "I followed the instructions we found to initially build the thing, but I'm no physicist. I handed the project over to Dr Millward and his team a while back."

Marshall looked at Medforth. "I knew Dr Millward was involved, but I didn't realise you had handed over the project entirely. Why didn't you tell me about this?" he asked his executive officer.

Medforth hesitated before replying. "Dr Millward is the best physicist we have on staff. I didn't think it mattered to you who was working on it as long as it was being done."

Marshall was frustrated, and his colleagues knew it. "If we lose the fight, I'll have to step into that thing. I want to know *everything* that's happening with it, no matter how minor.

Understood?" he said, the volume of his voice never rising but the tone unmistakably firm and irritable.

"Understood," Medforth replied formally.

"Captain," Howells interrupted. "Shall I escort you to see Dr Millward?"

Marshall nodded. Howells led the way out of the office and across the large open bay area. "Just so you know," Howells said, "Dr Millward is a bit, I don't know, all over the place. Unhinged is probably the best word. He's by far the most intelligent person I've ever met, but you will need to exercise patience with him. At least at first."

Marshall looked at Howells. He decided not to enquire further "Understood," he said.

Several minutes later, the men arrived at a room that outwardly appeared similar to Howell's office, but once inside it was quite different. In the centre of the square room was a large desk that was notably missing any chairs surrounding it. There was a computer screen covering much of the surface, and a large amount of paperwork scattered around the periphery. There was a small window along the right-hand wall that looked out on the hanger bay, though it had drawn blinds blocking the view. There was an eerie yellow hue emanating from two floor-standing lamps situated in each of the opposite corners. The walls were painted plain white, but they were covered almost floor to ceiling with what reminded Marshall of the scribbling of prisoners who had lost their mind. Looking around the room in amazement,

Marshall realised the "gibberish" was a series of long equations; each symbol flowed seamlessly into the next.

The room initially appeared to be empty, but Marshall then spotted a man in his late forties behind the door, pen in hand, staring at one of the markings. The arrival of the visitors startled him, and he shouted with alarm. "Doesn't anyone knock in this place?"

He turned to face the group, and immediately recognised Marshall. "Captain!" he said. A look of nervousness replaced his initial agitation. "I-I-I'm sorry, sir. I didn't... I was concentrating and didn't..."

"It's okay doctor. Please, finish what you were doing."

"Oh it doesn't matter now. That ship has sailed. I have lost the train, probably forever. Anyway, yes, what can I do for you?" he asked as he scurried quickly to the table in the middle of the room. "I have no chairs. Sorry, you must stand. Would you like something to drink? I have nothing here. SARAH! SARAH! Where is she? She's never around when I need her. SARAH! Never mind. No drinks, sorry. I--"

"Dr Millward," Marshall interjected, feeling the doctor would continue endlessly otherwise. "We have come to speak to you about the time displacement device. How is your work going?"

Millward looked frantically around the room, seemingly checking the walls for an answer to the question. He moved quickly, finally coming to rest at the wall opposite Marshall. He pointed at the markings, tapping his forefinger on the wall rapidly and turned to face the Captain. "This is my progress. No progress. Well, progress but not real progress."

"What do you mean?" Marshall asked.

"You see this cup?" Millward asked, making no indication as to what he may be referring.

"What cup?" Marshall asked. He scanned the room but could see nothing.

"This one!" Doug said as he moved over to the table, bent down, and brandished a large cup from the floor behind the unit. "This is my favourite cup. Look, it says 'My other cup is a Ferrari'," he said as he started to laugh hysterically and held the cup aloft for the group to see.

"I thought this cup was the key, but it's not. It's just a cup," Millward said, bringing the object in close to his chest and looking at it intently. "I found this cup twelve years ago. It was on the floor over there," he pointed at the floor between Marshall and the table. "I put it on the table, and after a while it was gone! I didn't know where it went. I was working on my equation. I didn't see it go. I thought Sarah had taken it when I wasn't looking. Would you like a drink? SARAH!" he stopped speaking and stared past Marshall and out of the door.

Marshall took a deep breath before he spoke. "No drinks, thank you Doctor. Would you please tell me how your research into the time displacement device is going?" he asked with agitation.

"I am!" Millward shouted. His expression was one of equal annoyance to that which Marshall was giving him. "It's the cup! Don't you see? I didn't see that cup again until six years later. I was on Earth, on holiday in New York City. I like New York. It's busy. Keeps my mind alert. Sensory overload. Have you been? I saw this cup in a tourist shop. You know those shops that sell things that people don't need? One of those. I saw it there, and I bought it. That's when I knew I would get the machine working. I knew! I tested the machine with it. Sent it back in time. Targeted this office. Yes, it worked, and last month it reappeared. Right in the same place, only displaced in time." Millward stopped abruptly. He was beaming.

"Doctor, I am aware of your success. I read the report. What I'm here about is the live tests. Have you successfully used the device to send a living creature into the past without killing it?"

"What? No! No. Not at all. Failure. Only failure. This is all my work on the matter," he said whilst waving his arm around the room and glaring at Marshall. "No good. Doesn't work," he finished.

Marshall looked at Medforth and Howells for help. Howells spoke first. "Dr Millward, you were working on a new theory last week. Did you hit a dead end?"

"Yes. Dead end. And dead rabbit," Millward fell silent. His fingers began moving back and forth rapidly. "She arrived when and where I wanted, but she died minutes later. Very sad. I need a new rabbit. Perhaps Sarah can get me one. SARAH! Where is she? Would you like a drink?"

Marshall indicated to Medforth and Howells that it was time to leave. "Dr Millward, thank you for your efforts. If you learn anything more, please let me know without delay."

The trio left the office, and Medforth closed the door behind them.

"You call that 'a little unhinged'?" Medforth asked Howells.

Howells chuckled. "That was actually him on a good day. The guy is an absolute genius; he even keeps up with Professor Hawking when he visits! He's just a little unstable that's all."

"A little unstable? Ha!" Marshall said with a wide grin. "Anyway, he hasn't figured out how to get me back to ninety-eight and survive, so that's that."

"I guess we'll just have to win," Medforth said as they headed to Howells' office.

17. Invasion

i.

Howells' final two ships launched in March and joined the one hundred and twenty-one strong armada, which had been broken into squadrons of eleven. April arrived swiftly, and apprehension that had been building in Marshall reached its peak.

He had been told the Aletheans would be in scanner range long before they arrived, probably months before, and yet so far they were nowhere to be found. Although this could be construed as good news, Marshall was worried that the Aletheans were approaching from a vector that *Odyssey* and the rest of the fleet were not covering.

Marshall sat on the bridge staring figuratively and literally into space. Around him, the room buzzed louder than usual as people busied themselves with system checks.

Marshall had ordered Howells to return to *Odyssey* and take charge of Engineering. Medforth and Costello had left the bridge over an hour ago to oversee the last of the weapon tests personally, and Singh was reconfiguring the defensive and offensive flight patterns for what Marshall guessed was the hundredth time.

Looking over the communications console, he saw Smith slouching forward with the side of his head resting on the palm of his hand. Marshall crossed the room and stood behind Smith. "Are you getting anything?" he asked.

Smith was startled. "No. Nothing at all. I requested sensor reports from *Impetuous* and all listening posts on the outer rim. There's nothing in any direction yet."

"It makes no sense. We supposedly have two days left, but they aren't even in sensor range yet. Surely that means they must be months away?"

"Space is big, it's entirely possible we just aren't looking in the right direction."

"True."

"Don't worry, we'll find them," Smith said reassuringly.

Marshall nodded and headed back to his chair. "Engineering, Marshall. Weapons report please," he said once seated.

"They're as ready as they'll ever be," Medforth replied.

"Great," Marshall said. "What's our final arsenal?"

"Rail guns are loaded to capacity, and we've got ninety torpedoes. The ion cannon is the same as the day we got here. I'm not worried about ours, but the physics of it are so complicated I'm a bit worried about the replicas. If we got anything wrong, God knows what'll happen."

"We'll be fine. We've been fortunate to have some of the best minds on Earth working on them for over two decades," Marshall said dismissively.

"Well that's just it, the best minds on Earth. This ship didn't come from Earth. How long do you think it'll be before even our greatest minds have an inkling of how to build something like this?"

"You worry too much, John. Chris is more than capable."

Medforth sighed. "I know. Never mind, just been a stressful eighteen years," he said with a chuckle.

Marshall also smiled. "True. When this is over we'll go back to Vegas to celebrate. The whole crew this time."

"Deal," Medforth said, before Marshall closed the line.

ii.

It had been thirty hours since Captain Adam Graham of *EDF Excalibur* had last slept. *Excalibur* was the lead ship of the fourth fleet, and had been deployed to Mars as part of the perimeter watch.

As his medical officer approached from the lift to his left, Graham realised he had been slouching in the Captain's chair and sat upright abruptly.

"Captain, would you please tell me when you last got some sleep?" Dr Robson asked.

"I'm fine," he answered curtly.

"We cannot fight both an alien fleet *and* our own fatigue," Robson said sternly.

"I said I'm fine. They'll be here soon. I'll sleep after we win," he said with a strained smile.

"If you don't go to bed for the next six hours, I'll relieve you of command," the Doctor said with an unwavering stare.

"You wouldn't."

"I would."

With a sigh Graham stood to meet the unusually tall woman. His face was expressionless. "Did Commander Metcalfe put you up to this?" he demanded.

Robson hesitated. "I don't need to be told that you are tired, Captain. It's written all over your face. Get some rest, the Aletheans aren't even in scanner range yet."

Graham relaxed with resignation. "Okay, Doctor. I'll--"

"Captain, I'm picking up a disturbance of some kind," the helmsman interrupted.

Graham turned to face the helmsman less than a second before he was erased from existence.

iii.

Smith jumped when his console sprang to life. He scanned the readout intently. "Captain, we're receiving a distress signal from the fourth fleet," he said.

"Let's hear it," Marshall ordered.

"I have *Endurance*. There's a three-minute delay."

The main screen flickered from the emptiness of space to a picture of a man's bloody face.

"Captain Marshall, this is Commander Smallman of *Endurance*. We are under attack by Alethean forces. They—," the image winked out. Stars again filled the screen.

"Sir, there's a data download coming in. It's a video file."

"Let me see it," Marshall said instantly.

"It's downloading now, one moment."

"Stream it!" Marshall barked.

"Aye," Smith replied as his hands moved frantically across the controls.

The forward screen displayed a similar star field but Marshall could see a number of EDF vessels floating motionless in space. As the video played, Marshall felt a haunting uneasiness spread throughout his body. After several seconds, there was a flash and a portal larger than any Marshall had ever seen opened. The massive aperture formed among the flotilla of allied ships, tearing them apart. Marshall estimated it was at least thirty times larger than any EDF ship.

Moments after the portal was fully established, dozens of vessels emerged like darts and opened fire on their helpless prey that had been caught by surprise. Ion Cannons and torpedoes flooded the space between the fleets, scoring several hits before the EDF ships began taking evasive manoeuvres.

The portal itself had destroyed four ships, having cut through them as though they had no defences. The opening salvo from the emerging fleet destroyed another two before they could react. The remaining craft evaded and fought back. The visual feed was from one of the survivors of the initial onslaught, but with the enemy armada now fully through the portal it was a short battle. The image shook violently and blinked out.

The bridge was silent. Marshall was still staring at the deactivated screen when Smith announced that they had received a second video file from another ship of the fourth fleet. Marshall ordered him to relay it to Costello at tactical and Howells in engineering, before he called his senior staff to the conference room.

iv.

"Analysis?" Marshall said to the gathering.

Howells was the first to speak. "The Aletheans have a portal technology that dwarves our own. I don't know where they came from, but it must have been outside our scanner range, which puts the source at least a light-year away. That portal they opened wasn't generated by any of their assault ships, it was created by a dedicated craft that followed their primary fleet."

"I didn't see anything like that?" Marshall said.

"It was visible on the second transmission. We've got footage of it emerging moments before the portal closed."

"Shit!" Smith exclaimed.

Marshall's eyebrow raised. "You have something to add?" he asked.

"Sorry," Smith said with embarrassment. "Medforth, do you remember S-327? The thing I found in the logs. It reportedly crashed on Earth in the forties?" Smith asked.

Medforth shook his head. "Sorry, I don't."

"The log only mentioned that it suffered from a system failure and crashed on Earth. We never managed to find out what it was. I bet it was a portal ship like the one the Aletheans are using. We never figured out how they made it all the way to Earth with the limited range of the portal drive, and that would explain it."

"How many more jumps will they need to reach Earth?" Marshall asked.

"One," Howells stated. "Earth must have been just outside the range of their last jump. Given how far they just covered in one go, we have to expect the next one will put them right on top of us."

Marshall nodded. "Agreed. I suppose all bets are off with the recharge time too? We've assumed they need an hour between jumps, but with a dedicated ship we can't assume anything."

Medforth tilted his head. "We were told they are due on the fourth. Assuming that's right and we take midnight as a target, we've got just over thirty hours."

Whilst victory was their primary goal, keeping the Aletheans outside the holo-mesh was also vitally important if the population of Earth were to be unaware of the battle.

For this reason, the fleet deployment had been planned such that the Aletheans would be enticed to arrive at a location that was far outside the holographic field. The downside to this was that if the Aletheans did not take the bait, the Earth Defence Force could find themselves with their enemy behind them. The plan had assumed that the Aletheans would be using the same portal technology as *Odyssey*, with a limited range that would assist in indicating their arrival point. With the portal ship, they were capable of appearing anywhere around Earth, so a change in tactics was required.

Another development that occurred to Marshall was that because of the longer range of the Alethean portals, they could potentially open a vortex in the middle of the fleet with the same devastating results that he had just witnessed.

Marshall leaned forward and rested his forearms on the table. "Okay, let's go with thirty hours and take anything after that as a bonus. We can't let them open a portal amongst the fleet like they did earlier. We need to disperse, but at the same time entice them to a place of our choosing. My suggestion would be to spread out the bulk of our fleet, leaving perhaps twenty per cent in a tight cluster on the outside of the mesh. If we do that, we give them an obvious point of attack. When they move in, we bring all of our forces back together using portals to catch them off-guard."

There were nods from everyone at the table. Medforth spoke first. "We need to work out the logistics, but conceptually it sounds good. There's a chance that they'll ignore the cluster and hit an undefended area."

"We can't do anything about that, it's an inherent problem of being in space. Costello, work with Smith to establish how exactly we're going to do this. We don't have long to get ready, and we need at least an hour to recharge the portal drive between trips."

"We'll get right on it," Costello responded, after which Marshall dismissed the meeting.

v.

The fleet dispersed an hour after the conference. The ships were scattered around Earth, with the twenty-two strong second and third fleets holding a defensive formation above the planet's northern magnetic pole.

Odyssey held position on the outer perimeter of the mesh, but over the equator. Marshall was pacing the bridge. The current tension in the command centre was tangible.

After four hours waiting for the Aletheans to make their move, Marshall hovered behind Costello at the tactical station with his eyes locked intently on the forward screen.

"Captain, a portal just opened two hundred thousand kilometres from the second and third fleets," Singh reported.

They took the bait, Marshall thought. "Stand by on portals," he ordered. The plan was to wait until the Aletheans had fully emerged before engaging them. He noticed his foot was tapping on the floor in anticipation of the battle to come.

Costello looked over his shoulder. "Their primary fleet is through. Only the portal ship left," he reported.

"That'll do. Signal the fleet to engage. Take us through Mr Singh."

"Aye," Singh replied as he executed the command. A portal was opened within seconds and *Odyssey* charged through.

vi.

The Laird had been travelling to Candidate 11 for one hundred and twenty-four years, of which Animus Vrix had been Regent for only eight.

"Regent, there are twenty-two vessels on an intercept course," the weapons officer reported on the bridge of *The Regent's Hand*.

"Despatch a squad to engage them," the Regent replied. He did not understand why the enemy would disperse their defences so widely. It made no tactical sense to him. In the end though, it would not matter. As with each of the previous candidates, this one would fall swiftly and his fleet would soon be on its way to the next target.

"Regent, I'm detecting portal signatures."

"Where?" he demanded.

"Directly ahead, my Lord."

A grid of portals opened in almost perfect formation. Ten by ten, the grid formed seconds before an EDF ship emerged from each one simultaneously. As they emerged, their Ion Cannons engaged and struck the hull of dozens of Laird vessels. Their targets reeled from the bombardment, and the Earth vessels flew into the maelstrom before veering off.

Coming about for another pass, the EDF cruisers fired torpedoes and rail guns while their Ion Cannons recharged. The Laird's initial surprise had now passed, and they were taking evasive manoeuvres whilst returning fire with their own cannons.

vii.

On the bridge of *Odyssey*, Marshall smiled at the outcome of their assault. "Report," he said.

Costello checked his readings before replying. "Seventeen Alethean ships destroyed; five disabled. We took no damage from the opening volley.

The deck lurched as *Odyssey* was struck by a torpedo. Marshall was thrown from his feet and landed hard on his back. The wind was knocked from his lungs but he was otherwise uninjured, so he climbed to his feet and made his way to the command chair.

"Damage report," he said.

"The shields deflected the majority of the energy. We've suffered structural damage to the outer hull on decks four and five. All systems operational," Smith reported.

"Costello, can you determine which ship holds their flag?" Marshall asked.

"Negative," Costello replied.

"Smith, open a wide-band comm channel," Marshall ordered.

There was a pause before Smith confirmed an open channel. Marshall stood and began speaking. "Alethean fleet, this is Captain Ryan Marshall of the Earth Defence Force. You have violated our territory and engaged us in unprovoked hostility. We offer a truce, so that we may discuss the terms of a peace treaty between our species. If you do not respond, we will have no option but to treat your incursion as an act of war."

He turned to Smith and indicated with a swipe across his throat that he wanted the channel closed. Smith nodded and followed the silent order.

On the main screen, Marshall could see the battle outside continuing as though he had never made the transmission. After a delay of almost a minute, Smith signalled that the Aletheans were responding.

Marshall waited for the screen to show him the face of the enemy, but only a voice was offered. "Captain Marshall of the Earth Defence Force. You will lower your shields and surrender your ships. The mandate of the Laird Kingdom requires that your planet be cleansed. If you surrender, we will ensure that your deaths are swift and painless."

The transmission ended abruptly.

Marshall's mind raced. Could another species have found an Alethean ship just as he had? He had not considered that. It would change nothing, as their plans were based upon their fighting Alethean technology rather than their war strategy.

Medforth looked at Marshall with a raised eyebrow. "The Laird Kingdom?" he asked.

"No idea," Marshall replied, shaking his head. "It doesn't matter for now. Smith, locate the source of that transmission and feed the coordinates to the helm. Singh, when you have them lay in a course and engage engines. Costello, as soon as we're in range you know what to do."

The group acknowledged and waited for Smith to find the enemy vessel. Singh weaved *Odyssey* between the enemy ships, and successfully avoided the blaze of their Ion Cannons that streaked past the hull.

"Captain," Singh said. "Eight enemy ships are heading directly toward us. Intercept in twenty-five seconds."

"Shit," Marshall said. "They must've had the same idea."

viii.

Captain Batson was at the helm of the *Intrepid*, having replaced Lieutenant Ramaswamy who had been relieved of his head and most of his upper body by a falling crossbeam. "Eight enemy vessels have changed course to intercept *Odyssey*," the tactical officer shouted.

"Bringing us about," Batson replied. "Put *Odyssey* on the main screen and order any ships in range to join us."

The screen changed from the battlefield to a vision of *Odyssey* moving through space at full speed toward the approaching squadron. *What the hell is he doing?*" Batson thought. A warning signal was triggered on the console in front of him as he increased speed beyond safety limits. "Intercept in twenty seconds, do we have any backup?" he asked.

"Yes sir, the *Venture* is the right behind us."

"Ready weapons. We-" Batson was interrupted by a loud shriek as *Intrepid* was hit by the combined force of Ion Cannon blasts to starboard and a torpedo to aft. Batson was thrown from his station and landed hard on his right shoulder. The room was filled with shouts from the crew. Batson checked that no bones were broken and climbed to his feet. Looking around the bridge, a sight greeted him that he would never forget. The tactical officer, who had seconds earlier been just a metre to his left, had been caught by an exploding conduit running along the port bulkhead. He had been sprayed with its corrosive contents, which were now melting the flesh from his bones as he writhed in agony.

Batson jumped to his feet and caught the officer as he fell out of his chair and collapsed to the floor. He reached for the helm and activated the internal comm system. "Medical bay, Bridge!" he screamed. "Get a team up here now! We have a man down with severe chemical burns!"

"Captain, look!" Bellion shouted as she pointed at the forward screen. Approaching fast was a Laird ship that was quickly filling the display.

"Bellion, get on tactical!" Batson shouted as he picked up the helm chair that was still lying on its side. It took less than three-seconds to enter an evasive pattern before the ship veered away, narrowly missing enemy ion cannon fire.

"I need weapons," Batson barked.

Bellion had removed her jacket and used it as a cloth to clear the tactical console. With the controls now accessible, she was leaning over the station and frantically entering commands despite the chemical residue burning her fingers. "We've got rail guns, but that's all," she said.

"They'll have to do. We can't outrun them; we've taken damage somewhere that's significantly affecting engine output."

Intrepid flipped one hundred and eighty degrees vertically and opened fire. Bullets flew silently through space and ricocheted harmlessly off the shields of the pursuing Laird vessel. The Laird re-entered weapons range seconds later and engaged their Ion Cannon, disabling *Intrepid's* shields and crippling her engines.

On the bridge, Batson punched the helm when the readout confirmed his ship was dead in space.

"We've lost sensors and weapons. Shield emitters on the port side of decks four, five and six are completely destroyed," Bellion reported.

"Shit," Batson said resignedly. "They're probably coming around for another pass, there's no way to tell. Everyone, report to escape pods!"

He reached for the intercom controls. "All hands, abandon ship. Repeat, all hands abandon ship," he said before turning back to look at the bridge and assess the evacuation requirements. The crew had begun to leave, but his tactical officer was still on the deck. He made his way over to him, and reluctantly checked the officer's neck for a pulse. There was none.

As he stood up, Batson heard a noise from the centre of the room and looked across to see a portal open. Through it stepped a woman that he did not recognise.

"Everyone," she shouted. "Through here with me. Quickly, the reactor is going critical."

With that, the woman disappeared back through the portal and Batson ushered his crew through the vortex. Outside, a volley of enemy fire collided with the gravity drive and the deck lurched violently, throwing Batson onto his back. A second later the gravity system failed, and he found himself floating weightlessly with his momentum carrying him toward the ceiling.

The woman re-emerged from the portal and was caught by the lack of gravity. As she floated in mid-air below Batson, the

Captain rolled forward so that his feet touched the shaking ceiling, and he pushed off in the direction of the female officer.

The bridge lurched again as Batson reached the woman, who caught him and momentum propelled the pair through the vortex. They landed hard on the deck on the other side, which was the opposite of the carnage he had left behind. This bridge was undamaged and her crew were calmly manning their stations. Another female was standing in the centre of the room. She turned to face Batson as he rose to his feet, and offered her hand, which he shook. "Captain Batson, welcome aboard the *Venture*," Captain Baillie said with a smile.

"Thank you, Captain," Batson replied before he turned his attention back to the woman who had helped him through the portal. He grabbed her hand and helped her to her feet.

Baillie gestured to the forward screen where Batson saw his ship floating derelict for several seconds, before it exploded in a ball of fire that was instantly extinguished by the vacuum. There was only a flotilla of spreading debris in her place.

Batson gathered his thoughts. "What happened?" he asked.

"We were on course to intercept *Odyssey's* attackers when you were flanked by an enemy ship. You were already taking damage by the time we got to you, but we managed to disable their shields and take out their weapons before they could deliver the kill shot."

Batson was nodding in acknowledgement when realisation hit him. "What about *Odyssey*?" he asked with alarm.

We've lost contact with her. Once we'd dealt with the Laird ship, we looked for *Odyssey* but she's no longer registering on sensors. There's a debris field where she was some time ago, but we cannot confirm it's her. We detected your core was going critical, so we diverted from the search."

The woman who had assisted *Intrepid's* crew turned to her Captain from the tactical station. "We've got Laird ships breaking off from the kill zone and heading directly for us. ETA thirty seconds," she reported.

"Take us back into the fight," Baillie ordered. Batson moved to protest but Baillie raised her hand before he could speak. "We may or may not have lost *Odyssey*, but regardless of that we cannot also lose this ship. Our numbers are dwindling as it is."

Batson nodded as the female officer left the two Captains alone in the centre of the bridge.

"The ship is obviously yours, but with *Odyssey* M.I.A. I'm taking command of the fleet," Batson said to Baillie. After a slight pause, his colleague nodded. Without hesitation, Batson turned to face the comm station and ordered the officer to send a fleet-wide message informing them that phase two of Captain Marshall's plan should be initiated on his command. The officer glanced at Baillie before responding, but swiftly followed his orders.

Venture re-joined the fleet, bringing the total number of remaining vessels to eighty-four. The Laird were losing ships at a marginally faster rate, however their superior initial size meant they still outnumbered the Earth Defence Force, with one hundred and eight still active.

ix.

"Regent," the weapons officer of the Laird flagship said nervously. "I believe I have found a weakness in the enemy shield system," he said quickly.

The Regent was not a patient individual. He turned and glared at the man, willing him to continue.

The officer obliged hastily. "Their ships are of the same design as our own, however I believe their replication of the shield generators has a flaw that we can exploit."

As his hands moved quickly around his console, a schematic of the shield grid of the Earth Defence Force vessels appeared as the Regent approached and stood over his shoulder.

"Here," he said pointing at the screen. The image showed a ventral view of an Earth vessel, with blue rectangles scattered around the hull to indicate the positions of the shield emitters. Surrounding each marking there was a circle to signify the area of the ship that was protected by the emitter.

Pointing at the starboard aft of the ship, he explained his discovery further. "There is a gap in the crossover point between these two emitters. I believe a carefully placed torpedo in this location would have sufficient power to penetrate the shields and destroy the ship."

"One torpedo would suffice?" the Regent asked.

"A direct hit in this location should be sufficient to get through, yes. We may need more if it is off target," the officer assured his leader.

"Do we suffer a similar flaw?" the Regent asked as he walked around the officer, his gaze never breaking contact with the tactical screen.

"No, Regent. Our shields have no such defect. Although our ships originate from Alethean templates, there are minor differences in their implementation."

The Regent nodded. "Target torpedoes at the defect of the nearest enemy ship. Fire when ready," he commanded.

The Regent's Hand changed course, and within seconds was within firing range of its intended victim. A torpedo left its firing tube and accelerated toward its target, then exploded on impact with her shields.

The Regent did not know, or care, that the ship was named the *Destiny*, that she had a crew of thirty-five, or that she and Captain Orton were among the first to join *Odyssey* as founding members of the Earth Defence Force. The only fact that concerned him was that in the last few seconds one of his torpedoes made contact with her hull, there was an explosion, and the vessel was reduced to nothing more than a flotilla of debris.

x.

"Captain, Destiny is gone," the helmsman of the *Venture* reported.

Batson glanced at Baillie from the tactical station where he was shadowing the stationed officer. Apprehension was evident in his expression. He turned to the woman, who was sitting to his left. "Order the fleet to execute defensive pattern Charlie," he said.

The tactical officer, whose name Batson did not know, nodded and entered a number of commands. Moments later, *Venture* changed course and joined the remaining ships of the Earth Defence Force in the prearranged manoeuvres.

xi.

"Seventeen," the weapons officer of the Laird flagship reported to the Regent when asked how many Earth vessels had succumbed to their design flaw.

The Regent had ordered a squadron to engage the enemy flank and target the gap in their shields. It had yielded impressive results and he fully intended to press the advantage further.

"Order the rest of the fleet to exploit their weakness. Now!" he barked.

"Yes, Regent," the officer said quickly.

The Regent watched as his fleet launched a volley of torpedoes, and his eyes widened in satisfaction as the enemy disintegrated around him.

xii.

Over the course of only thirty minutes, the numbers of the Earth Defence Force dwindled to only twenty-four vessels. The Regent, who smiled with smug satisfaction, walked to the forward section of the bridge of the flagship. His eyes never wavered from the image of victory in front of him.

"Regent, the remaining enemy vessels are retreating toward the planet's natural satellite," the helmsman reported.

Victory, he thought. *The fourth candidate will fall without its alien defences, and cleansing can begin.*

"Regroup, and pursue," he commanded the helm.

xiii.

The Laird fleet took a diamond formation and pursued the retreating Earth ships.

As the armada arrived at Earth's moon, they detected the remainder of the Earth Defence Force waiting in a defensive posture.

"I will speak to them," the Regent said.

A chime indicated that the communication channel was open, and the Regent lifted his chin to look down at the camera. "The Laird Kingdom has declared this system subject to purification. Your attempt to resist has failed. Surrender, you will be given no further warnings," he stated.

The bridge fell silent as the crew awaited a response. None came, and the Regent balled his hands into fists as rage overcame him. "Insolence!" he shouted. "Destroy them all!"

As the weapon's officer readied the flagship's arsenal, a signal on his station indicated the enemy fleet as within firing range. He was about to engage the ion canon, when without notice a klaxon sounded all around him.

Frantically checking his readings, his jaw slackened at what he saw. "Regent!" he shouted. "Incoming vessels to aft!"

"How many?" the Regent demanded.

"Fifty-Six!"

xiv.

40 minutes earlier.

Captain Orton stood on the bridge and watched *Destiny* manoeuvre through the battlefield, scoring hits on enemy vessels as she went. On the main screen, he saw his allies following suit and revelled in their superior battle tactics over the enemy. Despite this however, the Laird still outnumbered the Earth

Defence Force three-to-two, so victory was still nothing more than a desperate hope.

"Sir," the communications officer said, interrupting his thoughts. "With the loss of the *Odyssey*, Captain Batson has taken command of the fleet. He has ordered all ships to execute phase two of the defence plan."

A knot formed in Orton's stomach. Phase two was simultaneously the most dangerous and the most critical part of the battle. With split-second timing and some precision flying required from the helm, there was a significant chance that many ships would fail to complete the manoeuvre successfully and be destroyed.

He sat down and checked the ship's status on his personal console, and then initiated a ship-wide announcement. "This is the Captain. All hands, prepare for phase two. Update the first officer with department status within five minutes. Orton out," he said before closing the channel.

Several minutes passed before the first officer confirmed that all sections had reported in. Orton acknowledged him and gave his tactical officer the order to begin.

Patience had always been a virtue for Orton. Throughout his career he had used it to his advantage, but today he felt that this particular skill had abandoned him.

Five minutes passed, and his uneasiness was growing. "What are they waiting for?" he asked himself aloud. "Ho," he said as he turned to face his tactical officer. "You did reconfigure the shields?" he asked.

"Yes, sir."

The first part of phase two was to open a hole in the shields that was just wide enough for a torpedo to pass through. Orton had expected the Aletheans to notice the defect and exploit it immediately, so the delay was making him nervous.

"We've got an enemy ship making a beeline directly for us!" Ho reported.

"All right, here we go. Take evasive measures. Keep them on the right side of the ship so they can get a lock on the gap, but don't make it obvious."

The woman at the helm turned and looked at the Captain with a look of amused confusion.

"I don't know, just don't wave our starboard side like a flag," Orton replied with a smile.

The helmsman chuckled and turned back to her station. Seconds later the ship lurched as she veered away from the incoming attacker.

"They're firing," Ho reported. "A single torpedo incoming."

"This is it," Orton said.

The events that followed were precisely co-ordinated. A fraction of a second before the torpedo reached the shields, the computer resealed the hole. The torpedo collided with a fully powered shield and exploded. At the exact moment of detonation, *Destiny* simultaneously engaged her cloaking grid and jettisoned a pile of debris from the shuttle bay into space. The final stage was to engage full thrusters to move away from any subsequent incoming fire.

To the naked eye, and to the sensor array of any nearby ship, the vessel had been destroyed.

On the bridge Captain Orton realised he was holding his breath, and had been doing so for the duration of the manoeuvre.

"It worked!" Ho exclaimed.

Orton was awash with relief. He let out a long breath and slumped in his chair. "Helm, take us to the rendezvous point and hold position until we receive word from Captain Batson. Well done, everyone."

xv.

30 minutes later

Captain Orton stood behind the helm with his hands clasped behind his back, staring intently at the screen that showed the Laird fleet moving away from *Destiny* and toward the last of the visible Earth Defence Force.

"The Laird will be in firing range in one minute," the tactical officer reported.

It was the longest minute of Orton's life. The cloaked ships could not communicate with either each other or the visible fleet as it may reveal their presence. For this reason, Orton and his crew were unaware of how many ships had successfully completed the cloaking manoeuvre, and how many had been destroyed in the process.

"Thirty seconds," the officer updated.

Orton returned to his seat and sat down. Apprehension caused a tightness in his chest that had become a familiar companion over the last few hours.

"Ten seconds."

"Captain, we are receiving a wide-beam signal from the Venture," the communications officer reported.

"That's our cue. Disengage cloak and open fire, all batteries," he ordered, leaning forward in his chair with his wrists loosely resting on the arms.

xvi.

Dozens of EDF vessels de-cloaked and opened fire. The vacuum between the Laird armada and their attackers was ablaze with ion cannon beams and the darting glow of torpedoes racing toward their targets.

While their new allies engaged from the rear, the decoy fleet accelerated at full speed toward the enemy flotilla. Weapon fire streaked through space and collided with Laird shields.

The Laird fleet was caught in crossfire. Before the fleet could react to the change in circumstances, their shields began to fail.

Rail gun fire joined the bombardment, and cut through their hull to expose critical sections to empty space.

The Laird fleet evaded and began to escape the flanking attackers, but not before they had lost forty-three ships.

xvii.

The bridge of the Venture erupted in cheers as the Laird lines crumbled. Captain Batson shook Baillie's hand and congratulated her before making his way back to the tactical station.

"Captain, we are receiving a transmission from *Odyssey*!" the communication officer shouted over the noise of the bridge crew.

Baillie immediately ordered the man to open a channel, and a moment later the image on the forward screen was replaced with Captain Marshall's smiling face.

"Captain Baillie, it's good to see you are alright," he said.

"You too, sir," Baillie replied, beaming.

"We saw what happened to *Intrepid*. Did Captain Batson and his crew make it out?" Marshall asked.

"We did, thanks to Adele," Batson said as he entered the camera's peripheral range. "What happened to *Odyssey*?" he asked.

"We made a run for the incoming ships. When they opened fire we executed the cloaking manoeuvre. It was a risk, as we hadn't exposed the shield weakness, but we didn't have much choice."

"Thank God it worked. We thought you were destroyed," Batson replied.

"That was the idea!" Marshall said. "This isn't over yet, but for the first time we've got the Laird on the back foot. We outnumber them now, which should give them pause for thought. While cloaked we found their flagship. I'm issuing orders to regroup at rendezvous point Bravo, and from there we'll go after her. Let's end this as quickly as possible."

The two Captains nodded and the transmission was terminated.

18. Intruders

i.

The Laird fleet continued their assault relentlessly. Marshall was surprised at how little effect the decimation of their armada had been reflected in their attitude toward the battle.

"Squadron ready, sir," Costello reported after he had confirmed that the first fleet was in position to make a run at the Laird flagship.

"Smith, open a channel to the Laird."

Smith acknowledged before Marshall began. "This is Captain Ryan Marshall of the Earth Defence Force. Your fleet is crippled, and you are outnumbered. Stand down and we will allow you to leave our territory peacefully. You have one of our minutes. In the event that you do not understand our timing intervals, a data stream will accompany this transmission. Marshall out," he said and nodded to Smith who transmitted the specified data before closing the channel.

The bridge shook violently as a torpedo impacted the shields. Marshall glanced at his readouts to confirm that the Laird were still engaged in battle.

"Costello, prepare to initiate the attack on the flagship and proceed as soon as their minute is up."

"Yes, sir."

Odyssey lead a squad of ten directly toward the Laird flagship. Several ships were intercepted by enemy forces and had no choice but to disengage from their original course, but *Odyssey* and five others made it into firing range.

The flagship had three vessels guarding it. A combination of ion cannon fire and torpedoes was exchanged between the squadrons before the distance between them disappeared and both had to take evasive action to avoid a collision.

The closest EDF ship to *Odyssey* was disabled by ion cannon and rail gun fire before she could manoeuvre successfully out of the enemy flight path. She lost main power and drifted toward a Laird ship at pace. Moments later the ships collided and without shields there was no way to prevent the force of their collision from pulverising the hull. Both ships were destroyed, and the debris field scattered rapidly in all directions.

With a burst of thrusters, *Odyssey* spun one hundred and eighty degrees to face the Laird flagship. At full burn she raced toward her target with all weapons firing, and the ion cannon bombardment was taxing the enemy shields to the point of failure.

The Laird ship was severely damaged, and her shields failed seconds before *Protector* peppered her aft hull with bullets from her rail guns. As the piercings decompressed numerous sections of the ship, the Laird flagship launched a volley of torpedoes toward *Odyssey*. Singh evaded all but one, which blasted into the shields.

Marshall tightly held onto the arms of his chair as the bridge shook violently from the detonation.

"Shields are down!" Costello shouted, "We still have weapons and thrusters. The Laird ship is disabled."

Marshall ran to the tactical station where he observed the sensor readings from the enemy.

"Cease fire," he ordered. "Smith, get me a direct line to that ship."

"On it," Smith said.

"Captain," Costello said. "Their reactor is--" he started before being interrupted by a flash on the forward screen as the Laird flagship exploded. The flash lasted only a second before extinguishing to reveal a flotsam of particulate matter.

Marshall exhaled sharply. Before he had time to process the sight before him, a klaxon wailed.

"Intruder alert! Engineering section," Costello reported.

Marshall glanced at Medforth and then ran for the lift. "Costello, you're with me!" he shouted as he moved.

"Ryan!" Medforth shouted with a tone Marshall had never heard from him before. It stopped him mid stride. He turned to face his executive officer, who was approaching him quickly.

"You can't go down there," Medforth said as he reached the Captain alongside Costello who had joined the pair. "Your place is on the bridge. Let Simpson and his people take care of it."

"I'm not going to waste time on a debate. My ship is under attack and I'm going to defend it," he replied.

Medforth sighed resignedly. "I'm not going to talk you out of this am I?" he said.

"No. You're welcome to join us if you want, but I'm going."

Medforth nodded. The three men were already armed with rifles that were strapped to their backs. They quickly checked them before entering the lift.

ii.

Marshall and Medforth stood with their backs against the wall on the left side of the lift door. Costello was opposite.

The lift came to a halt and the doors opened. The sound of distant gunfire immediately filled the corridor.

Marshall gestured for Costello to move through the opening. The three men quickly stepped onto the deck, which had a corridor leading away to the left and another directly ahead. Marshall waved two fingers toward the forward corridor and the team moved on with their rifles raised.

Arriving at a T-junction at the end of the corridor, they stopped and crouched against the wall to their left. Marshall knew that the engine room was around this corner, and that it was the source of the weapon fire.

Marshall was about to give instructions to his team when he heard shouts from *Odyssey's* chief of security. Within seconds the chief appeared at the junction, his weapon was raised and firing toward the engineering section.

"Simpson!" Marshall shouted. The security chief stopped suddenly and turned to the three men with a look of confusion and shock. "Captain!" he exclaimed. He quickly sidestepped to join them and took a crouched position.

"How many are there?" Marshall asked.

"Seven came aboard. They've killed three of my men but we got four of theirs. Two were moving in on my position, I lost the other one."

"What about the engineering staff?" Marshall said.

Simpson shook his head. "They're all dead."

Marshall was filled with anger as he addressed his men. "Show no fucking mercy," he said. "Costello, you and Simpson go back down that corridor, look for the missing tango and then come in from the left. Medforth, you wanted to keep an eye on me. Now's your chance. We'll take this corridor and catch them on the flank."

Costello and Simpson stood and ran down the corridor toward the lift. Marshall nodded to Medforth and the pair rounded the corner from their cover and made their way toward the engine room.

Arriving at a junction with the entrance to the primary core on the right, Marshall and Medforth stood with their backs to the wall as Marshall peered around the corner. He spotted one figure standing at a console in the centre of the room but he was unable to find the other.

Simpson and Costello arrived at the other side of the entrance. Simpson shook his head to indicate they had not found the missing intruder.

Marshall nodded and leaned into engineering. He raised his rifle and took aim at the alien's head while Medforth moved around him and prepared to enter the room. Marshall fired, and while the enemy dropped as his head was split by the bullet, Medforth ran across the room and took cover behind a console. As he moved, the remaining assailant opened fire and missed him by no more than an inch.

Marshall let out a held breath, and turned to face the door as he prepared to join Medforth. He was moments from beginning his sprint, when a shriek sounded from his left. He looked to the other side of the entrance to see Costello being lifted in the air by a large blade that had pierced his back and emerged from his chest.

Behind Costello, a tall pale man gripped the sword. He swung his other arm toward Simpson and hit him square in the face, throwing him to the deck unconscious.

Marshall raised his weapon and took aim at the intruder's head, but was unable to get a clear shot past Costello. He lowered the rifle and ran toward the alien, slamming his body weight into the pair and narrowly missing the blade that had been pointing in his direction.

The trio fell to the deck. Costello rolled onto his side and Marshall scrambled on top of the Laird before he could recover.

Marshall pounded his fists into the face of his enemy, his anger fuelling the strikes. After successfully landing four rapid punches, the Laird grabbed Marshall's shoulders and used his left leg to throw Marshall over his head. Marshall landed on his back, but quickly recovered by rolling onto his front and jumping to his feet. By now, the Laird was also standing. The rivals stood motionless for a second before Marshall lunged at the alien and swung his arm into his opponent's stomach, or at least where Marshall assumed his stomach would be.

The alien was unhurt by the hit to his abdomen, as his leather-like armour absorbed the impact entirely. He quickly raised his arm and grabbed Marshall by the throat, lifting him into the air. He slammed the human against a bulkhead and squeezed his captive's neck.

"Retdhfaw'ert rwaa'ghytaw eewe'k aaarbna'th," he said to Marshall, who without a translator had no idea what he was saying.

Marshall struggled against the strong grip of his adversary, and attempted to pry his arms apart whilst kicking out his legs. He was quickly losing strength as his brain was deprived of oxygen, and he began to feel consciousness slip away. His vision blurred, and his arms started to fail him.

His eyes were almost closed, and he could no longer see his assailant. There was a sudden loud bang, and then the grip around his neck loosened before he dropped to the ground in a heap. As his vision slowly returned, he looked up to see the Laird standing motionless with his arms hanging loosely by his side. After a moment of confusion, he noticed that the back of the alien's head was missing, with the remainder of his brain exposed and the wound still smouldering. The Laird fell sideways to the deck with a loud thud. His lifeless expression was one of surprise, with wide eyes and a slack jaw.

Marshall coughed, and dragged himself into a seated position. He scanned the corridor until his eyes came to rest on a small hatch that opened to the entrance of a maintenance tunnel. The opening was no more than a metre square, and the cover was haphazardly lying on the deck in the middle of the corridor with Chris Howells lying halfway out holding a rifle in his hands.

Marshall smiled at Howells. "Nice timing."

"Always," Howells replied as he climbed out of the tunnel and rose to his feet. He crossed the corridor and helped Marshall up. "I managed to get into a crawlspace when the Laird came aboard. Lucky for you I did, too."

"The rest of your team?" Marshall asked.

"I was on the upper level when they attacked, the others were in the primary core. I don't know if they made it out."

Marshall picked up his rifle and ran toward Simpson and Costello. He checked Simpson for a pulse, which he found to be strong. Next he moved over to Costello, but he did not need to check for signs of life as the chest wound had bled out and Marshall knew immediately that it had been fatal.

Medforth emerged from the primary core. "I got him, there's only the missing one left," he said. He looked past Marshall to the alien corpse. "Ah, you found him!" he added. He looked at Simpson and Costello, his light expression changed instantly when he saw the pool of blood surrounding the tactical officer. "What happened?" he asked.

"We were outflanked. Costello paid the price," Marshall replied. Simpson began to move as he regained consciousness.

"That one is dressed differently to the two in there," Medforth said as he pointed to the adjacent room. "You think he was the leader?"

"Maybe. He was a tough son of a bitch, that's for sure." Marshall replied. He looked at the dead alien, then glanced at Costello's body and Simpson's semiconscious form before he addressed Medforth. "See to them, I'm going back to the bridge," Marshall ordered, and without waiting for acknowledgement he turned and headed for the lift.

iii.

Marshall arrived on the bridge several minutes later. Singh reported that the Laird fleet had retreated out of weapons range and were holding position. The battle was effectively on pause, so Marshall sat down and read through the combat log from the point where he left the bridge.

"Where's Medforth and Costello?" Singh asked. Other bridge crew had also turned to look at the Captain.

Marshall looked up at the communications officer, his face was shadowed by grief. "Medforth is tending to Simpson, who was injured during the attack. Costello was mortally wounded," he said quickly, hoping to finish the sentence before his voice broke.

The bridge fell silent. Marshall knew the crew had been elated with the success of the cloaking manoeuvre just thirty minutes ago, and he intended to maintain that level of morale. "Costello gave his life for the cause. We need to finish what we've started so that we may honour his memory."

Singh nodded, "Aye, Captain," he said before turning back to his station. Smith followed suit, and within seconds every member of the bridge crew was back at work.

Marshall composed himself, straightened his t-shirt, and sat upright in his chair. "Let's finish these bastards off. Smith, where is the Laird portal ship?" he asked.

Smith checked his console. "It's been holding position since it arrived. It hasn't joined the rest of their fleet."

"Get me Captain Batson," Marshall ordered.

Seconds later, the former Captain of *Intrepid* was on the main screen standing next to Captain Baillie. "Tom, I need you to lead a squad to the Laird portal ship. Send a team aboard to capture the vessel and eliminate the crew. Did your infiltration team make it off *Intrepid*?"

"They did, they can be deployed immediately," the American replied.

"Good. You shouldn't need more than three escort ships. Take your pick. The squads we started the day with are pretty much irrelevant now."

"Acknowledged. Batson out."

The screen flickered back to empty space. Marshall stood and approached the helm. "Singh, enter an intercept course for the Laird fleet. Smith, order all ships to regroup with us for a final assault. When we're in range, throw everything you've got at them. I'm not interested in prisoners, we need to neutralise the Laird threat once and for all."

The officers acknowledged and the ship accelerated away.

"We are entering weapons range," Singh reported.

"Full stop," Marshall ordered. "Smith, how is *Venture* doing?" he asked.

"They've reached the portal ship and send in their team," Smith reported.

"We'll wait here until that ship is secured," Marshall said. "We may as well get something out of this," he added to himself.

The *Odyssey* crew waited until a signal arrived from *Venture*. They had successfully captured the portal ship with no casualties, and the enemy crew had been neutralised.

"Open a channel to the Laird fleet," Marshall said to Smith.

The communication channel was established. "Laird fleet, this is Captain Marshall of the Earth Defence Force. You are outnumbered and outgunned, your flagship has been destroyed, your portal ship has been captured, and your leader is dead. Your fleet is forfeit, but if you surrender now we will allow your crew to return home unharmed."

Marshall signalled for Smith to close the channel. The crew waited for a response, but none was forthcoming.

The man who had taken Costello's tactical station spoke up. "Captain, there's an energy build-up in the Laird engine cores. They're overloading!" he said with alarm.

Marshall's gaze darted to the forward screen, his mind racing. "Singh, get us out of here. Smith tell all ships to fall back immediately!"

Odyssey flipped vertically and fired thrusters. She sped away from the Laird fleet and was joined by her sister ships. The entire Laird armada exploded in a fireball that lit up every window and sensor display of the Earth fleet, then went dark in a heartbeat.

"I think you got your answer," Smith said.

"Hmm," Marshall replied.

Medforth stepped onto the bridge moments after the detonation. He approached Marshall and reported that Simpson had a concussion but no permanent injuries.

Marshall sat down and composed his thoughts for a moment before opening a ship-wide announcement. "Attention all hands. The Laird invasion force has been defeated. Congratulations on a fine job. You are ordered to secure your stations and report to the construction hangar at nineteen hundred for the biggest piss-up of your lives. Marshall out."

He closed the channel and ordered Smith to broadcast the message to the entire fleet.

19. Ouroboros

i.

There was a wrap at the door. Marshall was lying flat on his bed, staring at the ceiling. He sat up, and wandered over to the hatch.

After pressing the contact to the right of the entryway, the door slid aside to reveal Medforth in the threshold.

"The party is missing its guest of honour," Medforth said with a smile. In one hand he was carrying a litre of whiskey, and in the other was a pair of tumblers. He raised them for Marshall to see.

"I'm sure they can manage without me for a little while," Marshall said as he gestured for Medforth to enter his quarters.

Medforth dropped onto the sofa that lined the rear wall under the window. He placed the tumblers on the table in front of him, and unwrapped the bottle.

Marshall sat in the chair to Medforth's right. "I wasn't planning on staying here all night, you know. I have every intention of coming to the party."

"So why are you loitering around your quarters?" Medforth asked as he poured two generous helpings of whiskey.

"Just got a few things to think about," Marshall replied curtly.

Medforth handed Marshall a drink then raised his own. "To victory," he said.

Marshall smiled for the first time since Medforth's arrival. "To victory," he repeated before the pair sipped the single malt.

"Relax," Medforth said firmly. "It's over, you can unwind."

Marshall's glass hovered in front of his lips. "Almost," was all he said before draining the golden liquid.

Medforth waited for Marshall to continue.

"I still have one thing left to do."

Medforth's brow furrowed.

"Eighteen years ago we were warned about the Alethean invasion. Well, the Laird invasion. I suppose I must have decided not to confuse matters by introducing a third party. Anyway, ever since then we've planned and built a fleet that has just successfully repelled their attack. If we hadn't been warned, we would have plodded along researching the technology of *Odyssey* and would have built a few more ships here and there. When the Laird arrived, we would have been wiped out almost immediately."

"Yes, I know. I was there. What's your point?" Medforth interrupted.

"Think about it," Marshall continued. "We won, so I don't need to go back. Which means we won't be warned, so we will be wiped out. Then, because we lose, I will go back and warn myself. So, we do prepare, and we win. Because we win, I don't need to go back. It's an infinite loop. I've been talking at length with Dr

Millward about this. It's something called temporal causality. Fuck knows what that means, but the gist is that I have to go back and deliver the warning despite our victory. It's the only way to maintain the timeline."

"You can't be serious?" Marshall scoffed. "You know from what you saw that it's suicide. I can understand the decision if we'd lost, but this is based on the ramblings of a man who is barely sane!"

Marshall lifted his glass and gestured for Medforth to give him a refill. "It's not just that. I was in the bathroom earlier and caught my reflection. Do you know what I saw? I saw the exact same Ryan Marshall that appeared all those years ago."

Medforth had filled both glasses and was returning the bottle to the table. "So what? You are him, after all."

Marshall shook his head. "I don't just mean I was eighteen years older. I mean this tear." He grabbed a gap in his jacket. "This cut." He tapped a line across his forehead. "This gash." He touched a hole in his trousers. "They are all precisely as I remember. I realised in that moment that the Marshall I saw, the man who warned me about our destruction, was probably telling the same lies that I need to go back and tell now."

Medforth stared at Marshall incredulously. "You mean we never lost?"

"Millward theorises that in the original loop we did in fact lose, and that without a warning we weren't prepared for the Laird and were wiped out. Ever since then, I've been maintaining the timeline by going back and delivering the message. I don't know much about temporal physics, but he made it clear to me years ago that no matter the outcome today, I need to go back. And that's what I'm going to do."

"It's suicide. Just get on with your life and don't worry about it," Medforth demanded.

"It's not as simple as that. We need to maintain the flow of time, and this is my role in making that happen. I'm doing this, and that's final."

Medforth's face turned pale. "When?"

"Millward is having the time displacement unit moved from the hangar to *Odyssey* as we speak. When he's ready, we'll head to the exact co-ordinates we occupied eighteen years ago. The device will send me back in time, but my location will be fixed so we need to be in the precise spot or I could appear inside a bulkhead. That wouldn't be ideal."

Medforth nodded slowly. "Do you have a rough timescale?"

Marshall checked his watch. "A little over two hours," he said.

Medforth looked down at his glass and fell silent. "I think it would be good for you to see the crew one last time, eh?"

Marshall's lip curled as he found himself uncharacteristically emotional. "Yes."

ii.

Every member of the Earth Defence Force wore a smile. Marshall had arranged for a plethora of drinks and snacks to be ready aboard the hangar for the unlikely event of their victory. He saw no harm, as if they had lost they would be dead anyway so the waste wouldn't burden him.

Walking through one of the many construction areas of the hangar, he and Medforth were greeted warmly by numerous officers who insisted on shaking their hands and congratulating them. The pair reminded each person they met that it was a team effort, and returned the congratulations.

Marshall was elated with their victory, but his thoughts persistently returned to the loss of Costello and the hundreds of officers who died for the cause. He felt the weight of their sacrifice, and also continued to ponder the task that lay before him.

When they arrived at the large cavernous room that hosted the festivities, Marshall could hear loud music resonating off the bulkheads. There were lights flashing and people everywhere. Some were already merry from the ale, while others were more sombre. *Not so easy to party when you just lost close friends*, he thought.

Marshall spotted Howells standing with Smith next to a large stack of drink pallets. He nudged Medforth and pointed at the engineer, before making a beeline for him. They were hounded most of the way by more crew members offering congratulations and thanks.

"I should have known you would be near the booze," Marshall shouted to Smith over the music. "And I hope you're only guarding it," he added, pointing toward Howells.

Both men laughed and raised their glasses to him. He could tell that Howells' drink was not his customary orange juice, but a brown liquid that Marshall guessed was whiskey.

Marshall's poker face had helped him many times, but Howells clearly saw what he was thinking. "Fuck it, mate. We just saved the world!" he said.

"You know how this ends, Chris," Marshall warned.

Howells raised his free hand in the air. "Don't worry. Tonight I'm going to enjoy myself with the rest of these heroes, and then I'll be back on the dull stuff," he said with a cheeky grin.

Marshall returned the smile but looked sternly at Smith. "Keep an eye on him," he ordered. Smith raised two fingers to his temple and flicked them in mock salute.

Marshall looked around the room and was pleased with how many familiar faces had survived the battle. There would be time to count the dead later, but for now his crew deserved a celebration.

"Ryan!" a voice sounded over the crowd. Marshall turned to see Batson approaching fast. Batson arrived and offered his hand, which Marshall gripped. Marshall then embraced the Captain firmly. "Good job," he said into Batson's ear.

"You too," Batson replied.

The group gradually dispersed amongst the crowd, and for the next hour both Marshall and Medforth forgot about the task ahead.

Marshall was discussing the recent season premiere of Game of Thrones, when his phone buzzed. He pulled the device from the pocket of his jeans and read the message on the display.

Ready when you are, was all it said. He made excuses, before retrieving Medforth from the other side of the hangar.

As the pair made their way toward one of the designated portal areas, Marshall heard his name being called. He turned to see Howells jogging toward them.

"You aren't getting away that easily," Howells said.

"What do you mean?"

"You're going back into the past, aren't you?"

Marshall and Medforth exchanged a glance.

"I knew it!" Howells shouted triumphantly. "Well, I'm coming to see you off. Wouldn't miss it for the world."

Marshall was surprised. "You aren't going to try to talk me out of it?"

"What's the point? If you've made it this far and are still intending to go, then your mind is made up. I'm coming to make sure that Millward doesn't screw it up, that's all."

Marshall scoffed. "Come on, then," he said with a smile.

iii.

Marshall emerged from the portal at the rear of *Odyssey's* bridge and made his way to the helm. He was followed closely by Medforth and Howells. "Singh, have you been briefed?" he asked the pilot.

"I have. The portal drive is on standby; we can go on your order."

"Then by all means," said Marshall.

With a single key press, *Odyssey's* engines flared to life and a portal enveloped the ship.

iv.

"Engines are offline. We're in position," Singh reported.

"Great job," Marshall said as he stepped closer to the pilot's workstation. He rested his hand on the helmsman's shoulder. "Singh, it's been an honour."

Singh stood and turned to face Marshall. "The honour was mine," he said as he held out his hand. Tears were welling in his eyes, but he held them back. Marshall took his hand and smiled warmly.

"Until next time," Marshall said. He released his grip and strode toward the lift. "Medforth, Howells, with me," he commanded as he stepped onto the lift.

v.

The door slid aside to reveal the large cavernous shuttle bay. In the middle was a myriad of monitors and workstations that were resting haphazardly on makeshift shelves and cabinets.

There were cables strewn across the deck, and large pipes overhead leading from the bulkhead to the time displacement device that was standing alone in the dead centre. The device looked like a solid metal shower cubicle. There was a spotlight pointing toward an open aperture, the beam from which was reflecting off the shiny metallic surface. This was not the first time Marshall had seen the device, but it was the first time that it filled him with dread.

"Jesus," Howells said when he laid eyes on the setup.

Dr Millward was standing to the left of the device. He was holding a tablet in his hand, which he was staring at intently. He looked up at the new arrivals but did not offer a greeting.

The trio approached the device, which was still some distance away.

"Stop!" Millward screamed as he shot forth the palm of his hand.

All three men stopped walking instantly, and waited for an explanation that they were not sure would ever come.

Millward's gaze returned the device without another word. Marshall was about to resume his journey when he heard a low pitched hum emanate from the contraption ahead of him.

Millward had powered up the device. The hum was getting louder, and Marshall's already notable apprehension increased even further.

"Millward!" Marshall shouted over the hum when he reached the physicist. "Have you made any progress on its safety?" he asked nervously.

Millward's stare shot up toward Marshall. "Sorry. No. Definitely fatal. Nothing more I can do. Done what I can. Not enough. Did my best. Sorry, no." he said frantically.

Marshall glanced at Medforth with pursed lips. "This is it then," he said. "I've left a log recommending the council install you as chair and commander of the fleet. I think that after today's events they'll listen," he said.

"Thanks," Medforth said solemnly. He was genuinely grateful, but at this moment he couldn't have cared less.

Marshall shook Howells' hand before stepping toward Medforth. The two men shook hands, and there was a pause before they embraced. After a few seconds they stepped away from each other, and Marshall nodded before he turned around to face the machine. He stepped forward into the aperture and spun on his heel to face the room.

"Look after the ship, she deserves it," he shouted to Medforth, who nodded.

"And Howells, I'll come back to haunt you if you fall off the wagon," he added.

Without hesitation Marshall nodded to Millward, who entered a command on his console that closed the door.

Medforth watched intently as the hum from the device increased in volume to an almost deafening level. A field of electrical energy began to surround the tube, and the intensity increased even further.

"Five-seconds!" Millward screamed over the ambient noise. "Four, three, two, one, mark!" he finished, and with a flash Marshall was gone. The machine instantly powered down and the room fell silent. Medforth looked upon the empty tube with a combination of amazement, bewilderment, pride and sorrow.

vi.

The world was a blur. Marshall couldn't see anything and his hearing was muffled as though he were underwater.

Pain!

It overwhelmed him, a sharp pain throughout the right side of his body.

"Jeezzzzz," he heard a muffled voice say, followed soon after by someone grabbing his shoulder and pushing against his limp body.

His senses began to clear. He was thinking clearly but his vision had still not returned to focus.

"What the fuck is going on? Who are you?" he heard from a familiar voice. His mind was clear now, and he remembered where he was supposed to be. He had arrived successfully. He chuckled as the reality of the situation hit him hard.

"It's funny being on this side of the conversation," he managed to say. He smiled, or at least he thought he smiled.

"What?" the voice said.

"Never mind. Help me get into a chair," he said. His vision was improving but he could still barely make out his surroundings.

Someone helped him up, and dropped him onto a cushioned surface.

"I asked who you are," the voice stated abruptly.

He tried to remember what he had been told by the strange visitor from the future, but he couldn't formulate the thoughts properly. He decided to improvise and hope it was right. "I am Captain Ryan Marshall, Earth Defence Force," he said.

"Earth Defence Force?" the voice asked.

"That's what we called the fleet, once we had enough ships to genuinely consider it a 'force'," he said before he winced as a bolt of pain shot through his entire body.

"I knew this would hurt, but not this much…" he said.

"What would hurt? Would you just tell me what the fuck is happening here?" the voice demanded.

He sat for a moment and stared at the table as the pain became increasingly severe. Almost at once, his vision clarified and his memories and thought processes regained coherence.

Composing a makeshift script in his mind, he began. "I have come here from 2016, using a device that we found schematics for in the ship's library a few years ago. 2011 to be exact. My past, your future.

"By 2016, we had built a fleet of twenty ships. Over the years we learned a lot more about the inner workings of *Odyssey*, and we even managed to improve some of her systems beyond what we found back in ninety-three. We were proud of our accomplishments, and ultimately this led to complacency.

"We had a number of extra-terrestrial encounters over the years. Fortunately, there was only one that turned hostile, and the rest were either friendly or disinterested in Earth or it's people.

"We should have known, especially after our first encounter, that one day we would face a hostile alien force that would require more powerful defences than we had at our disposal. But we were overconfident, and when that day came we were totally unprepared.

"The Aletheans, the same race who built *Odyssey*, dispatched a fleet to Earth to eradicate us. Not to take our resources, enslave our people, or occupy our planet, just pure and simple extermination. We have no idea why. They simply stated their intentions and attacked us.

"They arrived this week. We didn't see them coming, and after a short battle they destroyed the fleet. *Odyssey* and *Trojan* escaped, and I used the time displacement system to bring myself back here to warn you of the Alethean invasion, and to tell you this story."

He could make out his counterpart now, he was amazed by how young he looked. "Everyone is dead?" the man asked.

"I don't know what happened after I left, but the fleet was gone and there was nothing to stop the Aletheans from destroying Earth's population. They sent a transmission when they arrived ordering us to surrender, they were very clear about their intentions."

"Wow," his younger self said, standing up and walking toward the window. "What can we do?"

"Build the fleet faster than we did. Much faster. We built ships and made some incredible scientific discoveries, but we weren't prepared for an invasion. The Aletheans brought one hundred and fifty-seven ships, to face our twenty. We had no chance."

"One hundred and fifty-seven ships in eighteen years? That's impossible. We don't have the resources or the manpower," was the reply.

He winced and dropped his head, remaining still for several seconds before looking up. "Yeah, with your current setup. You need to increase the ship building capabilities of the current facility, and almost certainly you will need another one, or more. Look, I can't give you a strategy, this only just happened to me. I haven't had time to prepare anything for you, I used the displacement thing as a last resort."

"Are you all right?" he was asked.

"No. Our scientists told me this trip would almost certainly be one-way, and they couldn't say how long I would have. The pain is getting worse. I don't have long."

"Shit. I'll get Dr Harrison."

The older Marshall doubled over and coughed. He took a full minute to regain his composure. "No, don't waste time, just listen. Prepare the fleet, build as many ships as you can. The Aletheans' armour and weapons capabilities are the same as ours so you need to get as close to a hundred and fifty-seven as you can. They will be here on April 4th 2016, so you have eighteen years. The schematics for the time displacement machine are in a memory stick secured behind a wall panel in the science lab. Build the machine, and if you don't stop them you must do as I have and try again. Hopefully with a thirteen-year head start you might figure out a way of not killing yourself doing it too."

He smiled, but it soon turned to a grimace as the pain returned.

"I need to get you to the doctor, he can at least ease the pain."

With a cry of pain, he lurched forward and collapsed to the deck.

Thoughts ran through his head. *Tell him about the intruder and save Costello. Tell him about Fracaro. Tell him about the portal ship.* But he knew he couldn't and wouldn't, because that isn't what happened before. He had delivered his message; the fleet would be ready. The Earth Defence Force would prevail, and humanity would be saved. He had succeeded, and now the fate that had been awaiting him for eighteen years was here.

The End

Epilogue

"The damage is worse than we predicted. His cells are phasing in and out of our temporal plane."

"Flux. Yes, all over. Unable to stabilise. Don't know the cure. Research wasted. Thought we were ready."

"He appeared as expected. Why is everything else not as we thought?"

"Physics complicated. Not simple. Army types are stupid."

Marshall awoke in a room filled with blinding light. He squinted and attempted to sit upright. He failed, and he realised that his entire body was numb.

Turning his head from left to right, he saw various people working around him.

"He's regaining consciousness," he heard.

"Perhaps we should sedate him until we determine the full extent of the cellular damage?" a second voice offered.

"Do what you must."

There was silence. The third voice had ended the dialog.

There was a sharp pinch in his arm, and reality faded into nothingness once more.

"Vital signs are strong. I think it's working," he heard.

Opening his eyes, Marshall saw a face looking down upon him from his left. He didn't recognise it at first, but he came to realise it was Dr Millward.

"Wh—," he uttered.

"Don't speak. Not ready," Millward said.

He looked around the unnaturally white room, and saw what looked like nurses tending to patients, but he couldn't see who was on the beds. He continued to scan, and his gaze fell upon three men standing to his right.

"Med--"

"Don't try to speak!" Millward repeated urgently.

They were Medforth, Batson and a middle-aged man who looked familiar. But what had happened to them? They looked so different.

"It's okay Ryan, take it easy," Medforth said.

He never calls me Ryan, Marshall thought. He looked at Medforth, and was about to ask him a question when the world went white and he lost consciousness.

"He's coming around," Millward said.

Marshall opened his eyes and scanned the room again. Medforth was still there, as were the other two men.

"How are you feeling?" Medforth asked.

Marshall's mind was clearing, but his confusion over Medforth and Batson's appearance overrode all thought.

He composed himself and fought to formulate a question. "What the fuck happened to you two?" he asked the duo.

Medforth and Batson exchanged a look. Marshall wondered if his question had sounded correct but they soon looked back at him. "Ryan, it's been eighteen years since you stepped into that machine," Medforth said.

Marshall contemplated the words but could not believe them. He had expected to die whilst going back to 1998, but ending up in the future had not occurred to him.

Medforth continued. "It's 2034, and you've got us two out of retirement to come and see you," he said with a smile.

"How--," Marshall began, but a jolt of pain stopped him.

"You went back to ninety-eight, delivered your message, died, and were slingshot forward to the present. Dr Millward figured out after you left that you would travel forward by an equal amount of time. Something to do with a mug? I'm not sure, he was rambling. Anyway, he spent the last eighteen years figuring out how to save your life when you returned. You were dead when you reappeared two hours ago. You're lucky this guy is a genius," Medforth said with a friendly smile toward Millward.

"Holy f——," he started when the towering insect-like creature came into full view. Its arm was extended, and enclosed in its claw was a small device.

A loud, high-pitched sound erupted from the creature's mouth. Marshall winced momentarily, but quickly subdued his instinctive reaction.

The device came to life. A calm voice emanated from it as the alien's words were translated. "Greetings, Ryan Marshall. My name is Controller."